BEARERS OF THE
BLACK STAFF

By Terry Brooks

TERRY BROOKS

BEARERS OF THE BLACK STAFF

LEGENDS OF SHANNARA: Book One

www.orbitbooks.net

ORBIT

First published in the United States in 2010 by Del Rey,
an imprint of The Random House Publishing Group
First published in Great Britain in 2010 by Orbit

A CIP catalogue record for this book
is available from the British Library.

HB ISBN 978-1-84149-583-5
C-format 978-1-84149-584-2

Printed and bound in Great Britain by
Clays Ltd, St Ives plc

Papers used by Orbit are natural, renewable and
recyclable products sourced from well-managed forests and certified
in accordance with the rules of the Forest Stewardship Council.

FOR STUART FINNIE

Courage Under Fire

1

BLACK ICE COATED EARTH FROZEN HARD BY NIGHT temperatures that had dropped below freezing, a thin skein of slickness that challenged the grip of his toughened-rawhide boot soles. Yet the Gray Man stepped with grace and ease across the treacherous smoothness, not oblivious to the danger so much as accustomed to it. He passed through the woods along the snow line close by the valley's rim, only slightly less transparent than the wraiths to which he was so often compared. Amid the dark of the trunks and limbs and the deep green of the conifer needles, he was another of night's shadows.

Until you got close enough to realize he wasn't a figment of the imagination, but as substantial as the rumors that tracked him in whispers and long silences, and then he was something much more.

Through the night's slow retreat he passed, watching daybreak lighten the sky above the eastern rim of the valley, so far away it was little more than a hazy glow. He had been walking for several hours, his sleep ended early. Each day found him someplace else, and even though he followed the same route over and over, tracking the rim of the valley from mountain peak to barren ridge to escarpment and back again, he was never bothered by time or speed; only with order. It was given to him to navigate the heights from one mountain pass to another, one valley's passage to the next, always in search of an opening that led out—or in. The mists that had sealed the valley since the time of the Hawk had not yet receded, but that would change and it would do so in his lifetime.

His dreams had told him so.

The wall that kept the survivors of the Great Wars safely sealed in, and the things that roamed the world beyond locked out, would not hold forever, although there were many who thought differently. The wall was a conjuration of power unlike any he could imagine, although he wielded considerable power of his own. But nothing was permanent; all things must change. And no matter the beliefs of some and the wishes of others, life had a way of surprising you.

A hawk screamed from somewhere high above, soaring across the snowfields and rocky promontories, and something in the sound of that cry reminded the Gray Man that time slipped away and the past was catching up.

He quickened his pace, moving silently through the deep woods, his tattered robes trailing from his lean form. He did not stride through the trees so much as flow, a spectral creature formed of bits and pieces of color and smoke, of aether and light. He touched things as he went, small brushings and tiny rubs of fingertips, nothing more, reading from each something of the world about him. He sniffed the air and studied the look of the tiny ends of branches. Everything spoke to him. A Koden had passed here. There was fresh springwater not far away over there. Fledgling ravens had departed the nest last summer and flown off to breed families of their own. A family of black squirrels lived within that stand of blue spruce, perhaps watching him as he passed. It was all there for those who might read it, but he was one of only a handful who could.

After all, it was in his blood.

He was tall and rangy in the way of mountain men and long-range Trackers from the communities of Men and Elves alike, and broad-shouldered and hard in the way of the Lizards, though not burdened with the armor of their skin. He was quick when he needed to be and slow when quickness could get you killed. He was dangerous all the time. There were stories about him in every settlement, every village, every safehold and way station, and he had heard them all. Some were partly true, though none told all his tale. He was one of a kind and the last, as well—unless he found the next bearer. It was something he thought of now and then. But time allowed for little deviation from his duty, least of all seeking out and training the successor whom he fervently hoped he would not need for some years to come.

His hands tightened about the black staff that marked him for who and what he was, conscious of the deep carving of its runes and the pulse of the magic they commanded. He did not call upon the power much these days, did not have cause to do so, but it was comforting to know that it was there. The Word's magic was given to him by his predecessor and before that by his, and so on over a span of five centuries. He knew the story of its origins; all those who carried the staff knew. They passed it on dutifully. Or when time and events did not allow for an orderly passage, they learned it another way. The Gray Man was not familiar with the experiences of those others who had borne the staff; he knew only his own. He had never been visited by the Lady who served as the voice of the staff's maker. She had never come to him in his dreams as she had sometimes come to others.

Ahead, the trees thinned as the valley slope lifted toward a tall, narrow gap in the cliff face farther up. There, hidden within the rocks, the pass at Declan Reach opened through to the larger world. He had stood in its shelter at the edge of his and looked past into the gray nothingness beyond, wondering what that world might look like if he could pass through. He had attempted passage once or twice in the beginning, when he was young and not yet convinced that things were as everyone claimed. But his efforts were always rebuffed; the mists turned him around and sent him back again, no matter how straight he believed the path on which he had set his feet, no matter how determined his attempt. The magic was inexorable, and it refused all equally.

But now he had the dreams to consider, and the dreams told him that five centuries of what had once seemed forever were coming to a close.

He left the trees and began to climb. Fresh snow had fallen a day earlier, and its white carpet was pristine and unmarked. But he sensed something nevertheless, a presence hidden below, just out of sight. He could not tell what it was yet, but it was nothing he recognized. He quickened his pace, suddenly worried. He climbed swiftly through the rocky outcroppings and narrow defiles, testing the air as he went, trailing his hands across the rocks. Something had passed this way, descending from the heights. Two, perhaps three days ago, it had made its way down into the valley. Down, not up.

But down from where?

His worst fears were realized as he reached the entrance to the pass and found his wards not simply broken, but shredded. The wards had been strong, a network of forbidding he had placed there himself not a month earlier. Wards of the same strength and consistency he used at every such passage leading into the valley, wards intended to warn him of breaches in the wall, wards meant to keep the inhabitants safe from the unthinkable.

And now the unthinkable was here.

He knelt to study the area surrounding the tattered remains that still clung to the rocks where he had attached them. He took a long time, wanting to make certain of what he was sensing. There was no mistake. Something had come through from the larger world, from beyond his valley. More than one something, he revised. Two, he judged—a hunting pair come in search of food, huge, dangerous creatures from the size and depth of the claw marks on the rocks and the apparent ease with which they had destroyed the wards.

He stood up, shaking his head at the irony of it. Even as he had tried to measure the time allotted before the dreams would come to pass, they had arrived full-blown. In the blink of an eye, the past was upon them.

He looked out from his vantage point high upon the snow line to the spread of the valley. Mist and clouds hid much of it this morning, and it would be midday before that haze burned off enough to permit a view of even the closest of the communities. To which of these would the intruders go? It was impossible to say. They might stay high up on the protective slopes of the mountains. Whatever their choice, he would have to hunt them down and dispatch them before it was too late.

Which it might already be.

He turned back into the pass and with the aid of his staff began to rebuild the wards. He summoned the magic, holding out the staff before him and using the words of power and small movements of his hands. The runes began to glow, luminous against the still-dark early morning, pulsing softly in response to his commands. He felt the power flow from the staff into his body, and as always he was transported to another plateau of sensation, one that was too close to euphoria for comfort, a warning of an addiction he had already embraced too closely. The magic was an elixir, each time giving him such fulfillment, such satisfaction, that he could barely stand the thought of letting it go. But he had learned what the lure could result in, and by now, he knew the ways in which to keep from falling prey.

Or so he told himself.

He layered the pass with the wards, preventing the creatures that had broken through from escaping the valley without his knowing. It took him a while to complete the task, for he understood the importance of being thorough. But when at last he finished, the wards were set. He let the magic retreat back into the staff. The brightness of the runes faded, the glaze of the magic's euphoria dissipated, and the world returned to normal.

The Gray Man stood where he was for long moments afterward, savoring the memories, and then he turned his back on the pass and the wards and set out along the valley rim, tracking the creatures.

It was not difficult to do so. They were big and slow, and their tracks were distinct where imprinted in muddy patches on the rocks and within the snowfield. They were moving west now, opposite the direction from which he had come. They followed the snow line for only a short distance before dropping down to the deep woods and their protective cover. They were hunting still, the Gray Man guessed, but keeping close to the safety of the heights and some assurance of the way back. They were thinking creatures, though he doubted their ability to reason overrode their primal instincts. They were brutes, and they would react as such. A lack of caution did not make them any less dangerous. If anything, it made them more so. He would need to find them quickly.

He considered for a moment the ramifications of their presence. It

meant that after all these years, the wall was failing and their time of
isolation was at an end. This would be difficult for many of the valley's
inhabitants to accept—Men, Elves, Lizards, Spiders, and those singular
creatures that lacked a group identity. It would be impossible for some.
The sect of Men who called themselves the Children of the Hawk, and
who awaited the return of the leader who had brought them to the valley to protect them, would resist any suggestion of an end to the mists
that did not involve his coming. Their dogma prophesied that the wall
would endure until it was safe to leave the valley and the Hawk returned to lead them out again. Anything else they would call heresy;
they would fight against it until the evidence stood before them, and
even then they might not believe. Nothing anyone could say would
change minds so settled; belief in the invisible, belief founded solely on
faith, did not allow for that.

Yet he would have to try. There was no one else who would do so,
if he did not.

He glanced downslope out of habit, recalling that the Seraphic
who led the Children of the Hawk made his home in Glensk Wood.
How ironic it would be if the creatures from the outer world were to
somehow make their way to his community and introduce themselves.
Would the members of the sect believe then?

Bittersweet memories flooded his mind in a sudden rush and then
dissipated like morning mist.

The day brightened as the hours passed, and the sun broke through
the clouds to warm the air. The brume clung to the higher elevations,
catching on peaks and nestling in defiles, and shadows gathered in the
deep woods in dark pools. Now that the creatures had left the snow,
the Gray Man could track them less easily. But they left traces of their
scent and surface marks so that following them was possible for someone with his skills.

By now he had concluded that he was at least twenty-four hours
behind them. It was too long for creatures of this size not to have
found something to eat. He had to hope that whatever they had found
did not walk on two legs, and that was hoping for a lot. Trappers and
hunters roamed these hills year-round in search of game. Some made
their homes in cabins up along the snow line; some had their families

with them. They were tough, experienced men and women, but they were no match for the ones he tracked.

It frustrated him to think that this was happening now, that the ending of the barrier had come about so abruptly. There should have been some warning, some hint that change was at hand. Wasn't that what the Seraphic preached? But no one was prepared for this; no one would know what to do. Not even himself, he acknowledged. How do you prepare for the intrusion of a world you had escaped because it was too monstrous to live in? How do you prepare for an end to everything you had believed to be permanent?

He smiled grimly. It was too bad he couldn't ask his predecessors, those fortunate few who had found a way to survive the horrors of the Great Wars when it had seemed survival was impossible. They would know.

The ground ahead had turned damp and spongy, the snowmelt trickling off the heights in dozens of tiny streams. The Gray Man studied the ground carefully as he went, seeking the tiny indicators of his quarry's passing, finding them less quickly now, their presence faded with the changes in temperature and time's passage. As he slipped silently through the trees, he could hear birds singing and tiny animals rushing about, and he knew that they would not be doing so if any sort of danger were present. He had not lost ground; he had simply failed to make it up. The creatures were traveling faster at this point, perhaps because they sensed the possibility of food. He increased his own pace, worried anew.

His worry turned quickly to fear. Not a quarter of a mile farther on, he encountered a set of fresh tracks intersecting with those he followed. They were so faint he almost missed them. He knelt to study the sign, making certain of what he was seeing. These new tracks belonged to humans. It wasn't that the makers were trying to hide their passing; it was that they knew how to walk without leaving much to follow. They were experienced at keeping their passage hidden, and they had done so here out of habit. They had come up out of the valley, perhaps from Glensk Wood, two of them. They had found the tracks of the creatures, and now they were following them also.

He brushed at the two sets of tracks with his fingertips. The tracks

of the intruders were more than a day old. The new tracks had been
made less than three hours ago.

The Gray Man straightened as he rose, not liking what this meant.
It was entirely possible the two from the valley had no idea what it was
they were tracking. They may have had enough experience to suspect
the nature of their quarry, but it was unlikely they knew of its origins.
The best he could hope for now was that they appreciated the possibility of the danger they were facing so that they would be cautious in
their efforts.

But he couldn't assume anything. He could only hope.

He would have to reach them as quickly as possible if he was to
save them.

He set out again, this time at a steady lope that covered the ground
in long, sweeping strides.

Time was slipping away.

2

PANTERRA QU CROUCHED IN A THICK CLUSTER OF spruce at the edge of the snow line not two hundred feet from where the bodies lay sprawled and waited for his senses to tell him it was safe to approach. Shadows pooled across the killing ground, mingling with the bloodstains that had soaked into the half-frozen earth. He studied the bodies—or more correctly, what was left of the bodies—trying to make sense of what he was seeing. It wasn't that he hadn't seen dead people before; it was that he had never seen them so thoroughly dismembered.

He glanced through the trees at Prue, a wisp of darkness against the deep green of the woods, barely visible, even from so close. She could disappear in the blink of an eye when she chose, and no one could find her—not even him, not if she didn't want him to. It was a trick he had never been able to master. Just now, she looked as if she wanted to disappear to some other place entirely. Her eyes were wide and frightened, waiting to see what he wanted her to do. He gave her a quick sign not to move until he called her out. He waited until he saw her nod, wanting to be sure she understood. She was only fifteen, still learning how to be a Tracker, and he was determined to be the teacher she needed. It didn't matter that he was only two years her senior; he was still the one responsible for them both.

He turned his attention back to the bodies, waiting. Whatever had done such terrible damage might still be lurking about, and he wanted to be sure it had moved on before he revealed himself. He kept perfectly still for long minutes, watching the surrounding trees, especially higher up on the slope, where it appeared from the blood trail that the killers had gone. Kodens, maybe. Or a wolf pack at hunt. But nothing he could imagine seemed quite right.

Finally, giving Prue a quick glance and motioning once again for her to stay where she was, he stepped out into the open and advanced on the dead. The hairs on the back of his neck rose as he approached and saw more clearly the extent of the damage that had been inflicted. Not only had the bodies been torn to pieces, but large parts were missing entirely. The bodies were so mutilated that he wasn't even sure identification was possible. He kept switching his gaze from the dead to the upper slopes, still not sure it was safe.

When he stopped finally, he was right next to the remains. A hand and arm here, a foot there, a piece of a torso off to one side. Two bodies, he guessed. They might have fought hard to stay alive, but he didn't think they'd ever had a chance. It looked as if they had been caught sleeping; there were blanket fragments scattered about, and the remnants of a fire pit were visible. They might have been dead almost before they knew what was happening.

He found himself hoping so.

He took a deep breath of the cold morning air to clear his head, then knelt for a closer look. His tracking skills took over instantly. He sorted through the remains more carefully now, more intensely. Two bodies, a man and a woman who had been wearing gear very much like his own. Were they Trackers? He tried to think if he knew of anyone who was missing. There were always Trackers patrolling the upper heights of the valley, always at least half a dozen at work.

Then he caught sight of the bracelet on the wrist of the severed hand a few feet off. He rose, walked over, and knelt again. The bracelet was gold, and there was a tiny bird charm dangling from a clasp.

He closed his eyes and looked away. *Bayleen.*

That meant the other body was Rausha's. He knew them both. Trackers, like himself, but older and much more experienced. He had known them for years. Prue had known them, too. Bayleen had lived a few cottages away and had often looked after Prue when she was very little.

He thought about how this might have happened, scanning the ground for a sign that would confirm his suspicions. Rausha was a big man and very strong; whatever did this would have been much stronger and would have caught him off guard completely.

He slipped the bracelet off the severed wrist and got to his feet. He looked around once more, more cautious now than ever, more aware of what it was they were up against. "Come out, Prue," he called over to her.

He met her halfway, not letting her get any closer to the remains. When she was standing in front of him, green eyes mirroring the horror in his own, freckled face trying to look brave, he held out the bracelet.

"Oh, no, Pan," she whispered. Tears appeared in her eyes and trickled down her cheeks.

"Rausha, too," he said. He slid the bracelet into his pocket. "They must have been asleep when it happened."

Prue put her hands over her face and began to sob. He put his arms around her and pulled her close. "Shhh, Prue, shhh. It's all right."

It wasn't, of course, but it was all he could think to say. As he held her, he was reminded of how small she was. Her head barely reached his shoulders, and her body was so slight it was almost not there. He patted her head and stroked her hair. It had been a long time since he had seen her cry.

Finally she stopped and stepped back, brushing at her face with her sleeve. "What are we going to do?" she asked quietly.

"We're going after whoever did this," he said at once.

She looked up at him in disbelief. "You and me? We can't do that! We're still in training!"

"Technically," he agreed. "But we have the authority to make decisions on our own when we're scouting."

The tears were gone entirely now, and a hard look had replaced them. "I don't think Trow Ravenlock would agree with you."

"I'm sure he wouldn't."

"But then he isn't here, is he?"

Panterra gave her a quick smile. "No, he isn't."

She took a deep breath and exhaled. "And we're the best ones for a job like this, aren't we?"

She was alluding to their special talents, the ones responsible for gaining them Tracker standing at such a young age. Even at seventeen, he could decipher a trail better than anyone. He had an uncanny knack for knowing what had left it, and how long before, when others wouldn't even know it was there. Even Trow, who was the leader of the Trackers, acknowledged as much—although he still referred to Panterra as a boy. Prue was more gifted still. She had been born with preternatural instincts that warned of impending danger even when it was not visible. It was a talent she was rumored to have inherited from someone who had come into the valley with the Hawk. She had sensed the presence of the bodies that very morning, while they were still almost a hundred yards away. Young as they were, Panterra Qu and Prue Liss were the most effective pair of Trackers in Glensk Wood and perhaps the entire valley.

"We are the best," Panterra affirmed. "Anyone else who tries will be at much greater risk."

"What do we do if we find the things that did this?" She gestured toward the bodies.

"Mostly, I just want to get a look at them. A larger force can always hunt them down later." He held up one hand in a warding gesture. "I'm not suggesting you and I should try to take them on by ourselves."

"No, I shouldn't think so. Nor do I think we want what we're hunting to catch us out. We have to be very careful. I don't want to end up like Bayleen and Rausha."

He shifted his shoulder pack, looking out across the snowy expanse and the trail of blood. "Don't worry, we won't."

They set out at once, skirting the killing ground as quickly as possible, trying not to think about their friends and what it must have been like for them. They trudged up the slope in the wake of the blood spots, no longer bothering to hide their footprints, which would have been difficult in any case given the crusty covering of snow. The things they were tracking were making no effort to hide their passing, either, their huge splayed footprints clearly outlined where their feet had sunk deep into the white. Panterra gave them a quick glance, processing the information they offered. Great fleshy pads provided balance, claws the size of a Koden's allowed for ready purchase against the rock and frozen ground, two legs rather than four meant that they walked upright, and long strides suggested each one was well over six or even seven feet tall. Prue was right: he did not want these things to find out they were being tracked.

He glanced over at his youthful companion. He had grown up with Prue Liss; they had lived next door to each other and spent their childhoods together. The source and extent of their gifts was an open secret within their families, but otherwise kept private. Trow Ravenlock let them pair up because they had come to the Tracker cadre together and asked to be trained as a team. He might have preferred assigning each to someone older but quickly saw that they functioned best as a unit. More often than not, each knew what the other was thinking without either having spoken; each could finish the other's sentences as if they shared the same voice.

They had been together for so long, it seemed impossible that it would ever be otherwise.

"They're going back up into the mountains," Prue observed. She brushed back a lock of her flaming-red hair, tucking it under her cap. "Do you think they might be Kodens?"

The great bears lived at the higher elevations, solitary and reclusive, appearing now and then to hunters and trappers but hardly ever coming close to the communities. Certainly Kodens were big and strong enough to kill a pair of unsuspecting Trackers, as Panterra had surmised earlier.

But it still didn't feel right. "Kodens don't hunt in pairs," he pointed out. "Nor would they savage a body that way. They only kill to eat or protect their young. There were no signs of young Kodens and no reason for the savaging. Unless they were maddened by some disease or chance brought them together at the campsite, it doesn't make sense."

Prue didn't say anything for a minute, her breath clouding the air, her footfalls silent in the soft snow. "But what else could do something like this?"

He gave her a shake of his head. He didn't know. He glanced over and saw the mask of determination etched on her face. They were so different, Prue and he. For all that they shared talents that bound them closer than if they were siblings, they were still polar opposites in almost every way. He was tall and broad-shouldered and much stronger than he looked. She was slight, almost frail—although she could also be very tough when it was called for. She was emotional about everything, and he was emotional about almost nothing, a cerebral thinker, a planner and calculator. He was cautious while she was quick to act. He was forward thinking while she preferred to live in the moment.

He could list other differences, other contrasts, but in truth they were still more alike than not. They shared a love of life lived outside walls, a life of exploration and discovery. They were skilled survivalists, able to convert almost anything at hand into tools and shelter. They were athletic and good with weapons. They were of a like mind about the ways in which the world was changing, too, here within the valley, where the once united peoples who had been saved were splintering into groups that no longer had much to do with one another and who, in some instances, were openly hostile to those who were not like them.

They were in agreement about the one they called Hawk, who had brought their people here five centuries ago, and about those who now called themselves his children.

Ahead, the blood trail, which had diminished steadily the farther they got from the killing ground, bloomed anew amid a line of thinning trees. Pan slowed their pace, trying to make sense of what he was seeing, searching the shadows for signs of their quarry. But nothing moved on the landscape or amid the trees and rocks.

The silence was deafening.

"Do you sense anything?" he asked Prue.

"Nothing that I didn't sense before." She glanced over, her fine-boned features tense beneath her cap. "Is that stain ahead what I think it is?"

He chose not to answer. "Wait here," he told her.

He edged ahead toward the smear, already as certain as she must have been that it was blood. But as he neared, he saw that there were bones, too. There were bits of flesh and clothing.

There was part of a head.

Prue, who had come up beside him, silent as a shadow, threw up on the spot, unable to help herself, choking and gasping as she knelt in the snow. Panterra gripped her shoulders, bending close. "Take deep breaths," he whispered.

She did as she was told, and the sickness appeared to dissipate and her head to clear. "Don't look," he told her.

"Too late," she replied.

He helped her to her feet. "They ate them here, didn't they?" she murmured.

He nodded, forcing himself to look anew at the mess, studying the ground carefully, reading the signs. "They ate them, and then they slept. Over there." He pointed.

They walked over to a pair of depressions in the snow that gave a clear indication of the size and bulk of their quarry. Panterra knelt once more, touching the packed snow, trailing his fingers across its surface.

"They slept here after eating, then rose and went that way." He pointed off to the west and back down the slopes. "They're not done hunting."

"How far ahead?" she asked.

He rose and stood looking bleakly down into the deep woods that spread out below them. "Only an hour or so."

They set out once more, neither of them saying anything now, both of them concentrating on the task at hand. The air was growing warmer as the sun moved higher, the morning inching toward midday. They had been tracking for more than seven hours, and Panterra was aware of the need for food and rest. But they couldn't afford to stop for either until they finished this. The risk of losing their quarry, now that they were so close, was too great to set aside in favor of personal needs.

The snow line had been left behind more than a mile back, and the frozen ground of earlier had softened. Traces of footprints reaffirmed that there were two of them, and the width and depth of their prints was worrisome. Panterra was growing steadily less comfortable with every step they took. If they inadvertently stumbled onto these beasts or if the beasts happened to catch sight of them following, he did not like to think of the consequences. Both Prue and he carried long knives and bows, but these were poor weapons against opponents of this size. A spear or sword would better serve them, but Trackers did not like to be burdened with heavy weapons and neither Pan nor Prue bore them.

He thought some more about what they were doing, hunting creatures strong enough to kill two older and more experienced Trackers. He felt his reasons for doing so were good ones, but he had to wonder if he was displaying sufficient common sense. He knew that he and Prue were blessed with unusual talent and excellent instincts, but it would only take one slip for them to end up as two additional casualties with no one the wiser. He glanced momentarily at the girl, but she was concentrating on studying the way forward and paid him no attention. He did not see any doubt on her face.

He quickly erased his own.

The woods ahead grew increasingly dense, and the shadows dark. It was harder to see much of anything in the gloom, the sun unable to penetrate the heavy canopy. But that was where the tracks led.

He slowed anyway, signaling to Prue. She looked over. "What?"

He shook his head, not sure "what." Something, though, was not right. He could feel it in his bones.

"Still don't sense anything?" he pressed.

She shook her head no.

He hesitated, wondering if she might be mistaken. But she had never been mistaken before. It was foolish to start doubting her now. "Let's keep moving," he said.

They entered the woods, slipping noiselessly between the trunks of the trees, through the weeds and tall grasses. Because of the denseness of the foliage, they were forced to separate to avoid traveling in single file where only one could see ahead, working their way forward perhaps ten or twelve feet apart. The light faded, and the gloom deepened. There were no longer any tracks to follow, but broken stalks and scrapes on the bark marked the way. *Good enough for now*, Panterra thought. These were sufficient to keep them on the trail.

Then abruptly the woods opened onto a swamp, a morass of grasses alive with buzzing insects and groundwater thick with pond scum. A wind blew foul and sour across the waters and into the trees, carrying the scents of death and decay.

Panterra knew at once that he had made a mistake. He sank into a crouch, watching Prue, now almost fifteen feet away, do the same. While they had been tracking the creatures that had killed Bayleen and Rausha, the creatures had sensed them and led them to this bog. Swampy water ahead and a choking forest all about—it was a trap.

A quick shiver ran down his spine. How had Prue missed this? Had the stench of the swamp somehow masked their presence? Was that why her instincts had failed her? He reached for his knife and slowly drew it from its sheath. Prue was too far away, he realized suddenly— too distant for him to protect. He cast about swiftly, searching for a sign that would tell him from which direction the attack would come.

He found it almost immediately.

The creatures were right behind him.

3

PANTERRA QU TOOK A DEEP BREATH AND STARTED to turn around to face whatever was there. But a voice as cold and hard as winter stopped him where he was.

"Stay still. They know you're here, but they don't know exactly where yet. If you move, they will."

Pan was so shocked that he did what he was told without thinking. Whoever was speaking was right behind him, but obviously it wasn't one of the creatures he was tracking. He had been mistaken about that.

"Where are they?" he whispered, keeping his eyes focused on the swamp and its dense foliage. "I don't see them."

"It's a standoff then, boy. You don't see them, and they don't see you. No one sees anyone, do they? No, don't move. Don't try to turn around. Just stay still and listen to me."

Panterra shot a quick look over at Prue, who was staring at him in bewilderment. She didn't see the speaker, either, and couldn't figure out what Pan was doing just crouching there, staring out at the swamp. He made a small gesture for her to stay where she was.

"Will she do as you say?" the speaker asked. "That was a Tracker sign. Are you both Trackers?"

Pan nodded. "Yes."

"Kind of young for that sort of work. You must be good or know someone in the council. Do you come from Glensk Wood?"

Pan nodded again. "Who are you?"

"A friend. A good friend, as it turns out. I might even be able to save your life. Another few minutes, though, and I might have been too late. They've set you a trap."

"Have you been following them, too?" Pan tried to reason it through. "Or were you following us?"

"Don't flatter yourself, boy. I was following them, but you cut across their tracks ahead of me. Anyone else, another Tracker, would have gone back to the village for help. Not you, though. Are you brave or stupid?"

"Neither," Pan answered, a flush rising from his neck to his face. "I knew the two that were killed. They were Trackers, too. But I don't think what did it is anything we've ever seen before. So I thought we ought to get a look so we would know what it is that we're hunting later on when there are more of us."

The speaker was quiet for a moment. "You must be pretty good at the Tracker business. The girl, too. I had trouble following your prints where there wasn't snow to mark the way. Even then, it was easier following the tracks of the creatures than your own."

He had shifted somehow while he talked, gone more to the left. Pan could tell this by the change in the direction of his voice. But he hadn't heard the other move at all, not a single rustle. He studied the swamp again, and then cast another glance over at Prue.

To his horror, he saw that she had left her position and was coming toward him in a stealthy crouch.

"Tell her to stop!" the speaker hissed.

But Prue ignored his hand signals, seeing something now that he couldn't, which meant that the speaker had done something to give himself away and she was now aware of him.

"Can you fight as well as you track?" the speaker asked hurriedly.

A sword was shoved over Panterra's shoulder, handle-first. "Take this. You'll need it if you hope to stay alive. Don't engage—just fend it off, keep it at bay. I'll help you if I can, but the girl will need me more."

"What are we fight—" Pan started to ask.

The rest of his question was cut short by an explosion of movement from two different points at the edges of the swamp, one directly across from him, the other from his far left no more than fifty feet behind Prue. The brush and grasses burst apart, stagnant water geysered skyward into the low-hanging branches of the trees, and two monstrous apparitions came charging out of the gloom. They were down on all fours now, great hulking beasts that were barely visible through the gouts of swamp water and flying bits and pieces of plants and might have been almost anything.

Pan came to his feet, bracing himself. Out of the corner of his eye he caught sight of a gray shadow as it whipped through the grasses behind him, heading for Prue. A man, but so quick and light on his feet that it seemed to the boy he must be an apparition. He reached Prue ahead of the attacking beast, picked her up in one smooth motion, and bolted toward a huge old cedar. A second later he had tossed the girl ten feet into the air, her outstretched arms catching hold of a nest of thick branches from which she then hung desperately.

Pan liked the idea of a big tree, not wishing to climb it so much as to put it between himself and the monster that was now almost on top of him, tearing through the swamp as if it could sense where there was solid footing. Its head was wedge-shaped and armored with thick scales, and its maw was a mass of blackened teeth ready to rend its quarry. Pan fled at once, racing for a second cedar, aware of the closeness of the thing behind him. It moved more quickly than something that big should have been able to, and it was terrifying. Pan got to the tree just ahead of the beast, wheeled around, and struck the creature as its momentum carried it past him.

It was like striking a rock. His blade bounced off without effect, and the force of the blow numbed his arms all the way from his hands to his shoulders. He ducked back around the tree once more, watching the beast skid to a halt amid tufts of flying earth and grass. He needed a better plan than this one, he thought, and he didn't have one.

Then the stranger was suddenly there once more, flashing out of nowhere to stand between the beast and Pan. He held a black staff with markings that glowed as white as brilliant sunlight. The armored monster never hesitated when it saw the man. It came at him at once, a juggernaut thundering through gloom and tall grasses with singular intent. The man faced it without trying to escape, the staff held vertically before him, its entire length on fire now.

Run! Pan wanted to scream, but the word wouldn't come.

An instant later white fire erupted from the staff, lancing like a great, long spear into the attacker. It caught the creature just below its armored head, just inside one huge front shoulder. It picked the creature up as if it were a rag doll and threw it backward in a sprawling heap where it lay twitching and smoking.

Panterra stared in disbelief.

The man was moving again, vaulting through the foliage toward the second beast, not once looking back. Prue was under attack, the beast that had come around the swamp from the back trying to climb into the tree in which she perched. It reared up on its hind legs, becoming fully fifteen feet tall by doing so, and was clawing and tearing at the bark of the cedar, trying to reach the girl. Prue, realizing the danger, had climbed into the highest branches. But the tree was shaking and swaying so badly that she was in danger of being dislodged, and she wouldn't last long if the beast succeeded in tearing the tree out by its roots.

Then her rescuer was there, the staff afire once more, whirling and twisting in his hands, a weapon of wild magic. He sent the white fire slamming into the beast, knocking it away from the tree, tumbling it head-over-heels into the dense foliage. The beast came back to its feet, shook itself, roared in fury, and struck anew.

When it attacked directly, Panterra saw, you couldn't see much of anything past the armor of the head and shoulders. It was the creature's main defense. But their rescuer seemed ready for this, and he let the beast almost reach him before dodging aside and avoiding its rush. It said something about his skills that Pan was unable to tell which way the man was going to jump until after he had done so. Apparently the beast was fooled as well, because it failed to change direction until it was too late.

Exposed now from the rear, it tried to turn back around to protect itself, its strange voice sounding like the rasp of metal on metal. But it was far too slow. The white fire lanced from the staff, caught it mid-stride and hammered it backward in a fresh explosion of power. The force of the blow knocked it off its solid footing on the forested ground and into the mire of the swamp. Thrashing amid the fouled waters, it tried to rise. But the stranger used the staff a final time, striking at the big head, pinning it down, keeping it submerged. The beast fought to rise again and again, but finally it could no longer manage to lift its head and sank.

The stranger turned back, and Panterra did the same, searching for the second beast. But it was gone. Pan would not have thought it possible, given the damage it had sustained, but somehow it had risen and lumbered off, finding its way back through the trees toward the upper slopes of the mountain, backtracking in the direction it had originally come.

Ignoring Panterra, the stranger walked over to the cedar and directed Prue down, lifting her gently off the lower branches when she reached them.

"It will try to go back the way it came," he advised, nodding in the direction of the second creature.

"What are those things?" Prue asked, unable to suppress a shiver.

The man shook his head. "Beasts from another world, things we don't yet have a name for. What are *your* names?"

Pan told him, adding that they were sorry they hadn't been more careful in their efforts to track the creatures. He was seeing the man clearly for the first time, a tall, lean hunter wearing a strange combination of well-made boots and harness and clothes that were loose and tattered, the sleeves and pant legs ragged at the ends and the cloak shredded through. It lent him a ghostly appearance, even though his face was bearded, his black hair worn long, and his wind-burned, sun-browned skin as dusky as damp earth. He carried himself in a relaxed, easy fashion and seemed very much at ease, barely breathing hard even after his battle with the creatures. But his eyes never stopped moving, keeping watch.

"You're Sider Ament," Panterra said finally. "The one they call the Gray Man."

The stranger nodded. "Have we met before? How do you know me?"

Pan shrugged, glancing at Prue. "I don't know you. But we both know of you. We've heard the stories; Trow Ravenlock, who leads the Trackers of Glensk Wood, has told them to us. He described you. Especially that black staff. He says it was a talisman once. He says you are descended from the old Knights of the Word who served the Hawk."

Sider Ament shook his head. "He says a lot of things about me, doesn't he? For someone I've never met. I don't know the truth of most of what you say. I've heard the stories, too. But no one asked me to whom I was related or any of that. I'm a hunter born, a wanderer by nature, and I was given this staff by the one who carried it before me on the day he died. Now you know more of the truth than Trow what's-his-name and you can tell the stories better."

He looked off into the distance in the direction of the fleeing creature. "I'm going to have to go after it. I can't let it get out of the valley and let others know we're here. But I guess there's time enough for that when we're done speaking. This is important, too."

"Out of the valley?" Prue repeated, disbelief in her voice.

For the first time, the stranger smiled. "You are quick, little one. How is it you're a Tracker, though? You seem very young and small for such work." He glanced back at Panterra. "Even your protector seems a bit young, although at least he seems strong enough. And you both have some skills, that's clear. Tell me about them. About yourselves."

Ordinarily, neither would have told anyone anything unless they knew the person well enough to call him a friend. But the Gray Man's reputation was such that it never even occurred to them not to reply. So Prue revealed the truth about their talents and how these had set them apart from the other members of the community since they were children. Pan listened without saying anything, vaguely uncertain about whether Prue was wise in revealing all this, but unwilling to intervene.

When she was done, Sider Ament nodded slowly. "There were others like you once," he said. "Others who came into this valley back in the beginning." He looked as if he might say more, then made a dismissive gesture. "But that's the past, and the past can't help us. It's the present that matters, and you two seem capable enough of doing what's needed in my absence. Will you agree to help me?"

"If we can," Pan agreed carefully.

"Then go back to Glensk Wood and tell its council what's hap-

pened. Describe everything. Leave nothing out. Make them understand that what you are telling them is no exaggeration. Tell them that
these things are just the first of others that are coming. Tell them
that—"

He stopped suddenly. "Well, tell them what I am about to tell you.
You have to know first, and you have to believe what I'm going to tell
you for this to work. Here, sit a moment."

He took them over to a fallen log where they seated themselves.
Sider Ament's gray eyes held them pinned as he spoke.

"The world you know is ending, young ones. It isn't happening in
the way that the Children of the Hawk have foretold and that many
others would like. There's no return of the one who sealed us in here,
no resurrection of the dead, and no turning back to what's long past.
The mists that have sealed the valley away and kept us safe are dissipating. Soon they will be gone entirely. The world outside, the one we
left behind all those centuries ago, is going to come in to have a look
around. Those creatures we just fought were only the first that will
find their way here."

He paused. "Actually, they aren't even the first. There have been
others before them. But they were less dangerous and did little real damage. They took a few wild creatures, a stray farm animal or two—that
was it. Even then, I thought the mists would re-form and strengthen. But
they didn't and they won't. I know that now. They will only continue to
weaken."

Panterra and Prue exchanged a quick glance. "We don't believe as
do the Seraphic sect," Pan said. "We're Trackers, and we believe in a
world outside this valley. But we didn't know about the mists. We didn't
know anything had changed."

"No one does. Yet." Sider Ament rocked back slightly, cradling the
black staff in his arms. "But they need to. They need to prepare themselves. Not only for the emotional shock, but for the fighting, as well.
There will be dangerous things out there in the wastelands of the old
world. What was left behind was caught in a world of poisons and savagery, and only the worst and the strongest will have survived. It won't
be easy keeping them out."

He paused. "Let's be honest. We won't be *able* to keep them out.

Some will get through. Our chances for survival will depend on how few manage to do that."

Neither Panterra nor Prue said anything for a moment. Then Prue shifted uncomfortably on the log. "They won't believe us," she said. "The members of the council, the members of the sect, the Seraphic, none of them."

"Most won't. But one or two will. Enough to nurture a seed of doubt that will start to grow in the others. There will be other incursions into the valley, other killings, and then more will believe. But we don't want to wait on that. We have to start telling people now."

"What about the Elves and Lizards and the others?" Pan asked quickly. "Especially the Elves. We know some of their Trackers and Hunters are already looking to finding a way to leave the valley. They just don't know it's possible yet. But they will be quicker to believe."

The Gray Man nodded. "Then tell them. Or someone else from your village can. But I would think you would do the job best, if you can persuade your unit commander to let you."

The boy and the girl exchanged a doubtful look. Trow Ravenlock was a member of the sect and not likely to receive their news with an open mind.

"We'll do what we can," Prue said quickly.

Sider Ament smiled for the second time. "That's all I can ask. Spread the word, ask people to prepare." He rose. "I must be going."

Panterra and Prue stood up with him. "Will we see you again?" the girl asked.

"I imagine so." The Gray Man stretched his lean frame and rolled his shoulders. "Once I've tracked down that other beast, I'll come looking for you." He paused. "It might take a while, though. If it goes through the mists. It came in that way, after all. I imagine it will try to go back out."

"You haven't been there yourself?" Panterra asked.

Sider Ament shook his head. "Not yet. No reason to go looking for trouble when it will find you all on its own. I was hoping, of course, that I wouldn't have to go out at all, that a healing would take place. But it hasn't, so now maybe I'll have to go."

He gave Pan an enigmatic smile. "Maybe all of us will."

The boy's throat tightened in response, and he tried to imagine just for a moment what that would mean. He could not.

Sider Ament stepped close to them. "Now you listen. You're young, but you're capable. I regret having to ask this of you, though sometimes life doesn't give us the choices we might like. You have to do what needs doing here, but you can be careful about it. This is a dangerous time, and some of what's dangerous about it might not come from the direction you're looking, if you take my meaning."

Pan nodded. He understood.

"So you watch out for each other and you do what's right in this. Don't doubt yourselves and don't be turned aside from what's needed. A lot is going to depend on how quickly people of all the Races come around to seeing the truth of things. You can help make that happen, and what you do might make all the difference."

"We can do what's needed," Prue volunteered. "Can't we, Pan?"

Panterra nodded. "We can."

"I'll tell you more about all this the next time we meet." Sider Ament stepped away again. "One thing more. Remember what it felt like today, having one of those things bearing down on you like a landslide. Remember what it made you feel. That was real. And those things aren't the worst of what's waiting out there. I don't know that for sure, you understand. But I feel it in my bones."

He hefted the black staff and turned away. "Walk softly, Trackers, until we meet again."

They watched him stride off into the trees, a tattered wraith wrapped in what might have been the trappings of the dead, sliding from trunk to trunk, silent as dust falling, until at last he was gone.

The woods were silent now, the swamp a vast graveyard of dead things, the air rank with their smells. Panterra took a deep breath and looked over at Prue. Her small face was set with that familiar determined look, and her green eyes were serious.

"This isn't going to be easy," she told him.

He nodded. "I know."

"We have to think it through."

"I know that, too."

"Then we better get to it."

4

NEITHER PANTERRA NOR PRUE SPOKE UNTIL THEY had retraced their steps through the deep woods and were back in the relatively clear stretch below the snow line, and then they both began talking at once.

"I should have asked him about that staff . . ."

"He's nothing like the stories we've heard . . ."

They stopped speaking and looked at each other, and then Prue said, "He doesn't seem at all like the person in the stories." She wrinkled her freckled nose. "What does that suggest?"

"That the stories are either mistaken or lies." Pan walked with his eyes sweeping the woods along the lower slopes and the craggy rock along the upper. He didn't intend to get caught off guard again, even if he supposed that the danger was past. "Or maybe some of each."

"Trow told us most of them," she said.

"Most, but not all. And the stories are always the same. The Gray Man is a wild man, a recluse living in the upper reaches of the valley, keeping apart from everyone. He wanders from this place to that, his clothes ragged and torn, his face haunted by memories that no one knows but him. He carries that black staff, a remnant of the old world, a talisman once, but an outdated symbol of something long since turned to dust. He scavenges to stay alive, and you don't want him near your children because it is said he sometimes takes them and they are never seen again."

"That isn't what we saw," she pressed.

He glanced over. "No, it isn't. But we only saw him for a short time, so we don't know all that much."

"We know enough."

When Prue made up her mind about something, that was the end of it. That seemed to be the case here. Besides, Panterra wasn't inclined to disagree. What they had seen of Sider Ament was not in keeping with the stories. The Gray Man was wild enough, but he seemed sane and directed, and what he had to say about those beasts and the other creatures breaking through the mists could not be ignored.

"What do you suppose he does, living out there by himself?" Prue asked, interrupting his thoughts.

Pan shook his head. "I don't know. Watches, mostly. He seemed to know about those creatures quick enough to come after them. He must watch the passes, too. Otherwise he wouldn't know about the collapse of the barriers. Weren't the Knights of the Word dedicated to doing something like that once?"

"They were servants of the Word, Aislinne says. They fought against the demons that tried to destroy everything. So I guess they must have kept watch over our ancestors just like Sider Ament is keeping watch over us." She paused. "If Sider Ament is one of them, as the stories say, he would be doing the same thing, wouldn't he? He's certainly more than what they claim. You saw what he did with that black staff. He threw those beasts aside as if they were made of straw. I've never heard any stories about him being able to do that."

In truth, Panterra thought, they had never heard any stories about the black staff that didn't refer to it as a useless relic. The tales noted that he carried the staff, but used it only as a walking stick.

He found himself wishing he had the Gray Man back again so he could ask him about the power it contained. Was it a form of magic or science? It could have been either, but it was still from another era and something no one in the valley had ever seen before.

"Anyway, I don't care what the stories say, he was keeping watch over us," Prue finished, putting emphasis on her words. She gave Panterra a look.

"He did what I should have done," Pan admitted. "I led us right into a trap that would have gotten us killed."

"You did the best you could. How could you know what those creatures were like? How could you know they were from outside the valley?" She put a hand on his arm. "I should have sensed we were in danger, and I missed it."

"You don't have to take responsibility for my mistake," Pan insisted. "I know what I did."

She shrugged. "Let it go, Pan. We're safe now, and we have other things to worry about."

They talked for a while about how they were going to approach carrying out the charge given to them by Sider Ament. It would not be easy. Only a few were likely to accept that the world was changing in such a drastic way, and not many of them were in a position to do anything about it.

Trow Ravenlock might be one. He was a member of the Hawk sect and a subscriber to the belief that the Hawk would return to lead them out of the valley when it was time. But he was also a man who could be persuaded to a cause where there was evidence it was right to do so. He might hew to the party line, but he was independent enough in his thinking to listen to what Pan and Prue would tell him.

The other possibility was Aislinne. But getting her to help them would be tricky. She was impossible to predict; she might choose to do everything in her power to help or she might do nothing at all.

The hours slipped by, midday turning into afternoon and afternoon to dusk. By the time they had come down out of the high regions and onto the flats at the west end of the valley, the sun had dropped behind the rim of the mountains and the sky was coloring to gold and pink. On another day, the boy and the girl would have stopped to admire it. But the news they brought of the deaths of their friends and the charge they had been given did not allow for pauses.

So they crossed the grassy foothills to the thick woodlands beyond and made their way down familiar paths to their destination. The windows of the cottages and longhouses shone as firefly lights through the trees long before they arrived, and they could hear the sounds of voices and evening tasks being carried out as they approached, familiar and comforting.

"I could eat something," Prue observed.

"Right after we give our report," Panterra agreed.

They entered the village and made their way to the longhouse that served both as a gathering point for the Trackers of Glensk Wood and as a residence for their leader, Trow Ravenlock. It was early still, and there were torches burning at the entrance and candlelight flickering from within. But when they climbed the steps of the porch and peered through the door, they found the common rooms empty of everyone but Trow himself.

The Tracker leader was seated at one of the tables, studying a collection of hand-drawn maps. His short, lean body was hunched over as he worked, and his angular features were tightened in concentration. But he looked up quickly as they entered and hesitated only a moment before getting to his feet. "What's happened?"

Clearly he had read something in their faces. They walked over until they were standing in front of him. "Bayleen and Rausha are dead," Panterra said. "Killed before sunrise, probably in their sleep."

"Before sunrise," the other repeated. He looked from face to face. "So you've been tracking the killers?"

Pan nodded. "Since early this morning, up the slopes of Declan Reach and back down again. We cut the trail of the killers first and then discovered the killing ground. We kept tracking until we found where they had bedded down amid the remains. Then, toward midday, we caught up to them."

He stopped, waiting to see if Trow had heard clearly. The Tracker leader ran his hand through his iron-gray hair and blinked. "They killed them and then ate them later?" he asked slowly. "Is that what you're saying?"

"They dismembered them so that they were all but unrecognizable," Prue answered. "Show him, Pan."

Panterra reached in his pocket and produced Bayleen's bracelet. "That was how we know who it was," he said.

Trow Ravenlock sat back down slowly. "What sort of creatures would do something like that? Were they Kodens?"

Pan shook his head. "We thought they might be Kodens, but they weren't. They weren't like anything we've ever seen. Like anything anyone in this valley has ever seen. We tracked them, Trow, but they caught our scent or heard us. They set a trap for us; they were waiting in ambush. We almost died. But someone saved us."

He told the Tracker leader then about their encounter with Sider Ament and how the Gray Man had done battle with the creatures, killing one and driving off the other. They told him, as well, of the Gray Man's warning that the wall of the protective mists that had kept them safe for five centuries was breaking down. Prue added her own opinion: that Sider Ament was right and the things that had killed their friends had not come from within the valley but from somewhere without, from the world their ancestors had abandoned, because nothing so terrible had ever been seen in their own world.

Trow Ravenlock listened silently, and when Panterra and Prue were done, he looked at them a moment before shaking his head. "It isn't possible. What you're telling me about the mists? It isn't possible. The legend says—"

"It doesn't matter what the legend *says*!" Prue interrupted heatedly. "What matters is what we *saw*! Those things, Trow, were clear proof of what the Gray Man says is happening."

"Maybe, maybe not." Trow held up his hand as they both started to argue anew. "It doesn't matter what you or I think, in any case. What matters is what the members of the council think, and they're going to listen to the Seraphic. His voice is the law on matters concerning the Hawk and the future of this community's people beyond the valley. We can argue this until the cows come home and beyond, but it doesn't change things." He paused, looking from one face to the other. "Does it."

He made it a statement of fact. He sounded so calm about it Panterra was immediately angry.

"No, it doesn't," he agreed. "But we are obligated to make our report to you, and you are obligated to carry it before the council."

Trow shook his head. "I am obligated to do what I feel is best. In this case, giving a report to the council is not a wise idea. What I will do is to send other Trackers back up into Declan Reach to see if we can make sense of things. I will even order them to test the strength of the mists, so far as we are able to do so."

"'To see if we can make sense of things'?" the boy repeated.

"Don't make it sound like that. It's just a precaution to make sure you didn't miss something, that what you think you saw is what you actually did see."

Panterra started to respond and then hesitated, glancing back at the open longhouse door. Had he heard something? He walked across the room to the door and looked outside. The porch was empty, and there was no sign of anyone beyond. He searched the darkness for a moment, and then closed the door and walked back to Trow.

"If you won't give my report to the council, will you give it to Pogue Kray, at least?"

"The council chair will have the same reaction as mine, Panterra, only more so. He hews to the teachings of the sect much more closely than I do. It will accomplish nothing to tell him something he will not accept. You have to face the truth about this. No one is going to believe something so radical. They'll think you're seeing things and are unfit for your position."

Panterra and Prue exchanged a glance. "I request that I be allowed to make the report for you," Pan said. "I have the right to speak before the council on matters that concern the safety of the community. I am exercising that right now."

There was a tight silence as the two faced each other. "You have to let him," Prue agreed.

"I know what I have to do, young lady," Trow Ravenlock replied, looking over at her sharply. "I don't need you to remind me." He paused, turning his gaze back on Pan. "Why don't you sleep on this and we'll talk in the morning?"

Panterra shook his head. "A night's sleep won't change the truth of what we saw. We're wasting time. I want to give my report to the full council. Let them hear me out and decide for themselves."

"And hear me out, as well," Prue added bravely.

Trow looked from one to the other. "Don't put yourself in a position where you'll end up looking like fools. Worse, don't jeopardize your careers as Trackers. You might be throwing everything away by insisting on this. You're talented, but you're young still; you have some things to learn yet about prudence and common sense. This one time, listen to me. Let this go."

"We would be cowards if we did that," the boy said. "Bayleen and Rausha were friends; they deserve better."

"They were my friends, too. But they're dead and gone, and you can't change that." The Tracker's sharp eyes held them. "If you can find some hard evidence to support your statement, then you can give it."

Pan shook his head. "If we wait on this, people will wonder why we held our tongues. If it's true, why did we keep it from them?"

"We risk people finding out the hard way what we already know," Prue added. "We risk watching others die." She threw up her hands. "Why not just tell them? These people know us! They know we don't lie!"

Trow Ravenlock shook his head. "Skeal Eile might make them think otherwise. He has the skills to do that; I've seen it happen before. If you make him your enemy, he has the power to turn everyone against you. By giving this report, you might as well call him a fraud and a liar. You are declaring to everyone that the Children of the Hawk have been mistaken in their beliefs for five centuries. You can't do that and not expect retaliation. And you aren't ready for that."

"What I am not ready for," Panterra declared, "is sitting on my hands and doing nothing. I saw what I saw. We both did. These creatures we encountered were not from this valley. The Gray Man may be right—the wall of protection may be eroding. Whatever the case, he asked us to tell the people of Glensk Wood what he believes is happening, and we agreed to do so. I won't go back on my word."

The Tracker leader rose and stood looking at Pan. "You're making a mistake, but it's your mistake to make. Don't say you weren't warned. I'll give it until morning, in the unlikely case you change your mind. Then I'll speak to Pogue Kray and arrange for you to appear before the council tomorrow night."

He shook his head. "Now go—get out of here."

THE BOY AND THE GIRL WALKED from the longhouse and stood
together on the porch for a moment, staring out at the lighted windows of the community buildings where they glimmered in the darkness. As if by accord, neither spoke for a very long time.

"Maybe he's right," Prue said finally.

Pan gave her a look. "Maybe he's not."

"I'm just saying."

"Well, don't."

She tightened her lips petulantly. "Maybe we should just go to
bed."

"Maybe we should get something to eat first. Like we planned."

They went down off the steps and followed the path toward their
homes. It was growing late, and there were only a few people still
out and about at this hour. Those they passed nodded politely or said
hello, safe in the knowledge that all was right with the world, oblivious
to the truth. For reasons that he found hard to explain, it irritated
Panterra immensely.

"Will you come to my house and eat with me?" Pan asked finally.

Prue shook her head. "No, I think I'll just go home and find something there. I want to go to bed."

They didn't say anything more until their lane, with its neat row of
cottages, appeared through the trees. Lights flickered in a few windows, but none of them were theirs. Prue's parents were visiting her
mother's sister in the neighboring community of Fair Glade End.
Panterra's parents were two years dead from a wasting sickness that no
one had known how to treat.

They stopped in front of Prue's cottage, looking at everything but
each other. "I didn't mean to snap at you," Panterra told her. "I'm sorry
I did."

She shrugged. "I know that. You don't have to apologize to me.
I don't need you to do that ever, Pan."

"Maybe I need to hear myself say it."

She gave him a small smile. "See you tomorrow. Sleep well."

She turned and walked down the path to her doorway. Panterra waited until she had entered and closed the door, then turned and started for his own home. His older brother and sisters had shared the house with him until the last of them married and moved away. Now he lived alone, not quite certain what to do with either the house or himself when he wasn't tracking. Trow was right about that much: tracking was his life, and he didn't want to do anything that would force him to give it up.

He was almost to his doorstep when he heard someone call out in a low voice. He turned to find a small figure darting out of the trees to catch up to him. At first he thought it might be Prue—even though there was no reason for her to be appearing out of the forest when he had seen her go into her house. But as the figure neared, he realized who it was.

"Brickey," he said with as much enthusiasm as he could muster. "I was just going to bed."

The little man slowed to a walk but continued to approach until he was close enough that his whispers could only be heard by Pan. "Big day, I imagine, tracking monsters and what-have-you. Tiring work. Can you tell me what they looked like?"

Panterra snatched him by his tunic front and hauled him close. "That was you I heard outside the longhouse, listening in!"

Brickey managed a crooked smile, his features twisting uncomfortably. "Another wouldn't have heard me at all, Panterra. You are to be commended for your sharp senses."

Pan held him fast. "How did you even know we were back?"

"I saw you coming through the woods and decided to follow. I have an instinct for that sort of thing. Like you and the lovely little Prue, my instincts tell me what to do and I tend to listen to them."

Panterra studied him silently for a moment. Brickey had a shock of black hair, knotted, unattractive features, a gnarled little body, and scruffy clothes. They all screamed *thief* and they weren't lying. Brickey was a thief down to the soles of his boots, and the best that could be said about him was that he was very good at what he did. No one knew where he came from; he had just appeared, seemingly out of nowhere, a little more than two years ago. He had taken a liking to Pan for reasons that escaped the latter, showing up on his doorstep and at places he frequented, always acting as if they shared something approaching a friendship.

Pan let him get away with this because it appeared that Brickey had few friends, and there wasn't any harm in letting him act as if he were an exception. Brickey was in trouble a good deal of the time, his reach exceeding his grasp more often than not, but he never involved Pan and never asked for his help. Mostly, he just seemed to want someone he could talk to now and then.

"Let me give you some good advice, Brickey," Pan said, releasing his tunic front and brushing out the wrinkles. "Don't repeat anything you've heard tonight. Not to anyone. If anyone hears it, I better know that it came from me."

Brickey held up his hands defensively. "Oh, you don't have to worry about that! I won't breathe a word of it." He raised a cautionary finger. "But listen now. Let me give you some good advice in return for yours. Pay attention to what Trow Ravenlock told you. Don't give this report. Let things be for now—until you have hard evidence of what you claim to have seen."

"What I *did* see, you mean!" Pan snapped.

"Yes, yes, what you did see. But what no one else saw, you might want to remember." He leaned close. "I know Skeal Eile and his kind. I know how they think. You anger them, and you will live to regret it. You don't want to find out what that means by giving this report. Leave it with Trow."

Panterra nodded. "I appreciate your advice, but I've made up my mind."

Brickey backed away, shaking his head with disappointment. "Strong-willed and stubborn is what you are, Pan. But I can admire that in a man. Even when it's wrongheaded. Good night."

He gave a perfunctory wave and disappeared back into the trees. Pan watched him go, then turned back to his home and went inside.

It took him a long time to get to sleep.

5

PANTERRA WOKE AT SUNRISE. THE AIR WAS BITTER cold and he could see his breath cloud the air in front of his face. He rose quickly, walked to the front windows and looked out. The ground was thick with frost, a white coating of icy powder that sparkled in the faint first light. He moved to a different position, where he could see part of the upper stretches of Declan Reach. The snow line was down far enough that it was below the false horizon created by the cover of the trees.

He stared out at the mountains and the snow and the mist that hung like gauze across both and wondered that spring was so slow in coming.

Then he turned and hurried to the big stone hearth to make a fire, thinking back to another time. When he was a boy, his mother rose early to make the fire. It was always burning long before Pan woke, so that the house was warm and welcoming for him. His mother would be in the kitchen cooking, making him cakes or fry bread or some other sweet he favored. He'd smell sausage or a side of ham cooking, and there would be cold milk and hot ale set out on the table in large pitchers.

His mother would leave what she was doing and come to him at once, hugging him close, telling him good morning and letting him know how happy she was to have him.

He shook his head. It all seemed so long ago.

He knelt by the hearth, nursing sparks from the flint and tinder until the fire was going, and then added larger logs so that it would burn hot while he cooked. He brought out bread and meat and cheese and set them out. He boiled water for hot tea and set out two plates, cups, and cutlery. Everything was almost ready by the time Prue knocked on the door and peeked inside, as he knew she would.

"Is that for me?" she asked, indicating the second plate.

She knew it was, of course. It was their morning ritual when they were home after a long tracking. But she liked asking the question and he liked hearing her do so, so they continued to play the game long after it had grown familiar. Besides, he thought, there was no one else who would come to eat with him. Not uninvited, at least.

"Sit," he invited, pulling over a thick cushion and tossing her a throw his mother had made.

She was still wearing the same clothes from last night, and she looked as if sleep might have been as difficult for her as it had been for him. She closed the door and hurried over, arms wrapped about her slender body.

"It's freezing out there. Not like yesterday." She sat, holding her hands out to the fire. "Do you think spring will ever get here? Or is nature just playing games with us?"

He shrugged. "Can't be sure, but my guess is that winter's pretty much done. You saw how the leaves were budding on the hardwoods lower down off the high country. Faster than usual and thicker. You saw the sky at sunset. The cold still deepens each morning, but I don't expect it to be like that much longer."

He poured hot water from the pot into a cup and held it out for her, then took one for himself. They sipped in silence, taking pleasure in the warming air of the cottage and in the comfort they found in the presence of each other. There was no reason to say much of anything right away. There would be time for talking later.

He served up the food and they ate it in silence, sitting cross-legged in front of the fire. Panterra was fully awake now and alert, thinking about what lay ahead come nightfall. He would go before the council and speak of what had happened yesterday. He would ask Prue not to speak, just to support him by her silent presence so that perhaps she would not be tainted by the remarks he would make. But he knew she would refuse. Keeping silent was the coward's way, and Prue was never a coward. She would stand up for him and herself and for what she knew was right. That was how she was, how she had always been.

After breakfast was finished, they took the dishes to the kitchen and washed them in the old metal sink, using water that was hand-pumped from the well out back. The water was good in Glensk Wood. Wells were plentiful and tapped into a large aquifer that lay just to the northwest, toward the foothills. Food was easy to come by, too. Most of it grew wild, both fruits and vegetables, and hunting was a skill acquired by most at an early age. The balance of what was needed was grown in gardens and on small farms. Some of the communities struggled a bit more than Glensk Wood in the matter of food, but they had developed the skill to make tools and implements and so exchanged their goods for what they required. Trade among the villages of Men satisfied everyone's needs, and when it didn't there were always the Elves and the Lizards to provide what was missing. When the valley was first settled, it had taken a while for the communities to establish an order to things, to find their places in a supportive construct that let everyone live reasonably comfortably. But once they had settled in, trade had flourished.

Pan thought about the history of his valley world, a history that every child was taught nearly from birth. Not the part about the Hawk and his role in the past and future of the Saved, but of the way the relationships among the Races had evolved. The Races had separated shortly after their arrival, moving away from one another to establish their own boundaries within the confines of their new home. Men had settled in the south and west, the Elves had gone northeast, and the Lizards and Spiders, with their numbers much smaller, had made their homes in small corners in between.

The valley allowed for this separation because it was actually more than a single valley. It was a series of smaller valleys separated by natural barriers—woods, hills, lakes, and rivers, some smaller mountain ranges—all of it enclosed by the high peaks around which the mists formed their impassable barriers. The enclosure ran more than fifty miles west to east and almost a hundred north to south. Not an imposing distance, but one that allowed for territorial claims. It was said that there were countless more miles of land beyond the mists, and great bodies of water, as well. But no one living had ever seen them because no one living had ever been outside the mists.

This confinement had troubled no one for most of the time the Races had lived together. But that was changing. Even given the long period of adjustment and the strong network of relationships created through trade, a steady number had begun to wonder what lay beyond and if it could somehow be reached. The Children of the Hawk were a creation of Men, after all, and the other Races did not subscribe to its teachings. That was a reason for some of the tension that had built among the differing peoples. The Elves, for instance, believed it was their duty to go out into the world and restore it to what it had been before they were driven here by the massive destruction of the Great Wars. The Lizards were nomads, and the Spiders deeply reclusive. It was a poor fit, these disparate Races confined as they were, even given their acceptance of their fate. Their network of alliances and interdependencies would fly apart in a moment once they discovered the mists were breaking down.

As they were sure to do, Pan thought, if the Gray Man was right about what was happening.

"I've been thinking," Prue said suddenly. They were putting away the last of the dishes they had washed. "Maybe we ought to reconsider speaking before the council."

Her suggestion was so out of character that for a moment he just stared at her.

"Don't look at me like that," she said, frowning. "I don't much like the idea, either. But it might be better to do as Trow suggested and to wait and see. Saying the wrong thing now could land us in a lot of trouble, Pan."

She was right, of course, but they had known this from the first. "You've been speaking with Brickey, haven't you?" he said.

"He came to the door last night, after talking with you."

"I hope you didn't let him in."

She gave him a look. "He's not dangerous, Pan. But no, I didn't let him in; it was too late for that and I was tired. I did listen to what he had to say, though, and it makes some sense. Whatever else he is, he's not stupid. He sees things pretty clearly. And he's right about Skeal Eile. It's dangerous to question his teachings."

Pan had heard the rumors. Those who opposed the Seraphic almost always ended up changing their minds. Some were threatened with banishment from the community. Some suffered unfortunate accidents. Some went missing altogether. He looked down at his hands, still holding one of the plates. He set it down carefully. "I don't intend to question his teachings or his beliefs. I don't intend to do anything but repeat what Sider Ament told us. I promised to give his warning, that's all."

"I know you. It won't stop there. You'll be questioned on your story and you'll fight back. It won't help; it will only make things worse."

He sighed. "So you want me to do nothing, Prue? That doesn't sound like you."

"I want you to think about asking Trow for Trackers to go up into the passes. If we had evidence, we could go before the council with a little more assurance that we wouldn't be dismissed as children."

"You think that's how we'll be seen?"

She nodded slowly. "I do."

He didn't say anything for a time, mulling it over. "Maybe you're right. But I can't back down just because of the way people might see me afterward. Not when it's this important. If even a few are persuaded that there might be something to what Sider Ament says, then that's reason enough."

She gave him a small smile. "I thought that's what you'd say. I told Brickey as much. You know what he said? He said it would surprise him if you said anything else."

Panterra reached out and put his hands on her shoulders. "Guess I'm becoming a little too predictable."

She moved between his arms and hugged him. "Well, that's not a bad thing, Pan. Not a bad thing, at all."

NIGHTFALL CAME SLOWLY, the day dragging in spite of Pan's an-
ticipation. He thought afterward about what he had done during its
long, seemingly endless hours, and could remember barely anything.
He spent some of it with Prue, but a lot of it alone, thinking. He
stopped by to reassure a dour Trow Ravenlock that he had not changed
his mind and intended to make his report as promised. The latter just
shook his head and turned away. He thought about visiting his oldest
sister, who lived with her husband and two boys in the next village
over, but rejected the idea out of hand. Visiting meant explaining and
explaining meant a whole new round of arguments about the advisa-
bility of what he had decided to do.

So the day passed and dusk descended, and all of a sudden it was
time.

He went looking for Prue and found her waiting for him at the end
of the walk, just come from her own house. She was wrapped in warm
furs and wore beneath them her Tracker's leathers. She smiled cheerfully and took his arm. "Are you all ready?" she asked.

"Me? I thought you were the one who was going to tell them," he
joked, and gave her a shove.

They walked over to Council House, the village meeting hall and
the building in which most community business was conducted. It was
another longhouse, similar to the one in which the Trackers gathered,
only much larger. This one could easily hold five hundred people, if
you filled the balcony seats as well as the floor benches. Panterra had
expected a reasonable turnout; meetings such as these were open to
the public and always drew some interested parties. But he was surprised to find the hall packed to the rafters. Every seat was taken, and
those who had come late were forced to stand in the back or on the
sides against the walls, where they crowded in two- and three-deep.

Apparently word had gotten out that he intended to speak. Those
attending had at least an inkling of his news. He saw in the looks directed at him and the whispers exchanged that they were not happy
about it.

His gaze swept the hall swiftly, taking everything in. The room was
hot with bodies crammed together and the fire that blazed out of the

massive stone hearth at the far end. Torches threw down pools of flickering yellow light from brackets affixed to the walls around the room.
Great ceiling fans carried the smoke away through ceiling vents, their
blades turning slowly on pulleys hand-operated by men in the corners.
The ceiling itself was high and dark, and the rafters were dim forms in
the shadows of the center beam's vaulted peak.

Panterra glanced at Prue, who suddenly looked scared. She was a
loner who preferred life lived outside villages in the wild, where she
felt free and unencumbered. This was more people than she had seen
in one place in years. Clearly, she didn't like it.

"Don't look at them," he whispered to her, bending close. "Look at
me, if you have to look at someone."

They saw Trow, who beckoned them forward to chairs directly opposite the council table. Several members of the council were already
gathered, chatting with one another until they caught sight of him;
then conversation ceased momentarily as they stared. Pan didn't like
how that made him feel. He already sensed an undercurrent of discon-
tent from those gathered. He kept reminding himself he was only the
messenger, and the message was not his own.

But Panterra Qu was no fool. He knew this was not going to make
any difference, that the message was going to become his the moment
he voiced it.

Prue gripped his arm and hung on to it as he made his way forward.
They sat down next to Trow, who nodded without speaking and looked
away. Panterra felt a pang of disappointment in the Tracker leader. He
should have been more supportive; he should have tried to do more
for the men and women he led. It seemed to Pan that he had decided
to do nothing, that he had made a conscious choice to distance himself
from this entire business.

He looked around for Aislinne, but there was no sign of her. The
only ally he might find at this gathering, and she wasn't even there.
He wanted to ask Trow where she was, but he resisted the impulse.

A little more time passed as other members of the community
pushed into the packed hall, their voices raising the volume in the already noisy room. Panterra tried not to listen; he tried to calm himself
in the way his mother had taught him—by thinking of other things. He
fixed his eyes on the great hearth and its roaring fire, blazing up from

behind the huddled council members, and let himself disappear into the flames. He tried thinking of his family when he was young, of the happiness he had enjoyed growing up. When that didn't work, he tried thinking of the woods and the mountains, of his life as a Tracker.

He was still working at staying calm and centered in his thoughts when Pogue Kray entered the hall from a side door and took his seat at the center of the council table. He was a big, burly man with a black-smith's arms and shoulders, his movements slow and ponderous. Once, he had been a formidable figure, all muscle and hard planes. But his belly had taken over as his predominant feature, and now he looked settled and soft. His bluff face was black-bearded and sun-scorched, and he had the look of someone eternally dissatisfied with life's lot.

He was trailed by the Seraphic, Skeal Eile, wrapped in his white robes, his strong face held high and proud as he kept his eyes on a place just above the faces of all who turned to study him, unaffected by and distanced from their prying looks. He remained standing, placing him-self just behind and to the right of Pogue Kray.

The council leader rapped his huge hand on the hard surface of the table and signaled for attention. Slowly but surely, the hall quieted to silence.

"This room will come to order and remain so," the big man de-clared, sweeping the chamber with his black gaze. "The business of the council will not be interrupted by voices speaking out of turn or by ill-advised demonstrations. Should any of this come to pass, my keepers of the peace will act swiftly. Is that understood?"

Apparently, it was. No one said anything.

"Very well." Kray was satisfied. "We are here at the request of one of Trow Ravenlock's Trackers, who has asked to give us his report per-sonally. Is that Tracker present and ready?"

He looked at Trow, who got to his feet. "He is, Council Leader."

"Then let him speak."

All eyes fixed on Panterra as he rose. He glanced about quickly, but there was still no sign of Aislinne. He didn't hesitate further; he started talking at once—before he had a chance to lose his courage—relating the events of the previous day. He kept his eyes on Pogue Kray as he spoke and did not look at Skeal Eile, aware that the Seraphic was studying him intently from behind the council leader's chair. He tried not to hurry his report or to make it too sensational, but to keep it straightforward and accurate. He started with how Prue and he had come across the tracks of the creatures—tracks they could not identify—and begun following them. He continued with their discovery of the remains of Bayleen and Rausha, their efforts at further tracking their friends' killers, the ambush and attack by the creatures, and their rescue at the hands of the Gray Man.

He closed by repeating the latter's warning, and when he finished the entire assembly broke out in a wild cacophony of voices shouting and crying out in a mix of anger and doubt and fear.

Pogue Kray rose to his feet, his giant frame looming over everyone. He gave it only a moment, and then roared for silence, pounding his fist on the table once again. The quieting took longer this time, but eventually the room was still once more.

"There will be no more of that!" the council leader snapped, looking from face to face, eyes dark and fierce. "I told you what would happen, and if there is another such outburst I will empty the room and the rest will be heard by the council alone!"

"Perhaps that is best in any case?" Skeal Eile suggested in his low, compelling voice from over the other's shoulder.

Pogue Kray shook his head. "This session will continue as before. Young man. Panterra Qu, isn't it? You seem certain of your story. But its parts are both clear and yet still vague in my mind. Enlighten me on a few of its points. How is it that Sider Ament came to find you when he hasn't been seen in the valley in months?"

"He had been tracking the creatures, too—from where he found they had breached the mists," Panterra answered. "He caught up to us just in time to keep us from being killed."

"You and this young lady," the big man said. He turned to Prue. "Is this boy's story as you remember it? Or are there things you wish to add or subtract?"

Prue rose to stand next to Pan. "Everything happened exactly as he said it did. I would change nothing."

"Still, it is an incredible tale, with ramifications that I don't think either of you appreciate," Pogue Kray pointed out. "Perhaps you need further time to consider the reliability of your memories."

Skeal Eile stepped forward once more. "Your advice is well given,

Council Leader," he said. "These are young people with little experience in the world. They tell a wild tale, one that suits their age and inexperience but strains belief. What they remember might not be exactly what they saw at the time. Is there any physical proof of what they tell us?"

Pogue Kray nodded at Panterra. "Answer him."

Panterra shook his head reluctantly. "No, we have no physical proof. The swamp swallowed the creature that was killed. The other escaped. Sider Ament went after him."

"The wild man who lives as a hermit on the high slopes of our valley, the man who disdains the company of other men and pretends at being our guardian, carrying a relic that may or may not have come from another time." He shook his head in dismay. "No one has ever seen this staff do the things you say you saw it do, young Panterra. Things of magic from out of the old world, things no one has seen in centuries. Not even the Elves. Isn't it possible that you are mistaken in what you saw?"

Panterra shook his head. "I know what I saw. I am a Tracker. I am not easily deceived."

"But you admit that deception is a possibility, even for a Tracker as skilled as you?" Skeal Eile stepped in smoothly, eyes locking on Panterra. "I know your reputation. You have special talent. But all of us can be tricked by our own senses and the deliberate deceptive efforts of others. That could have happened here."

Without waiting for Pan's response, Skeal Eile turned to the assembled members of the community, raising his hands to draw their eyes and hold them.

"Listen to me, now. Listen carefully. This story lacks foundation in the teachings of the Hawk. It goes contrary to everything we know to be true. For centuries, we have been kept safe by following those teachings, by studying them as we would the rules of life, by keeping them close to our hearts. To dismiss them now, to toss them aside as if they meant nothing, would be a travesty beyond understanding. And all on the word of a boy and a girl who rely heavily on what they heard and saw while in the company of a man whose origins and purposes are suspect in the extreme?"

His hands swept the air and came down again. "We are the Children of the Hawk, and we know what the Hawk promised us. We know that he led us here to keep us safe and that when it is time to go out into the larger world again, when it is safe for us to do so, he will come for us. He will come as a sign or in the flesh reborn, but he will come. There will be no ending of the mists, no falling down of the protective wall, no intrusion of the world left behind, until the madness shut outside our homeland is dispelled forever. And he will be the one to bring us this message, not some hermit who has no better sense than to spread wild rumors."

A slow muttering had grown to a low chanting that filled the room and drew together the assemblage. Panterra glanced around uneasily, not able to quite grasp the words, but disliking their tone. Prue took his arm to catch his attention and shook her head, apparently thinking he was about to do something. Was he? He turned back to Pogue Kray.

"What if he's right?" he asked the council leader, lifting his voice so that everyone could hear it. "What if Sider Ament speaks the truth?"

"Careful, boy," Skeal Eile said quickly. "Your words verge on blasphemy. You risk your salvation as a Child of the Hawk."

Again the voices rose to shouts, sprinkled now with epithets that were clearly audible. Pogue Kray rose yet again, and yet again slammed his fist on the table.

The crowd quieted, but the dark looks remained.

"If you would speak, do so one at a time!" Pogue Kray rumbled blackly, his eyes sweeping the assemblage. "And do so with some care."

"I would speak," a voice from the very back of the room declared, a voice that caused Panterra to turn at once.

Aislinne Kray stepped out of the crowd at the back of the room and made her way forward. She was a tall, striking woman with long blond hair gone almost white, finely chiseled features that made her appear much younger than she was, and a determined walk that brooked no interference. Those in her way stepped back quickly, and voices went silent once more.

When she reached the front of the room, she turned slightly so that she was addressing everyone. "I am ashamed for you," she said quietly but firmly. "Ashamed and disappointed. What kind of people would attack a boy and a girl like this? I stand among you and hear you speak words like *heretic* and *demon-spawn*. I hear you suggest that they be cast out if they refuse to recant. A boy and a girl you have known all your lives. A boy and a girl who have proven themselves among the best of our Trackers, who have time and again done service to this village and its people by carrying out their duties with skill and dedication. Never once have their actions been questioned. Never once have they done anything to earn your scorn."

She paused, looking directly at Skeal Eile. "But now, for doing nothing more than bringing before you a message that could have significance for us all—and for keeping a promise made to a man who saved their lives—you would cast all that aside? You would declare them villains and worse?"

"Enough, wife," Pogue Kray interrupted wearily. "We take your point. But you must consider ours. This message casts doubt on everything we have held as truth for five centuries. We cannot accept that lightly."

"Nor do I say you should, *husband*," Aislinne replied pointedly. "Incidentally, I am a member of this council, too. It would be reasonable for you to give me notice of these meetings."

"You were fifteen miles hence, in Woodstone Glen." But Pogue Kray looked uncomfortable.

"Too far for someone to come fetch me, I guess." She was looking at Skeal Eile again. "But someone did fetch me, so here I am, and now I will be heard. Seraphic, you seem threatened by what this boy has to say. Can that be so? Are his words too dangerous to hear?"

"His words directly contradict the teachings of our sect," the other man replied, his voice gone smooth and pleasant once more. "We know our teachings to be truth. His words, therefore, must be lies."

"There is no objective scale by which to measure truth, Skeal Eile, when that truth is not written down. What we have are teachings passed by word of mouth over five centuries. There is room for error."

The muttering resumed suddenly, a low and sullen murmur, and Aislinne Kray wheeled on the crowd. "Are you thinking that I'm a heretic, too? Is anyone who questions the teachings of Skeal Eile automatically a heretic? Must we hew to the doctrine of the sect without question, or are we allowed to think for ourselves? Those the Hawk brought into this valley were people smart enough and strong enough to think for themselves or they would not have gotten here. Are we, their descendants, expected to do differently?"

The voices died away. The silence was huge. "No one questions others' right to think for themselves, Aislinne Kray," Skeal Eile said softly, his smooth, calming voice drawing everyone back. "But we are not given the right or the leeway to blindly accept that for which there is no basis in fact. I do not dismiss the boy's story. I do not brand him a heretic. I simply point out the obvious. His message flies in the face of our teachings and is delivered by a man who has not been one of us for many years."

"Then this council session should end here and now, with no further disparagement of young Panterra," she snapped. "He has kept his promise and delivered the message, and that is the end of it. If something more needs doing, I am sure our council leader will see to it that it is done."

"You do not decide when this council adjourns or when its work is done!" Pogue Kray thundered.

She gave him a look and then wheeled away, long hair fanning out as she turned. "Come, Panterra. You look as if you could use a glass of ale and a hot meal. Prue Liss, you come with me, too. Whatever else needs doing, it can keep until tomorrow."

"I have further questions to ask of these Trackers, Aislinne," Skeal Eile called after her, stepping forward as if he might try to detain them. "There are issues raised by their message that clearly fall within the purview of the Children of the Hawk. Our jurisdiction in such matters is not—"

"Tomorrow will be soon enough for your questions," Aislinne called back to him over her shoulder. She didn't slow or look around. "Good night to you. Panterra? Prue?"

Panterra glanced quickly at Pogue Kray, whose black brows were lowered and glowering. He waved them off with one beefy hand, dismissing them. "Go with her," he ordered, ignoring the fresh protestations of Skeal Eile, who was bent over his shoulder and whispering in his ear. He rose to his feet and slammed his fist on the table. "Council is dismissed."

Panterra and Prue hurried to catch up with Aislinne, and in seconds they were through the door and into the empty black night.

6

ISLINNE KRAY STEPPED DOWN OFF THE VERANDA that fronted the council hall and looked over her shoulder at Panterra and Prue. "That wasn't the smartest thing you've ever done," she said, and they could see the anger glittering in her green eyes.

"So we've been told," Pan admitted. "But don't blame Prue; it was my idea. I knew what the reaction was likely to be."

Aislinne grunted. "I doubt that you have any idea even now what the reaction is likely to be."

"Pan just did what Sider Ament told him he needed to do," Prue declared defensively. "He wasn't trying to cause trouble. They didn't have to attack him that way."

Panterra put a hand on her shoulder and squeezed lightly. "Maybe we ought to just go to bed."

"Not just yet," Aislinne said at once. "I'm not finished with you. Is your house empty, Pan? Good. We'll go there. We need to talk."

She led the way through the village, long hair fanning out like a veil, stride quick and sure on the familiar paths. The boy and the girl followed obediently, pulling their cloaks close as the chill night air bit at them, cold enough that it burned their exposed faces. Overhead, the sky was clear and filled with stars that spread across the firmament in a wash of white specks, thickly clustered and brilliant. The moon was down this night, and the stars shone brightly in its absence.

When they reached Panterra's lane, Aislinne paused while still within the cover of the trees to study the houses ahead. Saying nothing, she signaled to the boy and the girl to wait; then she stood silent and motionless for long minutes, watching.

"Come," she said finally, and started ahead once more.

Moments later they were down the path and up the walkway to Panterra's front door. The boy used his key and the three slipped inside to stand in the darkness.

"Lock it behind you," Aislinne ordered, her voice only slightly louder than a whisper. "Don't turn on any lights. Where can we talk without someone outside being able to see us?"

Pan led the way through the cottage, winding past the hearth with its now cold ashes from the morning's fire, through the kitchen to the back stairway, and up the stairs to the loft where he made his bedroom. There, in a darkness broken only by the pale wash of starlight through windows beneath low-hanging eaves, they seated themselves on the floor in a tight circle.

"Is there a reason for all this caution?" Panterra asked. He was careful to keep his own voice low. He found Aislinne's green eyes in the near-dark.

She gave him a look. "Don't be stupid, Panterra. Of course there's a reason!" She saw his bewilderment and shook her head. "You can't possibly be that naïve. Your revelations have stirred up poisonous waters. Do you really not see it?"

"You mean Skeal Eile?" Prue asked.

Aislinne sighed. "Child, child. I mean five centuries of traditions and beliefs that have become a bedrock of faith for far too many of our people. You cannot challenge something so deeply ingrained without arousing strong resentment. Look now. How much do you know of the history of the Children of the Hawk?"

Panterra and Prue exchanged a quick look. "Not much," the boy admitted. "Only that they think the Hawk brought them here and that he will come for them again when it is time to leave the valley."

"That merely scratches the surface. Yes, they believe that. But they also believe that they are the chosen people, the ones who were saved when the rest of the world perished in the Great Wars. They see themselves as the future of civilization. They think that theirs is the way—the only way. The Seraphics have told them so for five centuries, and for five centuries they have been thought right because no challenge to their teachings has succeeded. Or should I say, no challenge has survived its voicing."

Prue shook her head. "What do you mean?"

"I mean that the challengers have all recanted, fallen victim to unfortunate accidents or simply disappeared. Understand: the continued survival of the Children of the Hawk requires a surmounting of all attacks, real or perceived. This is about power and its usage—about the influence it generates and the coin it collects in the form of tithes and property. This is about who controls the populace and the land. On the surface of things, it would appear that my husband and the council do so, here in Glensk Wood. But underneath, where the truth of things lies hidden, it is another matter entirely. Skeal Eile and his minions hold all the power because the Seraphic speaks for the Hawk. In other times and places, it was other Seraphics. It has been so in the villages of Men since we came into this valley."

"So they see us as a danger?" Panterra asked in disbelief. "Just for bringing Sider Ament's message?"

"They see you as a *perceived* danger," Aislinne corrected. "And that is enough for them to want to do something about you."

"They will want us to recant?"

"At best—and I wouldn't be too quick to assume the best." She gave him a long look. "It is because of who sent the message that I say this, Panterra. Sider Ament is an unusual man with unusual abilities. Most think him a wanderer of strange habits and wild imaginings. They think he might even be demented. They know nothing of the truth of him, as I do. But what matters here is that his distancing of himself from the communities does not always serve him well. Not just in his lack of appreciation of the power of the Children of the Hawk. But also in his failure to realize what even the simple delivery of a message could result in for the messenger. He should not have asked of you what he did."

She rocked back. "If I hadn't discovered what was happening and returned to intervene, I think you might be spending this night under very different circumstances."

"Were you sent away deliberately?" Prue asked. "Or tricked into leaving?"

"No, it was nothing like that. My husband, for all he lacks in backbone and common sense, would not stoop to that." She allowed herself a small smile. "He is not the man he was, I regret, not the man I married all those years ago before he fell under the influence of the sect. But neither is he duplicitous or cunning. Circumstances put me in another place, not Pogue Kray, although he would have been happy if I had stayed where I was. Especially since I am certain Skeal Eile suggested that no harm could come of it, that the balance of the council members would act in my stead."

"How did you find out what was happening?" Panterra was confused. "Barely twenty-four hours passed between our return and the meeting."

She rocked back slightly, and the smile returned. "I have friends, Panterra. Some of them are your friends, too. One, in particular. One who cares about you both. He brought me warning of what was to happen, and I came back at once."

"Brickey," Prue guessed.

She nodded. "You can thank him when you see him again. But that might not be right away. After we've finished here, you will need to pack and leave Glensk Wood."

The boy and the girl stared at her. "Leave?" Prue repeated. "We can't do that!"

Panterra nodded quickly. "We have to stay and convince the council of what—"

"The time for that has come and gone," Aislinne interrupted, brushing aside his objection with a wave of her hand. "You had your chance this evening, such as it was, and you failed. It won't get any better from here on out. Not without physical proof of what you claim. Or what Sider Ament claims, although now you're perceived to be his agent and the message as much yours as his."

"But that's not . . ."

She held up a finger in warning, silencing him once more. "The problem confronting you is much greater than the message itself. Skeal Eile fears the message, but he fears you, as well. You have seen things that could be a threat to his power. You might continue to report what you've seen to others, and eventually someone might start to listen. It would be best, he'll reason soon enough—if he hasn't already—if you were no longer around to talk about it."

"He would kill me?" Panterra asked incredulously, and he almost laughed at the idea.

"But that's ridiculous!" Prue exclaimed. "He wouldn't do that! Everyone knows Pan! They wouldn't stand for it!"

"He won't do it himself; he will have it done by others. It will not appear as if he had a hand in it." She paused. "He has done this before to those by whom he felt threatened. He is a dangerous man, and you have crossed him."

Panterra stared at her, peering through the shadows to catch the reflection of her eyes, trying to see something of the truth he could not quite accept. "Then we have to tell that to Pogue Kray or Trow Ravenlock. Others have to know."

She smiled and shook her head. "That's been tried. How much have you heard about its success?"

Panterra looked away, thinking, and then turned back quickly. "Wait a minute. If he eliminates his enemies, aren't you at risk, too? Aren't you a bigger danger to him than Prue or I?"

"If he goes after me, he will have to deal with my husband. He's not yet willing to chance that sort of confrontation. Pogue might be under his influence, but he is not going to sit by and let me be harmed. I suspect he has made that clear already."

She paused. "Besides, I'm not viewed as being much more reliable than Sider Ament. I'm not held in high regard. Too quick to speak my mind, not so quick to recognize my place. I am indulged by my husband, and there are few who admire his patience or his wisdom where

I am concerned. But my family is old and well placed, and they protect their own. Even me."

"Does Sider Ament know any of this?" Panterra pressed. "Is he really so ignorant of Skeal Eile's ambitions?"

"The Gray Man has no time for such nonsense. Know this, Panterra. Sider Ament is not what he seems. You've already had a glimpse of that. He is a warrior, a fighter of great strength and skill. He protects us all by patrolling the valley rim and keeping watch against the things that might come through from the outside world. When he tells you that those things are coming, you should believe him. When he tells you they are here, you should not doubt. We can do nothing about those who do, those fools who think that dogma equates with truth. Sider Ament knows this, too. He can't change what is by speaking against it. Only the sort of confrontation you experienced below the heights of Declan Reach can do that."

"So we must run," Panterra finished. "But where will we run to?"

"You have friends and family in other places," she answered. "Go to them."

"We could go to the Elves!" Prue exclaimed suddenly. "The Orullian brothers would help us! Didn't Sider Ament say we should take his warning to the Elves, too?"

Aislinne nodded approvingly. "A good plan. Just choose carefully who to tell, and be careful not to draw undue attention. The Elves will be less likely to doubt. They don't embrace the teachings of the Children of the Hawk. Perhaps they'll send a contingent of Elven Hunters up into the passes to see if the barrier still holds, or you can persuade them to come with you in search of Sider. You will have to find him now, and bring back some kind of physical proof to show the council. Until then, it won't be safe for you here."

Panterra hunkered down in the darkness of his bedroom, dismayed. "I can't believe any of this. All I did was what I have been trained to do."

"Nevertheless," Aislinne said softly, and she let the word hang in the ensuing silence.

Aislinne wouldn't tell him to run if it weren't necessary, Panterra knew. She was his friend; whatever she thought of his actions, she

wouldn't give him advice that she didn't believe was in his best interests. Ever since she had befriended him, not long after his parents died,
she had counseled him. She seemed to understand him, even without
knowing precisely how he was gifted. Or maybe she had intuited his
innate abilities; her own instincts were not to be underestimated.

What to do? He thought back to the council meeting and the way
Skeal Eile had looked at him. The memory did not give him a good
feeling. He glanced at Prue. She was in as much danger as he was, given
what Aislinne had said. She had seen everything he had and been firm
in backing his story. Skeal Eile would have no use for her, either.

Still, the idea of fleeing his home troubled him. There was a final-
ity to it that was deeply unsettling. Trackers roamed far and wide and
sometimes for long periods, but they always knew they could return
when their tasks were completed. That would not be the case here.

"I don't know," he said softly.

"No one said it would be easy," Aislinne began, leaning forward to
take his hands in her own. "But sometimes—"

"Hssst!" Prue said sharply, freezing them both in place. Her eyes
were wide and bright in the darkness. "There's someone out there!"

She gestured toward the window that faced north, a vague, almost
disconnected movement. Her eyes were fixed; she seemed to be seeing
something hidden from them. Panterra knew that look. It was the near-
trance she entered when she sensed that danger threatened.

It was there and gone again in a moment, and she was looking right
at Pan. "We have to get out of here!" she whispered. "Right now!"

Panterra hesitated, just for a second, and in that momentary pause
he heard a scuffling and a quick intake of breath, tiny sounds audible
only to someone with hearing and instincts as keen as his own.

Aislinne rose, then stood motionless in the dark. "Wait. Don't move."
Seconds later there was a soft tapping at the back door. Three short raps,
and then silence. "Come with me," she said, starting for the stairs.

They went down the steps together, moving slowly and silently
through the shadows. Panterra strained to hear more, but there were
no further sounds. The world outside the walls of his cottage stayed
silent and dark.

At the door, Aislinne motioned for them to stand behind her.

She released the lock and cracked the door slightly. Then she opened it wide.

Brickey was standing there, wrapped in a black cloak. "There's been an accident," he told them.

Aislinne nodded as if she expected as much. "What sort of accident?"

"A man has fallen on his knife. He was hunting mushrooms or perhaps night-blooming rashia in the trees, just in back of the cottage. He must have tripped." He glanced past her at Panterra and Prue. "Good evening, friends. You're up late. I hear that the council session was difficult."

A man hunting mushrooms had fallen on his knife? Panterra knew at once that the little man was lying, that what had happened had nothing to do with mushrooms. In all likelihood, an assassin had been sent to dispatch him, but had ended up being dispatched himself. He looked with new respect at Brickey, who somehow managed to look deeply saddened.

"Dangerous work, night hunting," Aislinne observed, as if she accepted what the little man was saying without question. "Will you see that his body is taken elsewhere?"

Brickey bowed slightly. "Of course." He paused. "This unfortunate death might bring unwanted attention. It might be well if all of you went somewhere else as soon as possible."

"We were just discussing that," Aislinne observed. "Thank you, Brickey."

She closed the door and turned to the boy and the girl. "Pack what you need, Panterra, and then we'll cross to Prue's home and she will do the same. It will be safe enough now; another will not be sent in this man's place right away. In any case, Brickey will continue to keep watch."

"I thought he was merely a thief," Panterra observed. "It seems he is something more."

"Brickey is many things. But he keeps what he is to himself." Aislinne motioned impatiently. "Pack, Panterra. You have to leave."

It took them only a short time to gather the clothes, weapons, and supplies they needed to set out. They were practiced at this, good at packing on short notice, efficient at collecting what was needed. Aislinne trailed after them, glancing outside now and then, studying the darkness as if to uncover its secrets. The rustle of their packing efforts were all the noise any of them made. They saw and heard nothing further of Brickey, who had faded back into the night. Panterra found himself wondering how much of the other's interest in him was fostered by his relationship to Aislinne. How had the little man come to know Aislinne so well? He wanted to ask her, but decided against it.

When they were ready, Aislinne walked them outside to the edge of the trees. All around them, the night provided a dark, silent cloaking. There were few lights in the windows of houses and no one about. Overhead, the sky was clear and filled with stars.

"I'll tell your parents, Prue, and anyone else who needs to know that you have gone to visit friends and will return in a week. If you don't come back by then, I'll make up something else to keep them from worrying. Try to convince the Elves to help you. Perhaps events will dictate when you'll be able to come back again. It might not be very long at all if Sider is right; another intrusion from the outside world is more likely than not if the protective wall is failing. Still, we can't count on that; we have to rely on our own resourcefulness."

She sounded as if she meant to place herself in their company, as if she shared the danger they faced. Panterra shook his head. He didn't want Aislinne to do anything more for them, anything that might put her at further risk. But he knew she would do whatever she felt she must, and that his admonitions against doing so would be wasted effort.

"We'll get word to you," he promised.

"Walk softly," she cautioned, and he was struck by the familiarity of that phrase: Sider Ament had used it as well.

"Thank you for everything." Prue embraced the tall woman and held her close. "We owe you so much."

Aislinne broke away. "You owe me nothing. Just keep safe until we meet again. Now go."

They moved into the trees. Panterra looked back and waved goodbye to her. She was already turning away.

When he looked back again, she was gone.

7

AFTER LEAVING PRUE LISS AND PANTERRA, SIDER
Ament set out to track down the second of the two creatures that had broken through his wards.

He was struggling with a number of issues. The weightiest of these
was accepting that after all these years, the barrier that had kept his
valley home safe was crumbling. It wasn't that he found the idea impossible to believe; it was that it felt so personal. It had been five centuries, and there had been dozens of others who had patrolled the
valley before him, all descendants of the old Knights of the Word. In all
that time, the mists that barred passage in or out had held firm against
intrusion. But now, in his time, while it was his turn to bear the black
staff of power, they were breaking down.

He couldn't know this for certain yet, even given what he believed
to be clear evidence. But if the creature he tracked was attempting to
get back to where it had come from, and if he failed to catch up to it
before it succeeded, he would soon learn the truth. He supposed that
he would find out in any case, because he had no choice now but to

test the barrier no matter where he found the creature. The creature's appearance might have been unexpected and hence unforeseeable, but that didn't change the inevitable consequences. Depending on where it had come from, either the inhabitants of the valley were still safe from the outside world or they were not. Either life would go on as before or it would be changed forever.

It was his realization of what this meant that was so overwhelming. Like most, he knew something of what had happened five hundred years earlier to bring their ancestors here. The Great Wars—the wars of power, the wars of science—had destroyed civilization. They had leveled governments and institutions, obliterated cities and entire nations, poisoned air and water and earth, and left the larger world virtually uninhabitable. No one who had come into the valley had ever been able to go back out again to see what that meant. But the stories had persisted—the old world was lost and it wasn't coming back; the new world was the world they would make here, within the confines of the mountain walls and the protective mists.

Yet the question persisted in the minds of everyone: What was it really like outside the valley?

He had tried to imagine it on more occasions than he could remember. He had tried to extrapolate, from the fragments of memories passed down through the years, what a world cast into chaos might be like five hundred years later. Would anything have survived? Was there any sort of population? There had been mutants at the end; some of them had come into the valley with Men and Elves. The Lizards and the Spiders were the largest part of these. But wouldn't there have been others, too—others that were left behind or developed later, like the creature he tracked? Wouldn't there be things he could not begin to imagine, born of life twisted into new shapes and forms?

It would all be so different from what any of them knew. There would be an entire world to discover, to interpret, and ultimately to embrace.

But few, he added quickly, would be eager to do so.

Certainly not the Children of the Hawk, who would regard as anathema any form of assimilation that did not hew to their teachings.

Not the larger population of Men. Whether they were members of the sect or not, they had always been inclined to stay put, to resist movement even beyond the boundaries of their own communities.

Not the Lizards or the Spiders, who were so reclusive and mistrustful of others to begin with.

Only the Elves would embrace this opportunity—which was ironic, if you knew their history. The Elves had once been the most reclusive of all, a Faerie people come from so far in the distant past that they witnessed the birth of the Race of Men. But their choice to isolate themselves from Men had come at a price. Men procreated much more quickly than did the Elves, and eventually the latter began to see their numbers diminish by comparison. A stubborn insistence on isolationism had only pushed them farther from the rest of the world. Had it not been for the Great Wars and the concerted efforts of the Void and its demons to annihilate their Race, they might have been lost completely.

It was a lesson that had not escaped the ones who survived. Having found their way into this valley, they had chosen to pursue a greater involvement with their new home, embracing the teachings of the members of the Belloruus family who had served as their Kings and Queens for nearly the whole of the first four centuries. Much more so than the other Races, they were committed to sharing with others the opportunity that had been given to them. Instead of returning to a life of isolation, they had chosen to dedicate themselves to the restoration and nurture of their world and its creatures. It was a commitment they had made repeatedly not only to the valley but also to whatever lay beyond. And so they talked openly about what would happen when they could go out into the larger world once more.

But still, nothing would be as they had imagined, and coming to grips with the truth of things—even for those who were willing to try—would not be easy.

The Gray Man walked on through the afternoon and early evening, passing out of the woods that concealed the swamp and its battleground to the open slopes of the foothills and the mountains beyond. He climbed steadily through scrub brush and tall grasses to the beginnings of the mountain's open rock with its patches of lichen and scattering of tiny conifers. By sunset, he was nearing the snow line where it formed a threshold leading into the pass.

There he lost the creature's trail.

He had been tracking it without difficulty all that time, simply by following the droplets of blood. Even after the blood began to diminish—the wounds closing over, he supposed—markings remained from the passage that read clear to him. Then all of a sudden there was nothing, even after he had scoured the ground thoroughly. Because it was growing dark and he could no longer be certain that he wasn't missing something, he decided to stop and make camp for the night.

Although the path of the tracks clearly pointed toward the pass at the head of Declan Reach, he could not assume that this was where the creature had gone. His greatest fear was that it had somehow circled back and gotten behind him, perhaps even backtracked down into the villages. Wounded or not, it was still much too dangerous to be confronted by anyone but him. But for now there was nothing he could do. He would have to wait until morning.

He sat within the sparse shelter of a small grove of spruce and boulders, black staff cradled in his lap. He ate his meal cold, deciding against a fire, wrapped himself in his tattered cloak and the one blanket he allowed himself, and went to sleep.

He dreamed that night, something he seldom did these days, and the dreams were filled with dark images and fleeting shadows that lacked specific identity or purpose, but whispered of secrets. He tracked after them, using all his skills, but somehow they were always quicker than he was, always smarter. And at some point, he came to the terrifying realization that his efforts were failing because it was the images and shadows that were tracking him.

When he woke, the sun was cresting the horizon of jagged mountain peaks in a wash of crimson light and he was bathed in his own sweat.

He set out at once.

He swept the area in all four directions, but his search yielded nothing. He found himself wishing he had that boy with him—what was his name? Panterra? He might have found something with his young eyes that Sider, with his old, had not. A talented youth, with good instincts and skills and not afraid even when that beast came right at him. He liked the girl, too. The pair made a good match. He wished there were more like those two, but he knew there weren't.

Too bad he had to send them back down into Glensk Wood without him. They would not have been received well by the Seraphic and his followers. Maybe not by anyone. But it had to be done. Even if their efforts failed. Even if almost everyone refused to believe, there would be one or two who would. Word of mouth would spread, and eventually someone in a position to do so would act. It was the most he could expect, and it would have to be enough.

He abandoned his sweeping search of the lower slopes, deciding that no creature could hide its passing on such soft ground and so the one he tracked must have gone up into the rocks. He struck out in a deliberately straight line, looking to cut the creature's trail at some point between where he was and the head of the pass or, failing that, to find its tracks inside the pass itself. He went quickly, climbing steadily with the sun's rising, pushing aside the lingering memories of last night's dreams.

It took him about forty minutes to find the trail again. It came in from the west, which meant the creature had deviated for some reason. The tracks were scrapes from claw marks on the stone and small disturbances of the loose rock. There was no sign of blood. The creature might be wounded, but it was not bleeding. Nor did it appear to be disoriented or desperate. It was choosing its way with intent to hide its passage and escape any pursuit.

Sider Ament picked up the pace.

The morning stretched on, but he reached the head of the pass by midday. The creature was no longer bothering to conceal its trail by then, clearly believing that a quick escape back into its own world would be its best course of action. Sider was surprised to find traces of blood again on the rocks; the creature's wounds had reopened. He followed blood drops and tracks to where his wards hung in tatters from the rocks, stopped to examine them, and quickly determined that the damage had been caused by his quarry exiting rather than something else entering.

It bothered him that the creature could reason as well as it did. This wasn't some dumb brute. Its deliberate efforts at concealing its tracks, doing something to stanch its wounds, and making a conscious decision to get out of the valley, now that its companion was dead, demonstrated the depth of its intelligence. Sider knew that he would have to be careful. A creature like this would know how to set an ambush, how to hide and catch by surprise anything that threatened.

He left the wards down, took a deep, steadying breath, and started into the pass.

The mists closed about him almost instantly, but the dampness did not feel as heavy as it had when he had tested the barrier on other occasions. There was a difference of another sort, as well, but he could not immediately define it. He pressed ahead, hands gripping his black staff as they might a lifeline, aware that he could see little and hear nothing and that almost anything might be waiting for him in the haze. His instincts should warn him, but he could never be sure. In his line of work, in his life, it was often so.

He slowed, and his eyes swept the wall of mist ahead for signs of movement or a hidden presence and found nothing. The runes of his staff, which would glow in warning if there were danger threatening, remained dark. He pushed on, thinking suddenly that the reason the mist felt different was that it was warmer than he remembered. The air, in fact, was warmer. He was several thousand feet up from the valley floor and well above the snow line, and within the valley it was verging on bitter cold. Yet here, within the pass, the temperature was thirty degrees higher.

He shook his head and continued on.

The defile he followed twisted and turned through walls of rock, layered in shadows and the curtain of the mists. He could see nothing of the sky or the mountain peaks, nothing ahead or behind. It seemed to him that the ground climbed for a long time and then leveled out. If things progressed in the way that they had for the past five centuries, the mists would turn him around and send him back to where he had started. Or they would swallow him completely, as they had others who had come this way without the magic he possessed, and he would never be seen again.

But he did not turn back. He had penetrated much farther than ever before, and he was beginning to believe that this time he would make it all the way through.

He would be the first to do so in five centuries. The very thought was overwhelming.

Then, almost imperceptibly, the way ahead grew brighter. At first, he thought he was imagining it, that it was an illusion brought on by his own wish for something—anything—to change. But as the brightness heightened, he realized that he was coming out of the heavy brume into whatever lay beyond. He slowed automatically, still on watch against unexpected attacks.

Abruptly, the brume began to fade, and he passed through the last faint traces, walked out onto an uneven ledge—and caught his breath.

He was facing row after row of mountains, their sharp-edged peaks backlit by a sunset that refracted across the western sky in bands of crimson, scarlet, and azure, their colors so bright it almost hurt his eyes to look at them. Behind him and overhead, the night sky was engulfing the last of the light, ink black and thick with stars. All around, the air was chill and clear and sharp. He was not back where he had started, not back inside the valley.

He was through the pass and in another place entirely.

He looked more closely at the mountains that stretched westward ahead of him. Some were heavily forested, green and fresh with trees. Some were choked with ruined masses of trunks and brush and that exposed a bare and blasted earth that was as dead as yesterday. The two environments were juxtaposed in patchwork fashion, although he knew that each patch stretched for miles and miles. He peered more closely, trying to make out anything else. But from where he stood, he could not see any rivers or lakes and could not find even small glimpses of flatlands. There were only the mountains, the haven of both the living and the dead, and the fire of the sunset with its wild colors blazing bright against the black of night's coming.

He looked at his immediate surroundings, studying them carefully. The ledge he stood upon was flat and wide and dipped downward on his left to become the threshold to a long rocky slide that in turn appeared to angle through a split in the towering peaks. Although in the fading light it was hard to be certain, he knew there had to be a passage out of this maze somewhere. If those creatures could find a way in, he could find a way out.

But not this night—not in this growing darkness in a land with which he was totally unfamiliar.

He moved into the shelter of the rocks, close to where he had emerged from the valley, and sat down with his back against the mountain and his staff cradled in his arms.

For a long time, he just stared out at this new country, this world that had belonged to his ancestors and now would belong to their descendants. If they wanted it badly enough. If they could make a place for themselves. A lot of *ifs* littered the path into the future. But there it was, anyway—the future they had always known would one day come around.

He looked out over the countryside, marveling at how widespread it was, how enormous. And that was only what he could see. He had never imagined how much larger the outside world would be than their valley home. No one had imagined it could be like this. When they saw it for themselves, they would be stunned—just as he was. He wondered if they were equal to what it would demand of them. He wondered if he was.

He was still wondering when he fell asleep.

HE WOKE AT DAYBREAK, the sunrise no more than a faint gray glow against the rugged outline of the peaks behind him. Ahead, the land was still dark and empty feeling. He rummaged in his pack for food and ate quickly, watching the light slowly begin to etch out the lines and angles of what waited ahead. By the time he was finished and packed up anew, it was light enough for him to set out.

He descended the rocky slide he had spied the previous night, working his way downward to where it became a trail that ran between those two peaks. He scanned the ground for signs of the creature, but saw nothing. He kept his eyes and ears trained on his surroundings, knowing that the emptiness of the land was only an illusion, that there would be life of some sort.

But nothing showed itself, and after a while he wondered if he was mistaken in his assumption. Maybe the life he presumed he would find was small and scattered, and its numbers were tiny. Maybe the destruction of the Great Wars had done more lasting damage than he wanted to believe, and only a handful of life-forms had survived. Maybe those that were left were like those creatures—mutants and freaks. He could not assume anything about what he was going to find, he told himself. He must keep an open mind.

He must also remember the way back.

He glanced around, searching the slide until he found the dark slit in the rocks that marked the opening back into the pass. Not so difficult from here, but it would become more so the farther he went.

Nevertheless, he did not consider turning back. He pushed on, making his way along the trail, covering ground steadily as the sun rose and the daylight brightened. He followed the trail all the way through to the other side of the mountain wall, and there he found his first fresh traces of the creature he tracked. It was bleeding again, and the pattern of its footprints suggested that its wounds were bothering it more than before. He looked ahead, finding changes in the terrain only a short distance off. The mountains he traversed ended in woods that were barren and dead, the trees stripped of life and toppled onto one another.

Beyond that, he could see nothing but the hazy roll of a landscape that stretched on for miles and miles until it reached another range of mountains.

He made a fresh determination of where he was, taking mental notes of landmarks he knew he must find again on his return, and started walking once more.

Ahead, the skies were beginning to darken with towering rain clouds that were streaked with lightning and filled the horizon. A storm was coming on, and it was coming on quickly. Sider picked up his pace. A heavy rain now would wash away all trace of his quarry's tracks, and he would have virtually no chance of finding it after that. It wouldn't be the worst thing that could happen; it seemed unlikely that the creature would be eager to venture back into the valley after having suffered its injuries. But he couldn't afford to chance it.

His thoughts drifted randomly, as thoughts will do, to memories of his early years, before he carried the black staff, before his predecessor sought him out and told him he was the one who was meant to carry it next, before he was anything but a boy not as old as Panterra Qu was now. It was a long time ago, both in years and experience, and much he could just barely remember. But there was one memory that he kept, one that he would never lose. It surfaced unexpectedly now and then, a long slow teasing of what might have been if he had taken another path than the one he was on. Life would have been so different. Everything would have been changed.

He gazed off into the distance, seeing not the landscape but the promise of something he had let pass by.

There was a girl . . .

He sensed the creature an instant before it attacked him, his instincts warning him as they always did, if only barely this time. The beast catapulted out of the rocks like a juggernaut set loose on a steep downhill run, all speed and bulk and power as it came at him. He brought up the black staff, runes blazing to life in response, a protection that reacted more quickly than thought. His magic surged about him in a shield that kept him from being trampled into the earth and instead resulted in a glancing blow that flung him twenty feet to one side. He struck the ground with stunning force, but scrambled up anyway, fighting to orient himself as the creature swung back around.

Sider Ament roared at it as he fought to bring his magic to bear, but the creature was on him too quickly, and he managed only to keep his defenses in place long enough to save his life for a second time. The creature, a thousand pounds if it weighed an ounce, caught him up with its lowered head and threw him again. This time he slammed into the hardwood trunk and branches of an oak and dropped like a stone. Pain lanced through his left side, and he could feel rib bones crack. He only barely managed to hang on to the staff. Nausea swept through him, followed by a hot searing agony that caused him to cry out.

He was a fool, he thought, struggling to rise, making it to one knee. The creature had done exactly what he had warned himself it might. Sensing that it was being followed—or perhaps catching sight of him at some point in his pursuit—it had circled back and waited in ambush. He had aided the beast in its efforts by allowing his attention to wander. He had allowed himself to think of her, when thinking of her was always dangerous, always and always . . .

The creature struck again, and his thoughts scattered. Whipping the black staff about so that one blunt end pointed directly at his attacker, he sent a sharp burst of magic exploding into its muzzle. The beast barely slowed. Shaking off the attack, grunting in a heavy rumble that generated deep in its belly, it lowered its head further and came on. Sider watched through the screen of his pain and desperation, knowing he lacked strength enough to stop it.

In the final seconds before the creature reached him, he shrugged off his backpack, struggled the rest of the way up, and staggered two steps to his right to find what protection he could behind the huge oak, then used the staff to generate clouds of black smoke and fire to try to confuse his attacker.

He knew even as he tried this final ruse that it wasn't enough. The beast was too big and too enraged to be turned aside. Enveloped in smoke and the thunder of its charge, it brushed off Sider's defenses, shattered the oak tree, caught him with its snout and tossed him.

The last thing he remembered after that was the strange sound of multiple explosions. One, two, three in quick succession. There was rage and pain in the huffing roar that the beast emitted, and it seemed to him that the sounds were all one and all right on top of him.

Then he lost consciousness and didn't hear anything more.

8

H E IS FIFTEEN YEARS OLD AND LIVING IN THE HIGH
country with his parents and his younger brother, the family
home settled below the snow line but not so close to the
communities that they have to worry about more than occasional contact
with other people. No one comes into the high country save trappers and
hunters, and these people keep to themselves. It is the way his parents like
things; company is welcome when invited but not otherwise encouraged.

He does not know what has fostered this attitude, but he accepts it as
reasonable. His parents are good and kind people, but they like living
apart. They are self-sufficient folk content with their own company. On
some days, they exchange barely two dozen words between dawn and
dusk. They assign him chores and responsibilities and expect him to follow
through. He is as reliable and self-sufficient as they are. He does not need
minding and prefers his own company. He seldom fails to do what is asked
of him.

The hunters and trappers who come by now and then sometimes stop
but more often do no more than wave as they pass. Everyone living in the

high country knows everyone else; there are few enough of them that it isn't hard. They look out for one another in a haphazard sort of way, mostly when it is convenient and they think to do so. No one expects anything more. Self-sufficiency is a code of living that all embrace and accept.

It is a good life.

Now and then, he is dispatched to the villages of Glensk Wood or Calling Wells for supplies the members of the family cannot fashion or grow on their own. A trip to one of the villages happens perhaps once a month in good weather, less in bad. It has become his task to make these trips; he is good at bartering and cautious in his dealings. When he is sent to procure something, he is usually successful. Because he is less annoyed by the communities and their larger populations than are his parents, he is not unhappy about being sent. He finds that although he is happy living alone, he likes people, too. He comes to know a handful of those who live on the valley floor, and a very few become his friends.

One of them is a girl.

He meets her by accident, just a few days shy of his fourteenth birthday, while walking home from Glensk Wood. She is coming down the trail as he is going up, and when he sees her he thinks his heart will stop beating and never start up again. She is tall and strong and beautiful, and he has never seen anyone like her. He slows without thinking, captivated for reasons he will never be able to fully explain, but she seems not to notice. She approaches, nods a greeting, and passes by. She does not say a word. She does not look back as she walks away.

He knows because he looks back at her.

It is several weeks before he is able to return to Glensk Wood, and then only because he finds an excuse that will hide his real purpose in going. He does not know the girl's name. He does not know where she lives. But he is confident, in the way young people are, that he will find her. He sets out early, eagerly. He walks quickly to Glensk Wood and then spends several hours looking for her in a random sort of way, thinking that somehow he will stumble on her. When that proves unsuccessful, he begins asking about her, hinting at a business transaction he hopes to conduct. Again, he fails. The day ends, and he is forced to return home knowing nothing more than he did when he came down out of the high country—save one thing.

No matter how long it takes or what he must do, he will find her.

It is another month before he makes a second try. By then he is begin-
ning to believe that he is fooling himself about what is and is not possible.
The girl might have been visiting. She might have passed through one time
and then gone back to wherever she came from. She might never return. He
begins to question his behavior. Thinking it over in a more rational state of
mind, he feels both foolish and strangely unsettled. He has never felt this
way about anyone. He barely knows any girls his age, and none of them af-
fect him in this way. Why are things so different with this girl? He does
not like it that he so obsessed with her when in truth he has no reason for
being so.

But still he goes and still he looks, and this time he finds her.

Once again, it happens by accident. He arrives in Glensk Wood not
long after sunrise, having set out while it was still dark in order to make the
most of his day. He is just passing through the cottages at the north end, not
even really looking for her yet, just making his way toward the center of the
village, and suddenly there she is. She is standing in a garden digging rows
in the freshly hoed earth and planting seedlings for her flowers. He stops at
the edge of the stone pathway leading to her doorway and watches, not
sure what he should do next.

After a moment, without looking up from her work, she says, "Do you
prefer azaleas or sweet peas?"

He hesitates. "Azaleas are the more hardy, sweet peas the more fragrant."

He cannot believe he has just said this. He knows almost nothing about
flowers and does not have strong feelings one way or the other about most
of them. He admires them but has seldom voiced any kind of opinion on
the matter, even to his mother, who adores them.

"Do you have a garden?" she asks.

"My mother does."

"Your mother. Where do you live?"

"North of here, just below the snow line."

"Cold, hard country up there. What brings you to Glensk Wood?"

He hesitates once more. "Errands."

"Errands," she repeats, and now she looks up. She has long, honey-
blond hair, startling green eyes, and fine strong features. "Is it possible that
I am mistaken about you? Are you really come here only for the purpose of
running errands?"

He swallows what he is feeling and smiles bravely. "No. I was hoping to find you."

She smiles. "That's a much better answer. It is best to be direct with me. Anyway, I saw it in your eyes that time we met on the trail. So you don't need to pretend."

He shakes his head, confused and embarrassed. "I wasn't . . . wasn't really . . ."

She stands now. She is tall, almost as tall as he is. "To be here at this hour, you must have left your home very early. Would you like to come inside and have something to eat and drink? My parents aren't home. We could talk."

She stares right at him as she waits for his answer. Bold and challenging. He finds that there is nothing he wants more than to accept her invitation, but he is not sure he should do that.

"We could talk out here," he says, trying to hold her gaze.

She studies him a moment, perhaps wondering if he is worth the effort. Then she marches across to where he stands and takes him by the arm.

"We could," she says. "But we aren't going to."

He allows himself to be steered toward the cottage. He is surprised to discover that her grip on his arm is very strong.

"Are you afraid of me?" she asks him suddenly.

He shrugs and manages a quick grin. "I think you already know the answer to that."

She returns the grin. "You're right. I do."

* * *

SIDER AMENT REGAINED AWARENESS SLOWLY. He rose out of his slumber in a lethargic waking that seemed to take forever. But the pain and his memories of what had brought him to this state helped speed his efforts, and mustering what strength of body and will he could, he dragged himself back into consciousness.

He opened his eyes and looked around.

The first thing he saw was the corpse of his attacker, head thrown back and body blown open and bloodied. He stared at it a moment, trying to make sense of what he was seeing, to imagine what sort of weapon could do such damage.

Then he noticed the splints and bandages that wrapped various parts of his own body. His tattered gray robes had been cut away in several places, exposing part of his torso and his damaged left arm. The bulk of his pain seemed centered on those two places in particular, but the rest of him had not been spared.

His pack lay to one side, untouched.

His right hand still gripped his black staff.

"Awake at last, are you?" a voice boomed. "Welcome back to the land of the living!"

A man moved into view from behind him. He was big and power-fully built, face bronzed by sun and wind, his features crosshatched with scars and his hands missing several fingers. It was difficult to deter-mine his age, but he had clearly seen the years of his youth come and go a while back. He was dressed in black, his clothing a mix of thick leather and heavy metal fastenings, the material as scarred and beaten as he was.

He smiled cheerfully at Sider and knelt down next to him, tangled black hair falling down about his face. "I thought maybe you wouldn't wake up. I thought maybe my bandaging job wasn't enough to save you."

Sider wet his lips. "Good enough, thanks. Do you have any water?"

The big man rose and walked back to where the other couldn't see him, then returned carrying a soft leather pouch. He held it up to Sider's lips and let the water trickle down his throat. "Just a little," he said. "Until I'm sure your injuries aren't worse than what they seem, we don't want to rush things."

Sider nodded and drank gratefully.

"There, that's enough." The man took the skin away and rocked back on his heels. "You ought to be dead, you know. I saw what that beastie did to you. Ugly stuff. But you took a couple of blows that would have crushed an ordinary man and barely flinched. So you must not be so ordinary, huh?"

Sider closed his eyes. "What do you call that thing I killed? Does it have a name?"

"It's called an agenahl. A brute, but smart enough to out-think you if you're not careful."

"So I discovered. Are there a lot of them?"

The big man shook his head. "Not so many anymore. They're freaks, mutants left over from the Great Wars. Me and others like me are working hard at making them extinct, but it's not so easy." He paused. "Usually, they hunt in mating pairs. Odd to find a mature one traveling alone."

Sider nodded. "I killed its mate a couple of days ago, then came looking for this one to finish the job. I didn't want it leading any others back to where I come from."

"Smart of you. If they find a place they like, plenty of food they can hunt, they bring all their friends and relatives to the feast." He paused. "You come from somewhere in those mountains east, do you?"

Sider hesitated, and then nodded. "Quite a way off."

"Never been back there. No reason to go. My work is all down here, on the flats and in the woods, working for the fastholds. You look like you might do work of that sort."

"What sort of work would that be?"

"Mercenary. Work for hire. You do any of that? Never mind, don't answer. I'm asking questions when I should be thinking of fixing you some food. You hungry? Like a little something to eat? Storm passed us by a while back, moving north, so we don't have to worry about shelter right away. How about it?"

With Sider's tacit blessing, the big man set about building a fire and cooking a mix of beans, vegetables, and salted meat he fetched from his backpack. It was one of the best meals Sider could remember, and he ate it all in spite of his injuries. He accepted a bit of root the other man offered, as well, an herb that he was told would help dull the pain, but needed to be taken on a full stomach to avoid cramps. Sider found that it worked.

"My name's Deladion Inch," the other offered when the meal was done and they were back to conversing.

"Sider Ament," Sider replied, offering his hand.

Inch shook it. "So what do you call that piece of black wood you're carrying? I tried to take it out of your hand while I was working on you—just to make things easier, not to try to steal it, you understand—but you had a death grip on it. It started glowing when I touched it. I didn't think that was a good sign, given what I saw it do to the agenahl."

The Gray Man hesitated, still not certain how much he wanted to tell his newfound companion, even if he had saved his life. It wasn't his manner to reveal anything more than he had to. He instinctively liked this man, but he really didn't know enough about him. Trusting people you didn't know was never a good idea.

"Oh, you don't need to worry about giving anything away," Inch declared before Sider could make up his mind. "I know magic when I see it. It's still around, even after all these years of people living like animals and beating each other to death with clubs. Don't trust it, myself. But others do, and some seem able to make it work. I guess you must be one. What's different about you is the staff. I was just curious about it, is all."

"The staff was given to me by my predecessor, one in a long line of bearers," Sider replied, making up his mind to trust Deladion Inch that far. "It's complicated. In the old days, those bearers would have been called Knights of the Word. Do you know the name?"

The big man shook his head. "Never heard of them. People did talk about the Word in the old days. A few still do. Not many, though. No reason for it. But tell me more about the staff." He paused. "Look, I know you think I'm being more than a little too curious. But I like weapons. I use them all the time in my line of work and see others use them, too, and I've never seen anything like that staff."

Sider shrugged. "There isn't another like it, so far as I know. There used to be two in the valley where I live, but one was destroyed. Now there's only this one, and I'm the only one who can use it. So it's not of much use to anyone else."

The big man seemed to think about that for a moment. Then he grinned, reached over his shoulder, and pulled a wicked-looking black-barreled weapon from a sheath strapped across his back. "Ever see one of these?"

The Gray Man shook his head. "But I've heard about weapons like it that date back to the time of the Great Wars. They were used by government armies and then later by rogue militias after the armies were destroyed. They fired metal projectiles of some sort, didn't they?"

"Shells filled with metal bits." The big man reached into his pocket and pulled one out. It was about three inches long and an inch thick, metal-jacketed and banded with red circles. "One of these, fired from this gun, will blow a fist-size hole completely through you. Nothing stands up to it. Not even agenahls. You have the last of those black staffs? Well, I have the last of these. A Tyson Flechette, best gun ever made. Passed down through various families until it came to my dad and then to me. I take good care of this sweetheart."

He handed it over to Sider to examine. The Gray Man hesitated and then accepted the gesture with a nod. He looked at the flechette, remembering what he had heard about them from the people in the valley who claimed their ancestors had brought a handful with them before the mists sealed everyone in. But all those weapons had become rusted or broken over the years or simply been put away and forgotten. The shells, he remembered, lost potency over time and eventually became worthless. They were all gone, too.

"You can have your magic," Deladion Inch declared. "I'll take my flechette. It's never let me down, and it never will."

He seemed pretty certain about this. Sider handed the weapon back. "Well, I don't know much about it, except that it saved my life. Seems to have worked well enough for you."

The big man nodded. "Every time. I got some other stuff, too—other weapons and explosives. Thing is, I know how to take care of this kind of equipment, how to maintain it in good, working condition so it does what it's supposed to do. Most people, they think you don't have to do anything but point and shoot whenever you feel like it and that's all it takes. Those people are all dead or on their way to being dead. Not me." He grinned. "How about you, Sider? You have to do anything to protect that black staff of yours? Does it need any special treatment?"

There it was again, Deladion Inch's insistence on knowing about the staff. Sider studied him a moment and then said, "I usually don't talk about such things, Inch. It's not that I don't trust people; it's just a habit. But you saved my life and you seem a good sort. So I'll make a bargain with you. I'll tell you about the staff if you'll tell me about the

world you've been living in. Because I don't know about your world.
I've been shut away in the mountains for so long that I haven't any idea
what's going on out here. Those agenahls? Never saw or heard of one
before today. I don't know what things are like, and I need to."

The big man stared. "You don't know *anything?*"

"No more than what I've seen since I left the mountains a day or
two ago. No more than what I've heard you talk about."

Deladion Inch shook his head. "That would be funny if it weren't
so sad. You're lucky you're still alive, even given my help." He paused,
studying Sider. "So what you suggest is that we spend some time together swapping information—me about this world and what lives in
it, you about your staff and its magic? That about it?"

Sider nodded. "I can't travel right away, not on my own. I don't
know that I can even find a safe place while I heal. I owe you my life,
but that makes you responsible for me. Ever hear of that before? So if
you can find us a place to hole up and agree to stay with me for a day
or so, I would be grateful. But if you can't, I'll understand."

"Oh, I can stay with you. I can do whatever I choose. And I know
where all the safe places are in this part of the country. This is my territory, Sider—I know everything there is to know." He scratched his chin
and shrugged. "All right, I'll accept your bargain. I like you. And I don't
want to think I had anything to do with you dying out here alone.
You're right—you wouldn't know where to begin to find a safe place
on your own. Even if you were well enough to travel, I don't know that
you would make it back without help. Not knowing as little as you do."

Sider said nothing; there was nothing to say.

The big man rose. "All right, then. First thing we need to do is find
a place to shelter. Then we can talk. How are you for walking?"

IT TURNED OUT THAT SIDER WASN'T MUCH even for standing.
He tried it with Deladion Inch's help, but he collapsed almost immediately, dizzy and weak. The big man told him to stay where he was,
that there was a better way. He disappeared into the woods, but was
back again in minutes with a pair of saplings he had cut down. It took

him a little less than twenty minutes to rig up a sled consisting of his cloak stretched over and secured to poles that he fashioned from the saplings with an enormous knife. Once the sled was ready, he placed Sider on it, hitched up the ends with his big hands, and set out. It was an uncomfortable ride, bumping along over uneven ground strewn with rocks and debris, and Sider wasn't sure he wouldn't have been better off walking. But Inch seemed to feel he wasn't ready for it, voicing again his concerns that there might be internal injuries he couldn't know about. So Sider left it alone. He lay back and silently endured, hands clutching the black staff and feeling the magic respond. He knew that healing came more quickly to a bearer of the staff than to ordinary people, and he could already feel himself knitting inside.

The journey lasted a little more than two hours and took them down out of the rocks and into woods that were green and fresh and smelled of living things and sweet water. Sider saw nothing of either water or life, but he could sense that they were there, just out of sight. Breezes blew out of the south, clean and cool. Sunlight dappled the woods and spilled in bright streamers through gaps in the canopy, and Inch hummed and sang to himself as he trudged along.

But every now and then there were hints of darker things, of the past that Sider had expected to find. Smells of decay and harsh chemicals wafting in the wake of the fresher breezes, there for only a second or two and then gone. He caught glimpses of ruined forest and blasted land through the trunks of the trees his bearer negotiated, barren and stark. Once, off in the distance, he saw the remains of what might have been a fortress reduced to rubble. He took all this in and wished he could scratch the itch of his curiosity by setting out for a closer look. But his healing was not complete and his strength still suspect. He would have to bide his time.

"Not so far now," Deladion Inch advised after they had traveled for some time, but he said nothing more after that.

Finally, they broke clear of the woods and emerged onto flats that were all hardpan and scrub, stretching away for miles until they disappeared into the horizon south. Gullies and ravines had been carved out of the hardpan over time by weather and water, and clusters of rocks formed strange monuments amid the emptiness.

Dominating the whole of this wasteland was a massive walled ruin

that climbed from one level to the next, buildings crumbling, roofs collapsed, and doors and windows black holes into the spaces beyond.
Towers and parts of the outer walls that were still standing attested to
the size of what had once been a huge fortress.

It was the fortress he had seen earlier, Sider realized.

"We're here," Deladion Inch declared, setting down the ends of the
sled and rolling his shoulders wearily. "You know, you weigh a lot more
than I thought you would."

Sider was still staring at the fortress as he eased himself into a sitting position. It looked like something out of a time he had heard
about from those who still kept track of the history of the old world.
But it wasn't from the time of the Great Wars; it was much older than
that.

Or newer, he thought suddenly.

"When was this built?" he asked Inch.

The other man shrugged. "Maybe two, three hundred years ago," he
answered, confirming what Sider had suspected. "Built by once-men
that survived long enough to complete it and then be wiped out by a
plague." He shook his head. "Legend has it the plague killed more than
half of whoever was left after the firestorm that killed almost everyone
before that."

He looked back at Sider. "We have a lot to talk about."

"In there?" Sider gestured toward the ruins.

"Safe enough."

"Doesn't look it."

"What does? In this world, nothing's really safe. Didn't you know
that?" He laughed. "Let's take a look inside."

9

THE SUNSET LACED THE WESTERN SKYLINE WITH streaks of crimson against a backdrop of cobalt, a vast and awesome stretch of stark color turned ragged where it brushed against the mountains. Sider thought that for all of his years of wandering the valley steeps, where his vistas frequently extended from wall to mountain wall, he had never seen anything so beautiful. He mentioned it to Deladion Inch, the big man sitting next to him on the parapets of the fortress ruins, both of them propped up on blankets laid out over stone blocks, sipping glasses of ale and watching the day come to a spectacular end.

"I'm told by those who might know that it's only the chemicals in the air, the pollution of the wars, that gives that color," he said. "The silver lining you find in every dark cloud."

Sider said nothing, his eyes shifting north to where the storm that had missed them earlier was backed up against the range of peaks fronting his valley, thunder a distant booming. Lightning formed quick, intricate patterns, there and then gone again in an instant, each jagged flash more spectacular than the ones before. The storm was huge and walled away the northern horizon as if to forbid all entry.

"We get these storms all the time," Inch observed.

"Much bigger than what we see in the valley," Sider said. "More impressive."

He was feeling more at ease than he had when the big man had brought him here. Sider didn't like being shut away, no matter what claims of safety were offered. He knew the history of the compounds during the Great Wars, where being shut away was a death sentence. He preferred open spaces that offered several routes of escape. But Inch had assured him that the ruins possessed as many bolt-holes as anything they would find out in the open. The ruins, he advised, were filled with tunnels and passages that honeycombed the walls from one end to the other. If anything invaded that they were not able to stand against, it was a simple matter to find a way out before they could be trapped.

It didn't hurt Sider's sense of confidence, either, that the staff's magic was working away at healing his wounds, and that even now he was feeling much stronger.

The two men sat side by side as the last of the light faded from the western sky and the night descended like a shroud. Overhead, clouds that hung on the fringes of the storm north hid stars and moon, and the night's blackness was thick and impenetrable. Inch still wore his black leather armor, the stays and fastenings undone here and there to allow for comfort. Sider was wrapped in the remains of his tattered cloak and soft tunic and pants, all of them torn and shredded and in places cut away entirely to allow for the bandages. They had eaten and drunk and were now settled as comfortably as conditions would allow on a broad section of battlements that faced out to the west.

"I found this place maybe five years ago," Deladion Inch said. "I had kept myself mostly west of here, just above the hardpan and toward the forests where there were communities that needed my services. But I was looking to keep moving east, to find what else was out there. This was what I found, maybe the last of its kind in this part of the world. Or anywhere. There are other ruins when you travel farther west, cities mostly, but those have collapsed into rubble and are overgrown to a point where you can hardly tell what they were. If I didn't know something of the history, I wouldn't be able to put a name to them."

"You have any one place you call home?" Sider asked.

The big man's smile was barely visible in the darkness. "Don't stay anywhere long enough for that. You should know, Sider. What you do, I imagine you don't have a home, either, do you?"

The Gray Man shook his head, wondering what it was that Inch thought he did. "Not since I was a boy. My parents had a small farm up in the high country. I left when I was sixteen."

He shifted positions on the blankets, searching for a more comfortable one. "We haven't really talked about what it is we do, you and I. You seem to think we do the same thing. But I'm not so sure."

"No?"

"Let me try this out on you. You're what they used to call a mercenary. You hire out for a price—maybe the highest price, maybe not. But you've got skills everyone needs, so you're in demand. Have I got that much right?"

He could hear Inch chuckle softly. "Partly. I do have skills and everyone wants them, so finding work is easy. But I have a lot of different skills, ones that no one else has. That makes what I can do unique. So sometimes I don't work for anyone; sometimes, I'm my own employer. Sometimes the price is coin or goods, and sometimes it's just what I feel like doing. It's a harsh world, Sider, and I stay sane in it by making sure all the choices are mine and not someone else's."

Sider nodded. "You don't want to wake up the next morning knowing you made a bad one."

"Something like that." Deladion Inch took a long drink of his ale. It was bitter stuff, Sider found, but after a while it grew on you. "I like finding people and causes that need a strong hand to set things right. I like making my own judgments about who's bad and who's good. If I get paid, fine. If not, that's fine, too. We're all stuck in this world, and none of us made it the way it is. We don't like much about it, and I think if you want to live in it with some sense of responsibility, you have to find ways to keep it this side of becoming too insane. It wasn't like that for too many years. It's still dangerous, but at least it's understandable."

He took another pull on the ale. "So isn't that what you do? You sound like maybe it might not be. Do you think a different way about things than me?"

Sider shook his head. "I just don't follow the same calling, Inch. Mine comes from a long way back in time and tracks a different path. It's the staff's legacy, really. You wanted to know more about it? Well, here's something I can tell you. You don't inherit this staff; you earn the right to carry it. It is bequeathed to you along with a set of rules about how it's to be used. The primary obligation of its bearer is to protect those for whom it was created, way back when the Great Wars were just a possibility. When it was given to me, when I was chosen by my predecessor, it was with the understanding that I would carry on the work of all those men and women who bore the staff before me."

"What sort of work? It's not like mine?"

Sider shrugged. "I don't know enough yet about the specifics of your work to be able to judge. But I'm not for hire, and I don't get to choose my path. I am the protector of a group of people who escaped the Great Wars and haven't come back out into the world again since. Except that now they might have to because the world is threatening to intrude on them. I've kept them safe and patrolled the perimeter of their safehold since it was given to me to do so, and I see it beginning to crumble. They always knew there would come a time when this would happen, when they would have to come back into your world, their old world. But knowing it and accepting it are two different things. Now that it's happening, they won't necessarily believe it or trust me to make the call for them."

"So you work for free and you don't get any respect from those you serve." Inch arched one eyebrow. "I think I'd rather be doing what I'm doing. At least that makes sense."

Sider smiled. "Well, I don't know that what I'm doing makes much sense; I'll give you that. People are strange creatures, and they don't always have a clear eye toward how things stand."

"No different out here, my friend." Inch made a sweeping gesture toward the countryside. "That's our history, if you think about it. Look at how we got to where we are. The Great Wars killed almost everyone, and those they didn't kill they left homeless and disconnected.

Everyone made new families. Everyone had to band together to survive. It wasn't easy. Or so the stories that got passed down through the years tell us. It was pretty bad. Pretty terrible."

He hunched forward. "Here's what I know from the stories I've heard. The end of the Great Wars came in a series of huge explosions that tore up the land and poisoned everything in it for two hundred years. Almost no one survived. Those who did went north or south or hid out in places that escaped the worst of it. Some went underground. Some went deep into the mountains. Some stayed put and got lucky. Others turned into freaks and mutants and worse things than that. But there weren't many of any kind who made it. Most never got through the first five years."

He shrugged, looking off into the darkness. "It was a long time ago, Sider, and now it's just old stories. We live in the here and now, not the past. But the present's not so good, either. You wanted to know what things are like? All right, I'm going to tell you."

He paused, as if gathering his thoughts or searching for a starting point. "Well, there's no good place to begin. For about a hundred years after the end of the Great Wars, people lived like animals. Some still do, but almost everyone did then. They scrapped and clawed to stay alive. They killed each other if they felt threatened. They ate each other, too, I'm told. Food was hard to find, and starvation was an everyday occurrence. Men who hadn't changed into something else and Men who had, they were all in the same situation. There was no longer anything resembling civilization, nothing of order or moral imperative or a sense of right and wrong. There must have been some who still held those values and tried to practice them, but most gave in to the demands of their environment and became what they needed to become to stay alive."

"I'd thought that might have been what happened," Sider said.

"Happened for more than two centuries, and then things started to right themselves. The people who had escaped the worst of the plagues and poisons and firestorms had formed communities that were fortified and protected. Men armed themselves wherever they went, but at least they weren't afraid to go. Weapons were rudimentary for the most part. There were some flechettes and sprays and other leftovers from before the Great Wars, but most quit working or rusted up. Men forgot how to fix them and then how to use them and then forgot them altogether. The time for that kind of weapon was over. Men began making weapons in the old way, forging blades for swords and spears and javelins, shaping bows out of ash and tying flint to oak shafts for arrows, and they learned how to use them. They formed hunting parties and set watch over their women and children, and they stood up with some success against the predators and ravers that still roamed the land. The difference was that they were beginning to organize themselves."

"Still wasn't enough, though, was it?" Sider guessed.

Inch shook his head. "Not by a thirty-foot jump, it wasn't. There were battles fought all over the landscape, dozens every day, and whole communities were wiped out. Some of the mutants that grew out of the poisonous effects of the Great Wars had evolved into monsters that almost nothing could stop. Some were worse than the agenahls, but most of those couldn't breed and died out early on. There wasn't enough food for them, and they weren't smart enough to avoid eating things infused with poisons and chemicals. But that wasn't the worst of what was out there, Sider. You know what was? What still is?"

"I guess I don't."

"Demons that survived along with the humans and other creatures. There weren't many, but there were a few. They escaped in the same way everything else escaped—by being somewhere other than the worst of the destruction. But they were still what they always had been when it was over, and they went right back to doing what they had been doing all along—working hard at wiping out everything but their own kind. They subverted what creatures they could and turned them to their own uses. It wasn't like before; their numbers were small and their reach short. They were starting over, just like everyone else. But it was enough."

"Wait one minute." Sider held up one hand. "I've heard the stories about demons fomenting the madness of the Great Wars and forming armies to wipe out the human race. I only half believed them. But you're saying it's the truth? And you're saying there are *still* demons out here? Demons of the sort that destroyed—well, *almost* destroyed—humankind in the first place?"

Deladion Inch rocked back slightly. He was sitting cross-legged now, his cloak wrapped close as the air grew cool with the deepening of night. His smile was ironic, filled with mirth but lacking in warmth, and when he stared off into the darkness it was as if he were seeing and hearing things that his companion could not.

"Sider, here's the truth of things. After all that's happened since the Great Wars, after time's passage these past five centuries, nothing much has changed. Oh, the old world's gone, right enough. All those cities and factories and war machines and everything else that the old sciences created to make the world a better place have disappeared, and we've got nothing worth talking about to show for it. They might as well never have existed, any of them. Centuries of enlightenment and progress vanished virtually overnight because Men couldn't find a way to use it wisely and purposefully. Gone, the whole of it, and to what end? Was there a lesson learned? Was there a fresh perspective reached that might somehow help avoid it all happening again? You show it to me."

Sider shrugged. "History repeats itself, Inch. It's an old lesson, but no one ever seems able to put it to use."

The big man grunted. "Well, there it is, then. You take my point. Change comes in the form of repetition. We are doomed to repeat the mistakes of the past, and no amount of education gleaned from our propensity for self-destruction and misguided thinking ever teaches us anything. Not anything that we remember for more than a generation or two, in any case. It's been so in the past, it's so now, and I would be willing to bet it'll be so forever."

Sider shook his head, more in puzzlement than disagreement. "I think maybe we learn a few things each time that we don't forget. A few things that stick with us. It's just hard to pass those things on to those who come after us because if they didn't live through it, they don't view it the same way we do. If you don't experience something firsthand, it's a lot harder to accept."

He sighed. "But demons? Now, that's something I didn't think anyone would ever forget, given all the damage they did, the hurt and the destruction they caused. I wouldn't think the survivors of the Great Wars would ever let that lesson be lost, even if all the others were."

"Oh, they didn't forget it themselves, I don't think, and they taught it to their children." Deladion Inch drank again from his cup of ale. "But things like demons don't come around the same way each time. They're like nightmares; they take on new shapes and come at you from different places. They're changelings and shape-shifters, and they have the consistency and presence of ghosts."

He gave a quick warning gesture. "Don't misunderstand me. Demons might be the most dangerous enemy, but they're not the only worry. Not from what I've seen. The larger worry is the unsettled state of the different kinds of people who were the survivors of the Great Wars. Those people—those Races, more properly—took on different forms and developed different languages, and they barely knew of one another until a little more than a century ago when they stopped living in caves and hideaways and came out for a closer look around. Instead of trying to band together in a common cause, they did the exact opposite. They created new barriers to any sort of joining, making clear to anyone who wasn't exactly like them that they didn't trust or need their kind. It was the past all over again. Just like always, men are their own worst enemies."

"Are you saying that what you've got out here is a smaller version of what we left behind five hundred years ago?" Sider stared at him. "That nothing has changed except the number of participants?"

Inch nodded. "Pretty much. Sad, huh?"

Sider rocked back and looked off into the distance. It was dark and silent and peaceful, and there was nothing to indicate anything different. Yet there it was, the truth of things from someone who ought to know. The Great Wars might be over and the Races might have changed their look and makeup, but the hostilities that had plagued the world since day one continued. It would never change, he thought. No surprise, but it was hard to acknowledge nevertheless.

"How do you fit into all this, Inch?" he asked finally. "I know what you do, but how do you choose who you work for? You said it wasn't just the money; it was a freedom of choice. But how do you make that choice?"

"Oh, that." Deladion Inch shrugged. "It's not so hard, really. The communities are small, poorly trained, and not well educated, but they're tough-minded and determined. I find one that has a problem I can relate to and I offer to solve it. Sometimes I don't even make the offer; I just go ahead and do it. It depends on the situation. I want things to get better; this is how I make that happen. It's pretty clear to me, mostly."

Sider wasn't so sure it would be all that clear to him, but he let it go. Deladion Inch was a confident, self-assured man, and if he was any judge of ability, a dangerous one. He was probably more than a match for any two normal men and maybe more. Sider didn't think he ever wanted to find out.

Besides, as he had said to Inch earlier, he liked him.

"What about enemies that threaten everyone?" he asked. "Any of those still out there?"

The big man shook his head. "Maybe, but we don't know about them yet. The Trolls are the most populous people. Used to call themselves Lizards, but quit doing that a long time back. Something about wanting more respect. They live in tribes to the north. Thousands of them belong to each tribe; these are big communities. They did better after the Great Wars than the other Races, maybe because they were better protected by their mutations, maybe because they were farther away from the worst of things. In any case, they came out of it better and propagated quicker. I've been up that way a few times, met a few of their leaders, and seen their cities. They're smiths and ironworkers, for the most part. They make their own weapons and armor. No one in his right mind would go up against them.

"Other than that?" He furrowed his brow. "There are rumors . . ." He trailed off. "But there are always rumors, aren't there? I haven't seen anything of the sort that you're asking about, and neither has anyone I've talked to."

"I was just wondering how big a threat those of us living in the valley might face from those of you who don't. If agenahls are the worst of it, maybe it isn't so bad, after all."

Deladion Inch was silent for a moment, his eyes fixed on Sider. "Well, I wouldn't be too quick to make that presumption from anything that I've told you," he said finally. "Ask yourself this. Do your people have weapons and armor? Do they have training in the use of both? Do they know how to conduct themselves in a fight where the loser gets wiped out and the village gets burned back into the earth? If the answer is no, you're all in a lot of trouble."

Sider Ament didn't say anything in response. He nodded wordlessly and thought that the other man had an important point to make. He didn't know this world and its inhabitants, and any presumptions about what they might do or not do to his own community, once they found out about it, were reckless. The only thing he could be certain about was that if some of the former found their way into the valley and discovered some of the latter, it would happen again. The mists had dissipated, the protective walls were down, and his wards had been violated more than once. It was the beginning of the end of their old way of life and a signal that a new way must be found.

He wondered how the boy Panterra and his young friend were doing in convincing anyone in the village of Glensk Wood or in any other place they might choose to visit that this was true.

"You've given me a lot to think about," he said finally, looking over at Inch. "I thank you for doing so."

The big man smiled. "My pleasure. I hope it helped." He reached over and touched Sider gently on the arm. "One more thing. Something I have to ask. When you've healed sufficiently to leave here, will you go back to the mountains and your valley home? Back to where you came from?"

Sider nodded. "I expect I will."

"Do you have family there? A wife or children? I have none, so I have nothing to go back to and moving ahead is all I know. No ties of any sort. But is that so for you or is there someone back there who still means something to you? A loved one you think about when you're out alone and far away from your people?"

"No, no one." Sider hesitated. "Once, but not anymore. Not for a long time now."

Deladion Inch shrugged. "Doesn't matter. Doesn't change what I want to say. You speak of the way you watch over the people of your home, of the commitment that black staff requires of you once you choose to carry it. That sort of dedication, that's very rare. I don't know that I've ever seen it before. I just thought that maybe . . ."

He trailed off, the sentence left unfinished. "Do yourself a favor. When you get there and you've told your people whatever you think you need to tell them, stay there. Keep your people there, too. Don't come out here again until you're better prepared for it. You haven't seen enough of what's out here. You've no idea how dangerous it is. I do. And I'm telling you that you're not ready for it."

"Maybe that's so," Sider acknowledged. "But maybe I won't have a choice in the matter."

The big man chuckled softly. "You always have a choice, Sider. Do what I say. Stay in your valley and stay safe."

After that, they were quiet for a long time.

10

I DON'T LIKE IT THAT WE RAN AWAY," PANTERRA WAS saying as they climbed out of the valley in which Glensk Wood was now little more than a darker shading of color amid the green of the trees. "It makes it look like we did something wrong."

Prue, walking to his right and just ahead, gave him a look. "It doesn't matter what anyone thinks. What matters is the truth, and the truth is that we were just trying to help."

"You and I and Aislinne know that. But no one else does. No one else even heard me once I got to the part about the protective wall breaking down. No one wanted to hear that the things that killed Bayleen and Rausha were from outside that wall and might be just the first of an entire world of monsters trying to break in. Who can blame them? They're terrified of the possibility. Aren't you?"

"I'm fifteen. Everything terrifies me."

He laughed in spite of himself.

The sun was just cresting the jagged line of the mountains east, spearing the retreating dark with lances of gold and silver daylight, the clouds of the previous night dissipating and leaving only heavy fog that pooled in the gaps of the peaks. The boy and the girl had been walking steadily since they had left home during the night, heading east and north toward the Elven city of Arborlon. It was a two-day walk at best, but there was no reason for them to believe that anything ahead might obstruct their passage or anyone behind find their carefully hidden tracks.

"Do you think they'll send someone after us?" Prue asked suddenly, as if reading his thoughts.

He shook his head. "Skeal Eile? No, I think he'll be content to have us gone. If we're not there, we can't repeat our story. Eile doesn't care about us specifically—only what we might do if we continue to stir things up. He might like to have some private time with us, maybe find a way to make us recant. But he won't waste time trying to track us down."

"What makes you think that?" She looked irritated at the idea. "He's already tried to kill us. Why do you think he'll stop there?"

Pan shrugged. "I just do. All he worries about is protecting his place as leader of the Children of the Hawk. Last night is over and done with."

They walked on in silence, concentrating on the terrain ahead, their climb steepening as they approached the rim, their eyes lowering to avoid the rising sun's glare. The land about them was a mix of bare rock, tough mountain grasses, and small, sturdy conifers that could only live at great heights. Birds flitted past, and now and then a ground squirrel or chipmunk, but nothing bigger. Behind them, the valley that had been their home stretched away in a broad green sweep, its night-shrouded lines taking on clearer definition with the sun's rapid approach.

Once, a hawk passed directly overhead, sailing out of the valley and toward the rim to which they were headed. They stopped as one and watched its progress as it flew east and disappeared.

"A good omen, don't you think?" Panterra said.

Prue frowned. "Maybe."

She didn't say anything more, and he let the conversation lapse. But his thoughts drifted to the legend of the Hawk, to the boy who had brought their ancestors out of the destruction of the Great Wars and into the safe haven of these connected valleys. He wished sometimes he could have been there to see it, although he had a feeling that he wouldn't have much liked the experience if he were living it. A lot of people had died, and the survivors had endured tremendous hardship. The transition from the old life to the new must have been difficult, as well. Nothing would have been easy, even after they were safely closed away.

But why he really wished he could have been there was that he might better understand how things had come to their present state of affairs. The Children of the Hawk had been formed originally to honor the father of all the generations of survivors who had followed after the first. It had been a celebration of life and love and the durability of the human spirit. When so many had died, these few had lived. It was a wonderfully inspiring story of the human condition.

And yet it had come to this: a cult that followed a dogmatic hard line of exclusion and repression, believed its teachings alone were the way that others must follow, and claimed special knowledge of something that had happened more than five centuries ago. It did nothing to soften its rigid stance, nothing to heal wounds that it had helped to create by deliberately shunning people of other Races, and nothing to explore the possibility of other beliefs. It held its ground even in the face of hard evidence that perhaps it had misjudged and refused to consider that it was courting a danger that might destroy everyone.

How could something so wrong grow out of something that had started out so right?

They climbed on until they reached the rim, the sun now well above the horizon and moving toward midday, and turned north where the rim flattened into a narrow trail that wound through clusters of rock and small stands of alpine. The air was cold, and the winds blew in sudden, unexpected gusts that required travelers to pay attention and mind the placing of their feet. But the boy and the girl had come this way many times before, and so they knew what was required.

By midday, they had reached a point where they were starting down the other side, and in the distance they could see the gathering of lakes that marked the Eldemere, the forested waterways that formed the western boundary of Elven country.

In the distance, a rain squall was blowing across the lakes and through the woods, a ragged gray curtain that hung from towering masses of cumulus clouds.

"I think we might get wet," Prue observed.

Panterra nodded. "I think we might also get some help from Mother Nature in covering our tracks."

She glanced over quickly. "I thought you said Skeal Eile wouldn't bother coming after us."

"I did. But in case I'm wrong, it doesn't hurt to have help."

Prue gave him a disgusted look. "In case you're wrong, huh."

"Not that it's likely, but even so."

She grimaced. "No wonder I'm afraid of everything."

They took some time to eat a quick lunch, watching the storm roll across the Eldemere, the clouds thick and roiling and deep. There was no lightning or thunder, and except for the sound of the wind gusting, it was oddly silent. There was movement in the leaves on the trees, from the bushes and grasses below, and on the surface of the water. The scudding clouds and breaks of sun that streamed over the canopy of the woods cast legions of moving shadows, an entire community of dark wraiths that lacked substance and purpose. The boy and the girl sat eating and watching, not quite mesmerized, but definitely captivated. It was moments like this that made them feel at home and welcome in the world. It was here in the wild, outside of walls and open to the elements, that they had always felt most at peace.

"What do you think the Elves will say when we give them Sider's message?" Prue asked.

Pan shrugged. "I don't know. I think they'll listen without calling us names and looking at us like we're bad people, though."

He began packing up their gear, burying the remains of their lunch, scuffing over the earth, and doing what he could to hide their passing. He didn't think anyone would find the site, since it was well off the pathway and back in the rocks where no one was likely to venture by accident, but there was no point in taking chances.

"So we start with the Orullians?" Prue rose to help him, glancing down toward the Eldemere. "The rain is getting worse. I can't see an end to the storm driving it, either. Maybe we should make camp here."

"That wastes half a day we don't have," Pan replied, shouldering his pack. "I think we need to reach Arborlon as soon as possible. The things trying to break in from the outside world aren't going to wait on the weather."

She nodded, shouldering her own pack, and together they set out once more, regaining the path leading down and making their way toward the dark sweep of the storm.

"The Orullians will be more willing than anyone else to hear us out," Pan said finally. "Since they are cousins to the Belloruus family, they can get us an audience with the King and the High Council. If we deliver Sider's message to them, we will have done as much as we can."

"Do you think he'll be able to find us there? Sider, I mean? He said he would find us, but I don't see how he can do that. We aren't in Glensk Wood anymore, and no one knows where we've gone. Except for Aislinne."

Panterra shook his head. "I don't know. I keep saying that, don't I? I guess there's a lot we don't know, when you come right down to it."

Afternoon eased toward evening, and soon they had reached the edges of the storm; rain was falling all around them. They were wrapped in their all-weather cloaks as they pushed ahead, heads bent against wind and water, eyes blinking away both. The ground softened as they finished their descent and began to cross the valley floor into the Eldemere. Earth and grass replaced stone and crushed rock, but while their boots left clear tracks in the muddied ground they knew surface water would fill and smooth over their footprints by morning. Already sprawling ponds were collecting on the flats, connected by a network of streams that crisscrossed the valley like silver snakes.

Ahead, the country shimmered like a mirage.

"We better find somewhere to make camp," Panterra said finally, noting that the light was beginning to fail and the misty rain to thicken.

"There's that big chestnut," Prue suggested, and he knew at once the one she meant.

They made their way through the steadily falling rain, into the woods and around the lakes and waterways, angling slightly north above the largest of the meres, the name given to the lakes. The dampness was turning colder, and the air was filled with the smell of rain-soaked wood and grasses, rich and pungent. Panterra glanced back a final time to see if their tracks were visible, out of force of habit more than need, and he could see nothing of their passage beneath the slick of rainwater. Satisfied, he put the matter from his mind and slogged on.

It took them another hour to reach their destination, a huge old shade tree with a thick, almost impenetrable canopy that even in a steady rain such as this one kept the earth around the trunk dry for twenty feet in all directions. Smaller trees clustered close about the larger, a brood nurtured by their mother, and while the storm raged without it was calm and dry within their shelter. Tired and cold, the boy and the girl moved over to the trunk and dropped their gear. Wordlessly, they separated, moving to opposite sides of the trunk where they stripped off their wet clothing, dried off as best they could, and put on the spare set of clothes they had packed before leaving.

"Can we have a fire?" Prue asked when they had rejoined each other. "It would help us to dry out and warm up. If you think we're safe now."

He did, so he agreed. He gathered stray wood from within the shelter of the grove, and then ranged a little farther out to add some more. He kindled the wood with his flint and soon had flames curling up from a small pile of shavings and mosses. The fire was cheerful and welcome in the darkness and damp, crackling in steady counterpoint to the patter of the rain. Prue set out food for them to eat, and soon they were consuming a meal they hadn't quite realized they were so hungry for.

Pan's thoughts drifted once more to home and the series of events that had led them to flee it, wondering how it was that circumstance and chance played so large a part in the twists and turns his life had taken. He didn't regret what had happened, though; he knew it was their good fortune to discover the danger because at least they were doing something about it where others might have done nothing. That they were fugitives was unfortunate, but not permanent; the situation would correct itself eventually when they were proven right. He had the confidence and faith of the young that there was time and space enough for anything. You just had to be patient; you just had to believe.

"It isn't right that they can do this to us," Prue said softly, her eyes lowered as they cleaned the dishes. "Skeal Eile and his followers, chasing us away like this. You know it isn't."

"I know. And Eile doesn't seem the sort to let something like that bother him, either. What's right for him is whatever's necessary to keep him leader of the Children of the Hawk."

"You would think someone would notice that his moral compass is broken. Are his followers all blind?"

Panterra shrugged. "In a way, I think maybe they are. They want so hard to believe in what they've been taught that they find ways to rationalize things they wouldn't stand for otherwise. They need to keep their faith intact or risk losing it. No one likes letting go of what they have always believed, even when they know it's right to do so."

"But you think the Elves will see things differently." She made it a statement of fact.

"I think the Orullians will. I think some of their family will. If we convince even those few, we have a chance of convincing the others."

They talked some more about the future, agreeing that on their arrival later tomorrow they needed to sit the Orullian siblings down and tell them everything. No delays, no standing on ceremony, no equivocation—just lay it out there and let them ponder on it.

After a time, their eyes grew heavy and they curled up in their blankets. Because the skies were still overcast, the darkness was very nearly complete. The air remained chill and damp, and not even the dry ground beneath the chestnut could help with that. A shivering Prue hunched over to lie close against Pan, her small body knotted up. He took one end of his own blanket and wrapped them both.

"Thanks, Pan," she whispered.

He was reminded in that moment of how young she was. She might possess considerable talent and skill, but she was still only fifteen and barely more than a child.

He patted her hair gently, and then wrapped his arms about her, wanting her to be warm and safe. "Go to sleep," he whispered.

Then he fell asleep himself.

*　*　*

SKEAL EILE WALKED THROUGH THE VILLAGE of Glensk Wood in the darkness of the early morning, neither furtive nor fearful of discovery but confident, a man who knew his way and had tested his limits.

He was many things, was the Seraphic, but above all he was careful. He was ambitious, ruthless, and vengeful. He was fanatical in his commitment to the teachings of his sect and consumed by the struggle within himself to differentiate between what he knew was right and what he believed was necessary. But all of these were tempered by his caution. He had always understood how necessary it was to be cautious, how important never to act in haste. Others might act in the heat of the moment, might choose to disdain patience, might think that power alone was enough to protect against those who wished them harm, but he knew better.

Unfortunately, he had forgotten that lesson yesterday when he had sent his assassin to eliminate the boy and the girl who had brought their wild, desperate tales of creatures from the outer world. Such tales could only cause dissent among the faithful and foster cracks in the beliefs he had instilled in them, and that could never be allowed.

So he had acted in haste and been left to repent at leisure. The assassin had failed—disappeared without a trace—and the boy and the girl were gone. Now he had to set things right, though not in haste and not without caution. He had to set them right in deliberate and purposeful fashion, and he knew how to do that.

He had been the leader of the Children of the Hawk for a long time. He had been a Seraphic even longer, although no one knew of this but him. He had been born with the talent, his ability clear to him from early on. Devoted to the teachings of the sect, he had waited to be noticed so that his talent might be employed in their service. But time had come and gone, and no one bothered to approach him. So he took it upon himself to gain their attention. He began speaking at meetings, usually unbidden, often barely tolerated. But his oratory was powerful, and his fervor infectious. While the leader of the sect and his followers dallied, the faithful began to gravitate toward him.

Leaders are all the same, however; they might profess otherwise, but they do not wish to give up their positions or their power. His predecessor had tried to ease him aside and, failing that, to eliminate him. The assassins who served the sect were always waiting for an opportunity, like jackals prowling at the edge of the pack for the weak and the injured. His predecessor mistook him for a victim and sent an assassin to make an example of him. The attempt failed, and the man ended up a victim himself. It caused Skeal Eile a certain amount of regret because he was not a bad man, he told himself, only a committed one. He understood what so many others did not—that he had been born to lead the faithful and that obstacles to his leadership needed to be removed. What was one life compared with the importance of the teachings of the sect?

So he became their leader, donning the mantle he had been born to wear. He was generous and helpful to all who embraced him; he was a teacher and a giver of hope. He possessed magic, but he kept that mostly to himself and only now and then revealed glimpses of his talent. His voice was strong and ubiquitous, and he was both expected and welcomed at all council meetings and gatherings. Even those who did not subscribe directly to the teachings of the sect respected his power and his ability. They might not accept him as their leader, but they understood that his dominance was unquestionable. In turn, he did not insist on their loyalty, only on their recognition of his place.

His influence began to reach beyond Glensk Wood to the surrounding villages, until soon he had solidified his place as Seraphic to the sect throughout the valley. It was enough for now, although his plans were grander and more far reaching and would in time elevate the place of the Children of the Hawk to one of unquestionable dominance.

It was the right thing for everyone, he knew. It was way the Hawk himself would have wanted it—the way he would expect to find things on his return. Disruption or denial of this truth was the great heresy of his time, and Skeal Eile could not abide it.

There had been some who had committed that heresy over the years, some who could not accept the truths embedded in the sect's teachings. Skeal Eile had dealt with each of them as need required. Some he had managed to convince of the error of their ways, and had turned them about. Some he had marginalized or simply destroyed by discovering their unpleasant secrets and revealing them to all. Some he had driven out through threats and intimidation.

Some he had been forced to eliminate in a more permanent fashion, their presence alone an abomination. These unfortunates had committed heresy that was beyond redemption, had spewed out poison that would infect others if left untreated. For those few, the assassins were required.

But even the assassins were not always sufficient to right matters. Witness their failure with the boy and the girl.

The mystery of that failure troubled him. He had heard that the two possessed special talent, although he had never witnessed it himself. He did not think they enjoyed the use of magic, as he did, but he could not be certain. Somehow they had managed to overcome and kill a skilled assassin, this boy and girl. He could not shake the feeling that Aislinne Kray was a part of what had happened, that somehow she had intervened in the matter. But even she was no match for a trained killer. Besides, she was mostly a bothersome presence. Her husband was the one that mattered, and he was firmly committed to the sect and its teachings and bonded to Skeal Eile, in particular. That didn't mean he didn't love his wife enough to turn it all around if something should happen to her. Pogue Kray knew it had happened to others who had defied the sect, and he had made it plain to the Seraphic that he would not allow it to happen to her. So the troublesome Aislinne had been tolerated up until now, although that might have to change.

This was not so when it came to Sider Ament, but Eile had never been able to get his hands on the Gray Man. A loner who seldom came down off the valley rim and never into open view, he was an elusive target. Someday, maybe. Eile looked forward to putting an end to that man. But for now he, too, had to be tolerated.

Not so the boy and the girl.

Yet he must be careful here. He must be creative in his efforts to resolve the matter. Something out of the ordinary was required if he didn't want to experience still another failure.

He was well back in the trees now, on the outskirts of the village. It was deeply wooded here, the path nearly nonexistent, the underbrush thick and tangled. He slipped through openings that few could find even in daylight, the way clear to him, as it would not be to others. Ahead, a small cabin appeared through the undergrowth, a dilapidated

structure with a sagging porch and blacked-out windows that gave it
the look of a dead thing. But there would be eyes watching. There always were.

Yet the eyes of the old man who met him at the door when he
stepped up on the porch were as milky and blind as a cave bat's, staring blankly at a point some six inches over Skeal Eile's head.

"Who's that?" the old man asked in a whisper.

"Tell him I'm here," the Seraphic ordered, ignoring the question.

"Ah, it's you!" the old man exclaimed in delight. He cackled and
turned away. "Always a pleasure to see you. Always a joy! I'll send him
right out. Just one minute."

Off he went, back into the darkened interior of the cabin. Skeal
Eile did not try to follow. He had never been inside the cabin and had
no wish to enter it now. He had a strong suspicion that he wouldn't
like it much in there. Not given what he knew of the occupants.

He waited a full five minutes for Bonnasaint to appear. By then, he
was standing out in the tiny yard, studying the weeds and the bare
ground and thinking of other things. The boy materialized silently,
emerging from the darkness of the cabin interior, pausing momentarily
in the doorway as if to take stock of things and then stepping down to
confront the Seraphic.

"Your Eminence," the boy greeted, bowing deeply. "How may I help
you?"

There wasn't a hint of irony in the other's voice, only a clear expression of abiding respect. Skeal Eile had always liked that about the
boy. Even when they'd first met and the boy was only twelve, that
respect was evident. Now Bonnasaint was more than twenty, and their
relationship was unchanged. Skeal Eile still thought of him as a boy because he looked barely older than one, his skin fair and unblemished,
his features fine, his face beardless, and his limbs slender and supple.
There was nothing of the man physically evident in the boy, but get
below the skin and you found a creature that was very, very old indeed.

"I require your services," the Seraphic said quietly, casting a quick
glance at the cabin.

"He knows better than to listen in," Bonnasaint advised, offering up
a dazzling smile.

"I trust no one, not your father, not even you."

"Not even me?" The smile disappeared. "I am hurt."

"You are never hurt. You are as cold and hard as the stones of the mountains. That is why you are my favorite."

"It has been a while since you came to see me, Eminence. I thought that perhaps I had fallen from favor."

"I only come to you when I have a problem lesser men cannot solve. I have one now."

The dazzling smile returned. The boyish face brightened. "Please enlighten me."

Skeal Eile stepped close to him. "A boy and a girl. I want them to disappear."

11

PANTERRA AND PRUE WOKE TO A MORNING FROSTY with cold, the ground crystalline white and the lakes of the Eldemere shedding mist and dampness in the soft glow of the sun's first light. The echo of birdcalls was sharp and ghostly, sounding out of the silence in forlorn reverberation across the wider expanse of the lakes before disappearing into the dark maze of the surrounding woods. Mist clung in thick blankets to the mountaintops. The air was sharp and clear, and you could see the details of clefts in the rocks of snow-cropped defiles that were miles away.

The boy and the girl didn't bother with breakfast, not yet awake enough to need or enjoy food. Instead, they packed up their gear and set out walking among the meres, gathering their still sleep-fogged thoughts for the trek ahead.

The sun rose, the air warmed, and the morning changed its look and feel as first light turned to full sunrise and the silence of sleep gave way to the noises of waking. Breezes gusted across the meres and through the leaves of the trees in steady rustlings, the still waters of the meres began to lap against the shores, and the birdcalls were joined by animal scurrying and voices, distant and indistinct, suddenly become audible.

"Elves," Panterra observed, referring to the voices, the first word either of them had spoken since waking.

Prue nodded agreement, but didn't reply.

They walked on, traversing the whole of the Eldemere, stopping once at midday, when hunger got the better of them, to eat a lunch of bread, cheese, dried fruits, and cold water before continuing on. They passed no one on the way, although they were now well into the territory of the Elves and could expect an encounter at any point.

But it was not until they reached the far eastern edge of the meres and came in sight of the forested bluff on which Arborlon had been settled that they saw their first Elf. A boy who was a little younger than Prue stepped out of the trees as they neared the switchbacked road leading up to the bluff and stared at them.

"Good day," Prue greeted him, giving a smile that would have melted ice.

The boy frowned, his already slanted brows slanting further, his narrow features narrowing further. "This is Elf country," he declared, as if in rebuke to their presence.

"Good. Then we are in the right place."

"Humans aren't welcome."

"We aren't entirely human."

"You look human to me."

"Well, you aren't very old and you haven't see all that much of the world, so you wouldn't know." She gave him a fresh smile for good measure. "What's your name?"

"Xac," he said, his look indicating that he was still wary of any trick they might be planning.

"I'm Prue," she answered. "Do you know the Orullian family?"

The boy nodded, confused now. "What do you mean, you aren't entirely human? I've never heard of that."

"See, now you've learned something new. Your education is improved. Can you take us where we need to go? That way, people will know we are being carefully watched and won't make any trouble."

"I don't know," Xac answered, still suspicious. "If you're not entirely human, what are you, then?"

Prue thought about it a moment. "Tell you what. Come with us to the Orullians and you can find out from them."

The boy studied her carefully for a few long moments. "All right," he said finally.

So with the boy Xac leading the way, they crossed out of the Eldemere and through hills covered in tall grasses and scattered clumps of rock to the road leading up to the bluff. They began to see other Elves in the trees and on the hills around them, coming and going about their business. Most spared them a glance and not much more, assuming they were with the boy, which was what Prue had intended. Visitors in the company of one of their own did not draw as much attention. Panterra, watching Prue continue her conversation with Xac, could not help but admire her way with people. She had an uncanny ability to win them over, all without any hint of her intentions. Only fifteen, and already she was more practiced at it than most of the adults he knew. Maybe, he decided, it was because she was more grown-up than so many of those same adults.

They climbed the switchbacks that led to the top of the bluffs, angling up steep stairs embedded amid rugged clusters of rocks and thick stands of trees and warded by stone walls and iron gates. The Elves called it the Elfitch, and it was intended to form a series of protective barriers against anyone trying to ascend the heights without permission. Ordinarily, this wasn't a problem. Sentries kept watch over visitors from posts overlooking the western approach, and if anything dangerous appeared an armed force of Elven Hunters would respond in moments. Panterra couldn't say when that had last happened—quite possibly not in his lifetime. But the argument went that the Elfitch was always meant to be a deterrent rather than a defense.

Even now, there would be eyes on them ascending the roadway. But since Xac was accompanying them and they only numbered two, there was little reason for concern.

When they reached the top of the Elfitch and turned onto the Carolan heights, they began to see a larger number of Elves going about their business. Now heads began to turn and gazes to focus. The presence of humans in Arborlon was rare, the result of isolating themselves from the other Races. Lizards and Spiders were frequent visitors, smaller in population and eager to make alliances. Elves were more willing to accommodate them than Men. Men couldn't seem to help wanting to attach conditions to their friendship, while Elves simply asked that you honor their ways and respect their place in the world. Men were the most numerous of the peoples residing in the valley, yet the most difficult to be around. Panterra found that both strange and unfortunate, but that was the way of things.

Some of it, he knew, had to do with the practices of the Children of the Hawk. But much of it was tied to a history that over the centuries had shaped the thinking of the Race of Men to such an extent that it was virtually impossible to change. Because Mankind had always been the dominant Race, the reasoning went, it was predestined that it always should be. Other Races were inferior, not of the same intelligence and ability or of the same high moral makeup or possessed of humans' innate appreciation of life's purpose. The excuses went on and on, and Panterra had heard them all, most often from members of the sect, but sometimes from those who ought to know better. It was the sort of thinking generated by hidden fears and doubts, by a nagging sense that maybe you weren't as special as you had been told and would like to think.

Neither Pan nor Prue—for they had discussed it many times when they were alone in the high country—had any use for that sort of rationalization. Nor was either particularly concerned with Man's insistence on establishing some order of dominance among the Races. It was enough if you knew where you stood with any individual from any Race, and the pecking order would have to sort itself out over time and through trial by fire. Everyone was trying to do the best they could, and success was predicated on things like determination and strength of character and even luck. It had always been so, and they kept clear of those who thought otherwise.

Of course, the Elves were not immune to this sort of one-upmanship, but they were less vocal about it and less inclined to make it known at every opportunity. Some among them believed that theirs was the dominant Race and always had been. They were the oldest of the Races and the most talented. They had been given the gift of magic, and they had used it to great effect until they had lost it through neglect and indecision. That their numbers were less than those of humans because they procreated so much more slowly was of little consequence in the larger scheme of things. What mattered was that they alone had found ways to survive since the time of Faerie. Some even believed that it had been a mistake to come out of hiding during the Great Wars, that if they had stayed hidden the other Races—Man, in particular—would have destroyed themselves, and the Elves would have been the better for it.

The upshot of all this was that neither Men nor Elves had a whole lot of use for the other and kept apart to the extent that it was possible, each casting a wary eye for the other to cause trouble. Only a handful of individuals within each Race understood that they were all rowing in the same boat and all likely to stand or fall on how willing they were to unite in the face of dangers that eclipsed their own petty squabbles.

But that sort of danger hadn't appeared until now, Panterra knew. So a testing of each Race was close at hand.

Pan flashed momentarily on all of this in response to the looks cast at him by some of the Elves they passed. He knew that his worldview wasn't particularly sophisticated or experienced. He was not schooled in reading and writing, and he owned no books himself. He had learned to read signs rather than books because teaching himself to be a Tracker was what really mattered to him. He was ignorant of many things, but he was not stupid. He was a keen observer, and he was well traveled throughout the valleys, so he understood a few things about the way the Races related to one another and had thought at length about what that meant. What you knew about people mostly came from coming in contact with them, he reasoned. If your instincts and your senses didn't lie to you, if your reasoning was sound, then you could draw your own conclusions about the human condition. All you needed to do was to pay attention to what was going on around you. That was what he had done.

His thoughts on the matter were only momentary and then they were gone as swiftly as they had come, and he moved on to what was always a fresh appreciation of the place to which they had journeyed.

Arborlon was an impressive city by any measure, the more so for being the largest and oldest of the centers of habitation in the safehold. Arborlon had been built in a time before Mankind itself was born, in the time of Faerie and magic, before humans and all their offspring. Built and rebuilt over the centuries, encapsulated by the magic of the Loden Elfstone so that it and its inhabitants might be preserved against the greatest of evils and moved when moving was the only option available, it was the only city of its kind still in existence. There were rumors of others, of cities vast and wondrous, all reduced to ruins and rubble, empty of life, testaments to what had come and gone in other times. But Arborlon was the real thing, a city of the most distant past, built by the oldest of Races, alive and well after all this time.

"Isn't it beautiful?" Prue said softly, as if reading his mind.

Beautiful, indeed, Panterra thought, and he gave her a smile of agreement.

There were no walls in Arborlon, once you got to the heights. The cottages and assembly halls, the amphitheater and the gardens, and even the royal palace and its grounds were open and accessible to all. Home Guard protected the Kings and Queens and their families, and Elven Hunters would defend against attacks when called upon, but the Elves were forest creatures and lived their lives in the open. Their dwellings reflected this. Though most were ground dwellings set within the forest and along the waterways, some were nestled high up in the trees and suspended by cables so that they appeared to be a part of their surroundings. The entire city blended into the woods, making each a part of the other, so that it had a natural feel unlike anything found in the villages of Men.

Panterra supposed that something of the reason he felt so comfortable among the Elves was his affinity for their way of life. Like them, he preferred living out in the open, part of nature and the larger world. He was at home in the woods, and he believed in practicing stewardship of the land. Elves embraced the world in a way Men had never learned to, and their magic, although mostly lost, had left them a legacy of trying to do whatever they could to keep all the living things around them healthy. The differences between Men and Elves were striking in many ways, but none more so than their differing approaches to maintenance of the territories they inhabited. Elves took a direct approach to caring for the land. Indeed, they were raised to believe it was a calling. Men practiced what was mostly a benign neglect, accepting the land as they found it but doing nothing much to preserve it. They lived on it, cultivated it, took what it had to offer, but did little to give anything back. It wasn't a deliberate, mean-spirited approach; it was simply the way they had always lived.

Of course, there were no absolutes, so some—Panterra and Prue among them—took a more direct interest in the land and spent time and effort doing what they could to preserve and sometimes restore it. But the Elves were more committed to that way of life than Men, and the boy and the girl felt closer to them for being so.

"If you're more than human, what else are you?" Xac asked suddenly, back again on that subject. "Why are you being so secret about it? Why can't you tell me?"

"We're Elves," Pan declared without thinking.

The boy stopped where he was and stared at him. "No, you're not. You don't look anything like Elves."

"We're in disguise. The part that's Elf is hidden on the inside. Isn't that right, Prue?"

The girl gave him a look and then nodded. "We were born human, Xac, but we have Elf blood."

Xac shook his head. "I don't think so. I think you're crazy." He gave them a suspicious look. "How do I know you're telling me the truth about the Orullians? Maybe you don't even know them. Maybe you're here to cause trouble."

"Tasha and Tenerife," Panterra said, giving the names of their friends. "Twins by birth, but they don't look a thing like each other. They have a sister who is about your age. Her name is Darsha. Is that enough to persuade you to take us to them? If not, just leave us here. We can find someone else who'll do the job."

"We aren't here to cause trouble," Prue added. "Tasha and Tenerife are friends."

Xac still looked doubtful. "Well, maybe."

"Come on, let's just go." Pan was impatient. "You can ask them when we get there. They'll tell you that we've got Elf blood."

The boy hesitated, but then started off once more. They maneuvered their way through the city streets, a maze of crosshatch byways and paths, all of it designed to confuse if you were not a resident familiar with the terrain. But Xac knew his way and led them. A number of Elves greeted him with calls and waves, some directing questioning looks at his companions, but no one actually saying anything. They passed through the center of the city and angled south past the palace and its extensive grounds, all of it planted with lush grasses and rainbow-bright flower beds, all of it carefully tended. Panterra found himself smiling in response to how the smells and colors made him feel, wishing as he always did that this could be his home. Even though he was committed to staying and serving as a Tracker with Prue, Glensk Wood was not where he wanted to spend his life. Besides, reality did not require that you forgo your dreams, and dreams sometimes revealed paths that led to new realities.

"They're up there," Xac said suddenly, breaking into his thoughts.

He looked at where the boy was pointing. A cluster of Elves was constructing a stairway that ran from the ground through a series of platforms to a house settled high in a thick stand of spruce. The stairway was framed and anchored, and the men were now engaged in setting the treads in place, all except for the Elf standing at the foot of the steps, who was issuing directions.

Tasha Orullian was large by any standard, but for an Elf he was huge. The Elves were not a big people, few standing over six feet. But Tasha stood six-five out of his boots, which meant that wherever he went in the city of Arborlon, he stood out. Broad-shouldered and long-limbed, he was strong beyond any measure Panterra had been able to devise and hard as iron.

He glanced around as Xac approached with his companions and gave a yelp. "Xac Wen! What have you done, you scullion's brat? Brought outsiders of obviously disreputable character into our midst? Have you lost your mind?"

The boy flushed bright red and before either Pan or Prue could say anything to discourage him, he had whirled on them, a razor-sharp long knife in hand, poised to fight. "It's not my fault; they lied to me!" he screamed back at the other.

"Wait, hold on, you little madman!" Tasha threw up his arms in dis-

may as he walked quickly over to the boy and snatched the knife away.
He was like a big cat, smooth and lithe and powerful. "Give me that
before you hurt yourself. Must you take everything I say so literally?"

The boy, who clearly had no idea by now what was going on, glared
at him. "They said they weren't entirely human! They claimed they
were Elves!"

Tasha gave Panterra and Prue a questioning look and then nodded
soberly. "Yes," he said, his dark face stern, "they are. I know they don't
look it, but deep down inside, where it matters, they are."

"But they . . ."

"Welcome home, little Elves," Tasha greeted Panterra and Prue, ignoring Xac's protestations. "I've missed you."

He reached out and gave each a bone-crushing hug, going only
slightly easier on the girl than the boy. His chiseled features brightened
with delight as he released them. "Hmm, you've still got some growing
up to do, but you seem more mature otherwise. There's a hint of intelligence in your otherwise dim-witted eyes. Been doing something
important, have you? Is that why you've come?"

"Something like that," Panterra answered. He glanced over at Xac.
"We need to talk about it."

Tasha Orullian untied the scarf that was holding back his long
black hair and wiped the sweat from his face. "Building stairways to
houses suspended in trees was getting boring anyway." He glanced over
his shoulder. "Tenerife!" he shouted. "Look who's come to visit!"

A slightly smaller figure appeared through the door of the tree cottage and waved before starting down. With deceptive ease, he swung
from one post to the next, one platform to the next, and vaulted the
last ten feet to the ground unaided. "Panterra Qu!" he cried, coming
over. "And little sister! What a nice surprise."

He embraced them both, not so roughly, but every bit as enthusi-
astically, slapping both on the back in the bargain. Tenerife was a smaller
version of his twin, lighter and shorter and less of a presence, but still
unmistakable. Not so physically imposing, he was also not so rough-
made, his features more finely wrought. Like his brother, he was dark-
complected and wore his black hair long and tied back from his face.

"Good to see you, Tenerife," Panterra greeted him.

"Come to the house," Tasha invited, sweeping them up like leaves with his long arms outstretched. "We can have something to eat and drink while we talk. Xac Wen!" he shouted, noticing that the boy was trying to tag along. "That's all for today. Go find a pack of wild dogs to play with. Go wrestle a Koden or something."

The boy glared at him. "You wait until I grow up!" he shouted at Tasha Orullian.

"I should live so long!" the tall man shouted back, but grinned nevertheless. "He's a handful now, that one," he said to his guests as they walked away, leaving the boy standing at the foot of the stairs. "I can't imagine what he'll be like when he gets bigger."

"The same, only more so," Tenerife grunted. "Imagine that."

They passed down several trails to a cottage nestled with a handful of others in a grove of towering oaks, seating themselves on benches at a table set to one side of the entry. Tasha excused himself to go inside and then returned almost immediately with tankards of ale and a platter of cheese, fruit, and bread.

"This will help us express ourselves more clearly," he announced, distributing the tankards first. "Or at least we'll think so."

They ate and drank and talked of old times. The Orullians were the Elven equivalent of Trackers, although they served at the King's pleasure and on behalf of the entire Elven nation rather than just the city of Arborlon. Panterra and Prue had met them more than three years ago, and the four had taken an instant liking to one another. The Orullian twins were fascinated by the then only twelve-year-old Prue, unable to believe that anyone could sense things unseen with such unerring accuracy and timing. They thought her better than what her people deserved and promptly declared her an honorary Elf. They made Panterra one, too, but mostly because it would have been rude to leave him out. Their standing with the brothers was what had prompted Pan to tell Xac that they were partly Elves. It seemed truer than not under the circumstances.

"Now then," Tasha said once they had finished eating and consumed a fair amount of smooth, sweet honey-lemon ale. "To business. You've come to visit us, of course. But you've come for another reason, as well. Tell us what it is, Pan."

So Panterra related the events that had brought them to Arborlon for refuge and help.

"There, you see?" Tasha declared to his brother, gesturing angrily. "I told you these two did not belong with the sorry excuse for human beings who occupy Glensk Wood. They belong here, with us. We are their people in more ways than they are."

Tenerife shrugged. "He's right. We may not be your people in terms of flesh and blood, but we are more so in our hearts and souls. You should do as Aislinne says and stay with us. Forever, if need be."

"I would like that," Prue declared rather a bit too boldly, and then caught herself. "I mean," she added quickly, "that it would be nice to live in such a beautiful place."

"Of course it would be nice!" Tasha exclaimed. "It would be wonderful! That's settled, then!"

"Not exactly," Panterra said, holding up both hands. "Finding a new home isn't why we came to you. We came to ask your help about the collapse of the protective wall. If it's really failing, we need to prepare ourselves for the possibility that whatever's out there is coming in here."

"We need to prepare ourselves for the possibility that we might have to go out *there*," Tenerife added pointedly. He looked at his brother. "We should tell all this to the High Council."

Tasha nodded, saying nothing for a moment. "But do we want to tell them now or later." He cocked one eyebrow at his brother. "Consider the circumstances. We know and trust Panterra and little sister, but the members of the High Council do not. They are humans, and many do not trust humans. Will they be believed or doubted? Will the High Council choose to act at once or will they debate the matter until the cows come home?"

"You think they will not be believed?"

"I think it is a distinct possibility."

"Do we take it directly to the King, instead? He may dither on it as well, as he does with so much these days."

Tasha shrugged. "That is the question, isn't it."

"Is Oparion Amarantyne still King?" Prue interjected.

The big man nodded slowly. "He is. But his Queen is new. And therein lies the problem." He took a deep breath and let it out slowly. "After all these years, little sister, he remarried. Abruptly and foolishly, if you ask us. His Queen is young and beautiful and fickle. In spite of his years of experience and his keen mind, she plays him like a musical instrument. He would do anything for her; if not for his close friends and the members of the High Council, he would likely do things he would later regret. She has his ear on all matters, and it is her firm intention to guide him in his decision making until the day he dies."

"At which time," Tenerife cut in, "there is a widespread suspicion that she intends to carry on without him."

Panterra and Prue exchanged a glance. "Is that possible?" the girl asked. "Will she be named Queen after him?"

"Another good question," Tasha replied, rubbing his chin as if to extract an answer. "Will she succeed him? Or will Phryne?"

Phryne Amarantyne. The King's daughter by his first wife was a formidable adversary. Panterra had met her only once, but that was enough. She was young but very tough. "I see the problem," he acknowledged.

"Not entirely, you don't," Tasha said.

"But likely you will before long," Tenerife added.

"So you don't think we should take this before the Elven High Council?" Prue asked.

Tasha leaned back, exchanged a look with his brother, and shook his head. "Not yet, at least. If we take it before the High Council at this point, we risk losing all credibility if they fail to believe any part of your story. As well, the Queen will find out, and as I've said there are a number of reasons for all of us not to want that to happen. I think we should keep this quiet until we know more."

"We need to make a trip up into the mountains and see what we can find out for ourselves about the passes," Tenerife declared. "After we've done that, we can decide how to attack this."

"But we'll need the King's permission to do that." Tasha drummed his fingers on the table.

"Yes, of course. But maybe we can gain that permission quietly."

"Without the Queen knowing what we're doing?"

Tenerife stretched his lean body, extending his legs and looking skyward contemplatively. "Difficult, but not impossible."

"The King will tell her."

"Not if we can find a way to persuade him not to. Of course, we can't just ask him outright. We might be his cousins, but he won't stand for that sort of interference."

They looked at one another in silence. Tasha drank some more ale and contemplated the tabletop. Tenerife kept looking up at the sky, and Prue stared down at her hands, folded in front of her. Panterra found himself wondering what they were getting themselves into.

"What we need is a bit of misdirection," Tenerife said suddenly.

When he had finished explaining what it was that he meant, everyone was smiling.

12

FOUR HOURS LATER, PHRYNE AMARANTYNE SAT SI-
lently across the table from the Orullian twins and the boy and
girl from Glensk Wood, studying their faces. She let them wait
on her, not wanting to respond too quickly. Their story was outlandish
and dangerous, and she hadn't yet decided how much of it she believed. If it had been the Orullians telling it, she would have dismissed
it out of hand. Cousins or not, they were well known for tall tales and
clever pranks, and this wouldn't be the first time they had tricked her
into believing something that wasn't true.

But the story had come from Panterra Qu, a boy she had met only
once before and didn't know much about. That he was friendly with
the Orullians didn't invest him with much credibility. But his de-
meanor and his presence suggested that tall tales and clever pranks
were not something he engaged in. So she had listened until his story
was finished. She liked the girl, too. Prue Liss. A tiny thing, but obviously self-possessed and able. She did not seem the sort to engage in
foolishness, either.

It was late in the evening by now, the sun two hours gone, the moon up, and the sky ablaze with stars. Neither clouds nor mist obscured the view this night, something exceedingly rare. Phryne was enjoying it, even knowing that she might be wasting her time at this meeting. But it was her time to waste, and she had discovered years ago that an Elven Princess could do pretty much what she wanted. Her parents had told her otherwise, but she quickly came to understand the reality of her situation. If she was discreet and caused no harm, she didn't need to answer to anyone.

She sighed as she gazed off into the trees, still keeping them waiting. It wasn't that simple, of course. Never had been. And certainly wasn't now, with her father married to the stepmother from the black pits of the dead. Sometimes she could barely make herself believe that things had come to this. She had loved and revered her mother. She still loved and revered her father, even after his remarriage. Her stepmother was a different story.

"This is all true, is it?" she asked Panterra Qu suddenly, shifting her eyes to his, pinning him against the darkness. "All of it?"

He didn't flinch. "It is."

"I would not like it very much if this turned out to be another Orullian trick performed at my expense."

He looked confused. "I wouldn't do that."

"It is all true, cousin," Tasha Orullian assured her, reaching out to pour a little more ale into her tankard. "This is no joke."

She thought about it a moment more. The possibility of the protective wall giving way, of the valley suddenly vulnerable to whatever lived without, whatever had survived the horrors of the Great Wars, was overwhelming. She imagined for a moment what might be out there, and her thoughts were not pleasant.

She was a practical girl—well, *girl* was not really the right term anymore—a practical young *woman*. She had become more so since her mother's death and her father's remarriage. She had grown up quickly in that new environment, learned how to adapt to unfavorable situations and difficult people. She had grown to accept unpleasantness as a part of life rather than to struggle futilely against truths that could not be changed. Admittedly, this new truth was of a different sort than anything she had encountered before, and she was still not quite sure she believed it. But the possibility of its existence was not something that could be dismissed out of hand.

"So your plan is to go up into the passes and find out if the barrier is still in place or if it is crumbling?"

"Yes," Panterra responded, and she liked it that he didn't equivocate.

"Just the four of us," Tenerife added. "A quick survey and a solid determination of what's happened. Once we know, we report back to the King and the High Council."

"I don't understand," she said. "What's stopping you?"

"We can't go without the King's permission."

"Then ask it of him!"

There was a collective hesitation. "We hoped maybe you could do that for us," Tenerife said finally.

She stared at him. "Why me instead of you, cousin?"

"Because we think whoever tells him needs to ask him to keep it to himself for a while and not confuse the matter by allowing other individuals to become involved," Tasha blurted out. "Cousin."

She hesitated only a moment. "You mean my stepmother and her lover. You're worried about them."

Panterra and Prue exchanged a quick glance. "'Her lover'?" the boy repeated carefully.

"Phryne, that sort of talk can get you in a lot of trouble," Tenerife said quietly. "Those are rumors, nothing more."

She made a dismissive gesture. "Maybe that's what you think, but I know the truth. I have to live with it every day. And I don't have to pretend it doesn't exist. My father may choose to do so, but that is his affair."

She turned to Panterra and Prue. "I better explain, since this obviously comes as a surprise. My beloved stepmother has taken a lover. First Minister Teonette, a man in a position of power second only to my father. The choice was calculated. Their affair is a carefully guarded secret from most, but not from me. My father knows, I think, but he pretends not to. At least, that is how I intuit things, since we have never discussed the matter openly. But I see it in his eyes. He is hurt and ashamed, but he chooses not to make it public. Maybe he thinks she will come back to him someday and be the good wife he thought she was."

She shrugged. "I'm not holding my breath. But back to the business at hand. You believe that I might better be able to persuade my father to keep your plans a secret from others, is that it?"

Tasha nodded. "In a word or two."

She shook her head. "I don't know that he will, Tasha. I can't depend on him that way anymore."

"But you could at least ask him. If we ask, he will not only stop us from going but likely refuse even to see us again for a very long time."

"Probably true." She thought about it. "I'm not sure I understand exactly what it is that you're afraid of, though. What is it that you think my stepmother and the first minister might do? Why would they even care?"

"I've been wondering that, too," Panterra cut in.

Tasha took a long pull on his tankard of ale and wiped his mouth with the back of his hand. "It's the nature of the beast," he said. "The lady and the man in question are ambitious and looking for opportunities to advance their own interests. This bit of news, if true, will change the lives of everyone living in the valley. All people, all Races. I don't want to give anyone a chance to exploit that before the King and the High Council are prepared to deal with it. That's all."

Phryne made a face. "I find it hard to argue with your logic. Very well, cousin, I will do it—but on one condition. I'm going with you."

She had made up her mind instantly, not bothering to think it through, just knowing that this was something she wanted to be a part of. If they wanted her to be their foil, they were going to have to make her a full member in their conspiracy.

"You most certainly are not," Tenerife declared at once.

"How quickly do you think the King will turn us down if he finds out you're involved?" Tasha added.

She gave them a look. "Leave that up to me. You trust me enough to speak to my father on your behalf. You'll have to trust me enough to persuade him to let me come with you."

They stared at one another in heated silence for a moment, their faces saying everything.

"I think it's a very good idea," Prue said finally, breaking the silence. "If I can go, Phryne ought to be able to go, too."

There were all sorts of arguments against such thinking, but no one was about to make them. Tasha threw up his hands, and his brother slumped back in his chair, frowning. Panterra, entirely on impulse, smiled encouragingly at Phryne Amarantyne, and she smiled back.

She found she was liking the boy and the girl from Glensk Wood better all the time.

◾ ◾ ◾

PHRYNE WAITED UNTIL THE FOLLOWING MORNING to approach her father, not wanting to disturb him when he might be sleeping. She had always been close to him and mindful of his needs, no more so than in the weeks right after her mother's death. But in the months after that, when both father and daughter began to find a new path through life, they had drifted apart. It was not done consciously or even with any real understanding at first that it was happening. At least, not on Phryne's part. She was never really sure about her father. But gradually he began to spend less time with her. There were obvious reasons for this. He was King, and as such he was busy with the affairs of the Elven people. After the death of her mother, he had immersed himself in work as a way to avoid dwelling on his loss. She had done the same, after all. She knew, as well, how difficult her father found it to be around her. She was a constant reminder to him of what he had lost, of how like her mother she looked—small-boned, fine-featured, her auburn hair a perfect match, her favorite expressions ones she had learned from her mother. It was likely that her father found her presence too painful to endure for more than short periods of time. It should have been the opposite, she had told herself when she realized what was happening. But then things didn't always work out the way you wanted them to.

As she'd discovered when, out of nowhere, Isoeld Severine appeared. Young and beautiful, she was a baker's daughter from Kelton Mews, a tiny village off to the far west, with a population that would barely make up half a dozen large families. How her father had met her was open to question; he told one story after another, charmed by the idea that it was their secret and no one else's. Isoeld had manners and poise as well as beauty, and she won over her doubters much more quickly than any objective measure would have found reasonable. After all, this was the King who was so besotted, and there were many reasons to wonder at how this had happened. Phryne had never been fooled; from the beginning, she had questioned what was happening. The age difference was troubling. The mysterious circumstances of their meeting were troubling. The way that Isoeld went so quickly from friend to lover to wife went so far beyond troubling that it brought Phryne and her father to their one and only shouting match.

But her father had made up his mind, and his daughter was not about to change it. He made it plain to her that this was his life and therefore his choice. If marrying Isoeld made him happy and if Isoeld proved a proper Queen for the Elven people, then no one had any right to object.

For a while, Phryne had left the matter alone, half willing to reconsider her dislike of this interloper, this marital bed thief who sought to take her mother's place. She knew she was jealous and protective and entirely unreasonable in her insistence that Isoeld was the wrong choice. She also knew that no one could ever be the right choice because in her heart no one could ever replace her mother.

Then, through a series of small recognitions and deductions, she had decided that Isoeld had taken a lover. First Minister Teonette was handsome and available; he was also ambitious and politically driven. They were right for each other—more so than she and the King—and the looks they directed at each other said as much. Such looks were few and cautiously exchanged in moments when they thought no one was looking, but Phryne was always looking because she had never stopped being suspicious.

She had thought to tell her father on more occasions than she cared to think about, but each time she pulled back. It was not her place. It would sound wrong coming from her, and her father would in all likelihood not believe her. After all, she had no real proof. She had never caught them in a compromising situation; she didn't know of anyone who had. Anyway, perhaps her father already knew, she decided. Perhaps he had chosen to let it be and expected others to do the same if they loved him.

Now too much time had passed for any real chance of ruining Isoeld. Phryne had waited too long. The relationships of all parties concerned were too settled for any of them to tolerate disruption. Her father loved Isoeld, and Isoeld loved being Queen. She had a good idea what the first minister loved as well, but she didn't care to ponder that.

Well, that last was a lie. Of course, she pondered it. She thought about it all the time. She just didn't know what to do.

Thinking back on all this, she walked out into the gardens and sat on a stone bench, staring down into the still waters of the lily pond that provided a focal point for the surrounding beds. Trees cast dappled shadows across the green sweep of the grounds, reaching beyond the gardens to the lawns and hedgerows, giving all of it an oddly secretive look on a day that was sunny and warm in spite of winter's lingering hold. She watched birds flit from branch to branch, everything from wrens and sparrows to tiny hummingbirds. She could hear their songs mix with the buzzing of dragonflies and bees and the rustle of leaves. In the solitude of the moment, she found she could forget everything.

She leaned forward and looked down at her reflection in the waters of the pond. Her short-cropped red hair softened the angular features of her sun-browned face, and her startling blue eyes stared back out of the watery depths, watching as she watched, as if she had divided herself.

"Do you see anything you like?" a familiar voice asked.

It took a certain amount of effort, but she forced herself to look around as if it were the most casual of acts, smiling at Isoeld. The Queen wore soft yellows and pale blues and with her nearly white-blond hair and delicate features looked stunning.

"Not really," Phryne replied, staring directly at the other.

To her credit, Isoeld smiled back, as if no insult had been given. "We none of us much care for the way we look, do we? Even if others sometimes do. Good morning to you, Phryne."

"Good morning, Stepmother," Phryne answered. She paused, taking in the basket the other woman carried over her right arm. "Off to the market for fresh fruits and vegetables?"

"No, off to work with the sick and injured this morning. The healers say I bring smiles to the faces of their patients, and I am happy enough if I can do that."

"Of course you are. My father says you bring a smile to his face just by walking in the room. I imagine you can do that for almost anyone, can't you?"

Isoeld looked off into the trees a moment. "Why do you dislike me so, Phryne? What do you think I have done that makes you so unhappy with me?" She looked back quickly, shaking her head. "You know, I had no intention of having this discussion now, but suddenly I find I cannot put it off another moment."

Phryne rose so that they were facing each other. "I don't like it that you are taking my mother's place in my father's affections. I don't like it that you are so quick to assume that you are entitled to be Queen in her place. I don't like anything at all about the way you insinuated yourself into my father's affections and took him away!"

It was out before she could think better of it, her anger rising instantly to the surface, released in a rush of vitriolic words. She stopped short of saying more, already knowing she had said too much.

"Why stop there, Phryne?" the other woman asked suddenly. "Do you think I am not aware of the rest? You don't like it that I am so young and your father is so much older. You don't like it that you think I am unfaithful to him and see another man behind his back. You don't like it that he spends so much time with me and so little with you. Isn't that right?"

Phryne compressed her mouth into a tight line. "Yes, that's right."

Isoeld nodded slowly, as if something important had been confirmed. "You have reason to feel as you do about some of what you've said, but not all. I have taken your mother's place, but only because your father does not want to be alone. I am a comfort to him, but I will never replace your mother, even though you might see it that way. If I have taken your father away from you, it is not because I intended for that to happen, and you must speak to him about his neglect. I am Queen because he fell in love with me and for no other reason; I am lucky to be Queen but more so to be his wife."

Phryne started to turn away, but the other woman grabbed her arm. "No, you let me finish! I can't help that the age difference between us is so great, but age does not necessarily determine the depth of a couple's love for each other. I have no consort and I do not betray my marriage vows. I am aware of your suspicions; others have voiced them, as well. But I am faithful to your father. The first minister is a friend and nothing more. Your father knows this; if you speak to him about it, he will tell you so."

She released Phryne's arm and stepped back, her face stricken. She was crying, and Phryne wondered suddenly if perhaps she had been wrong about her. What she was seeing was genuine; Isoeld was all but broken. Phryne had an almost overwhelming urge to embrace her, to tell her she was sorry, that she would think better of her after this. But instead she looked down at her feet, avoiding the other's eyes. She couldn't quite manage an apology. She wasn't ready to let go of the past just yet.

"We must put this behind us, Isoeld," she said, needing to say something. "We must be better friends."

Isoeld nodded quickly, wiping the tears from her eyes. "Yes, we must do that. We both love your father. That should be reason enough."

"Yes," Phryne agreed, "it should."

Isoeld tightened her grip on her basket. "I have to go. Can we talk more later?"

"Of course. Anytime you wish."

Phryne watched her walk away and wondered if maybe this was a turning point in their relationship.

TWENTY MINUTES LATER, she was standing in her father's office, speaking to him as she had promised her cousins and the pair from Glensk Wood that she would. But even given the importance of what she was attempting and her efforts to concentrate on the business at hand, she could not stop thinking about her confrontation with Isoeld. Something in the way the other woman had spoken to her had touched her heart and made her believe. But to have been so wrong and so mean-spirited was difficult to accept, and she was struggling with it.

"My cousins Tasha and Tenerife wish to hike up into the mountains north to Aphalion Pass, Father. They have visiting them a boy and girl from Glensk Wood, who are Trackers. They are sharing their skills and experience while here, and all of them want an outing where they can use those skills and that experience in a practical way. I was hoping you would give them permission to go."

Her father was a man of average size and looks, the sort of man you might pass by without a second look. He had kind eyes and a pleasant, open smile, and he looked to be someone you might want for a friend. What set him apart was not immediately apparent. His voice, for instance, was deep and rich and compelling, and when he spoke of how the world was and how it needed to be and what was good for the people and the creatures that inhabited it, you believed him. More important, he believed, and it showed in his commitment to his service as King. Born into the royal family, a Prince since birth, he had always known that one day he would be King, and he had prepared himself. First Minister Teonette looked more the part—tall, strong-featured, and athletic—but it was her father who was centered and reliable and who instilled confidence in a way that few others could. While growing, he had observed how others reacted to his own father's behavior and learned accordingly. But he had learned as well what it meant to win respect and admiration and gain real loyalty.

She was reminded of it now, as she was every time she stood before him, and the feeling generated was a mix of deep, abiding respect and love. Her father was a good and honorable man, and everyone who came in contact with him knew it.

He gave her a questioning smile. "And this was something they could not manage to ask me themselves?"

She shook her head. "No, Father, it isn't that. They were perfectly willing to ask you, but I suggested it would sound better coming from me. I haven't quite told you everything. I want to go with them."

Oparion Amarantyne frowned. "Why would you want to do that?"

"For many reasons. I want to be a part of their adventure, and they have offered to let me accompany them. I want to learn something about tracking and scouting. They can teach me better than anyone. I am tired of sitting around in the city; I haven't been anywhere in months. I need to do something, and I need to feel like it has meaning."

"Your studies here have meaning."

"My studies here are sedentary and boring. I am not saying they lack importance in my education. I know they don't. But I want practical experience, too. This is my chance to gain a little of that."

Her father pursed his lips. "No wonder you didn't want them to make this request. It would be easier for me to turn them down than you."

"I didn't want them to have to make my request for me. I thought it better to face you myself. I learned from you; if you have something you want, you should be the one to ask for it."

Her father studied her face without speaking for a moment, then rose and walked to the window. With his back to her, he said, "I know you pretty well, Phryne, and I think maybe there is something else at work here. Is there?"

She hesitated, her mind racing. He expected an answer, but she couldn't give him the one he was looking for. "You're right, Father," she said, making it sound like a reluctant admission. "There is something more. I thought I might not have to tell you everything; some things I like to keep to myself. But in this case maybe that's not best. So I will tell you. It is this boy, the one from Glensk Wood."

Her father turned back from the window. "What about him?"

"There's something different about him. I don't know what it is, but I want to find out. This is the best way. Here, in the city, that's difficult. He is aware that he is an outsider. He sees how everyone treats me. But in the mountains, I think it will be different. I think I will be able to tell more about him. I want to do that."

It was a game she had played with him all of her life. When she didn't want him to know her reasons exactly, she would give him a variation that contained just enough truth to make him believe.

"You've met him before this, haven't you?"

"Once, some time back." She was making it all up as she went, enjoying the game. "Don't you think I'm old enough for this?"

"A father never thinks a daughter is old enough for anything," he said. "Nor do I want to know what you mean when you ask that question." He shook his head. "You've grown up so quickly. I didn't really see it. I think I was somewhere else when it happened. If your mother were here . . ."

He trailed off, then suddenly smiled at her. "She would be very proud at the way you've turned out. All right, Phryne. You're old enough that you don't need me to tell you how to live your life. Go with your cousins and this boy."

She walked over to him and gave him a hug and a kiss on his cheek. "Thank you." She hesitated. "I've got one more request of you. I would like you to promise me that you won't speak of this to anyone until we return. Not even Isoeld."

He put his hands on her shoulders and moved her back from him so he could look her in the eye. "Why do you mention Isoeld, Phryne?"

"Not Isoeld, especially. I didn't say that. I said 'not even Isoeld' because she is closest to you. I'm asking that you speak of it to no one at all. The boy and the girl from Glensk Wood are here in spite of their own people. You know of the Children of the Hawk? Well, their Seraphic has forbidden them from coming here. But they came anyway. Their friendship with my cousins means something to them. Do you understand?"

"I think so. You would keep their presence a secret from those who would object to it?"

"Exactly. I don't want to be the one responsible for revealing the extent of their defiance of the leader of the sect. I've told you because I trust your discretion."

"But not Isoeld's?"

"You are my father."

He studied her face a moment, and she could read nothing in his dark eyes. Slowly, he nodded. "Fair enough. You have my word." Suddenly his eyes narrowed. "This expedition—it isn't dangerous, is it? You aren't keeping anything from me? I wouldn't agree to this if I thought there might be any risk involved."

She had no idea if there was risk of any sort, but she hoped so. A little bit, at least. Of course, she wasn't about to tell him that. "I'll be safe. The twins will look after me."

He nodded. "I'll leave it at that, then. But be certain you tell them I intend to hold them accountable if anything bad happens. Sometimes those two can be reckless, and I don't want them being so here."

She gave him her most reassuring smile. "You know I wouldn't do anything reckless."

A bigger lie had never been told, but her father wanted to believe her so it was left at that.

13

THE LITTLE COMPANY FROM ARBORLON SET OUT
shortly after dawn on the following morning, heading west
and north toward the towering peaks that cradled Aphalion
Pass. They traveled down off the heights and back onto the lowland
lake country of Eldemere that Pan and Prue had traversed on their way
to the Elves, angling north across the upper stretches of the meres. The
weather had changed during the night, clouds moving back in from the
rim of the valley, leaving the sky overcast and the light gray and hazy.
A thin mist was falling as they set out, and their clothing was soon layered in damp droplets that sparkled like tiny gemstones.

Panterra Qu breathed in the clear, sweet smell of the early-morning
air, fresh with the taste of earth and plants pungent with the ripeness
of new life. He was clearheaded and well rested after a good night's
sleep, excited by the prospect of exploring the pass and encouraged
by Phryne Amarantyne's success with her father. She walked beside
him now, her angular face bright with expectation, her eyes shifting
from place to place, taking everything in. She had an economical gait,

a measured way of walking that demonstrated she had hiked long distances before and knew how to conserve her energy. He liked the way she had refused to allow anyone to help her with her backpack, but insisted on carrying it herself. She had also made it clear that she would share in all the chores and tasks, would stand watch when it was needed, and would appreciate it if they called her by her first name and not her royal title. She had also advised that she expected to stand with them before her father when they returned with whatever information they were able to cull from their investigation, good or bad.

Clearly, she meant to be an equal member of their company and to do her own heavy lifting, figuratively and metaphorically.

He caught her smiling at him. "What?" he asked, smiling back.

"I was just thinking of what I told my father to persuade him to allow me to make this trip with you."

"Tell me. You haven't said a word to anyone about how you managed it."

She shrugged. "You wouldn't be interested."

"I would," he insisted. "I think you must have been very clever."

She gave him a look that suggested she thought he might be making fun of her. Then she seemed to decide otherwise. "All right. I told him I wanted to come because of you. I said I wanted to know more about you, that you were interesting. But I said you were not comfortable among the Elves and would reveal little while in Arborlon. Away from the city, up in the mountains with just the five of us, you might be more relaxed."

It was his turn to study her. "You told him I was interesting? He must have been curious about me after that. What else did you say to him?"

She laughed. "Not much. I just told him you were interesting. I hope it turns out to be true. It would be a shame if I had to admit I was wrong."

He couldn't quite read how she meant that, but he felt the gentle nudge of her teasing. She was testing him. Why would she do that? "I guess I don't want to be the one to prove you wrong. But I don't think I'm the best judge of whether or not I'm interesting."

"No, of course not," she agreed. "I have to decide that for myself.

Oh, I also told him you were here in spite of express orders not to come. I told him the Children of the Hawk did not approve of Elves, but that you cared more for your friendship with Tasha and Tenerife than you did for the disapproval of the sect."

"That much is certainly true." He wondered if she actually knew about his problems with Skeal Eile and the sect. Tasha might have said something, but that wasn't like Tasha. "I'm not really in any trouble."

"Well, my father doesn't need to know that. He just needs to know not to say or do anything that will cause you some."

They walked on in silence for a time, heads lowered against a gusting wind that had begun blowing down out of the mountains. Tasha was in the lead, his broad frame acting as a windbreak for the rest of them as they wound their way through the tangle of the meres. Tenerife walked beside Prue, talking to her in low tones, his eyes on his brother's back. Both Elves were heavily armed with javelins, longbows, hunting knives, and short swords. They carried small bags of throwing stars, as well, and daggers stuffed in their boots. He and Prue, on the other hand, carried only their longbows and knives. Phryne didn't seem to be carrying any sort of weapon. All five shouldered bedrolls, food, extra clothing, and medicines stuffed in backpacks.

The Elven Princess dropped back momentarily, apparently having lost interest in their conversation, but then suddenly she moved up next to him again, closer now than before, her eyes on his face. "Tell me something interesting about yourself."

He looked over at her to see if she was joking. "What sort of something?"

"Something I might not learn on my own without knowing you better than I do. Something no one else knows. Something about the sort of person you are. Maybe about why you're a Tracker and not a mushroom hunter or a farmer."

She looked at him expectantly, and he laughed. "If I were a mushroom hunter or a farmer, I would starve to death." He furrowed his brow. "Besides, there's not much of anything about me that Prue doesn't know already. So you might have to live with sharing any insights I offer."

"How did the two of you become so close, Pan? She's not related to you, is she?"

He shook his head. "No, we just grew up together, played together when we were little because we lived next door to each other. Our families were friends. We had the same interests, liked the same things. Being outside and exploring was what mattered to us." He smiled, thinking back on it. "She was special."

"Tasha says she can sense danger before she sees it. Before anyone sees it. Is that so?"

"It is. She's always had that gift."

"A useful gift. What's yours?"

"Maybe I don't have one." He shrugged. "I'm not anyone special, Phryne. I'm just someone who likes being a Tracker."

She linked her arm in his, pulling them close. "I don't think that's so, and I'm not usually wrong about these things. There is something different about you; I sensed it right away. I see the way my cousins defer to you at times, how they look to see what your response might be. I see how they talk to you. They think you're special. Tell me why."

He gave her a grin. "There isn't anything to tell."

"Tell me, Pan."

She wasn't going to give up. He sighed. "I'm good at tracking."

"Better than good, perhaps?" She cocked an eyebrow.

"Better than good. I can find sign where no one else can. I can sense it sometimes. I don't know why it is, but just like Prue knows of danger she can't see, I know of sign I can't see. I guess it's instinct."

She released his arm and went back to walking at his side without touching him. He missed it right away. "Tasha was right about you," she said. "You are more Elf than human. You should be one of us."

They walked on, stopping finally at midday for lunch at the edge of one of the larger meres, sitting on a grassy patch and watching the big fishing birds swoop and glide above the surface of the waters. They talked a little about what they were going to do when they got up into the mountains and reached Aphalion Pass, but mostly Tasha told stories, although Tenerife, who had heard them all before, was less enthralled than the others.

"Everyone knows about Kirisin Belloruus," Tasha said, beginning a fresh story as lunch was ending and the last of the ale was being consumed. "At least, everyone who is an Elf or has made even a cursory study of Elven history. He was the spiritual leader of the Elves when they came into this valley, the founder of the practice of accepting a commitment from birth on to maintaining and healing the land, and dedicated to the restoration of ancient magic lost sometime after the end of Faerie. He was the seminal force behind the Elven nation's evolution for many years. They say he'd made a pact with the shades of our ancestors to recover the lost arts and practices, which in large part had been forgotten. But who present knows of his sister?"

Tenerife raised his hand. "Besides you, enlightened one," Tasha amended. "And Phryne, of course. Who else?"

Neither Panterra nor Prue knew anything at all about a sister, although both had heard the story of Kirisin Belloruus countless times.

"Her name was Simralin, wasn't it?" Phryne offered.

"It was." Tasha beamed at her as a teacher might an exceptionally bright student, although Pan suspected that as the daughter of the King, she was at least as well versed as Tasha in Elven history. "A forgotten figure to some extent, but an equally important one. She was older than he was and something of a warrior. She fought against the demons and their minions countless times and helped in the recovery of what up until then had been the missing Elfstones."

"Aren't they still missing?" Phryne interrupted.

"The blue ones, the seeking-Stones, yes," Tasha agreed. "Although the Loden Elfstone remains in the possession of the royal family, as you well know." He gave her a look. "Can I finish my story now? Because it deals with that very subject."

He waited for her nod, and then continued. "She fell in love with a Knight of the Word, from the old order, one of the last. When they found their way here, she bound herself to him in the Elven way, and they lived together until he died. She took his staff then and gave it to his son. It was said that he instructed her to do so when he was gone, and so she did. His son, in turn, passed it on, and so things proceeded for generations until it was destroyed. Do you know how it was destroyed?"

Tenerife, who had poured himself a second cup of ale, shook his head in dismay. "Just tell the story and get on with things, Tasha," he admonished. "We have to be going."

Tasha ignored him. "It was destroyed in a struggle between the descendants of the only two Knights of the Word known to have survived

the Great Wars and made it safely into the valley. One was an Elf, the
other a human. Apparently, they knew each other well and had even
liked each other. But something triggered a deep-seated and long-
lasting dispute between the descendants, the source of which has been
forgotten over time. In the ensuing battle, the human prevailed. The
Elf was killed and his staff shattered in the bargain."

He paused. "The Gray Man now carries the remaining staff. It was
his predecessor who fought the Elf who bore the other."

"I hadn't heard that," Panterra said, thinking anew of his encounter
with Sider Ament. "How long ago was this?"

"Twenty years, at least." Tasha Orullian shrugged. "It's not well
known outside the Elven royal family. Even they never talk about it.
It's rumored that Sider Ament witnessed the struggle and took the last
staff from the hands of his predecessor, who died in the battle, as well."

There was a long silence as his listeners mulled over the details of
his story. "What about the blue Elfstones?" Prue asked.

"The blue Elfstones were in the possession of the descendants of
Kirisin and Simralin Belloruus and could be traced through the first
four centuries of our time in this valley. But a hundred years ago, they
disappeared again. Someone took them."

"Supposedly," Phryne interrupted suddenly. "No one knows for
sure. Isn't that so, Tasha?"

"It is. So you've heard the story?"

She shrugged, made a dismissive gesture. "It's just a story, a myth.
Except for the parts about the Elfstones being missing and the last staff
being in the hands of Sider Ament, which everyone knows, it's all speculation. No one was there to witness the battle between the bearers of
the staffs, or when the Elfstones disappeared."

"Tasha and I heard the story from our grandfather years ago, but admittedly he wasn't the most reliable source," Tenerife cut in. "Tasha
just likes it because it's strange."

His brother got to his feet abruptly. "As you say, it's just a story,
Phryne. No need to question it. Anyway, it's time to be going. Enough
of stories for now."

They packed up their gear and set out anew, striding off into the
mistiness of Eldemere, heading toward the mountains north and
Aphalion Pass.

XAC WEN WAS TRYING for what must have been the thousandth time to restring a bow that was several sizes too big for him, an effort that was generating new levels of frustration, when the old lady hobbled into view. Xac was sitting outside his cottage home, propped up on a stool, the bow clutched between his knees as he struggled to bring the loose end of the bowstring to the notch. He wouldn't have put so much into doing this if the bow hadn't belonged to his father, who had been killed when Xac was only four. The bow had been given to him by his mother as a gift to remember his father by. The boy remembered his father well enough anyway, a tall, kindly man with great patience and a decided lack of good sense, which was the reason he had gotten himself killed, choosing a thunderstorm to go looking for his missing dog. He found the dog, but a bolt of lightning found him. He died instantly, they said, didn't suffer, an unfortunate accident, but all Xac knew was that once you were dead you weren't coming back, so what did it matter how you died?

The old woman drew his attention immediately. She was stooped over and shuffling like she might not be too far off from joining his father in the world of shades. She was clothed in layers of blouses and skirts and scarves and such, a woman who apparently dressed without knowing when to stop. A cloth sack bundled full of something loose and soft was clutched under one arm, a change of clothes, perhaps. He stopped trying to do anything with the bow when he saw that she was making directly for him and instead set down his work and stood up.

"Good day, young man," the old lady greeted him, her voice high and querulous. "Is your name Xac Wen?"

Xac almost said no. The old lady was just this side of scary, a crone all the way from the frizzled tips of her thick black hair, where it escaped the scarf that was trying futilely to bind it, to the tips of her worn boots, the leather cracked and the iron-shod tips scuffed and worn. She barely looked at him as she spoke, her head lowered like a supplicant's, her eyes flicking up just momentarily to take him in before shifting away again. One mottled hand gestured at him like a claw.

"I'm Xac Wen," he admitted.

"I'm looking for my daughter," the old woman said. "Her name is

Prue. She came to Arborlon in the company of a young man from the village of Glensk Wood, some miles west of here. I've been looking for her for days. Do you know her?"

Xac hesitated, not certain he wanted to reveal anything. "How would I know her? Why are you asking me?"

"When I talked to some people in the city, they told me they might have seen her with you. Please, young man, it's very important. I need to tell her that her brother is very sick and ask her to come home right away."

Xac found the old woman repulsive, but that didn't give him the right to keep her from her daughter. Maybe the brother would die and the girl never get to see him, and it would all be his fault.

"She was here a couple of days ago, but she left again. She went up into the mountains with some friends of mine. But she'll probably be back before the week is out."

The old woman nodded without speaking, swaying a bit unsteadily. "I will wait for her, then. I'm too old to go searching in the mountains. Can you tell me one more thing? Where should I look for her when she returns?"

"She's been staying with the Orullian brothers, Tasha and Tenerife. That's who she left with."

The old woman turned and started away. Her boots made a scraping sound on the loose stone of the walkway. "I will look for her there, then. Thank you, young man."

Xac watched her go, wondering suddenly how she had managed to get this far, as hobbled as she was. Why had she even come, in fact? Why hadn't she sent someone in her place?

He wondered, as well, with the instinctive suspicion of the young for what any older person tells them, if he had done the right thing.

⬛ ⬛ ⬛

THE LITTLE COMPANY FROM ARBORLON slept that night at the foot of the northern peaks, sheltered in a copse of fir backed against the rock of the foothills, and though it rained, they stayed warm and dry in their blankets. At first light, they set out once more, beginning their climb into the mountains. The passes of the safehold were more numerous and easily reached to the west and south than to the north and east, and Aphalion was a particularly difficult ascent, even in good weather, which today's was not. They were on their second day out of Arborlon, and the weather had taken an unpleasant turn. It had begun raining before sunrise, and the rain got heavier as the day progressed, the skies remaining gray and unfriendly.

The climb was difficult under the best of conditions, steep and winding, the footing made treacherous by loose rock and sharp drops that fell away hundreds of feet as the five progressed. That it was raining and the ground slick made everything much worse, and the climbers were forced to keep their attention focused on where they placed their feet and found their handholds. They climbed in single file with Tasha and Tenerife trading off as leaders. Panterra and Prue knew the trail as well as the Elves, but deferred to their hosts. It was their country, after all.

Pan dropped back to the rear of the procession, glancing up periodically at Phryne Amarantyne as she climbed just ahead of him, nimble and sure-footed. He found her an enigma. The more time he spent with her, the more confused he became. Her admitted interest in him didn't make sense. Nor could he come to terms with her easy friendship. She barely knew him, had spent only a handful of hours with him, and yet she was acting as if she had known him all her life.

But then girls confused him, anyway. Prue was the exception, and that was probably because he had known her for so long. She was the "little sister" to him that she was to Tasha and Tenerife, and their familiarity with each other had been tested and earned. Phryne, on the other hand, just assumed it was there and that it needed no seasoning and no consideration. It was enough for her that they were together on this journey and shared a common purpose in being so. Panterra, who had spent so much of his life alone and away from other people, save for Prue, was more comfortable staying apart. He was more reticent, more measured in developing his relationships. Phryne Amarantyne seemed to find this unnecessary.

At one point in their climb, Prue dropped back beside him. She didn't say anything for a long time, but only kept him silent company.

Finally, she whispered, her voice so low he could barely hear it, "Do you see how she looks at you?" He knew right away whom she meant, so he simply shook his head no. In truth, he did not.

Prue cocked an eyebrow at him. "I think she likes you. A lot."

That was all she said, and moments later she moved ahead of him again, joining Tenerife at the front of the climb. Pan stared after her, wondering if she had lost her mind. Phryne was an Elf and a Princess. He was a human and a Tracker. Two different Races and two very different worlds. Any relationship beyond casual friendship was impossible. He put Prue's comments out of his mind.

The hours passed, and by early afternoon they had reached the summit of the mountain they were climbing and could see the head of Aphalion Pass through a defile in the higher peaks ahead. They pressed on, heads bent against a much stronger wind, out in the open as they crossed the vast expanse of the ridgeline toward the dark gap. The rain had tapered off and turned to a fine mist that verged on crystalline and stung when it struck their exposed skin. No one was talking now, all efforts directed at moving ahead as quickly and efficiently as possible.

It took them the better part of two hours to reach their destination, and when they did they collapsed in exhaustion inside the shelter of the split, dropping their packs and breathing hard. They drank water from their skins, ate some bread and cheese, and recovered themselves as the wind howled across the open spaces behind them.

Finally, as if of a single accord, they rose, shouldered their packs, and started into the pass.

Aphalion was much different from Declan Reach. The latter was twisty and narrow, and the terrain through the cliffs much more uneven. Aphalion was a broad, wide passage between a pair of towering peaks that shut out all but a narrow band of sky, the rock dropping away from the highest points overhead in straight, black curtains. The trail leading through twice angled sharply, once right and once left, but otherwise did not vary. Huge sections of stone that had split off the cliff walls in times past lay in massive shards, but did not entirely block the way. The wind, as it blew across the gap overhead, was a mournful howl that refused to let up, its cry like that of a creature in misery.

When they were deep into the pass, Tasha, who was in the lead, brought them to a halt, and they huddled close.

"This is where the pass has been closed in times past!" He had to shout to be heard as he gestured ahead of them. "Before, there was fog and darkness too heavy to penetrate! All that's gone! I think the wall has failed here, too! But we'll see!"

He turned away and started ahead once more, the others following. Almost at once the rain returned, sweeping down out of the split between the peaks in long, hard streamers that felt almost like waterfalls as they struck the travelers. Panterra was soaked in seconds, even with his heavy travel cloak for protection. He stumbled under the weight of the beating he was taking, only barely managing to keep himself upright. Ahead, Phryne went down, collapsing on her hands and knees, head lowered. Pan reached her in seconds, pulled her to him and straightened her up. Once on her feet, she glanced at him and nodded, and he released his grip. She went on without a word.

Now the wind was howling with fresh determination, the sound so overwhelming that it was all Pan could do not to put his hands over his ears. The five pushed ahead, but the effort it required increased and their progress slowed. Time ceased to have meaning, blown away in the wind, buried in wild sound.

Just ahead, there within the brume's roiling curtains, as faint and shadowy as a dim memory, something moved.

Prue must have seen it first, or at least sensed the danger, because she was racing ahead to catch up to Tasha, grabbing at his arm and gesturing. The others closed the gap, coming together just as the shadowy form suddenly blossomed into something much larger and more formidable. It seemed to unfold right in front of them, gaining size and weight. They stood frozen in place as they saw it grow, their weapons already drawn and held ready.

Tasha gestured them back with frantic movements, his big frame flattening against the stone of the cliff wall. Panterra tried to penetrate the concealing gloom to see what was there, but could not manage it.

Then the shadow surged into view with frightening quickness, lurching out of mist and rain and darkness, rising up to assume monolithic proportions and suddenly Pan could see clearly what they had stumbled upon, and the words were a cold, silent whisper in his head.

A dragon!

14

PANTERRA QU HAD NEVER SEEN A DRAGON. BUT HE knew what they were from tales he'd heard as a child, and he knew enough of how they looked to recognize one when he saw it. What he wasn't prepared for was how really terrifying it would be. It was a massive beast, squat and bulky through its midsections, but its neck and limbs long and sinewy. Scales covered its body in armored plates, and its back and tail were ridged with spikes. When it swung its head toward him, Pan could see bony protrusions on its snout, a beard hanging from its lower jaw, and teeth the size of his forearm protruding from its maw. It was black and slick with moisture, and its eyes had the feral gleam of a predator.

Every impulse screamed at Panterra to run. But Tasha remained flattened against the cliff face and was furtively gesturing for the others to do the same. All five were backed up against the rock, so still that they didn't even seem to be breathing. The dragon was huffing, as if trying to cough, the sound penetrating even the wind's shrill howl. It spread its huge wings, and they spanned the width of the pass. It arched its neck, its jaws split wide, and a huge, long tongue licked out at the rain.

Panterra could not look away from the beast. A part of him said he should, that he didn't want to see what was going to happen next. Another part said that so long as he kept watching, he had a chance of staying alive.

A dragon, he repeated over and over in the silence of his mind. There were no dragons in the valley. Dragons didn't exist in his world.

The dragon screamed—there was no other way to describe it, the sound high and shrill and bone chilling—causing Pan to press even harder against the impermeable stone. The monster's shadow fell over him as it surged forward, and in that instant he knew he was dead.

But then, a miracle. The dragon's wings flapped twice, the turbulence they generated sudden and massive, and the beast lifted away through the gap in the cliffs, rose skyward like a great bird of prey, and disappeared north away from the valley.

It all happened so quickly that for long moments afterward, no one moved. Pan kept thinking it might return, that it was only a trick to catch them out when they tried to run. He kept thinking there was no way it could be gone. Not really gone.

Then Phryne Amarantyne was next to him, pressing close, her blue eyes wild and excited. "Wasn't that wonderful?" she breathed. "Wasn't that the most beautiful and terrible thing you've ever seen?"

It was all of that, Pan thought, but mostly it was heart stopping. "Yes," he said, managing to look at her without something approaching disbelief. "But I never want to see it again."

"Oh, I do!" she said with a gasp, and she actually laughed.

Tasha was calling to them, and they hurried to group around him, casting anxious glances at the sliver of sky visible through the gap in the peaks. Prue's eyes were wide and her face white as she caught Pan's eye and shook her head in an unmistakable signal. She wanted nothing more to do with this business.

"Everyone's heart still beating?" Tasha asked, scanning their faces. When no one spoke, he continued, "Well, at least we know now that the protective barrier is truly down. That dragon—"

"Was that *really* a dragon?" Tenerife cut in, as if not quite ready to accept that it was. "When we know that dragons don't exist?"

"It was a dragon," Tasha assured him. "A clear signal that Panterra and little sister are in no way mistaken about those creatures they encountered and the warning of the Gray Man is not to be disregarded. We have to let the King and the Elven Council know. With five of us to testify, there can't be much room for doubt."

"I would like to see the outside world before we go back," Phryne cut in quickly. She looked from face to face, seeing reluctance and doubt mirrored in each. "If we follow the pass to its other end and see for ourselves that the outside world is open to us, we have even better proof of what's happened. I don't think we should underestimate those who will question our claims."

Tenerife shook his head. "I don't think we should do anything of the sort. We might get to the end of the pass, but there's nothing to say we'll be able to get back again. If that dragon returns, it could block our way."

"If that happens, we need only to wait until it flies out again. Or follow the mountains west along their outer perimeter to a different pass. If one is down, it stands to reason the rest are down, as well."

"I don't know *what* stands to reason." Tenerife shook his head. "It seems risky."

"Oh, and none of the rest of what we're doing is?" Phryne laughed. "That's very funny, cousin. What do you have to say on the matter, Tasha? Are you for turning back, as well?"

"There is a sound argument for doing so," the other replied, running his fingers through his long black hair. The scarf that had tied back his hair seemed to have disappeared. "But I see the merit of your argument. And I, too, would like to see what lies at the end of the pass. I'll go with you. The rest can go back, and no blame will attach to them for doing so. Brother? Pan? Little sister?"

"I'm going," Tenerife declared grudgingly. "I guess."

Prue grimaced. "I go where Pan goes."

They were all looking at Panterra now, so he shrugged away his discomfort with an irritated gesture. "Let's stop talking about it and just get it done."

They set out again quickly, keeping close to the cliff wall on the left side of the pass, looking skyward at every opportunity. No one was sure of anything after the unexpected appearance of the dragon, and no one wanted to be caught off guard again.

As they advanced, Pan moved up beside Prue. "That was pretty awful, wasn't it?"

She nodded. "It makes me wonder what else is out there. If I hadn't sensed the danger, we might have walked right into that thing."

"I saw you react. That was quick thinking. You saved us all."

"This time I did." She looked decidedly unhappy. "But maybe I won't the next. You should have said something back there when Phryne insisted on going ahead. She seems to think this is all a game. She might have listened to you."

She gave him a look and abruptly rushed ahead, rejoining Tasha. She was angry and no mistake. But he didn't know what to do about it. He wasn't responsible for Phryne; it hadn't been his suggestion that they keep going instead of turning back. Prue was being unreasonable, and that wasn't like her.

They slogged on through the steady rain, all of them on edge. Shadows, fluid and elongated, chased one another along the walls and floor of Aphalion Pass, seeping off rocky outcroppings, and the five companions constantly found themselves searching for things that weren't there. The wind continued to howl mournfully as it whipped across gaps in the peaks, its whistle shrill and unrelenting. Ahead and behind, the darkness had closed away all traces of where they were going and where they had been.

The pass wound through the mountains for a much longer time than Panterra had supposed it would, but after a while it narrowed to a width of less than twenty feet and began to angle first one way and then another. No dragon of the size they had encountered could hope to get through at this juncture, Panterra thought, taking some comfort from the fact. But he was bothered that his sense of direction had failed him some time back, and he had no clear idea where they were.

Finally, when it seemed there would never be an end to their trek, the way ahead brightened, the rock walls opened up, and the members of the little company found themselves climbing a slope of loose rock to a broad ridgeline swept by long streamers of rain and mist. Hunkering down within their travel cloaks, they stood together on the ridge and peered out into the grayish haze beyond. Clouds roiled across a patchwork collection of streams and rivers carved out of the earth by time and weather, waterways that interconnected and spread over terrain both blasted and barren. What trees there were looked stunted or dead, their branches withered and their greenery gone, bearing silent witness to the cataclysm that had destroyed the old world centuries ago. There was nothing for as far as the eye could see but dead things. Bare earth and rock, ruined forest and erosion, it was a more stark and empty landscape than Panterra would have imagined possible.

"Shades," whispered Phryne, standing next to him.

"Everything's dead." Prue voiced Panterra's unspoken thought. "Everything."

"Not quite," said Tenerife, pointing.

Far off in the distance, well beyond where specific details could be determined, dozens of columns of smoke rose through the deep gloom. With the weather as bad as it was, it was impossible to be certain, but that was how it appeared to them. They stood together staring at the smoke for a long time.

"I can't be sure what I'm seeing," Tasha said finally.

His eyes were the best of the five, so the others accepted that they would find nothing, either. "We should go find out," Phryne said suddenly. Again, she saw the looks on their faces. "We've come this far; why not go a little farther?"

"Because now we are setting out across country we know nothing about," Tasha pointed out. "That makes exploring a whole lot more dangerous. I can't imagine that your father would have much good to say about us if we follow your suggestion. I think we've done as much as we can. It's time to be going back."

"But what if those are people out there? What if they can tell us something about what's happened to the world?"

"What if they aren't and they can't and they only want to eat us?" Tenerife asked with a grunt. "Let it go, cousin."

She wheeled on him. "I don't want to let it go! I want to have a look for myself!"

Without a word, Tasha scooped her up in his long arms and threw her over his shoulder. "Time to be going, Princess. Satisfying your curiosity will have to wait for another day."

She struggled against him, demanding that he put her down, beating at him with her fists. Panterra had never imagined that a Princess would behave this way, and he didn't like how it made him feel. Clearly, Phryne Amarantyne was someone who was used to getting her way and didn't like it a bit when she didn't.

"This is foolish!" she snapped, continuing to thrash from her perch atop her cousin's broad shoulder. "We're supposed to be exploring! We're supposed to discover as much as we can!"

"We can come back and do that another time," Tenerife replied, walking alongside Tasha but staying out of range in case Phryne decided to take a swing at him. "When we're better prepared."

"When we have more men and more weapons and less confusion," Tasha added. "Stop struggling, will you?"

She stopped then, going limp, as if suddenly drained of the energy to resist. She hung there for a moment, and then said, "Put me down."

Tasha hesitated, but finally he lowered her to her feet and stepped back. "We came to find out about the barrier that wards us from the outer world, Phryne. We've done that. Now we need to go back and let your father and the High Council decide what is to be done about it."

"I know," she said, straightening her rumpled clothing and brushing herself off. "I just thought that since we were already here . . ." She trailed off. "I just thought we might do a little more, learn a little something else. But I understand your point, Tasha. I'll let it go for now. But I'm coming back."

"And we'll come with you," Tasha assured her.

Panterra hoped the big man didn't think he was speaking for all of them, because he wasn't at all sure he and Prue would be coming back. Having seen what they'd seen, he was inclined to believe that his own duty lay in reporting back to Pogue Kray and the people of Glensk Wood. It might not be easy to accept, but now they knew for sure. Everyone in the valley would have to be made aware that the barrier was down and the valley was open to the rest of the world. It would take time for people to get used to the idea, and the sooner they got started doing so, the better.

All of a sudden he caught sight of something he had missed before. Off to the left, close against the wall of the cliffs, a single column of smoke rose into the damp air. A solitary campfire, he decided instantly, not a quarter mile distant.

"Look there," he said to the others, pointing.

They peered through the gray twilight with him and spied the smoke immediately. "A campsite . . ." Tenerife said quietly, the words trailing off.

"Now we *have* to have a look!" Phryne insisted at once. "That's not too far for us to go! Is it, Tasha? It's not, is it?"

Her cousin did not reply at once. Panterra could tell that he was thinking it over. "It's not what we came to do, cousin," he repeated. "I don't know."

But he was clearly hesitating, and this did not escape Phryne. She turned to Pan. "We can go over there and take a quick look and come right back and go home. It won't take us that far out of our way and it won't use up hardly any time at all. You tell him, Pan. We can do this and maybe learn something important. Don't you want to know who's living out here after all these years?"

Pan did want to know, but he also didn't want to take one too many risks. They still had no idea how dangerous it was in this new world, and he didn't want to find out the hard way.

"We can go," Phryne pressed. "You and I. The others can wait here for us."

Prue stepped forward at once, her small frame stiff and her face set. "I will go with Pan," she declared. "He is my partner, and we know best how to look after each other." She took Panterra's arm. "Come on, let's get this over with. It's clear that you've made up your mind."

"Go on, then," Tasha called after them. "But watch yourself, the both of you!"

"Nothing will happen!" Pan called back bravely.

Prue dug her fingers into his arm so hard he flinched. "Not now, it won't," she muttered as she dragged him along.

*   *   *

PANTERRA WAITED JUST LONG ENOUGH to be certain they were out of hearing before wheeling on her. "Why are you acting like this?" he asked, careful to keep his voice low.

Her green eyes fixed him with a frosty glare. "Acting like what, Pan?"

"Like you're angry with me. Like it's somehow my fault. Why are you even going with me, anyway? You know you don't want to. You don't want anything to do with this!"

"True enough. But if I don't come with you, you'd go with Phryne and she might get you killed!"

He stared in shock. "Why do you say that? I'm not going to let anyone get me killed! I can take care of myself. Besides, who says I would go with Phryne?"

"You don't know yourself very well, do you? Not as well as I do, anyway. Trust me. You would go."

She turned away, as if dismissing him. He followed her in silence, seething. She was wrong, of course. He hadn't had any intention of going with Phryne, no matter what she thought. At least, he didn't think so. He would have told her no, and they would have turned back into the pass and started home. Even if she had insisted on going alone, he would have stopped her. Or Tasha would have. Even though he was interested in the source of the smoke and the possibility of contact with people living outside the valley, he wouldn't have gone. Prue was just wrong.

Yet now here he was, going with her instead of with Phryne. And he hadn't tried to stop her, either. What did that say about him?

He shrugged the matter off. It was too late to do anything about it now. Neither one of them would turn back at this point. They would have to sort it out later.

They stayed close to the rock walls of the cliffs as they made their cautious way toward the smoke, using clumps of scrub, piles of deadwood, and clusters of rock as cover, staying down in the gullies and ravines when they could. It was slow work made more difficult by the need to mask all sounds and keep their exposure to a minimum. They watched closely for unexpected dangers, aware that in this country there would be things they hadn't seen before, traps and pitfalls and predators they might miss if they weren't careful. They didn't talk anymore, but concentrated on the task at hand.

It took them less than an hour to reach a point where they were near enough to their destination to get a good look at the source of the smoke. Hidden in a shallow ravine grown thick with scrub, they were able to peer over the ravine's lip to where the smoke curled lazily

out of a campfire smoldering in a ring of stones not fifty feet away. Packs
of some sort were stacked to one side, and blankets lay neatly folded
next to them. The camp's occupants were nowhere to be seen. Panterra
cast an anxious glance in all directions, not liking that no one was visible and they couldn't be sure if anyone was close.

He looked over at Prue, and she shrugged. It was impossible for
them to determine much of anything from the little they could see. He
felt a keen sense of disappointment. This whole effort had been a
waste of time. There was nothing they had learned by coming here that
they didn't already know.

Except for one thing, he thought suddenly. They had determined
that someone like them was alive out here, someone who carried packs
and used blankets, which meant the world was still inhabited by beings
like themselves and not just the beasts and dragons they had encountered.

They remained where they were, undecided about whether to stay
or go, studying the camp, still hoping they would learn something
more. Time passed, and the darkness deepened. Nothing showed itself,
nothing moved, and no sounds broke the stillness save once when a
creature cried out sharply far off in the dark. The outside world felt
huge and empty.

Finally, Pan reached over and touched her arm.

We need to get out of here, he mouthed.

She nodded, and they began backing down the slope of the ravine, in-
tending to retrace their steps. But they had gotten only a few feet when
Prue suddenly grabbed him and shook her head sharply, warning him to
freeze. Something was wrong. She mouthed a silent explanation, but he
couldn't make out what it was. She was looking everywhere, sensing danger but unable to pinpoint its source. Panterra searched the shadows with
her, but the shadows fell in layers that filled the ravine. He couldn't see
anything. He glanced back at her, wanting her to tell him if they could go,
if they should flee, but Prue was still searching the darkness.

He dropped slowly into a crouch, steeling himself, trying to decide
what to do.

Then a huge shadow fell over him, crashing down on him like a
great weight and collapsing his world, and it was too late.

15

H E IS SIXTEEN, LITTLE MORE THAN A YEAR OLDER than when he fell in love, when the bearer of the black staff comes to him. The appearance of the old man is entirely unexpected. Sider Ament knows who the bearer is and has even seen him now and then, but he has never spoken to him, has never even come close. Nor has the old man ever approached him as he does now, coming out of the trees.

Sider's first thought will haunt him for the rest of his life.

What does he want with me?

It is a question, he will think later, that he should never have asked.

It has been a wondrous year for the boy. The days have been filled with dreams of the girl from Glensk Wood. When they are together, some of those dreams are realized. But this happens all too infrequently, for he still lives on his parents' farm and must still find excuses to go down into the valley to see her. Yet when he cannot be with her, he thinks of her constantly. He imagines a life together, married with a home and children, inseparable. He knows it will happen one day, and he is impatient for it. He is consumed by his dreams and his expectations, and lost to everything else.

And now the old man comes to him.

It is an ordinary day, and he is working in the north pasture repairing the fencing where the livestock had broken through some days earlier, forcing him to collect them and bring them home. It is mindless work, and he is free to dream of what really matters to him. He knows he will see her again in less than a week's time, a visit to the village for supplies and materials already planned, the opportunity he needs. She will be waiting for him; she is always waiting for him. From the first time he was with her, he knew what their future would be. And though she did not say so, he could tell that she knew it, too.

He turns from his work and stands waiting as the old man comes up to him. He has known of him from the time he was a small boy. His father has told him of the bearer of the black staff, of his solitary life as guardian of the people of the valley. He has told him of the old man's legacy, of the history of his staff and the Knights of the Word. It is not common knowledge, but somehow his father knows. Perhaps he learned it from the travelers who sometimes pass through, the men and women of the high country who live apart from the rest of the world. Perhaps the old man himself has told him.

Either way, Sider has given the matter little thought. It has nothing to do with him.

"Sider Ament?" the old man asks, stopping a few feet away. He is leaning on the black staff, gripping it tightly with both hands. He looks tired. Even more, he looks haunted. It is there in his eyes, in the lines of his face, in the way he holds himself.

Sider nods but says nothing.

"You and I must talk," the old man declares. His voice is surprisingly gentle. "Walk with me."

Together they set out across the grassy slopes of his farm, a slow, meandering wander that lacks discernible purpose and destination and, in the end, needs neither. The day is warm and the air smells sweet, and it feels as if time has slowed. The old man's voice is rich and full, and while he looks weary, he sounds strong.

"I have been watching you," the old man says. "When I find time, when it is possible. I have been measuring you. I like what I see. Others speak well of you, your father especially. You have a direct and purposeful way that reflects your character. When you are given something to do, you see it

through. You make no excuses for yourself. You accept work as a part of life and self-sacrifice as a part of work. You will make a fine life on this farm one day, should you choose to do so, but I think you are made for other things."

Sider does not understand what the old man means. He looks at him curiously, but the old man does not look back.

"This world we inhabit, here in the valley, is mostly good and nurturing, but it is fragile, too. It feels as if it will last forever, but it will not. No one wants to acknowledge this; no one ever wants to believe that what he has will not endure. This home was given to us as a safehold against the destruction of the old world, of the apocalypse that ended a civilization. It was given to us as a place in which we could survive until it was time to leave. That time approaches."

Now Sider is beginning to see what the old man means, but he cannot accept it. It makes no sense. "What are you saying?" he asks.

"I am saying that the end of our stay in this valley is coming, perhaps in your lifetime, and we must all prepare for it."

Sider shakes his head in disbelief. "How do we do that?"

"The transition will be difficult and not without cost. Coming into the valley was dangerous; leaving will be no less so. Almost no one will want to accept that it is necessary. But if they do not, it will be made clear to them in ways that are not pleasant. The outside world will not be as hesitant as they. The outside world will begin to encroach, and what lives there survived an almost total annihilation of life. Think what sort of creatures could manage to do that."

Sider does, and the images are not ones he cares to examine too closely. But he still does not see what the old man wants. "Shouldn't you discuss this with my father? He is a reasonable man. If you tell him what you have told me, I am sure he will do what he must to prepare our family."

He sounds so grown-up when he says it, as if he is the elder speaking to a young listener. The old man smiles. *"Good advice. But that is not the reason I have come to you."*

Sider studies the other quizzically. "Am I missing something?"

"Everything. But I find no fault in you for that. Why should you see so clearly in a matter of minutes what I have lived with for years? It will not be easy for you now or later. It will never be easy. But it will be important. It will matter."

He stops where he is and turns to face the boy. "This," he says, holding out the black staff, "is why I have come to you."

Sider looks at the staff, and then looks at the old man again. There is something in the other's eyes that borders on dangerous, but mostly there is that immense weariness, deep and abiding.

"Take it," the old man tells him. When Sider hesitates, he adds, "It will not harm you. But I want you to see what it feels like to hold it. There is a reason for this. Please do as I ask."

Sider is not afraid, but he is wary. He does not know the old man well enough to trust him completely. Nevertheless, he does not feel threatened by the request and does not want to refuse when there is no solid reason for doing so. He reaches out his hand and takes the staff.

As he does so, strange things begin to happen almost immediately. They are not so frightening or intimidating that he releases his grip, but they are both startling and unexpected. When he takes the staff from the old man, he finds it immensely heavy, as if it were cast in iron rather than carved from wood. But its weight changes almost immediately to something much lighter and more manageable. His grip, when he first grasps the staff, is uncertain and feels odd. But that changes, as well, and within seconds it feels comfortable, as if the staff is an old friend, as if it's something he has carried around for years and can't imagine being without.

Stranger still is the sudden reaction of the thousands of markings carved into the surface of the wood. He has not noticed them before, but when he takes the staff he can feel them. Now they flare to life, the etchings become bright with a pulsating light that outlines each against the dark surface of the wood. All up and down the staff, the markings glow as if alive with an inner fire. And there is heat—not one that scorches or burns, but a heat that warms first the palms of his hands and then spreads from his hands into his arms and then his body, filling him with something that approaches reassurance and comfort. It is hard to describe and harder still to accept. He flinches slightly, but still keeps his hold on the staff, letting the sensations wash through him, entranced now, enraptured, eager for more.

"Do you feel it?" the old man asks eagerly, recognizing the look on the boy's face. "The warming?"

Sider nods, speechless. He is looking down at the black staff with its markings, noting that their light has grown brighter, more insistent. The warmth is all through him now, and the staff feels so much a part of him that for one confusing instant he believes it now belongs to him and he will not be able to give it up. Magic, he thinks. There is a life to the staff fueled by magic. They say the old man wields it as the Knights of the Word once did, but until this moment he has never believed that it was so.

"What am I to do?" he asks the old man, uncertain of what is expected, of why this is happening.

The answer comes in three soft-spoken words. "Close your eyes."

He does so, relaxed now, reassured, and the images begin to flood his mind almost immediately. He sees a world he does not recognize, filled with huge buildings and strange objects that travel very fast and carry many people, some on the ground, some over water, and some in the air. He sees vast fields and valleys in which crops grow, covering miles of ground in all directions. He sees thousands upon thousands of people, some clustered close together in small spaces, some spread out over vast areas. He sees animals and plants and bodies of water and all of it is bright and shining and filled with life and color.

Then, in what seems an instant, it is all shattered. Explosions of unimaginable proportions obliterate everything in blinding flashes. Sickness and poison turn living things to dead husks. The air and earth and water turn foul and blackened. Everything fades, and he senses it happening not all at once, but over a period of time. What is left is wasteland. What remains are creatures both feral and desperate, hunter and hunted, and no law or behavioral code governs either. There is only a need to survive and the ways of making it happen. None of it promises anything good. None of it suggests that life will ever be the same.

The images disappear, and he opens his eyes. The old man is looking at him intently. "Did you see?"

He nods. "What was it?"

"The old world. A world that once existed and then ended and led to our migration to this valley. A world that will one day soon begin to intrude on our own and to which we must return."

Sider shudders. "I will never return to that."

The old man nods. "Not if you are prepared. Not if all those who live within the valley are prepared. Not if we are made ready." He pauses. "But we are not ready yet. Will you do your part to help?"

Sider stares at him. What is he asking? He still holds the staff in both hands, the feel of it comforting, even after the images. They are only images,

after all—only images from a past about which he knows little. The staff is
hard and real and present.

"What do you mean?" he asks finally. "What is my part?"

When the old man tells him, he knows instantly that if he agrees all of
his plans for the girl from Glensk Wood are finished.

SIDER AMENT STOOD SILENTLY in the shadows, watching the
lights in the cottages beyond the trees where he hid as night descended
on Glensk Wood. It had taken him two days to return from the ruins
in which Deladion Inch had kept him company while he recovered
from his injuries, and it felt now as if he had been away for years, rather
than days. Sider had healed quickly, a phenomenon that puzzled Inch
and about which he had asked repeatedly. But while they got on well
enough, Sider chose to keep the secrets of the staff to himself. It was
force of habit, for the most part, a natural caution he would have ex-
ercised under any circumstances. He liked and trusted Inch, but the
power of his staff wasn't a secret to be shared with anyone.

When he left the big man finally, healed and strong again, they
promised to meet at another place and time down the road. In parting,
the other gave him a small metal object with a single button. It was a
tracking device, he informed Sider. Press the button once and a red
light would come on. It would lead Inch right to him, wherever he was.
If he were ever in danger, if he ever needed help, if he just wanted to
find Inch, the device would bring him. It was small and easily hidden,
and Sider had placed it in a sleeve stitched to the inside of his belt.
After all, you never knew.

In truth, he felt he would indeed see Deladion Inch again, but he
could not have said when or where and there was no point making
plans when you lived the kind of life they lived. So he had taken his
leave and come back into the valley, returned from a world none of
those he had left behind had thought they would ever see. He was
back, and there was much for him to do.

But first he would do something he had not done in more than
twenty years. He would speak with her.

He stood in the shadows for a long time, watching the cottages around him, but hers particularly. He had chosen a spot where he was completely concealed from anyone looking but still able to see through her front windows into the room in which she sat, working on her sewing. She had always been clever, capable of looking after herself without needing to ask for help, and he supposed she still was. She looked after her husband as well now, a man he knew almost nothing about. He had kept it that way on purpose. It was difficult giving up something you loved so much. It was even more difficult accepting that someone else now possessed it. But that had been his choice, and the time for second-guessing himself had long since passed.

When he had waited long enough to be certain that she was alone, that her husband was either away or sleeping and no other people occupied the house, he stepped out of the shadows and walked to the door. He stood there for a moment, wondering if he was doing the right thing, then decided he was and knocked softly.

The seconds ticked away.

Then the door opened, and she was standing there.

"Aislinne," he said, speaking her name in a whisper.

She took a step back, her face shocked, her eyes blinking rapidly. He thought for just a second she might even collapse. But the second passed, and she was still standing there, staring at him. "Sider," she said in turn.

For a moment, neither said anything more. It had been so long. Perhaps she felt the same way he did, that just standing face-to-face like this was enough. She was still beautiful, still infused with a look of resolution that shone past the momentary surprise, and when she took his arm and pulled him inside, it was as if they had never parted.

He saw her glance at the black staff he carried, saw a flicker of distaste mar her soft features, and then she was looking back at him once more. "What do you want, Sider?" She closed the door behind him. "Why are you here?"

"To speak with you." He held her eyes with his own. "For just a moment, and then I'll go."

She hesitated, as if considering what the consequences of such a bargain might be. But then she nodded. "Wait here."

She was still holding her sewing, and she walked back across the room and set it down on the chair where she had been sitting, crossed again to a rack that held several cloaks, pulled one off and draped it over her shoulders, and returned to where he stood. "Not here. Pogue will be home soon, and I don't want to have to explain you."

She took him back outside and walked him away from the house then down a tiny lane that led through the cluster of homes to a small woodland honeycombed with trails. They walked without speaking, she leading, he following, the night about them silent and dark. They passed deep into the woods, angling this way and that along the trails until they reached an end to one and a wooden bench formed by a split tree trunk mounted horizontally on two stumps.

They sat down next to each other, not touching, but close enough that they could see each other's faces clearly, even in the darkness. "You've come about the breach in the protective wall, haven't you," she said.

She got right to the point, as always. Direct, purposeful. He almost smiled, pleased to find her still so much like the girl he had known. "I have. But how did you know?"

"We have friends in common. Panterra Qu and Prue Liss told me about your encounter with the creatures from the outside world and your suspicions that the wall was collapsing. Is it so, then?"

He nodded. "I have just returned through the pass in Declan Reach. The wall is down and may have been so for some time. Those creatures found their way through. I tracked them along the high slopes, killed one, and then tracked the other back out through the pass. But there are more, and many other things. Monsters, mutants, creatures we've never seen before. There are humans living in the outside world, too. Lizards, Spiders, and probably Elves, as well. Not so many yet; probably most were destroyed in the time when our ancestors first came into the valley. But enough of them, and they are finding their way to us, Aislinne. We cannot keep them out. Nor can we expect to stay safe within."

She shook her head in something like disapproval. "So Pan and Prue suggested. But your words—the words you so foolishly told them to carry to our village council—were a mistake. It did nothing to help; instead, it made them enemies. Now Skeal Eile and his minions hunt them." She was suddenly angry. "Have you no sense at all, Sider? Did you think they would be welcomed for bringing such heretical news?"

He was taken aback. "I did what I thought I had to do. Glensk Wood sits closest to the pass. The people had to be warned. I would have done it myself if I didn't think it more important to track down the second creature so that it wouldn't lead others of its kind back into the valley."

"Very noble of you. But your lack of foresight almost got those young people killed! After the council rejected their tale, Skeal Eile sent an assassin to make certain they never spoke of it again. They barely escaped him. If I had not been with them and foreseen—"

"You were there?" he interrupted, realizing what that meant.

"I was there, yes!" she snapped. "And after the assassin was dispatched, I sent them to the Elves to find safety. They have friends in Arborlon and intend to tell your story to them. Perhaps they will have better luck this time. Perhaps the Elven High Council will be more willing to listen than my own council members were. But if the Elves aren't better disposed toward them than the people of Glensk Wood, I won't be there to save them." She paused. "So tell me this. Will you?"

He hesitated. "I will go directly there after I leave you."

She nodded. The anger faded from her eyes. She reached out one hand and touched his cheek. "I'm sorry. You don't deserve my anger. You have enough of anger and distrust in your life without my adding to it. I am too hard on you." Her hand dropped away. "It's been a difficult road you've had to travel, hasn't it?"

He smiled and shrugged. "I made my choice." He looked at her anew, taking in the details of her face. Older now, but the girl he remembered was still there. "And you? How is your life?"

She laughed softly. "Not what I had expected it to be. I am married to a good man who looks after me, but I am not his passion as I was yours. Nor is he mine. We live together, childless and estranged in many ways, sharing space but little more. He governs the people of Glensk Wood; he heads the council. It gives him purpose, and I think that is enough for him."

"But there's not much of anything for you, is there?"

"I have my work in the community, helping where I can, trying to make things easier for people who don't have a voice of their own. Being married to the leader of the village doesn't hurt my efforts. Though Skeal Eile detests me."

"More so now, if he knows what you've done."

"He suspects but doesn't know. Not for certain. In any case, Pogue protects me from him."

The Gray Man wondered if that were so, but he let the matter drop. There was no point in voicing his doubts; Aislinne would do what she felt she must, and any words of caution from him would be wasted. "Tell me of the boy and girl. I met them; they seem capable enough, reliable and honorable. Am I right to think so?"

"You are. They will do what they say and attempt to convince the Elves of the danger. But they can only do so much. Word must still be gotten to the other villages, to the other communities, to all the Races. Everyone needs to come together and decide what to do."

He nodded. "Can you help me with that? Do you have friends whom you can trust and can send as messengers, warning of the danger? I know I ask a lot . . ."

She placed her fingers quickly to his lips. "You ask little enough, Sider. I will do what I can. But you must promise to go after our young friends and see to it that they are protected. They escaped once, but I am not sure they are safe yet. Skeal Eile is not one to forget. He knows the danger they represent, and he may try to do something to put an end to it—and to them—even as far away as they are. He is a ruthless man."

Sider nodded, and they were silent for a moment, looking at each other in the darkness. "I don't like leaving you here," he said finally. "I think you should come with me. To Arborlon or somewhere else. But away."

She shook her head. "You don't have the right to ask that of me anymore, Sider." Her smile was wan and tight. "You gave it up when you chose that staff over me."

He glanced down at the talisman, tightly gripped in one hand, and then he looked back at her. "I know what I gave up. A day doesn't pass that I don't think of it. Not a day that I don't regret it and wish it could have been otherwise. That I don't . . ."

He trailed off. "I just don't want anything to happen to you."

She gave him a perplexed look. "How strange to hear you say so. I've had that same worry about you every single day since you left me. You might want to consider that after you're gone."

He stared at her, his words all drained away.

Then she rose. "I think we've said all there is to say, Sider. Thank you for coming to let me know what's happened to the wall. And for promising to look after Panterra and Prue." She stepped back. "I should leave now. I can go back alone."

But she stood where she was, looking at him, as if undecided. "Please be careful," he said.

She nodded, but still said nothing and still did not move.

Without looking away, he laid the staff against the makeshift bench and reached for her, enfolding her in his arms, pressing her against him. He felt the softness and warmth of her, and for just an instant it was twenty years ago. "I never stopped loving you," he whispered. "I never will."

"I know," she whispered back, her head buried in his shoulder.

"I'm so sorry."

"There's no need. Not anymore."

She broke away from him, turned quickly, and went back down the path that had brought them. She took long, purposeful strides, and her long hair swung from side to side like a dusky curtain.

She did not look back.

16

"PAN! WAKE UP!"

A familiar voice, hushed and urgent. It was both close and at the same time a long way off, indistinct and fuzzy. He tried to put a name to it and failed.

"Pan! Please!"

Prue. He blinked against the woolly darkness that wrapped him like a blanket and opened his eyes. She was looking at him from only inches away, her eyes huge and gleaming in a wash of firelight. Her face was tight with fear.

"Are you all right?" she whispered.

Good question, he thought. His head was pounding and he was trussed hand and foot with ropes. He tried to remember what had happened. Something big and black had fallen on him while they were stalking the builders of the fire. Prue had sensed its presence, they had tried to escape, the black thing had . . .

A cloud of acrid smoke blew past him from the fire as the wind shifted. Sparks erupted from the blaze in a bright shower, and he caught a glimpse of huge bodies standing all around him, leaning on clubs and spears, shoulders hunched. Somewhere farther off voices argued. He could not make out the words, but there was no mistaking the tone.

Then a wolfish head swung into view directly in front of him, and he caught his breath. Yellow eyes fixed on him as jaws split wide in a lean muzzle to reveal rows of white teeth. A tongue licked and lolled alternately from between hooked incisors. He could smell the beast's fetid breath, could feel the heat of its humped, shaggy body as it moved to block his view, eyeing him as it might a piece of raw meat. Some sort of wolf? A feral dog? He couldn't tell; he only knew that he had never seen anything like it. He shrank from it, pressing himself up against Prue.

The beast regarded him a moment, looked deep into his eyes as if seeking something, and then turned away and moved off, joining another of its kind, a second beast that looked exactly the same, a few yards off. They touched noses, giving greeting. Tongues licked out, and muzzles rubbed affectionately.

"That was what jumped on you and knocked you down," Prue whispered over his shoulder. "You hit your head on a rock and lost consciousness. Then the Lizards took us both."

Lizards, Panterra repeated silently. He was conscious suddenly of the source of the insistent throbbing: a sharp pain that emanated from a point far up on his forehead. It was there he had hit his head; he could feel a small trickle of blood running down his face. He tried to reach up to feel the wound, but his hands were tied around his waist, and he couldn't raise them.

"It isn't too bad," Prue assured him. "Mostly, it's just a big knot."

Mostly. Pan shook his head. He wasn't sure if he was more angry or embarrassed, being caught like this. He should have known better than to listen to Phryne Amarantyne. There was no good reason for him to have done what he did, coming out of cover and exposing himself just to see who had built a fire. But it was wrong to blame the Elven Princess; he was the one who had made the decision, the one who had given in when he should have known better.

He wondered suddenly where she was, where the Orullians were, too, for that matter. Did they realize what had happened to Prue and himself? Had they tried to come after them when they didn't return?

Had they sought a way to save them? He looked around more care-fully, scanning the darkness, but he didn't see anything.

He felt Prue edge closer, positioning herself so that she could whis-per in his ear. "They were waiting for us, Pan. They built and lit the campfire as a trap. It's some kind of game, I think. There were dozens of them in hiding, but they were too far away and too well concealed for me to detect. It was those beasts that did all the work. It was too late to do anything by the time I sensed them. They stalked us, cor-nered us, and knocked you down, and then the Lizards came, too."

"Why do you say it's a game?" he asked. "Did they tell you this?"

She shook her head. "They haven't told me anything. They speak a language I don't understand. It isn't like the one the Lizards speak in the valley. These Lizards are different in other ways, too. They don't look or dress the same. Their skin is different—darker, coarser, like tree bark. They don't dress the same, either. They wear armor and carry shields." She paused. "I think maybe they are part of an army."

"But you think this was some sort of game that got us captured?"

"Just the way they acted when they saw us. Just how they moved and talked. They laughed a bit, pointed at us, made fun of the beasts that had us pinned. They seemed to be having fun." She gestured sud-denly. "Except for the two over there. Those two, they don't seem happy at all. I think from the way the others treat them they might be the leaders. They've been arguing ever since they found us. I don't know why."

Pan looked at the two figures standing nose-to-nose some distance off, the first a little taller than the second, the second a little more ag-gressive. They were shouting now, the second gesturing toward their captives, the first giving him a look and a shrug. The taller was very black and very lean, not so burly and massive as the shorter or the Lizards with them. In the darkness, the fire crackled as someone fed it wood while the others stood idly by, watching the argument.

"If I could loosen these knots . . ." Pan trailed off and began work-ing his wrists about experimentally, but the knots held.

"If you could loosen those knots and somehow make it to your feet, those beasts would be on top of you in about five seconds," Prue pointed out. "I don't think you want that."

He glanced over at the wolfish creatures. They were sitting on their haunches, gleaming eyes fixed and eager. As if anticipating that he might make the effort to flee and give them some sport. Pan watched them for a minute, and then gave up trying to free himself. Prue was right; there wasn't any point to it.

Then all at once the argument between the two Lizards ended, and the shorter of the two stomped over to where they were tied up and glowered down at them. There was a darkness in his gaze that left Pan feeling cold. He seemed very young, his skin still smooth in places and his features almost boyish. But there was nothing about him to suggest that he was in any way friendly or inclined to be helpful. Animosity radiated off him in bright waves. If Pan had wondered for a moment whether the Lizards might reconsider and let them go, he abandoned all such thoughts now.

All at once the Lizard began shouting at them, so furious that he was spitting. His words were indecipherable, although it seemed that he was asking them questions, demanding that they answer. Both pulled back in the face of his wrath, unable to respond in any other way. Furious, he kicked Pan in the ribs, glared at them one last time, and turned back to the other Lizard, shouting now at him.

The taller one walked over to join him, taking his time. The build of his body and the definition of his facial features suggested he was older, more mature, and he did not seem angry like the other. He was calm as he studied them, standing with his still-furious companion, his dark eyes taking in everything about them.

Then he spoke, a few words only in their own language, and the other, after a moment's hesitation, walked away. They saw him move over to the gimlet-eyed beasts and reach down to ruffle their ears. The beasts growled appreciatively.

The newcomer knelt next to them, bending close. "Can you understand me?" he asked, speaking their tongue in something that approached a mix of a growl and a cough.

Pan and Prue exchanged a surprised look. "How do you know our language when we don't know yours?" Pan asked quickly. "We have Lizards where we live, but they don't speak like you."

"Keep your voices down!" the other snapped, glancing back over his shoulder. He paused. "We're not Lizards. We don't call ourselves that anymore, or allow others to call us that. We call ourselves Trolls, as in Faerie time. Call us that. Remember. Trolls!" He sounded angry.

"Trolls," Pan repeated quickly. "Sorry. But how did you learn to speak like we do? How did you learn? Are there Men living out here?"

"Men, others. But I speak your tongue because my family kept the old language. Others mostly didn't; they only speak Troll. But there were always two languages in our history, old and new. I can talk to you, but Grosha and the others, no." He paused. "Who are you? What are your names?"

They gave them, speaking them in turn. "Arik Sarn," said the other, the name all rolling, guttural sounds run together.

"Arik Sarn," Pan repeated carefully.

"Where do you come from?" the Troll pressed. "No! No pointing! Hands down! Just answer."

Pan hesitated. "From inside the mountains behind us."

"Your people? A community?"

Pan nodded.

"Are there others?"

"Yes."

"Trolls, you said. Elves, too? Other Races?"

Pan nodded again, exchanging a fresh glance with Prue. "Why do you want to know?" the girl asked impulsively.

Arik Sarn ignored the question. "How long are you in the valley?" he asked instead.

"A long time," Pan answered. "Hundreds of years. We were brought there after the Great Wars and before the last destruction."

The Troll caught his breath sharply. "Brought there? You were led by someone?"

"Yes."

The Troll leaned very close, and his voice dropped to a whisper. "A boy? He was called Hawk? It was Hawk who led you?"

Panterra stared in disbelief. "How do you know about the Hawk?"

Sarn shook his head. "Later. Other things first. I am allowed to speak to you because I know your language, but Grosha will not allow it for long. Grosha Siq is my cousin. He is the son of the tribe Maturen, Taureq Siq. The tribe are Drouj, but they are not my tribe. A game of chance captured you. Grosha plays this game when he hunts. Now you belong to him. Mostly, after his Skaith Hounds have trapped prey, he gives the prey to his hounds to let them do with it whatever they want. But Men are scarce in this part, not found much. I persuaded him you must go to his father to be questioned. His father has first claim on you."

"Skaith Hounds," Prue repeated softly, shivering.

"Hunting beasts. Very dangerous. You would be dead, but the game requires you be alive for Grosha to view." He glanced over his shoulder anew. "We must finish this talk. No time left. I am not so much freer than you, understand? I am part of an exchange between Maturens to assure peace between their tribes. Taureq's eldest is with my father; I stay with Taureq. Five years I have to stay. I can do some things, but not much. I mentor Grosha, so I go along on this hunt. Good thing for you. I kept you alive, but maybe not for long." He paused, his black eyes fixed on them. "The truth? I don't know why I did so. Not for sure. A hunch, maybe. A foolish risk, too. But I did."

Grosha Siq had finished playing with his pets and was coming back over to them. Arik Sarn stood up. "We'll talk later."

NEARLY A QUARTER OF A MILE AWAY, but still within sight of the light from the campfire that Panterra and Prue had gone off to investigate, Phryne Amarantyne crouched in the shadows with Tasha Orullian, waiting for Tenerife. When Panterra and Prue had failed to return in a reasonable time and there were clear signs of activity around the fire—faint sounds of life and shadowy movements—Tenerife had decided to have a look. He was the most skilled of the three, the best suited for undertaking such a task, and there had been no argument that he should be the one to go. It might be that Pan and Prue were safe and that the sounds and movement signified nothing. Nevertheless, Tenerife had been quick to point out, they could not afford to take anything for granted.

But now Phryne was worried that perhaps something bad had happened to him, as well. She was furious with herself for urging Pan and Prue to go in the first place and frightened that her insistence might have brought harm to her new friends. Sometimes she didn't understand herself. Sometimes she acted in ways that were more self-indulgent than rational, and this appeared to be one of those times. She used her position as the daughter of the King; she used her beauty and her charm. She used everything she could find to use, and she did so almost offhandedly. She hadn't needed to know who'd built that fire or who might be tending it now. She could have left it alone, the answers she was eager to gather about the world outside the valley set aside for another day. But she had not wanted to wait, had not wanted to miss the chance of finding out something important and even vital about this world none of them had ever seen—that no one from the valley had seen. She wanted to be a part of that, to be at the forefront of this new discovery.

And so she had insisted, argued, and cajoled all four of her companions until Panterra and Prue had agreed to set out.

Stupid and willful—that was what she was.

"Do you see anything?" she whispered to Tasha.

He shook his head but said nothing in reply, his eyes fixed on the darkness beyond their place of concealment.

All this was her fault, her responsibility. She had demanded to be taken along as the price for getting permission from her father for her cousins and their Glensk Wood visitors to go. She had pushed them through the pass and then beyond. She had flirted with Panterra to win him over—not simply for that but because she was attracted to him as well, an attraction that was forbidden for an Elf and particularly for an Elven Princess, as she well knew and simply ignored—enjoying the way he was flustered and confused by her attentions. She had acted like a girl, not like the young woman she professed to be. It was a clear indicator of how much growing up she still had to do, she thought bitterly.

She wondered what her father would think of her if he discovered what she had done, but she didn't have to wonder about it long to know the answer.

"He's coming," Tasha whispered suddenly.

A second later his brother appeared out of the darkness, creeping through the rocks and scrub in quick, furtive movements until he was safely back in the shadows crouched next to them.

"Panterra and little sister have been taken by Lizards. How this happened, I can't tell. Or even what the reason for it was. But they are trussed and bound, and there are too many guards for us to attempt a rescue."

Phryne bit her lip, aware of his eyes on her, feeling his judgment settle on her like a weight. "I'm sorry," she whispered. "I didn't mean for this to happen."

Tasha glanced over. "This isn't your fault. We all agreed to let them go. None of us thought there was that much danger to it. Pan and little sister are Trackers, and she has the sight. That should have been enough to protect them. I don't understand it. Lizards aren't known for their ability to sneak up on people. They shouldn't have been able to get that close without giving themselves away."

"Whatever the case," Tenerife continued, "we have a bigger problem still. The Lizards are putting our friends in a cart and taking them away. They'll be moving out shortly for other parts."

Phryne felt her heart sink. Any chance at rescuing Panterra and Prue would disappear if they lost sight of them. There was no telling where the Lizards might take them or what they might do to them once they arrived at their destination. If anything was to be done, it had to be done now.

"I think we have to go for help," Tenerife said quietly, looking once more at her. "I don't think we can do this alone."

She shook her head quickly, adamantly. "No. I'm not going back without them." She met his gaze and held it. "I won't leave them."

"Your father would skin us alive if we let you do anything else, cousin. You know that."

"He's right," his brother agreed, shifting his bulk so that he, too, was facing her. "We can't afford to risk anything happening to you. We have to return and tell your father about this and come back with a larger, better-equipped rescue party."

"No," she repeated. "I won't do it."

Tasha gave her a rueful grin. "The choice may not be yours to make. We are the ones held responsible for your safety."

"I am the only one responsible for me!" she snapped. She realized how arrogant that sounded and immediately held up her hands in a placating gesture. "Listen to me, please. If I agree to go back now, without Panterra and Prue, and my father learns what has happened, it will be years before I am allowed to do anything of this sort again. It will simply reconfirm what he already suspects—that I am a child, a girl, and I must be coddled and watched over until I am someone's wife."

"Better that than ending up dead or a prisoner of those Lizards," Tenerife pointed out. "You didn't see them. I did. They aren't like the Lizards we know. These creatures are huge and dangerous beyond anything I've ever known. They wear armor and carry weapons of war. This isn't a group of travelers on a journey; this is a war party, and it is too much for three Elves to try to overcome."

"All right, I agree," she said quickly, not wanting to cede him any of the territory she had already made up her mind to claim. "But we could follow them, track them to wherever they are taking Panterra and Prue. We could look for a chance to rescue them. Then, if no opportunity shows itself, if nothing happens to allow us to free them, we can come back into the valley and tell my father."

"We lose time that way, cousin."

"We lose opportunity the other way, *cousin*."

"Following your advice the last time didn't work out so well. Perhaps this time you should defer to us."

"Thank you for pointing that out. I had forgotten completely. Now that I am reminded, I should probably crawl back into my hole and defer to your superior good judgment for the rest of my life!"

They glared at each other. Tasha, listening silently until now, gave a heavy sigh. "Enough. Both arguments have merit. No good purpose is served if we fight among ourselves. We must weigh the choices and decide. Time slips away."

"You decide, then," his brother ordered. "The vote is split between Phryne and me. She says we stay, and I say we go back. You choose, and we will abide by your choice."

He obviously felt that his brother would side with him. Phryne almost objected to the proposal, but decided to hold her tongue. Better to wait and hear what Tasha had to say before attacking him. She had done enough of that already, and she had a sense that any more of the same would only be counterproductive. Besides, he was going to have his say in any case. She desperately wanted to stay, to make right the things she had helped make wrong, to not return as the instigator of what could only be termed a disaster. But she had to accept that she could not make this happen by herself, that she needed the acquiescence and support of her cousins.

"What do you say, Tasha?" she asked him, forcing herself to look him in the eye. "What should we do?"

Tasha seemed to consider. "There is one aspect of all this that neither of you has mentioned, one that might be more important than any of the others we have discussed. If we do the smart thing, the reasonable thing, and we return to Arborlon and ask your father to let us return and search for Panterra and little sister, will he allow it? Not just you, cousin, but any of us. Or any Elves at all, for that matter."

He paused. "Because the people we are asking him to rescue, the people his Hunters must search out and do battle for, are humans. No, don't say anything yet, Phryne. I know your father is a reasonable and good man. But he differs not so much from other Elves in his dislike and mistrust of humans. He will weigh that against any obligation he feels toward you or us in making his decision. I cannot say for certain which way he will go, even knowing him as I do. That troubles me. If he refused to help our young friends, Tenerife and I would have to come back on our own, likely in direct disobedience of the King, and do what little we could to make things right."

He looked from his brother to Phryne. "What do you think?"

Phryne knew what she thought. She thought her father was a better man than that. She thought he would stand up for those his daughter had taken responsibility for. But she also knew Tasha was not wrong in his assessment. She shook her head, an indication of her own uncertainty.

Tenerife shrugged. "You make it all sound so reasonable, brother. As you always seem to. I find nothing to disagree with, so I withdraw my vote against abandoning our friends and suggest we go after them."

He walked over and put an arm around Phryne's shoulders. "We should leave now before they get any farther ahead, don't you think?"

She gave him a broad smile in response and kissed him lightly on the cheek.

17

THE TROLLS TRAVELED WEST AND NORTH FOR MOST of the remainder of the night, armored giants flanking the wagon that bore the prisoners, the sounds of creaking wheels and leather traces blending with the tromp of booted feet and guttural mutterings through a darkness barely broken by the pale light of moon and stars. Panterra and Prue were rolled and bounced about in the wooden bed by the jerky, swaying motion of the wagon, trying as best they could in their bound condition to brace themselves in its corners. Behind them, the mountains that hid their valley home slowly receded into darkness, swallowed by time and distance.

Prue eventually fell asleep, by then folded over and lying prone, her head in Pan's lap where he kept her as comfortable as he could manage. For himself, there could be no sleep. Not while his head ached and his anger burned. He spent his time trying to loosen his bonds, working them this way and that, twisting his wrists, using sweat and blood drawn from deep cuts incurred through efforts to lubricate the leather— all to no avail. The Trolls kept checking on him in any case, glancing in from where they walked alongside, keeping close enough that even if he were to break free there would be no chance of a successful flight.

Not that he would ever leave Prue. It was all just an exercise, just a way of passing the time and giving vent to his rage and frustration, the whole of it born of a deadening sense of futility.

He looked more than once for Arik Sarn, thinking to engage him in further conversation, wanting to learn more about what was happening to them. But there was no sign of the enigmatic Troll, no indication when or even if he would reappear, and Pan soon decided that help from that quarter was unlikely. He had thought from the other's knowledge of the Hawk and his journey to the valley, there might be some sort of kinship shared. In part, that feeling was fostered by the other's unexpected ability to speak their language and by his familiarity with their history. But in retrospect, Pan wondered if he were reading things into the encounter that weren't really there. Desperation sometimes fueled false hope. That could be so here.

He wondered anew if the Orullians and Phryne Amarantyne had any idea at all what had happened to them, if their friends even knew they were being taken away. A rescue seemed so unlikely given the odds of success that he found he couldn't give the idea serious consideration. If there was to be any chance of escape, it would have to come from his own efforts; reliance on others was a fool's game, and he knew it.

So he worked at his bonds and stared daggers at his captors when he caught them watching. But eventually, even that wasn't enough to fight off his fatigue, and with Prue's head still resting in his lap, he slept.

When he woke again, it was to shouts and cries and a rumble of activity all around him. The caravan was descending a long, rolling slope toward plains in which countless tents spread away in dark hummocks amid a sea of burned grasses, spindly weeds, and scattered clumps of rocks. It was daylight again, if only barely so, the eastern sky above the now very distant mountains silvery behind a thin layer of clouds, the landscape washed of color. No greens were visible from where this new encampment was settled, the whole of the land in all directions barren and empty of life. Only the Trolls—and there were thousands of them—populated the otherwise bleak landscape. They were gathered everywhere about night fires that mostly had burned out by now, leaving spirals of smoke rising into the air like the spirits of the dead. Bent to tasks that Pan could not decipher, to work that lacked recognizable definition or purpose, the Trolls went about their business. Only a few glanced up as the caravan approached, and those only for a quick look before turning away again.

Prue was awake, as well, hunched close against him. "There are so many of them. What are they doing here?"

Her words were barely audible above the rumble of their cart and the jumbled sounds of the camp. He shook his head in reply, saying nothing. Whatever the Trolls were about, it wasn't good. This was an army on the move, not a permanent camp. The Trolls were thousands strong, and there were arms and armor stacked everywhere. He saw beasts of burden that looked like nothing he had ever seen before, some of them vaguely resembling horses, many with horns and spikes jutting out of their heads and necks. Some were so burly that they had the look of battering rams, all covered in leather and metal clips. Some had the look of Kodens.

He saw a handful of the Skaith Hounds, as well, kenneled off to one side in a wire pen that rose fully eight feet high and was topped with spikes. The beasts pressed up against the wire, tongues lolling out from between rows of teeth. They whined and growled in steady cadence, and the two that had taken the boy and girl raced off to greet them, their master sauntering off in their wake, waving to someone in the distance.

"We can't stay here," Prue whispered. "We are in a lot of danger if we do. You know that, don't you?"

He did, of course, but he also knew he didn't have a way of changing the situation. "Just wait," he whispered back, not knowing what it was he expected her to wait for, short of a miracle.

The wagon with its prisoners rolled into the camp and through the tents, and waves of Trolls crowded around and peered in at them, discovering finally that there was something to see. Dozens more came quickly in response to the shouts of those closest. Panterra and Prue pressed together at the center of the wagon bed, trying to elude hands that poked and prodded at them, to evade the odors of sweat and heated breath washing over them. The Trolls laughed and joked with one another, and one or two brought out knives and gestured at the boy and the girl, taunting them.

Panterra kicked out, trying to drive them back. A powerful hand grabbed his leg and pulled him toward the side of the wagon, away from Prue. "Pan!" he heard her scream as his head banged down on the wooden slats and his head spun anew.

But a second later the Trolls fell back, the men of the escort forcing them away, and Arik Sarn was lowering the gate and reaching in to loosen their leg bonds and help them down. They could barely stand at first, their legs cramped from the binding. The Troll held them up, stronger than he looked, as the blood returned and twinges of pain shot through their lower limbs. Flanked by the men from the escort, the Troll guided them through the crowds and into a large tent at the center of the camp, into fresh darkness and a muffling of the sounds without.

"Stay here," he told them, steering them over to a pole at the center of a section of the tent that was curtained off from the rest.

As if to make clear that there wasn't a choice, he sat them down with their backs to the pole and chained them with ankle manacles that kept them in place.

Then he turned without a word and disappeared back the way they had come.

■ ● ■

THEY REMAINED WHERE THEY WERE for several hours, and at one point both fell asleep again. The sounds outside their place of confinement provided a steady thrum of noise, and no one came or went from their tent. Pan gave up on trying to free himself from his bonds, the ankle chain a new twist on their imprisonment that he had no way of overcoming. Their best hope now, he decided, was in awaiting the return of Arik Sarn.

When the Troll finally did reappear, he came bearing a tray of dried meat, hard bread, and a pitcher of ale with cups. He set down everything he had brought, knelt beside them, and released them from the bonds that secured their hands, but left the ankle chain in place.

He worked for a long time rubbing Prue's wrists, restoring her circulation, and then he produced a container of thick salve from his tunic and rubbed it into her abrasions and cuts. He let Panterra take care of himself, glancing over every now and then, his face impassive as he worked, his eyes giving nothing away of his feelings. He took a long time with Prue, curiously tender in his ministrations, then he pointed to the tray and motioned for them to eat. He sat watching silently as they did so, and when Pan started to speak, the Troll shook his head and gestured anew at the food and drink. *First things first*, he seemed to be saying, and Pan left it at that.

But as soon as they pushed back their plates and drained their cups, he was all business. "When your eating is done, Taureq Siq comes to question you. As Maturen of the Drouj, he will decide your fate. I ask the questions because I speak your tongue and can translate answers. But beware. You must answer fully and accurately. My oath as hostage and guest is part of the exchange of eldest sons. I am forbidden from hiding truth, even a little. Honor does not allow for it. Do you understand what I say?"

Panterra understood perfectly. "We should say nothing we would not want you to repeat."

Sarn nodded. "Yes. Grosha looks to feed you to his hounds. He considers you property that has been taken away from him, and he is angry about it. He blames me, but his father has first claim and Grosha knows this. Even so, I may not be able to do anything more for you. Taureq dotes on Grosha and mostly gives him what he wants. He has little reason here to deny Grosha. I will do what I can to help. But remember about giving answers to questions. Be careful how you speak and of what."

"Why are you helping us?" Pan asked impulsively. "You owe us nothing. You barely know who we are."

The Troll gave him an unreadable look. "Would it be better if I didn't help you?"

There was a sudden flurry of activity from just outside the chamber's closed flap, and Arik Sarn stood quickly and turned. A moment later a Troll's flat-featured face poked through, and the Troll spoke quickly to Sarn in their by-now-familiar guttural language. The latter nodded and gestured the messenger away. "They come for you. Stand up and meet them as equals. Show no fear; do as I told you."

Panterra had no idea how they were supposed to avoid showing fear when they were captives in a camp of thousands of Trolls, any of whom might choose to kill them with not much more than a momentary thought. But he took Prue's hand in his own and stood with her, facing the tent flap, holding himself erect. Sarn gave them a quick glance and then stepped to one side, distancing himself by doing so. It seemed an ominous sign.

"Watch me closely," Arik Sarn said quickly.

The sounds of footfalls and voices entering the outer portion of the tent froze them in place. Seconds later the tent flap was thrown back, and a clutch of armored black bodies strode through the opening and came to a halt. Panterra knew at once which of them was Taureq Siq just from the obvious deference paid him by all but one of the other Trolls who accompanied him. It was in their body language and their silence, but mostly it was in the way he dominated the room. Trolls were large to begin with, but Taureq Siq was a giant, standing fully eight feet tall and weighing well over three hundred pounds, all of it looking to Pan as if it were muscle and bone. Only Grosha, dark-browed and cold-eyed, standing at his father's right hand, showed no hesitation at crowding forward and then launching into a diatribe that was accompanied by angry gestures toward Panterra and Prue and his cousin. His father let him go on for a moment before backing him away with one massive arm and a single sharp command that turned the furious boy silent.

He took a step forward so that he stood at the forefront of the little assembly and close to the boy and the girl. His huge body was layered with scales as thick and rough as bark looming over them like a tree trunk, and his flat, empty face was ridged with scars. He studied them, letting the silence build for a moment before he shifted his gaze to his nephew and asked a quick question. Sarn answered briefly, and then there was a further exchange.

"Taureq says to tell him where you come from," he said quietly.

Panterra took a deep breath. "We come from deep in the mountains east of these plains. Those mountains are our home."

Another quick exchange among the Trolls followed. "Taureq says to tell him if you are a nation of Men only or of others, too."

"We are a nation of mixed Races. Men, Elves, Trolls"—he was quick to remember that the word *Lizards* was not to be used—"and Spiders."

Another exchange followed this translation. "How many?"

"Hundreds of thousands," Panterra lied.

There was a pause after his answer was given, then a flurry of words from the Maturen. "Taureq never heard of you. Why not, if your people are so many? Why live in the mountains and not in the grasslands south?"

Again, Panterra answered, embellishing the truth where it was needed. They had not come out of the mountains until now because they did not know if it was safe to do so or if the rest of the world had been destroyed. They were happy isolating themselves. They had found a home that could sustain them and that they could protect. He went on from there. He made it sound as if they were self-sufficient and well fortified against intruders, a united community of friends and neighbors deeply entrenched inside mountain passes only they knew how to navigate. He had no idea if he was saying the right thing; he only knew he needed to give the impression that an intrusion or attack of any sort would be a mistake.

Then, abruptly, the questions stopped. Taureq Siq stood quietly, looking at Panterra. He seemed to be considering. Pan waited, keeping his face expressionless, trying to convey a sense of calm. But as the seconds passed, he sensed in the spaces between their soft, slow fading that he had made a mistake.

As if in response to his fears, Taureq Siq made a quick, dismissive comment, and Arik Sarn turned to Pan and said, "He says you are lying. He wants to know why."

Panterra felt his throat tighten as he struggled to find the right response. "I don't lie. But I am worried that he intends to use his army to invade us and want to make clear that we are a poor choice for an attack."

A further exchange between Trolls followed. "He says no harm will come to your people, but you should not lie to him because if you do he will take his army into the mountains and find your people and kill them, but first he will kill you and the girl."

Sarn's words died away into silence. *So he means us no harm, but he's willing to kill us all if he decides he's being lied to?* Pan gave a mental shake of his head. He could trust nothing of what this man was saying, which was pretty much what Sarn had suggested in advising him to reveal nothing he did not wish repeated. Grosha was smiling, standing next to his father, hands clasped almost gleefully. He sensed he was about to have his way with them, that they would soon be entertainment for his Skaith Hounds.

"I have answered truthfully," Pan said, trying to deflect both Taureq Siq's threat and his own fear. "I don't know what more I can do. What else do you want to know?"

Beside him, he felt Prue inch closer.

Another long pause as Taureq Siq considered. Beside him, Grosha was growing more agitated, restless enough that he was trying to push forward again. His father, almost absently, shoved him back, and then spoke anew to Arik Sarn.

"He says you must take him to meet your leaders," the latter advised Pan. "Tomorrow."

Pan hesitated. *Now what am I supposed to do?* His mind raced, searching for an answer that wouldn't come. "I'm not allowed to do that," he said finally. "I don't have permission to take anyone into the mountains. But I could bring our leaders somewhere close to where your son captured us. I could arrange a meeting. I just need a little time."

He said all this without having the faintest idea if he could arrange a meeting or even with whom he might try to do so. Those in the valley didn't have any unity of the sort he had described, and there was no one who could speak for all of the various peoples. But it didn't matter. He would tell the Maturen anything to keep him at bay. Whatever happened, he must not take these Trolls into the passes or he would forfeit whatever measure of security those living in the valley might still enjoy now that the protective barriers were down.

He watched Taureq Siq's face as Sarn translated his words, but could read nothing in the Troll's impassive expression. The Maturen said something in reply, and then the two went back and forth for a few minutes in what appeared to be either an argument or an attempt to clarify. Whichever it was, Pan didn't like the feel of it.

Arik Sarn turned back to him. "Taureq Siq will think on your suggestion and give you his answer before the day ends. He says you must think some more on the answers you have given him. Maybe you will want to change some of them. He orders me to stay with you until you do."

Pan exhaled softly. "Tell him I am grateful," he said, not knowing exactly why he was grateful for anything that was happening, but thinking he needed to say something encouraging. "I will do as he says."

The Maturen gave him a short nod, one that managed to convey both approval and menace, and then he beckoned the others after him and departed the way he had come without a glance back. Grosha, however, gave Panterra a long, hard look that promised that as far as he was concerned, nothing was settled.

Panterra felt Prue clasp his arm. "Maybe he'll let us go," she whispered. "Maybe he'll agree to your suggestion."

Pan didn't think so. He didn't know what would happen, but it wasn't that. He suspected that Taureq Siq had already made up his mind about what he was going to do, but had decided to wait to let Panterra's imagination take hold.

He started to say as much to Arik Sarn, but the Troll held up his hand in warning. They stood in silence for a long time, listening. Then Sarn walked to the tent flap and peered out.

"Spies stay behind sometimes. Hide and listen and then tell him things. Maybe not this time because they don't speak your language. Talk freely, but softly. Be quick. He will come back soon."

"You think he has decided, don't you?" Pan pressed.

"Yes."

"He won't let us go, will he?"

"No." The Troll glanced back over his shoulder, and then moved away from the tent flap to stand close. "He won't let you go until he has the answers he wants. Maybe not then, either. He wants to know how to get into your valley so he can decide for himself if he will oc-cupy it. This is what he is not telling you. He moves the Drouj from its traditional homelands, which have sickened. The Drouj avoided this for a long time after the Great Wars, but no longer. Things have changed. Taureq looks for a new homeland; that is what he is doing out here."

"But where are the women and children?" Prue interrupted. "Have they left them behind?"

"Doesn't matter what he's done with his women and children. Do you understand what I am telling you? Do you see the purpose of Taureq's questions? He seeks your home in the mountains. If he likes it, he will take it from you."

"And you don't approve?" Pan asked.

"It doesn't matter if I approve."

Panterra shook his head. "But I don't understand. Why are you telling us all this? Why are you helping us at all? Aren't you putting yourself in danger by doing so? If the Drouj find out what you are doing, won't they be angry?"

Arik Sarn nodded. "Very angry. Taureq Siq would kill me instantly, forget any agreement with my father and their shared blood. He would do it even if it meant sacrificing his eldest, in turn."

"Then I'll ask it again. Why are you helping us? With so much risk, so much at stake, why?"

The Troll's smile formed a small break in his impassive features. "It is complicated."

"Yes," Prue said at once. "But explain it anyway."

The Troll shrugged. "We have only a little time, so I have to hurry." He paused. "Wait."

He walked back over to the flap entry and peered out once more. "I thought I heard something," he said. "Maybe. Maybe not." He shook his head, walked back to them, and motioned for them to sit. "I think we are family," he said very softly. "Your people and ours."

"Family?" Panterra repeated in disbelief. "How?"

The other leaned close, and his words were barely audible. "Once," he said, "hundreds of years ago, at the finish of the Great Wars, our ancestors both were seeking a place to survive what would come after. Two of mine were street children led by a boy named Hawk. He gave to his family—to those children who followed him—a name. It was the same name my ancestors gave their own tribe when they formed it later."

He paused, and then leaned closer still. "In Troll, the name is Karriak. But in the old language, the language of Men, the name he gave them was Ghosts."

18

GHOSTS.

It was the name the old stories said the Hawk gave to the street children who followed him. A name out of their own history, repeated from generation to generation by those who had followed the boy leader into their valley home. Panterra and Prue both knew the name well; both had heard it many times.

Ghosts.

And so, closeted away in the shadowy, concealing confines of the tent, the activities of the Troll camp a distant rumble beyond the hide walls, they listened with rapt attention as Arik Sarn told them the strange story of his own people's history.

"Some Ghost children were killed along the way. Some got safely to the place that became their home then and is yours now. We know this. But one who lived did not go with the others, did not want to come into the valley, did not want to be confined by walls. Better out in the open, no matter the risk. This one was named Panther. He met a girl with mutation sickness that turned humans into what used to be

Lizards, and they went north where the fallout from the wars and poisons did not reach. Panther was still human, but the girl was changing. The old stories do not tell why they bonded. Perhaps love, as the legends say. Perhaps for convenience and sharing. But a partnership was made, and in the north Panther and the girl found others like themselves and formed a tribe, the Karriak. It was the first of the great Troll tribes, and Panther and the girl become its leaders."

"I've heard the story of Panther and the girl from my mother," Prue interrupted. "The girl was called Cat. They turned north, just as you've said, right before they reached the valley, and they were never seen again. The Hawk brought the others into the valley where we live, and the mists closed everyone away and kept us in and everything else out. So no one ever knew what happened."

Sarn nodded. "Our stories are silent about those who went with Hawk except to say they found a place in the mountains that Panther and the girl left behind. So, we have different parts of the same story. But the Karriak tribe survived and grew strong in a place that sickness and firestorms passed by. The legends say that Panther became a Troll, the first after the girl, and named them so, said they are like Elves—like Faerie creatures of old in books—creatures that have strength and pride and stand upright and do not crawl like insects. Panther fathered children with Cat, and became the first Maturen of his tribe. His children followed him and their children after."

He paused, considering. "All centuries back, a long time ago. The Karriak grew too large and split to form other tribes. The Drouj is one. In the beginning it was a lesser tribe, but it became the most powerful. Leadership changed in both tribes, new families took power. The Trolls number in the millions and hold the whole of the North Country from the Blue Divide to the Storm Seas. The other Races are still small, not so many members, Men, Spiders, and Elves—though hard to say about the Elves, who hid again after the wars. We don't see them anymore. Most settled on the western coasts and out on the islands, far away." He shrugged. "So they say. Other peoples survived, too—others than Elves and Spiders and Men. But mostly there are Trolls."

He paused. He was struggling with his words now. "My family's bloodlines are Panther's, come down to me through generations.

Others gave up caring about their ancestry. It is enough for them that they are Trolls. Not my family. Not me. I know the truth. I know that to be related is a difference. It is not meant for people to be apart and not care. The world is not a place where no one should care for anyone. It is a place where all are part of one family, all are related, all belong to what remains of what is long past, of what was lost to the wars."

He looked at them in turn, measuring them. "It is my belief, but maybe not yours. But I think so." He paused. "You say you know the story of Panther and the girl. Tell me if I am right. Were your ancestors called Ghosts at one time?"

Panterra and Prue exchanged a long look. It was hard to know what to do here, hard to be certain what should be revealed. Pan wanted to trust this Troll who had done so much to help them—or so it seemed, anyway—but was afraid that anything he gave away might come back to haunt him. In the end, he went with his heart.

"There is talk within our families, a claim made by those who feel most strongly about it, that both of us can trace our ancestries back to those who were called Ghosts," Panterra ventured, choosing his words carefully. "Prue's own claim is the stronger. She has the sight, the ability to sense danger when it cannot be seen. One of those children who traveled with the Hawk also possessed that sense. But there are no written records. No one can do more than make the claim. No one knows for sure."

"Still, whether we are direct descendants or not doesn't matter," Prue added quickly, indicating the three of them. "You are right, Arik Sarn. We are still family. We come from the blood of the same small group of travelers. We are here because of them. We share a common history, a common story. Perhaps that is enough in a world where everyone is starting over."

"Not for everyone," the Troll said quietly. "Not for Taureq Siq. Or for his tribe. A year's time among the Drouj taught me this. It is not the same with my people or the other Troll tribes. The Drouj think they are a people of destiny, meant to dominate the rest of us. Taureq's private ambitions are these; I hear him speak of it many times. I listen, understand, say nothing. But there is no mistaking. His army will do to your people what it has already does to other Troll tribes. His conviction is that he must rule, and he follows that path."

Panterra grimaced. "Where have we heard that before? That was the fate of the old world, the fuel that fed the fires of the Great Wars. Has no one learned anything? Those who ignore the mistakes of the past are doomed to repeat them in the future, but no one believes it."

Sarn glanced over his shoulder as if to make sure they were still alone. "I choose to help you because the Drouj are wrong. My people are not strong; they give way to him. Maybe all the tribes together are not strong enough to stop him. But your people should not be destroyed. Maybe they can flee, maybe hide. They should be given the chance."

"If we can get out of here and warn them, they will," Panterra promised, wondering at the same time just exactly what they would do.

"We should start by finding Sider," Prue started to say, stopping as she heard the sound of voices approaching from without.

The tent flap was thrown back, and Grosha stood in the opening. Arik Sarn was already on his feet and had assumed a position of dominance over the prisoners, as if he were in the act of questioning them. A fierce exchange took place between the cousins, the meaning of which the boy and the girl could not understand, but the tone of which was unmistakable.

"Stay here until I return," Sarn advised them abruptly. "Do what you are told."

He went out through the open flap without saying more, close on the heels of his cousin. Panterra and Prue felt their frail hopes of freedom go with him.

* * *

MORE THAN A MILE AWAY, safely removed from the sprawling Lizard encampment, Phryne Amarantyne crouched in the concealing shelter of a cluster of rocks atop a ridgeline that allowed her a perfect view of the camp below. The barren depression in which the Lizards had settled themselves was flat and wide and empty of any sort of cover. It told the brothers Orullian, who were familiar with this sort of thing, several important facts about the Lizards. First and foremost was that they considered themselves safe in an unprotected position, so they believed either that no enemy force large enough to challenge them was anywhere close, or that no such force even existed. Second, but of equal importance, this was an army on the move; even if something unexpected did threaten, the Lizards felt they were equipped to deal with it.

So any attempt at getting closer would be foolhardy, especially in daylight, which it now was and had been for the better part of six hours. A clear view of what was happening—of comings and goings that might involve their friends, in particular—was as much as they could hope for until it got dark.

Even then, Tasha allowed, it would be difficult to do much to help. Panterra and Prue were somewhere in the middle of thousands of armed soldiers, concealed in a sea of tents, and finding them under any circumstances was highly unlikely. The best they could hope for was that at some point the Lizards would attempt to move them again, and then a rescue of some sort might be mounted.

Or maybe flying sheep would swoop down and spirit the boy and the girl away and they would all go home happy, Tenerife added brightly.

But Phryne was not as pessimistic as her cousins, confident that an opportunity would present itself. They had gotten this far in spite of everything, tracking the caravan without difficulty through the night, reaching the encampment in time to see approximately where Pan and Prue were being taken. She was almost certain she knew the exact tent, although with time's passage she had grown somewhat less sure about this. But whatever the case, she was determined to find a way to get their friends back. If not today, then tomorrow. Or the following day, or at some point soon, because she had meant it when she said she was not going back to Arborlon without them.

Restless and keyed up, she let the brothers sleep while she kept watch, eyes fixed on the encampment and its surroundings, waiting for the chance she was sure would come. Her experience at search-and-rescue missions was nonexistent, so her thinking was not hampered by practical considerations. Even so, she had enough of an understanding of how life worked to know that whatever they attempted would be extremely dangerous and could easily fail.

She continued to blame herself for what had happened to Panterra and Prue, unable to absolve herself of her guilt for pressing them to go when they clearly hadn't wanted to. She hated herself for thinking that way because she wanted to believe what she had done was the right thing under the circumstances. That was why she needed to get them back, of course, because otherwise she would go on condemning herself over this business for the rest of her life.

She just wished something would happen. The hours dragged by, the day wore on, and they were no closer to rescuing the boy and the girl than before. Tasha had cautioned her that patience was necessary, that haste was what had landed them in the current mess. *Her haste*, he might just as well have said.

Which was true, so it was difficult to fault him for reminding her.

After a while, she found her eyes were growing heavy. She knew she should wake her cousins, but she hated asking them for anything and didn't want to appear to need help of any sort. She dug her foot into the rocks and twisted until it hurt, bringing tears to her eyes but sharpening her senses anew. She thought about Pan, about how she was drawn to him, about how much she liked him even without knowing him any better than she did. It was extremely rare for Elven royalty to bond with a commoner—forbidden when the commoner was a human—but she liked the idea of doing something shocking. It was attractive to her; it sent a small tingle up her spine just thinking about it.

Anyway, she didn't like doing what other people told her she had to do. Oh, it was one thing if it was her father, of course. He was the King. But not other people, and not when what they were telling her was tied to some outdated code of conduct that should have been cast out years ago. Not marry a commoner! What nonsense! She wasn't even thinking about marriage. She was only thinking about spending time with him, about getting to know him better. He was interesting in his withdrawn, taciturn sort of way. She liked how he seemed so flustered when she talked boldly to him. She liked how it made her feel.

She looked off into the distance at the Lizard camp. Nothing. She dug at the rocky earth with her boot for something to do, but grew quickly bored. Her eyes were still heavy. She could close them just for a minute, couldn't she? Why not? It wasn't as if anything was happening or even likely to happen in the next few minutes. That was all she needed—just a few minutes.

The sun was hazy and the land barren as she peered first skyward and then out across the horizon. Everything was so bleak. It looked as if nothing lived there, even given the presence of the Lizards. It was an ugly, barren stretch, and she was sorry she had ever thought about going outside the valley. When this was over, they should all go back and stay there. This was no fit land for humans or Elves or anyone else.

She shifted to a more comfortable position and let her eyes close.

When she felt the hand on her shoulder, she realized she had been sleeping.

But it was too late to do anything about it by then.

DEEP INSIDE THE MAZE of Troll encampment tents, Panterra and Prue sat waiting for Arik Sarn's return. They had no way of knowing how much time had passed, but to Pan it felt like hours. Little conversation passed between them as the minutes dragged on, most of it truncated and forced, a way to provide each other with some small measure of reassurance that whatever happened they were still together. They could hear the sounds of movement and voices from outside their enclosure, a rough-edged jumble unrecognizable as anything specific. It suggested things best not thought about too hard or long, and they did what they could to ignore it. Pan was less successful with thoughts of freedom; he could not stop having those, even knowing that escape was virtually impossible.

More mundane wishes intruded, as well.

He wished he could have a bath and a change of clothes.

He wished he could see the sun again.

He wished he had stayed inside his valley home.

He was wishing for a few other things when a stirring from outside their chamber brought his head up. His eyes fixed expectantly on Arik Sarn as the Troll reappeared. He came over to them without a backward glance at the tent flap—which was quickly closed by someone standing without—knelt where they sat, and bent close.

"Taureq Siq has decided. Your suggestion is accepted. You will go back to your people, back home." But there was something wrong with the way he said it, something troubling. "You will be released, Panterra Qu, to speak to your leaders, to tell them of the meeting. Taureq will come to them at midday on the first day of the next full moon, to the place where we found you, and they will talk."

Panterra grinned broadly, glancing over at Prue as he did so. He couldn't believe it! They were going let them go! "You see," he said quickly, working hard at keeping his voice low. "I told you that . . ."

But Prue had caught what he had missed. She shook her head. "You don't understand. Only you are being set free. Not me. Am I right?" she asked, her eyes shifting to the Troll.

Arik Sarn nodded in agreement. "Only you, Panterra. Your friend will be held hostage to make sure you come back."

The smile dropped from Pan's face. "No," he said at once. "We both go. Both of us. If not, I don't go, either. Tell him that!"

But the Troll was already shaking his head. "Then you will both die. Taureq has decided. No argument is allowed. You will go, the girl stays." He hesitated. "I will be going with you. To make sure you keep your word. Taureq says I must."

Pan shook his head in disbelief. He didn't mind if Sarn came along, but to leave Prue was unthinkable. "She's only fifteen," he hissed at the Troll. "She can't be left here—"

"Pan!" she interrupted quickly, grabbing his arm. "Stop. Don't demean me by arguing that I am a child. I am not. I haven't been since I became a Tracker. I am as grown-up as you are and in some ways more so. There's no point in arguing about this. Taureq has decided. You heard. I would have decided it the same way. He would be a fool to let us both go."

Arik Sarn was nodding. "Listen. She knows."

"You have to do this for both of us," Prue continued. "If we both die here, nothing will have been accomplished. If you are free, at least you can warn everyone about what is happening, and maybe you can find a way to come back for me." Her grip on his arm tightened. "I know you can do this, Pan. I believe in you."

Panterra dropped his head, running his hand across his brow and through his hair in an unmistakable gesture of dismay. "I should never have suggested going back," he muttered. "What a fool!"

Prue was having none of it. "You did the right thing and probably saved both our lives. Nothing else we said or did was going to make things any better. You can see that as well as I. This is the best way. I can wait for you; I won't be hurt. They won't do anything to me. Not until they know what's going to happen with the meeting you suggested."

Arik Sarn leaned forward. "We will come back for her," he said. "You and I. I promise. We will come."

Panterra Qu looked at them in turn, wishing he could think of something else to say, something that would change what was happening. But there was nothing to say, nothing to do. He knew that as well as they did. He took a deep breath. "They won't hurt her?" he asked the Troll. "Are you certain of this?"

The other nodded. "I am certain."

Pan shook his head one final time. "I don't know. I just don't."

But he did know, and the matter was decided by then. Sarn had fresh clothes brought for him, released him from his chains, and gave him time to dress. When the Troll returned with packs of supplies for them, Pan could barely make himself look at Prue, still clothed in rags, still chained in place.

He knelt next to her and hugged her close. "I'm so sorry," he whispered.

She hugged him back. "You do what's needed. I'll be waiting for you. I'll be ready when you come."

He didn't even consider mentioning the obvious, although they were both thinking it. *If he did come; if he would come at all.* But he had said he would, she was expecting him to keep his word, and so he had to. Nothing less was acceptable. It didn't matter what obstacles he faced. He would not leave her here to die.

He rose and gave her a long look. He wanted to say more, couldn't think what it should be, and so managed only a quick smile and good-bye before turning away so he wouldn't see her cry. Or, if he were honest about it, so that she wouldn't see him.

Arik Sarn led him through the tent flaps and back outside. He went obediently, as if walking in a dream. He could not seem to focus his thoughts, to gather his scattered wits. Everything felt surreal and disconnected. The day was winding down, the light gone gray and hazy east, the sunshine fading rapidly west, the surrounding land layered in shadows. He stood in the midst of the tents and the Trolls, a stranger in a hostile land, wondering how in the world he had gotten there. Sarn took his arm, guiding him through the tents, through a sea of watchful eyes and pointing fingers, the sounds of guttural Troll voices trailing after them, guilt and fear riddling him with wormholes that threatened to reduce him to dust.

"This feels wrong," he said at one point, but his companion ignored him.

A little later, the Troll spoke softly and motioned to one side. Taureq Siq and his son stood watching them, their Troll faces impassive, their ridged bodies statues against the moving backdrop of the camp. Neither attempted words or gestures, but simply observed as Panterra and his minder passed by. Again Panterra felt something tug at him in warning, a chance missed, a mistake made, a hidden regret that later would become obvious to him. He tried to think what it could be, to see it behind its concealment, but nothing would come to him.

Then they were through the camp and outside its perimeters, walking away from all the activity, the eyes, the pointing, the whispers and shouts that trailed after.

From the guilt and from Prue.

Panterra knew she would not want him to think this way, but a voice inside his head kept whispering that he could not pretend he didn't see the truth of things: that he was abandoning her, that he was leaving her to a fate he couldn't even begin to imagine.

That he would never see her again.

＊　＊　＊

THEY WALKED EAST FOR ALMOST A MILE without speaking, the darkness ahead growing stronger and deeper as the light faded away.

Panterra walked without thinking about what he was doing, beginning to ponder instead how he was going to explain himself to those he had left behind, how he could possibly justify his actions. It didn't matter to him what necessity required or common sense dictated or anything else that had to do with cause and effect. Seeking reason where there was no reason to be found was the last refuge of those who had acted inappropriately; that was what appeared to him to be true here. Nothing could explain leaving Prue. Nothing could make up for losing her.

Arik Sarn seemed to recognize what he was going through. The Troll walked apart and did not attempt to engage him in conversation. The trek occupied their efforts and kept them from needing to do more than to concentrate on putting one foot in front of the other, eating up the distance and time that remained between them and the mountains they were heading for.

Once, Panterra stopped completely, turned and looked back. "I can't do this," he said, as much to himself as to his companion.

He stood there in the ensuing silence, considering his options, weighing his chances if he turned around now and crept back under cover of darkness, sought out the tent in which Prue was imprisoned, broke apart her chains and set her free. It was possible, he thought. It was something he could do, an action he could take and complete.

He thought about it for a long time. Then reason intruded and prevailed.

The boy and the Troll walked on again.

They were still within sight of the camp as they climbed a rise through a scattering of large boulders and deep depressions when a cloaked form stepped from concealment and blocked their way. Panterra started wildly and Arik Sarn produced a short sword with serrated edges as if conjuring it out of thin air, but the appearance of a black staff carved through with runes froze both in place.

"Late for a twilight stroll, young Panterra," the newcomer offered mildly. "Or have you secured your freedom? Is your unexpected companion friend or foe?"

Sider Ament! Pan practically fell over himself with relief.

"I thought I would have to come get you on my own, but you've saved me the trouble," the Gray Man continued. "Your would-be rescuers and like-minded fools are back up in the rocks, waiting for us. We should join them." He gave Arik Sarn a sharp look. "What's become of Prue Liss?"

Panterra started to speak, couldn't, gestured back over his shoulder at the Troll camp and shook his head.

"Like that, is it?" Sider Ament walked over and put an arm around the boy's shoulder. "We'll have to go get her back then, won't we? But first you must tell me everything. Both of you. Come now."

And turning away, he led them up into the rocks and out of view.

19

IT WAS A WEARY AND DISPIRITED LITTLE GROUP THAT walked on past midnight and well into early morning before reaching the base of the mountains that warded their valley destination. By then, everyone was exhausted, all but one of them having slept little or not at all for the past two days.

But more disturbing to Panterra Qu than their lack of rest was their barely concealed distrust of Arik Sarn.

"I don't care what he did for you," Tasha whispered at one point when they were walking apart from the others during their homeward trek, the sky gone black and star-speckled and the wind a low wail across the flats. "He will revert to his own kind at some point; it's the nature of things. Don't trust him. I'm warning you."

"He troubles me," Tenerife added. "He has a look. Darker than what he shows on the surface, rougher-edged. He's hiding something."

Phryne wouldn't come close to either one of them, and even Sider Ament was not convinced. "You are right to feel grateful for his help," the Gray Man said. "But temper your gratitude with caution and remember that things aren't always what they seem. Remember that these are not people of the same sort as the ones you have known."

The Troll didn't do much to encourage them to feel differently. He barely spoke to any of them, relying on Pan to explain what had happened and make clear his part in the matter. He seemed wary of all of them, but particularly of Sider, from whom he continually shied away. Pan saw the way he looked at the black staff, saw the fear and uncertainty in his eyes, and realized that the Troll knew something of this part of their history, too.

When Pan asked him about it, the two of them briefly trailing the others, the Troll said, "You said nothing of a black staff wielder, of a user of magic. It is dangerous to be close to one. There are stories of them and their magic sticks, of fire that consumes, that burns everything to ash. They fought demons in the old days, the stories tell. All were supposed to be dead. Trolls don't like magic or magic wielders. We don't trust any of it."

There was nothing for it, of course. None of them had been there to see how the Troll had protected him. He could hardly expect that they would become instant friends, since Sarn was allied with the bunch that had made Prue and himself prisoners in the first place. Such friendships took time and required trust not easily given. But they did not send him back; nor did he ask to go. An uneasy acceptance of the situation was reached, an accord that would at least allow them to travel together as their shared purpose required.

Which, of course, was Taureq Siq's demand for a meeting. All involved clearly understood it to be a preliminary step to invading their homeland. But Panterra had not hesitated to tell them of it right from the start. It was necessary they know everything, that they be fully aware of what was at stake when they reentered the valley and stood before Oparion Amarantyne.

This was their intention, of course, agreed to from the beginning by all of them. The Elf King was the leader they had the best chance of convincing; there was no one better to approach. With Phryne and the Orullians spearheading the effort and the Gray Man and Panterra in support, the King would have to listen and consider. In the end, Panterra was willing to bet, he would have to act, as well. Oparion Amarantyne commanded the largest and most powerful fighting force in the valley; he could not just stand by if convinced of the impending invasion. And if he agreed to rouse the other Races to stand and fight with him, they had a chance of keeping Taureq Siq and his Drouj from the valley.

Of course, there was still the matter of getting Prue back safely, and their chances of doing that were less easily measured.

"Listen to me," the Gray Man had said to Pan after all was revealed and the question of Prue's fate was a cloud they could not get out from under. "Listen carefully, because this will not be easy for you to hear. We can't go back for her just yet. No, say nothing until I finish. We cannot go back because we must first go to our people and set them to the task of saving themselves. It is the life of one girl versus the lives of thousands. We must act responsibly and choose the latter. Once we have done what we can in the valley, then we can act to save Prue Liss. She will not be forgotten or abandoned. But she must wait her turn, and you must be patient."

There were a dozen arguments that Panterra could have made about this approach, though he knew that doing so would achieve nothing. The Gray Man was right about the importance of delivering a warning first. But Pan made up his mind that before any meeting with Taureq Siq and its inevitable fallout, he would go back for Prue. He didn't know what he would do when he found her. He did not know if anyone would go with him or if he would end up going alone. He only knew that whatever the case, he was going.

Besides, he could not shake the nagging feeling that Sider Ament would do whatever was expedient in all matters, this one included. If it became impractical for him to do something about Prue, he would find an excuse for abandoning her. It wasn't that he didn't mean what he said or didn't intend to do what he could; his work as a bearer of the black staff simply meant that he must always balance gains and losses in making his choices, and that sacrifices were inevitable. Panterra understood why this was so for the Gray Man. But he would not allow Prue to become one of those sacrifices.

When they stopped for the night—as Sider had decided they should, too much in need of rest to complete the journey on a single trek—Panterra took his doubts and his fears to one side, away from the others. He watched as the Orullians rolled themselves into their blankets and went straight to sleep. He watched Arik Sarn do the same. Phryne lay down close to him, her face turned away. Even Sider, positioning himself at the edge of their concealment where he could look back across the valley, found rest of a sort, his eyes fixed and staring, his gaze blank, his breathing slow and even in the silence. Pan needed to sleep, too, but he was still thinking of Prue, still caught up in his regret and shame at leaving her behind. Her skills and experience notwithstanding, she had been his responsibility in their partnership as Trackers and in their relationship as childhood friends, and he would never be able to get past that. It didn't matter that she had absolved him and told him to go; the guilt was still there, a raw wound that would not close.

For the first time since he had returned, he thought about having to tell her parents what he had done. How could he do that? What could he tell them? Anything he said, unless it was a lie, would be devastating.

He sat staring out at nothing, lost in thought, wrapped in his remorse and dismay.

"I'm sorry I told you to go," Phryne said suddenly, her voice not much more than a whisper.

He glanced down at her, startled. "What?"

"I shouldn't have been so insistent. This is my fault; I know that. I wish I could take it back."

"About Prue?" He shook his head. "No, I don't think so. Mostly, it's mine. I left her."

"But you wouldn't have had to do that if you hadn't gone to look at that fire, and you wouldn't have gone to look at that fire if I hadn't insisted."

Panterra edged over so that they were almost touching. He leaned down. "I made the choice to go, Phryne. I didn't have to do so. I didn't have to take Prue with me, either. So you don't need to blame yourself, or apologize to me."

"I feel like I do. I feel like I need to apologize to everyone."

He smiled in spite of himself. "I feel like I need to crawl into a hole."

She was silent a moment, retreating into herself. "I won't be satisfied until we get her back, Pan. I'm going to tell my father everything and insist that he do something."

"Well, I hope he listens to you. I hope he believes what you tell
him."

There was another pause. "I'll find a way to make him believe."

"I expect you will."

She was silent for a long time then, and he was about to find a place
to sleep—or at least try to—when she said, "Would you lie down next
to me? Just close enough that I can feel you?"

She didn't explain, and he didn't feel that he should ask her to. He
just did as she asked, sliding close as he lay down facing her back. Using
her blanket, she reached back with the trailing edge and covered them
both. She didn't say anything more, but soon he could hear the regular
rhythm of her breathing and feel the heat of her body.

He went to sleep not long after that.

WHEN HE WOKE, both Phryne and her blanket were gone, and he
was lying on the bare ground, the chill of early morning stiffening his
joints. He rose and stretched, finding the others grouped around a
small collection of foodstuffs produced from someone's stores, eating
quietly. He joined them without comment. He was pleased to see that
the Elves were sharing what they had with Arik Sarn. The Troll's impassive face revealed nothing of what he was thinking, but he gave a
quick nod as the boy sat down next to him.

Phryne Amarantyne never even glanced his way.

They set out again shortly afterward, but not until Sider had satisfied himself that no one was tracking them or trying to spy on where
they were going. Even so, he took them on a circuitous route that
wound through clusters of rock and deep ravines as they ascended the
mountains, effectively hiding them from view almost all the way up to
the entrance to Aphalion Pass. Once there, he paused them again, taking time to study the plains below. Only then did he allow them to
enter the pass and make their way back into the valley.

They were all relieved to discover that the dragon they had encountered on their way out was nowhere to be seen.

"A creature mutated from the old days, before the Great Wars," Sider opined when Panterra asked him about its origins. "Or, if you prefer something more magical, a creature that has survived from the time of Faerie, a mythical beast that was sleeping until we brought it awake again. Hard to tell without getting close enough to examine it. Difficult to tell even then."

No one was going to suggest attempting anything like that, even if they somehow found the dragon again, so solving the mystery of its origin would have to wait.

"How did you find us?" Panterra pressed as they descended out of the pass, not having thought to question the unexpectedness of it until then.

"Magic," the Gray Man deadpanned. Then he shrugged. "Or maybe something more like luck. I returned after chasing after that beast we fought, thinking to find you and see what success you'd had with the people of Glensk Wood. I spoke with Aislinne Kray and learned of your danger. She suggested I do something about it, since she felt I had caused the problem. So I went to Arborlon and discovered that you had gone up into the pass with the Orullians and Oparion Amarantyne's daughter. I guessed at the rest when I found all of you missing and your tracks leading off into the wasteland. One thing led to another."

"How do you know Aislinne?" The words were out before he could think better of them.

The Gray Man looked away. "I know her from a long time ago."

There was more to it than that, Pan sensed, a great deal more, but he knew better than to ask. Whatever their relationship might be, or might have once been, Aislinne wielded considerable influence over Sider Ament if she could tell him to do something and the Gray Man would do it.

"She kept us safe when Skeal Eile would have seen us dead," he ventured after a moment. Then he told the other about the assassination attempt and their escape from the village.

Sider Ament listened but said nothing, the subject apparently closed. Panterra knew enough to leave it there.

They walked on through the morning, and by midday they had

reached the outskirts of the city of Arborlon, come into view of its heights and the ramp leading up. Once within the city, the little company went straight to the King's home, quickly picking up an escort of Home Guard that had apparently been told to watch for them. Heads turned at the sight of Arik Sarn, but the presence of Lizards was not all that unusual in Arborlon, and so the gazes did not linger.

"Many Elves," the Troll said quietly at one point. "Thousands?"

"Thousands and more," Pan answered. "More Elves than Men in the valley. More than any of the other Races."

The Troll nodded, looking uneasy. "Dislike Trolls?"

Pan shook his head. "They like them well enough. But the Trolls choose to live apart."

Arik Sarn looked away. "Trolls always live apart."

Their escort grew larger, walling them away from those who crowded close enough to shout questions or to have a cautious look. That the Princess was among the newcomers must have raised a few eyebrows, but no one tried to speak with her, not even those in the Home Guard escort.

They reached the palace and were taken into one of the reception rooms, a chamber situated well back in the complex, windowless and dark until the smokeless lights were ignited and dominated by a large table and some twenty seats arranged around it. The walls were draped with tapestries portraying Elven legends and flags embroidered with the personal insignias of the Kings and Queens. Light seeped through skylights glassed over and screened with fabric, and paneled walls and flooring gleamed with fresh polish. Panterra felt out of place, ragged and unwashed, but he took a chair with the others to wait.

The Home Guard left them, save two, who took up positions outside the double doors leading in. Sider made a point of asking Arik Sarn to remain in their company.

Only moments passed before Oparion Amarantyne appeared, storming through the doors and slamming them shut behind him. He moved to the head of the table and stood glaring at the assembled. But when he met Sider Ament's gaze, he saw something in the latter's eyes that caused him to tamp down his anger.

He shifted his gaze to his daughter. "I am going to assume that things were not exactly as you described them to me earlier, Phryne. I would appreciate an explanation for that and a full accounting of what has transpired." His gaze shifted again as he took a seat. "My Elves, young Panterra, the Lizard visitor sitting outside the doors of this room, and the Gray Man. An odd company. And a story behind its making, I imagine. Sider Ament. Perhaps you should be the one to start?"

The Gray Man did so, telling the King everything. Pan saw Phryne wince once or twice at what she was hearing, and he would have winced, as well, if he hadn't been so busy trying to think of what he could add that might make a difference in the King's thinking. But Sider was thorough, and left nothing unsaid. The King did not interrupt, sitting back in his chair and taking in the story with rapt attention.

"There is no mistake about the protective barriers?" the King asked when the Gray Man had finished. "The walls are down? All of them?"

"All of them. The passes are open."

The King looked dismayed. "And now we are threatened by a Lizard army. Excuse me. By a *Troll* army. So then. Today is the first appearance of the quarter moon in the cycle leading to full. We have perhaps twenty days in which to act. Not a lot of time."

"Time enough," Sider replied quietly. He looked around the room. "I'm done talking. Does anyone care to add anything?"

The Orullians and Phryne all started speaking at once, then sorted themselves out and took turns. Phryne took full responsibility for everything, blaming herself for what had happened to Prue. She begged her father in full view of all assembled for a chance to make it right. The brothers spoke at length about the threat from the Troll army and Taureq Siq, arguing for an immediate mobilization of Elven Hunters to defend the passes. Pan wanted to speak, to say that they had to do something about Prue, that they had to save her. But such a demand would have sounded selfish and redundant in light of what had already been said, so he kept quiet.

Instead, he watched the faces of the others. He noticed the surreptitious looks that passed between Sider Ament and the King, glances that were furtive and expressionless and seemed to escape the others.

He noticed that Sider, when not appearing to pay attention to the speakers, was watching him. Closely.

"Enough," the King said finally, as the brothers Orullian repeated their argument for mobilization for what must have been the third or fourth time. "I think you've said all that needs saying and I have heard enough to give thought to what is needed.

"Phryne, clean up and wait on me. Tasha and Tenerife, take the Troll to your home and keep watch on him until I decide what needs doing. Eat, drink, and bathe yourselves. Better take Panterra Qu, as well. Go."

He gestured them up from their seats and ushered them out the doors into the hallway beyond, where Arik Sarn was sitting and the Home Guard were waiting to escort them out. No one said anything. They barely looked at one another. There was a shared feeling of uncertainty and dismay as they departed the building and emerged outside once more.

Panterra noticed that Sider Ament did not come with them.

*   *   *

OPARION AMARANTYNE WAITED until the others were gone, and then he took the Gray Man out of the reception chamber and down the halls of the palace to the small library that served as his private reception room. It was not entirely unexpected. The looks they had exchanged earlier had told Sider that the King would speak to him alone when the others were finished. They were not friends in the common sense, but had grown up in their valley world at the same time and were of a like age. They had been boys when Sider had become bearer of the last black staff and Oparion had been made King. The deaths of a mentor and a father had brought them together under awkward and difficult circumstances, which they had managed to surmount. An unconventional friendship had developed, one founded for the most part on mutual respect and a willingness to meet halfway. That friendship had lasted now for more than twenty years.

Even so, the Gray Man could not be certain what stance Oparion would take in this business.

When they reached the King's reception chamber, they took seats by a cold fireplace across from each other, sitting close in a wash of gray light that filtered through cracks in draped windows.

"I will tell you up front that I find this tale more than a little incredible," the King began. "But not so incredible that I don't believe it. Perhaps it is rather that I find it overwhelming. Five hundred years of safekeeping and now the protective walls are down. Without warning. Without apparent reason."

"Not a reason we can discern, although the Seraphic will tell you it signals the return of the Hawk."

The King made a dismissive gesture. "It signals the end of an age. It signals the beginning of a fresh struggle."

Sider nodded. "That it does. What will you do?"

"In truth? I don't know." The King leaned back in his chair. "The boy's promise to the Drouj that he would arrange a meeting is worthless. Even if I could identify who our leaders are, I could never manage such a thing. Most of them barely speak to one another. We'll have to think of something else."

"Agreed. The boy's promise was made under duress. Given the circumstances, he gave the best response he could manage."

The King shook his head. "Forgive me for asking, but is the threat from this Troll army as great as the boy thinks? Can we believe him?"

The Gray Man shrugged. "The threat is real enough. I saw the army, measured its size. It's as Panterra Qu described. Still, it's hard to be sure what to believe. The boy is young, and he doesn't have the wisdom and experience to see things as clearly as I'd like. He sees too much with his heart. Losing the girl as he did makes his observations less than reliable. But he is no fool, either. On the face of things, what he's told us makes sense."

"But you are not certain?"

"I'm not."

"About the Troll?"

"Not only the Troll, but the whole of what's happened. The boy showed courage and quick thinking in making the Trolls think us much stronger and more united than we actually are. But he is still only a boy. He may be seeing things that aren't really there, reaching conclusions that he shouldn't. I don't know. I'll need to spend time with him to determine that. I'll have to leave the valley again, as well. But first I'll go south. I'll take the boy with me."

"To the villages of Men?"

Sider nodded. "I have an obligation to warn them. Whether they listen or not is another matter. But the passes must be fortified and defended, no matter the outcome of this business with the Trolls. Others will follow, sooner or later. It is inevitable. I'll try to arrange for a defense of Declan Reach if you agree to send your Elves to Aphalion Pass. You had better fortify against an attack on your city, as well. Even if you can only manage to erect barriers on the ramp leading in, that will help. Send to the Lizards and Spiders, as well. Ask them to come join you. I don't think they would do so for Men, but they might for Elves."

The King smirked. "An irony that does not escape me." He sighed. "I will have to tell the High Council of this. Some will doubt the need for what you are asking."

"I won't be the one asking. You will. They won't challenge you."

"Of course they will. They challenge me on everything. I let them because tolerance is necessary when you are King. I might have thought otherwise when I was young, but no more. Sometimes it's like letting the fox into the henhouse." He gave the Gray Man a look. "Your task seems the harder of the two. How will you make anyone believe you? Few believe you now. Some don't even believe you exist."

Sider Ament smiled. "That's a problem. But we'll need help from everyone if we are to survive. Prejudice and animosity will have to give way to expediency and common sense. A banding together of all the Races will be necessary. The Trolls are merely our first test in what I can only think of as a collision between two very different worlds. We have to prepare ourselves before it's too late. Maybe I can make the councils of Men see as much."

"Maybe. Maybe not." The King cocked a questioning eyebrow. "What about our visitor. What do you suggest I do with him?"

"What you have already done. Give him over to the care of the Orullians. Let them spend time together. Perhaps the brothers will learn something useful. But watch him, too. Just to be certain we haven't made a mistake by bringing him here. I won't be gone more than two weeks, time enough to return for the meeting with Taureq Siq."

"That's being optimistic. You won't begin to reach all the southern villages before you have to come back."

Sider shrugged. "Can't be helped. I'll try to arrange for others to act as messengers in my place. It's the best I can do."

The King rose. "Rest here tonight, then, and leave in the morning. You won't be much good to anyone if you're exhausted, and you look it now." He sighed. "I have to have a talk with my impetuous daughter about the difference between the keeping and breaking of promises."

The Gray Man nodded, rising with him. "Allow me one more question. We face great dangers in reemerging from our safehold, High Lord. Some of these may hark back to the time of the Great Wars. Some may possess magic. Once, the Elves had use of magic, too. Is there none at hand now that you can call upon? Do you know nothing of the whereabouts of the blue Elfstones?"

There was a tense moment of silence as the King faced him, his features tightening. "Nothing," he said quietly. "The Elfstones were left in the hands of the Belloruus family, even after the Amarantynes became rulers of the Elves. As far as I know, that never changed. No one has heard anything of the Elfstones for years. Not since the Belloruusian line failed and the Amarantynes became rulers."

"But you married into the family, didn't you? Was your wife told anything about what happened to the Elfstones?"

"Not that she ever made known to me. By the time of our marriage, the Elfstones had long since gone missing. There was no reason to speak of them, no reason that anyone should bother."

Sider shifted his rangy frame as if to get a better view of things. "Is it possible the Stones could be found now, that whoever has them might consider producing them, when the need for their magic is so great?"

Oparion Amarantyne held his gaze a moment longer before turning away. "Anything is possible. It would be up to whoever took them to give them back." He gestured abruptly. "You had better rest now. You have much to do in the days ahead. I wish you luck."

The Gray Man knew better than to say anything more, even though he would have liked to. The matter of the missing Elfstones was troubling, but not as much so as the King's strange disinterest in their whereabouts. As if he couldn't care less; as if he couldn't be bothered. Such magic should not be dismissed so casually. Sider promised himself he would discover why Oparion Amarantyne seemed so willing to do so.

Later, when there was time.

Shouldering his black staff, he set the matter aside and followed the King from the room.

20

I T IS THREE YEARS SINCE THE OLD MAN WITH THE black staff appeared to him, a harbinger of a future that would change his life. The boy is mostly a man by now, though not yet twenty, grown tall and broad-shouldered, strong in body and self-confident. He has left his family and the farm to go with the old man, to study what the other would teach him, to be mentored in the usage of the magic of the black staff and in the ways of the larger world. He has left the girl he once thought he would never leave, but even now she shines in his memory with the clarity and brightness of crystalline dew in sunlight.

He thinks that this will never change. He will discover to his sadness and regret that he is right.

Sometimes he wants to go to her, to see her once more if only momentarily, to measure how she is and what her life is like. He does not do this, of course. Only once does he suggest this to the old man, in a moment of weakness that betrays him. The old man neither denies nor permits; he simply asks him to reconsider. Reason takes hold, and an awareness of consequence stills his eagerness. What would a visit accomplish other than *to reaffirm what he already knows he has lost? Quickly enough, he abandons the idea.*

He thinks often, however, of their last meeting and the way they left things as he said good-bye to her.

"I wish it could be different," he tells her, a trite and inadequate attempt at demonstrating regret he cannot begin to express.

"It could be different, Sider," she responds. "You need only make it so. No one has a claim on your life. No one but yourself. This is your decision, and it has not been forced on you. But once you make it, do so without regret or apology. Do so with commitment and determination."

"I love you," he manages, the words like sand in his mouth.

She smiles sadly, leans in and kisses him. She touches his cheek. She says nothing. Then she turns and walks away and does not look back.

He has not seen her since. Sometimes he thinks he will never see her again.

His studies provide succor, an escape from his emotions and his memories. The old man is a good teacher, giving him chances to discover what it is that the black staff can do and what it cannot. It is magic so powerful that he wonders how anyone, let alone himself, can manage to control it. Even so, he discovers, there are limits to what it can do. It is also unpredictable. Trial and error teaches him some of this. Mistakes teach him even more. The magic, he discovers, can protect him. But there is a price for using it, a depletion of the body and soul, a leaching away of life that accelerates aging. It happens in increments and it happens slowly, but it happens. Choices are necessary because sometimes using the magic exacts too heavy a toll to make the usage practical. An understanding of why this is so comes early in the course of his mentor's instructions when the old man explains it to him in what the boy has come to recognize as a familiar approach.

"Suppose you are attacked by something monstrous, a creature of enormous size and strength. Do you use the magic of the staff to defend yourself?" the old man asks him.

"Of course," he answers confidently.

"Then suppose you are attacked by a dozen men, all armed and ready to see you torn apart. Do you use the magic to defend yourself here, too?"

He nods again.

"Do you defend yourself at the cost of your attacker's life in each case? Or do you simply try to disable your attacker?"

"That would depend."

"What would it depend upon?"

"On how threatened I felt. On whether I believed my life was in such danger that only my attacker's death would save me."

"Is the price for both usages the same?"

He hesitates.

"Does the price differ depending on the attacker?"

"I think it might."

"What would determine the cost of using the magic in each case?"

Again, he hesitates.

The old man nods his approval. "Your hesitation is warranted. The answer is uncertain. The answer can only be discovered by use of the magic, and sometimes that is not a good thing. Understanding that there is a difference is important. Causing injury or death to monsters is different than it is to humans. It differs with species, as well. The emotional drain it exacts determines that cost. Each time you use the magic to harm or kill, you take away something from yourself. The ways in which you are connected to whom or what you attack determine how much is lost. Is this attack personal? Do you know anything about the attacker's circumstances and background? Do you have a history with the attacker? Is the attack quick and clean or drawn-out and messy? Have you reacted too quickly or too severely? Have you acted out of need or reacted out of fear and doubt? It all matters, young one. It all tallies in determining the cost, in exacting the price."

He understands, but at the same time he doesn't. He has no personal experience with what he is being taught. He is never given the staff to use in combat; he is not allowed to test its power against anything living. Everything is explained, but little experienced. He tries to extrapolate, but there is no substitute for the real thing. He chafes under the restraints placed upon his education. He listens and learns, but he continues to wonder what it will feel like when the staff and its magic belong to him.

Sometimes he thinks that the talisman will never be his, that the old man is simply keeping him on as a companion. He is aged and worn, but steady in his life. Nothing seems to threaten, nothing surfaces that would cause either of them to believe that a need to gift the black staff will ever be *more than a distant possibility against which they both guard. It distresses the boy to think that he gave up his dream of a life with the girl he loved so much for a promise that may never be fulfilled. It eats at him like a cancer that he may have sold himself so cheaply.*

Then one day, three years into his apprenticeship, the old man takes him aside from their daily routine and walks him down the hillside to a stream running below the cabin that serves as their present home. For the past six months, they have lived up along the ridgeline fronting the western peaks, occupying a campsite that has been used for years by trappers. It is an idyllic, pristine setting, carpeted with meadows grown thick with wildflowers in spring and covered deep with unblemished acres of snow in winter. The sun shines often here, as it does not in other parts of the valley where the mists hang in thick draperies and the clouds brush the peaks. Sider likes this place and wishes they could stay here longer, even knowing from experience that they will soon be leaving.

But today the old man does not speak to him of his lessons and their choice of camps.

"There is something we haven't talked about before," he tells the boy. "Something that we have to talk about now. There is another besides myself who bears the black staff. Another who is descended from the old Knights of the Word."

He has the boy's full attention as he pauses to gather his thoughts.

"An Elf," he says finally. He looks off across the countryside, as if across the span of his years. "There were two who came into the valley, who survived the Great Wars, carrying their staffs. Both were of the Race of Man, but one married an Elf girl; their descendants stayed with the Elven people and continued to intermarry so that eventually they were blooded Elves. Their staffs stayed with them, both Man and Elf, but because the protective mists shut out the threat of the old world there was no reason for the staffs or purpose for those who bore them. Their presence became marginalized, and they drifted into lives like my own. They were wanderers, objects of speculation and curiosity and sometimes mistrust. No one was sure what the black staffs were for or why anyone still carried them."

"You were sentries against the dangers that would arise when the mists faded and the world changed back to what it had been," the boy says. "Did no one remember?"

The old man shrugs. "A few. But most thought the world was fixed and would not change. They still think so, mostly. Or they believe in the teachings of the Children of the Hawk and wait to be saved. It is in the nature of things to want to believe that what's familiar and comfortable will last forever." He looks down at his hands. "In any case, there are two of us still, and the other is an Elf, and the Elf has grown dangerous. He was never as stable as he needed to be; he was a poor choice in the first place. But the choice was not mine to make, and I suppose it seemed a good one at the time."

"Why is he dangerous?"

"He lacks judgment and reason. He is seduced by the possibilities of extending the staff's magic to increase his own value and position. He has forgotten what it is he committed to. Because the Word no longer speaks to us, because we serve an ambiguous cause, we are more vulnerable to choosing paths we might otherwise avoid. The Elf has steadily lost his way, and now a kind of madness has surfaced and taken hold of him. I am afraid of what he might do, and I have to go to him and see if I can help him."

The boy shakes his head. "But what can you do?"

The old man smiles. "That is what I have to discover."

"Isn't this dangerous?"

The old man nods. "But there is no one else who can reach him, and if no one tries, the danger that he will do something harmful grows stronger."

The boy is quiet for a time. He thinks the matter through, aware that the old man is watching him. "I will go with you," he says finally.

But the old man shakes his head. "No, you will wait here for me. I will have a better chance of reasoning with him if I go alone. If he sees more than one of us, he will feel threatened. He lives in fear of betrayal. He trusts no one. He has no apprentice to serve as his companion and successor and no desire to find one. He sees himself as invulnerable, his life as infinite. He is seduced by the power of the magic and will not give it up. He thinks that others wish to take it from him. Perhaps there are some who do. But he will not fear that from me because I already have power of my own and do not need to acquire his."

"When will you return?" the boy asks.

The old man studies him and does not answer for a very long time. "When I can," he says finally.

They sit together in silence then, looking at each other and then at the countryside. The boy does not like what this last answer suggests. He does not like what he is feeling. But the decision is made, and he must accept it.

Even though it leaves him cold and empty.

The old man departs with the sunrise, bearing his black staff. The boy will only see him once more before the talisman, heavy with the weight of its responsibilities, passes to him.

THE MEMORY CAME AND WENT, a reflection of his thoughts of the future he would one day face. He might have carried on to the end of things, calling up the last of those memories of the old man, but Panterra Qu was speaking to him, whispering as they neared the village of Glensk Wood.

"What will you say to her?"

He was suddenly exasperated with the boy. Always wanting answers to his questions, even when they should have been obvious. But he supposed that he was like that once, young and uncertain, his fate in the hands of a man who was essentially a stranger to him yet would influence his future in ways he could only begin to imagine. He had wanted answers, too. He had been impatient for things to be revealed that were kept secret, that he was expected to simply accept. He had not been as aggressive about it as Panterra was, but then he had been given considerable time to adapt to his role as student.

And he had known from the beginning what was expected of him, which Panterra did not.

The nature of their relationship was at the crux of his exasperation, he supposed. For he had come to a slow and painstaking conclusion since meeting this boy that he was the one who should bear the staff after him. He had the necessary skills, required temperament, and sense of responsibility. He had something indefinable, too—something that set him apart, that marked him. Sider could not have explained how he knew this; he just did. Panterra Qu was the one he had been looking for. It had taken him a while to come to terms with this, but now it felt like a foregone conclusion.

The difficulty, of course, lay in explaining it to the boy and in persuading him that he should make the choice Sider had made all those years ago—to abandon his plans for his old life and form fresh ones for his new.

"We will ask her for her help," he answered the boy, keeping it short and vague. He wasn't sure himself, after all. But he would know when they found her.

"But what can she do? You've already seen how they have put her aside even as a member of the village council. If not for her marriage to Pogue Kray, she would have been banished or worse a long time ago. If she helps us now, Skeal Eile will look for a way to correct his earlier mistake."

True enough, Sider thought. "We won't let that happen." He glanced over. "My word on it."

The boy seemed to accept this reassurance, and they proceeded in silence, wending their way down the narrow path that took them into Glensk Wood the back way out of the mountains, avoiding the main road. Sider saw no reason to advertise their coming just yet. What he was hoping was that Aislinne would have something to say about how to proceed. She knew the village and its leaders far better than he did, and she would have a sense of what might gain their support while avoiding the machinations of Skeal Eile.

Darker thoughts took hold. He'd had the chance more than once to put an end to the Seraphic, to make him disappear as if he had never been. But he was not trained as an assassin, and his code of conduct did not allow him to harm those who did not directly threaten him or those he protected. Skeal Eile was skirting the edges of that distinction if he was responsible for the attempted assassination of Panterra and Prue at Pan's home. But the Seraphic's involvement remained only a suspicion, strong as it might be. There were many at the council meeting when Panterra spoke; one of them, aroused to the point of mindless rage, might have acted on impulse.

Still, he would have to find a way to assure himself that the Seraphic would not try to harm Aislinne after he and Panterra left. That he hadn't done so before was no guarantee of what he might do in the future. Especially after he heard what Sider had to say. Things would be changed irrevocably after that.

And with that thought completed, the answer to what he would do came to him in a flash of inspiration.

Even so, he kept it to himself. They were at the edge of the village now, passing close enough to cottages to see lights in the curtained windows and movement behind the curtains. A few villagers walked the main road off to their right, too far away to be recognized, but easy enough to avoid. He motioned the boy to stay close and slipped from tree to tree, from thicket to woodpile to outbuilding, steadily advancing into the heart of the village. *Not long now*, he thought. Her home was not more than several hundred yards farther on. He wondered if she would be alone or if Pogue would be there. In a way, it might be better if he was.

But he knew he didn't want that. For what brief time he was allowed, he wanted to have her alone.

The path they were following ended at a small copse of trees bordering the rear of a semicircle of cottages, and Panterra suddenly took hold of his arm and stopped him.

"My home," the boy whispered, pointing at one.

The cottage was dark and silent, and there appeared to be no one living there. But the grounds were neatly kept and the exterior of the house looked cared for. The boy stood where he was for a moment, studying the home as if he had never seen it before, and Sider wondered what he was thinking. Then the boy nodded and gestured that they could go on, apparently only wanting to take a quick look at it.

Minutes later, they were standing in the shadows outside Aislinne Kray's home while Sider studied it and waited for his instincts to tell him it was safe to go inside. He couldn't be certain who was there; no movement within was discernible from where they stood.

But he sensed that the house was not empty.

"Wait here," he told Panterra.

He left the cover of darkness, walked up to the front door of the cottage, and knocked. Now he could hear movement inside, the sounds of footsteps, the lifting of a latch, the creak of hinges.

The door opened, and Aislinne was there.

"You've returned," she said quietly.

She did not seem surprised, but there was something in her eyes that suggested she wasn't quite prepared, either. She was dressed, not yet ready for bed, her hair still tied up. The room behind her was empty.

"I'm sorry for the hour," he said.

"No, you're not. You're never sorry for anything, the lateness of an hour least of all. Did you do as I asked you? Did you find Panterra and Prue? Are they all right?"

Direct and purposeful. She was still the girl he had met when he was just fifteen. For a moment, he saw her that way again, composure in place, golden hair hanging down, her gaze fixed on him, tall enough to look him directly in the eyes. She could tell he was staring, and he didn't care that she did.

"I've brought Panterra to speak with you. Something has happened, and the people of Glensk Wood are in danger because of it." He hesitated. "Is Pogue here?"

She shook her head. "No. Does it matter?"

"Can we come inside?" He avoided answering her question, not wanting to risk what he might say.

She nodded. He looked back over his shoulder at the shadows where the boy was waiting, and beckoned. A moment later Panterra appeared, hurrying across the green space to the door and inside. "Well met, Aislinne," he greeted as he brushed past her.

"And you, Panterra. How is Prue? Not come with you?"

The boy's eyes flicked immediately to Sider, and the Gray Man knew he would have to answer the question directly, that Aislinne would not be fooled. "She stayed behind," he said. "Let me tell it."

He did so, a quick and efficient recapitulation of most of what had happened to Panterra and Prue and their Elven companions after leaving the valley, and then of his own part in attempting to bring them home again. He looked for condemnation and disappointment in Aislinne's eyes as he related how they had left Prue Liss behind, but he found none. She sat quietly as he talked and did not interrupt.

When he had finished, she looked down at her hands for a moment. "At least you tried to help them. At least you brought Panterra back with you." She looked up again. "Will you return for Prue? Will you try to save her, as well?"

"I have already promised that I would. But I had to come here first. I have to make certain that warning is given. Have you sent messengers to the other villages?"

She shook her head. "No one would go. Not without more than your word. They are afraid, Sider. Afraid of Skeal Eile, afraid of the sect. You can't blame them."

"No, I don't suppose I can." He gave her a wan smile. "I don't suppose assigning blame in this business serves any good purpose. Those who haven't seen it for themselves will find it hard to believe anything of what I have told you. But they will have to find a way to do so. The dangers they face will not allow them to do otherwise."

"Even then, what can anyone do?"

"If they are attacked by the Trolls, they must fight," he answered. "If they are fortunate enough to prevail, they must still find a way to fit themselves into the larger world. They must assimilate. They must adapt. They must forget everything they thought was true about their safe haven and rethink what it will take for them to survive."

She nodded. "What do you intend to do to help?" She paused. "By coming here, I assume that you intend to speak with Pogue."

"I intend it. And once I have done so, I intend to get word to those other villages. But I would ask your thoughts first. We already know how Skeal Eile and his followers will react. How should I go about this so that they cannot undermine me? I have to be certain that someone will listen to me and then act on what I am saying. Glensk Wood sits closest to Declan Reach. If the Trolls find the pass through, they will come here first."

She thought about it a moment. "A public announcement invites trouble. Something private might be better." She gave him a look. "What if I were to bring Pogue and Skeal Eile to you tonight. Just the two."

"Eile won't come," said Panterra, standing off to one side.

"He will if he doesn't know the reason he is being summoned."

"Bring Trow Ravenlock, as well," Sider said. "His Trackers are the closest thing you have to an organized fighting force, and two of them are directly involved in what's happened." He glanced at the boy. "Ravenlock will stand up for you, won't he? He believes in you and the girl?"

Panterra Qu nodded doubtfully. "But he believes in the teachings of the Children of the Hawk, as well. I don't know."

"Well." The word was a sigh of resignation. "We have to start somewhere."

"I'll go now." Aislinne stood. "Panterra, there's food in the kitchen. Go in and have something to eat and drink. Sider, I would speak with you alone for a minute."

She took him outside without further explanation, closing the door tightly behind them. She stood on the porch without looking at him for a moment, staring out into the night, but seeing something else entirely. Then she took him down the steps, across the yard, and into the shadows where they could not be easily seen. All around them, the village was dark and silent. Even the lights in the windows were beginning to disappear.

When she turned to face him, there was no friendliness in her eyes. "Why did you bring Panterra back with you?"

The question took him by surprise. "He's seen things I haven't; he brings another perspective and another voice to the discussion. I thought it would help."

She gave him a sardonic smile. "You are such a poor liar, Sider. All you say is probably true, but that isn't why he's come with you. I don't need you to tell me the reason, either. I can see it in your eyes, in the way you look at him. You want him for yourself. You've decided he's the one."

Sider hesitated, considering a lie. Then he gave it up. Not with her, he decided. "That's true. But he doesn't know it yet; I haven't spoken to him. I have no way of knowing what he will say."

She stepped close. "I know that boy. And the girl who partners with him. They aren't exactly like you and I once were, but close enough that I won't let you do this. Separating them would be worse than what you did in separating us. Do you realize what they mean to each other?"

He shook his head. "I know hardly anything about that. I only know what he makes me feel, and what he makes me feel is why I plan to speak to him."

"I forbid it!" she hissed sharply.

"It isn't your place to do that." The words were out before he could think better of them, too late to take back. "Aislinne, I don't want this, either. But if I am killed in this business, in this transition from the old world to the new, that boy will be needed to take the staff and go on. There must be someone to follow after me."

"Then find someone else."

He shook his head. "I haven't time for that. I haven't even got a place to start. I've been looking all these years, waiting, but there's been no one. Now I have to—"

"Stop." She spit out the word as if to rid herself of its bitterness, one hand lifting to emphasize her wish to silence him. "No more. I have to go. But we aren't finished. Do you understand me?"

He took a deep breath. "All too well. I'll wait on you. I can promise that much."

She stared him down, and then nodded. "I'll bring you your audience. Practice your speech to them while you wait. And practice one to me, as well."

Then she was gone.

21

WHEN SIDER CAME BACK INSIDE THE COTTAGE, Panterra Qu could feel the anger radiating off him. The Gray Man's face was rigid with it, and his posture warned against saying anything. So Pan sat quietly, ate the food he had found in the kitchen in the cold box, and waited for the anger to dissipate, the familiar calm to return.

After a while it did. "That looks good," Sider offered absently.

He rose, disappeared into the kitchen, and returned with a plate of his own. He ate hurriedly, obviously anxious to finish before Aislinne and the men returned, saying nothing further to Pan.

But when he was finished and had returned his empty plate to the kitchen and lowered himself into a chair across from the boy, he said, "Are you ready for this?"

Pan nodded. "What do you think will happen?"

The Gray Man shook his head. "No one will be happy to see us, Skeal Eile least of all. But they will stay and listen because they will know that our being here means we have something important to tell them. They'll listen, but maybe they won't believe. It depends."

"I guess it does," Pan agreed. He thought about it for a minute. "What will you do about Skeal Eile?"

Sider Ament shrugged. "That depends, too. If I don't like what I see in his eyes, I'll have to reconsider my thinking. Otherwise, I'll seek a promise of unconditional support in front of the other two. That sort of public oath carries weight. Since we won't be staying, we won't be at much risk. It's Aislinne who should worry."

"Aislinne seems able to take care of herself," Pan said. "And she has friends besides us who can protect her."

The Gray Man nodded and looked away, his gaze drifting toward the curtained windows and the night beyond. "She was always resourceful."

Panterra wanted to ask him about Aislinne, wanted to know more. There was a history between the two that went way back; any fool could tell as much. He wanted to know what that history was. But he knew that asking would be wrong and likely brushed aside. He would have to wait and hope that at some point Sider Ament would choose of his own volition to talk about it.

They waited in silence then, listening to the night's deep stillness, searching for sounds that would signal the coming of the others. It was not long before they heard footsteps and accompanying voices. Those approaching did not do so cautiously or with any indication that they knew who was waiting inside. Pan heard Pogue Kray's deep voice rumble in sharp cadence to Trow Ravenlock's quieter tones. But he did not hear Skeal Eile or Aislinne, and wondered if something had happened.

The door opened and both speakers stepped inside, drawing to an abrupt halt the moment they saw Panterra and Sider. Aislinne and Skeal Eile followed, Aislinne entering last and closing the door firmly behind her.

"What is the meaning of this, Aislinne?" her husband asked at once, never for a moment turning away from the two visitors, his dark eyes angry.

"We have a nice piece of trickery at work here, Pogue." Skeal Eile offered a guarded smile, but his voice was smooth and pleasant. "Your wife possesses depths of deception still unplumbed, it seems."

Only Trow showed any semblance of calm, giving Sider a nod and saying to Pan, "How are you, Tracker? We miss you and your partner. Have you come back to stay?"

Ignoring the others, Aislinne moved to the front, turning to face her husband. "I did not tell you who waited because you would not have come and it was important that you did. If you hear them out, I think you will agree with me and forgive me my deliberate omissions."

Pogue Kray glowered at her. "Sometimes, you step too far over the line with me, Aislinne. You should not presume—"

"I see no harm in hearing what they have to say," Skeal Eile said suddenly, cutting the other short. "We're here, after all. What harm can come from it?"

And right away, Panterra knew that something was amiss. For the Seraphic to be this calm suggested he was not altogether surprised to find them there, and that was troubling. No one should have known they were coming. No one should have been prepared for this.

But maybe it was simply the Seraphic's discipline and training that allowed him to give this impression, and he was simply disguising his real feelings beneath a façade of apparent calm.

In any case, there was no time to find out. An argument between Aislinne and Pogue Kray was pushing everything else aside.

"I don't like being deceived!" Pogue Kray snapped, his eyes flicking dark with anger. "Especially not by my wife! I expect better than that from her!"

"Any deception in this business exists only in your mind!" Aislinne replied quietly.

"Tricking me into this meeting does not count as deception?"

Sider Ament suddenly stepped between them. "Instead of attacking Aislinne, perhaps you would do better to listen to what I have to say."

"Keep your opinions to yourself, Gray Man!" the other snapped, coming forward to meet him. "You and your black staff, thinking you can do whatever you wish. Think again! I don't need to listen to anything you have to say, not now and not—"

"Perhaps it would suit you better if I simply left and you found out on your own that the protective wall you all believe in so strongly is broken and an army of thousands waits just on the other side of the pass at Declan Reach. Perhaps you would prefer to tell what's left of your people after that army destroys the village, kills the men, and makes slaves of the women and children that this was all Aislinne's fault. Perhaps they will understand your refusal to speak with me about it now. Perhaps. I won't be there to find out, however. Come, Panterra."

He pushed past Pogue Kray and moved toward the door. After a moment's hesitation, a stunned Panterra followed in his wake.

"Sider, wait!" Trow Ravenlock moved to block his way. Smaller than the other, he stood defiantly in place before him. "Don't go. Tell him to stay, Pogue."

The big man stood frozen in place, silent.

"Tell him," Skeal Eile advised quietly. He gathered his white robes closer about him and lifted his head slightly to emphasize his insistence. "This is no time for soothing your injured pride by acting the part of the child. We need to know what he's talking about."

Again, the voice of reason, and again Panterra felt the wrongness of it. But he avoided looking at the other, keeping his eyes averted.

Aislinne walked up to her husband, stood directly in front of him, and placed a hand on his shoulder. "I did what I thought needed doing to get all of you in this room. Now, please. Listen to Sider."

Pogue Kray took a deep breath. "All right, Aislinne." He turned about to find Sider facing him. "Speak, then. We will hear whatever you have to say on this."

It cost him something to do that, and Panterra thought he paid it mostly because of what he felt for Aislinne. It might have cost Sider Ament something, as well, and it was Aislinne who had exacted the price from him, too.

"Here is what the boy and I know," Sider began without preliminaries, still standing by the door, facing them. "We have been through the passes at Declan Reach and Aphalion and seen for ourselves that the protective walls are down. A handful of Elves went with us, and they know this, too. The outside world is open to us, and we are open to it. There are dangerous things out there, and some of them have already come into the valley, as the boy has told you. More of them are coming."

Then he told them of the Troll army under Taureq Siq and of Panterra's encounter of several days earlier, leaving out only the part about Prue's capture. He simply told them that the boy, once it was discovered who he was and where he was from, was released to come back and ask for a meeting between the Maturen and the leaders of those who lived in the valley. He added that the Drouj were migrating in search of a new home, and it might well be that Taureq Siq believed that this valley, with its mountain walls and natural defenses, would provide him with what he needed.

"I think they will try to force their way in if we refuse them entry. I think they intend to take the valley away from us. We have to prepare for this, without reliance on the barriers that have kept us safe, and we have to do so now."

Trow Ravenlock cocked an eyebrow at Panterra. "You told them where we were, Pan? You gave them that information willingly?"

The boy flushed at the rebuke. "I was a prisoner and under threat of being harmed. I didn't know their intentions at the time. I didn't even know that they were migrating."

"It isn't his fault; they would have discovered the truth easily enough without his help. You should be grateful that he had the presence of mind to deceive them as to your strength of numbers and preparedness." The Gray Man brushed the comments aside. "Concentrate your thinking on what's needed now. The three of you are the leaders of this community. The boy and I have chosen to come to you first because the danger to Glensk Wood is greatest. If the Trolls look to come into the valley, they will come through either Declan Reach or Aphalion. The Elves will set defenses at the latter; you should think of doing the same here."

"We have no army," Pogue Kray pointed out. "We have no skills or training at organized fighting. What can we do?"

"Whatever is needed." Sider Ament held his gaze. "Others will come to help you once they know of the danger, but while you wait for help to arrive you had better do what you can to prepare yourselves. Fortify the pass. Use your Trackers to show you how; they have training and skills. But if you just sit here . . ."

He trailed off and shook his head.

"You make your point." Skeal Eile looked around the room, measuring everyone. "If there were to be an objection to all of this, it should come from me. What Sider Ament says is a blasphemy on the teachings of the Children of the Hawk. But I say nothing against him.

It is clear he believes what he says and has seen what he claims. I was wrong to doubt him, and I am sorry for my mistake. We must rethink our beliefs—no one more than myself. I acknowledge this. I believe still that the Hawk will return when it is time, but until then he expects us to help ourselves. Gray Man, as Seraphic of this and many other villages I defer to you and to your best judgment in how this should be handled. I stand ready to help."

As if things couldn't possibly get any stranger than they already were, Panterra thought. Skeal Eile offering to help Sider Ament? Acknowledging that his teachings might be wrong? It was insane.

"My Trackers and I stand ready as well," Trow Ravenlock added, clearly spurred by the commitment from Skeal Eile. "Pogue, surely the council will rally behind us?"

For a long moment, Pogue Kray was silent, glowering at nothing in particular, his head lowered, his shoulders hunched. He looked to be a fighter in search of an opponent, not knowing where to find one. He seemed worn out, suddenly reduced in size in spite of his bulk. He shifted his gaze from one of them to the next, quick looks that refused to linger, as if he were dismayed.

"I don't know what to think," he said finally. "We have no proof of any of this. We have only the word of the Gray Man and this boy, who is already under a cloud of suspicion. How is it that we should believe either?"

"The boy has never lied to me before," Trow Ravenlock said quietly. "I doubt that he does so now. Tell us, Pan. Does the Gray Man speak for you, too, in this matter?"

Panterra nodded quickly. "He does. Everything he says is true. I was there; I saw it. Some of it, I told him myself."

Ravenlock looked back at Pogue Kray. "That's good enough for me. If the Seraphic and I are willing to look further into this, you should be willing to do so, too."

Pogue Kray shook his head, still doubtful.

"What have you got to lose?" Sider asked. "Send men up into the pass and see what you find there. If the protective barrier is down, you have your answer and can do what's needed about the rest of it. Doing nothing is what puts you at risk."

The big man looked at him, studied him carefully, but not in a good way, and then finally nodded. "I will look into it. Maybe you do speak the truth, although I question if that is possible."

Sider said nothing, but Panterra could tell that the antagonism between them had as much to do with Aislinne as it did with the news the Gray Man had brought. Their rivalry might be buried in the past, but Pogue Kray had unearthed it and set it out for everyone to view.

The Gray Man turned to Skeal Eile. "I want your word that neither you nor any of your followers will harm either Panterra or Aislinne for their part in all of this. If they have done anything to offend, put the blame on me. I encouraged it."

The Seraphic managed a shocked look. "I have already admitted my failings and promised that I would stand by you. That oath includes the boy and the woman. I give you my word that both are perfectly safe from any who serve or follow the teachings of the Children of the Hawk. I will see to it that my word is kept."

Something about the way he said it was immediately troubling to Panterra, much the way his attitude in all of this had been. But on the face of things, the oath seemed straightforward enough, and Sider apparently took it to be so, nodding in satisfaction.

"Very well," he said. He looked at the other two. "The boy and I will spend the night and leave in the morning for Calling Wells, Porterria, and Mountain View. We will warn the people there, their leaders and councils, and ask them to send you armed help. Two have small armies, as you know, which can stand with you against the Trolls. Will you send word to the small villages while I'm gone?"

"I will see that it is done," Trow Ravenlock said, apparently thinking to speak for all of them. "You needn't worry."

They probably *did* need to worry, Pan thought, but this was the best they could hope for.

Good nights were exchanged in an uneasy parting, and the boy followed the Gray Man out the door and into the dark.

* * *

THEY HAD GOTTEN ONLY AS FAR AS THE EDGE of the surrounding trees when Aislinne caught up with them. "A moment, Sider," she said, bringing him around to face her. "Panterra, stand over there and wait on us."

She pointed to one side, and the boy walked over obediently and turned his head away.

"What did you tell Pogue about running after me like this?" Sider asked at once.

She gave him a look. "Not everything that passes between us is about you, Sider. Pogue understands this, even if you don't. I told him that I needed to apologize to both Panterra and you for the way you were treated. I told him that this was in no way a threat to him and he should not take it so—that he and I are married and that whatever was between you and me was over and done with a long time ago. He accepts that."

Sider felt a sharp ache when he heard her speak those words, but he understood the need for them and simply nodded.

"What I want to say to you has nothing to do with an apology," she continued. "You require no apology; you knew what you were getting yourself into, as you mostly always do. But I want to remind you of what I said earlier. Leave Panterra alone. Let him live his life. Do not think to make him your apprentice. Don't try to take him away from Prue. He is not ready for that and neither is she. Find another apprentice or let the matter be until one comes along. I mean it, Sider. I am warning you."

He shook his head. "I wouldn't have thought that matters would ever come to this, Aislinne. Warnings are not required. We have always understood each other better than that. What's done is done between us, but I still read you like a Tracker can read a trail sign. I still know what's in your heart. Your caution is noted. Do not presume further."

She gave him a long, searching look. "I rather doubt you know as much as you think. I would guess you know almost nothing of me, even now. But I will take it that my warning is understood and you will act accordingly." She seemed about to say something more, then shook her head. "Good luck to you."

She started to turn away, then hesitated and looked back again. "Be careful, Sider. I do not trust Skeal Eile's word. You might have noticed that he did not give a promise of safety to you, only to Panterra and me. And I don't trust even that."

She walked away quickly, back toward the house, and he had to fight down the urge to go after her and claim her and take her away with him once and for all. But that ship had sailed a long time ago, and so he beckoned to Panterra and disappeared into the trees.

*   *   *

"SEE HOW THEY TALK WITH EACH OTHER?" Skeal Eile whispered. He was standing close to Pogue Kray, close enough to feel the heat of the other's anger as he watched his wife with the Gray Man. "See how they incline their heads so that they are almost touching?"

Trow Ravenlock was already gone, anxious to get back to his Trackers, already thinking ahead to what he must do on the morrow. But the Seraphic had lingered, sensing an opportunity.

"She has said it is nothing," Pogue Kray replied without conviction.

"She would say that, wouldn't she? I warned you, Pogue. I said she was duplicitous. I said she does not hold you as close as you believe she does. Now this."

The big man had not looked away once from the scene at the edge of the trees and did not do so now. "I believe her," he said.

"Your sense of loyalty is admirable." Skeal Eile let the moment pass, watching as the two former lovers parted and Aislinne started back toward the cottage. "Well, duty calls. Much needs doing yet this night."

He went out the door swiftly, moving down off the porch and turning away from the approaching woman, heading toward the center of the village. He had done as much as he could to sow the necessary seeds of distrust in Pogue Kray. The rest would have to wait. He could sense the big man weakening, growing doubtful, less confident of his wife's fidelity. He would continue to doubt her, even though he would hate himself for doing so, and would eventually cease to trust her altogether. The Seraphic would see to that. As her credibility with her husband waned, Aislinne Kray would become more vulnerable and ultimately cease to be a threat. All of which would permit him to pro-

ceed with his newly revised plan for domination of the valley's populace
without interference from either of the Krays.

But all that was for later. More pressing matters needed his attention just now.

He hurried on through the night, bypassing the main roadways in
favor of the more obscure paths, anxious not to be recognized. Soon he
was across the village and approaching its outskirts, the houses fewer
and population sparser. He was replaying in his mind Sider Ament's
words, considering how they impacted his plans, grateful that he had
known in advance that the Gray Man and the boy were coming, that
he had been prepared for them and able to think through carefully in
advance the nature of his response.

Every setback brought fresh opportunity. It was so here. He need
only make use of his skill and experience to take advantage of it.

When he was deep in the trees, he slowed, pacing himself, gathering his thoughts anew, wanting to be careful now, to be cautious. He
did not want to reveal what he was feeling—the excitement, the euphoria, and the intense sense of possibility that fed his ambitions. Not
to the boy, his killing tool.

He reached the dilapidated cottage, walked up to the sagging
porch, and stopped. The old man was nowhere in sight, and the cottage was as dark and silent as ever. Yet there was someone inside; there
was always someone inside. Even the old man, blind as he was, kept
watch in his own way and would know Skeal Eile was there.

But it was the boy who appeared this time, coming silently through
the doorway to greet him. "Your Eminence," he said, his smile bright
and expectant. "Did things go well for you?"

"You know of the meeting, then?"

The smile widened. "Tell me something of what was said, won't
you?"

Skeal Eile ignored the question. "It was helpful of you to advise me
of their coming. It makes it so much easier for me to forgive you for
your failure to carry out your assignment in Arborlon."

Bonnasaint shrugged. "Sometimes patience is the only alternative
to disaster. I did what I could. My disguise as an old woman got me
close to their quarters, but not to them. They were away from the city

when I arrived and remained gone for several days. When the boy returned, he was alone. The girl never did reappear. The boy was always in the company of others, including the King of the Elves. He stayed but one night, and then he was gone again. An opportunity that would have allowed me to perform my special services never presented itself. My apologies, again, if you are displeased."

Smooth and diffident, as always. Skeal Eile inclined his head. "I am in no way displeased. Matters have taken an unexpected turn, one that makes it wiser to let the boy and the girl live. They will cause no further trouble. The failure of the protective walls and the appearance of this Troll army require that I take a fresh approach. The Children of the Hawk are threatened, but in being threatened they are also offered an unexpected chance to enhance their standing and thereby my own among the citizens of the valley. It requires only a few nudges and a little luck for this to happen."

"You are ever vigilant in finding both," Bonnasaint observed, arching a perfectly formed eyebrow. "What is my role in advancing your special interests, Eminence?"

"My interests and yours run roughly parallel, Bonnasaint." He gave the youth a broad smile. "In the sense that I still have people who are obstacles to my efforts and you still have skills for removing such obstacles, nothing has changed. I still require you."

Bonnasaint executed a perfect bow, a graceful sweeping motion of one arm together with a downward cant of his slender body, an act of deference that could not be mistaken. "I am yours to command."

"Then listen carefully. The Gray Man and the boy travel south from Glensk Wood to the larger villages to enlist support for our own citizens. They do my work for me, although they do not realize it. They set the stage for my ascension as leader of all the peoples of the valley. The Races will be persuaded to stand with me when it matters, although ultimately it will be for purposes of my own. Do you see?"

The boy shrugged. "You seek to increase your hold over them?"

Skeal Eile smiled indulgently. Bonnasaint knew just enough to appreciate the opportunities, but cared nothing for the reasons. It was one of his best qualities. "The teachings of the Children of the Hawk are the way and the life. No other considerations or causes must be allowed to diminish those teachings or my own stature as leader of the sect. Simple enough."

"As you say," the other acknowledged. "It is an honor to serve you, a privilege."

"It is your calling, Bonnasaint. It is your destiny."

The other inclined his smooth, boyish face. "What is it you require of me this time, Your Eminence?"

"A great sacrifice, Bonnasaint. A great risk that might cost you your life if you are the least bit careless. For I intend to give you a challenge that no other would even dare consider. Does the idea suit you?"

There was a momentary pause as the boy regarded him. From within the cottage, the soft cackle of the old man wafted through the silence. Listening, of course. Always watching over his talented son. "Father," the boy said, an admonishing edge to the word. He kept his eyes fixed on Skeal Eile, and the latter could tell that the hesitation was born not of uncertainty, but of a desire to savor the moment.

"The idea suits me perfectly," he replied. "What is it you wish me to do?"

"To come with me on a journey of our own, the kind you best prefer."

Bonnasaint smiled. "Tell me more, Eminence."

The Seraphic bent close.

22

PHRYNE AMARANTYNE WAS IN SUCH DISFAVOR WITH her father that she was forbidden to leave the city for any reason, assigned instead to work with Isoeld in caring for the sick and injured. Phryne tried reasoning with him, but he talked right over her attempts at an explanation, fixated on his belief that she had not only disobeyed him but lied to him, as well. She thought his conclusions unfair and wrong, but he was having none of it. Her punishment was decided. She was confined to the city for as long as he decided she needed to be confined. When she asked how long that might be, he told her he would let her know.

With that, things quickly spiraled out of control. Her patience exhausted and her back well and truly up, Phryne lost her temper completely. She called her father pigheaded and obtuse. She called him other things, too, much worse things that came out of her mouth in the heat of a shouting match that brought retainers running. They arrived just in time to witness her father break a vase that had been given to him by her mother, sweeping it aside from its resting place on his desk in a wild gesture that was meant to emphasize the extent of his rage.

After that, it was pretty much over. She was sent to her room and told to stay there until she could conduct herself in a civil manner, and she told him that he should stay right where he was in his office until he could do the same. She stormed out, flinging final threats back at him in response to his own threats, and by the end of the day the tale of their confrontation had grown to epic proportions and was being recounted with imaginative embellishments throughout the city.

By the following morning, both Phryne and her father were speaking again, albeit without warmth or much eye contact.

Phryne was not unhappy to be working with Arborlon's healers, an undertaking she had engaged in on her own over the years, and she was rather pleased to be working with her stepmother, hoping that this might present a fresh opportunity to strengthen their relationship. She had all but decided that she had been wrong about Isoeld's infidelity and wanted to make amends. Here was the perfect opportunity, a chance to be with her for more than a few minutes at a time, working side by side in a shared effort to bring a little comfort and relief to those less fortunate. Doing so would allow them to know each other better and to find common ground that transcended Isoeld's marriage to her father.

But right away she noticed that her stepmother seemed less than pleased about her presence. It wasn't anything overt in her behavior or comments; on the contrary, she seemed to want to make Phryne feel welcome. It was mostly in her lack of enthusiasm and frequent periods of distraction. Phryne supposed these might be explained by the need for each of them to concentrate on the care each patient required. But the feeling persisted that something about having to share this time with Phryne was aggravating her. Something about her stepdaughter was nagging at her underneath all the pleasant words and friendly smiles.

Phryne wasn't sure what was going on, but she resolved to talk with Isoeld about it before the week was out in an effort to close this fresh breach that had opened between them. If that failed, she told herself, she might even choose to speak to her father about it, asking his advice on what to do.

But before she had a chance to act on this, she received a message from her grandmother summoning her for tea and conversation.

When it came to her grandmother it was never an *invitation*, it was always a *summoning*. Mistral Belloruus was her mother's mother, a formidable woman in her day, never a Queen herself, but the scion of a family of Kings and Queens reaching all the way back into the time before the Elves had uprooted and come to the valley. She had never approved of her daughter's marriage to Oparion Amarantyne, his crown and his impressive family history notwithstanding. She had not attended the wedding and not come into the palace or sat in the Council or attended official functions since. In point of fact, Phryne could not remember when she had last heard of her grandmother even leaving her home. Certainly she had never seen it happen herself.

Nor had Phryne gone to visit her grandmother or been invited—or summoned—to do so since the remarriage. It was as if their family ties had been so thoroughly severed that there was no point in even considering an effort at rebinding them. She accepted that she was as much to blame for this as her grandmother, since she had made virtually no effort to correct the situation, but whenever she had thought of trying to do so she had always come up with an excuse for putting it off to another time.

Now, it appeared, that other time was here.

The message was delivered as such messages always were—by one of the oldsters who still clustered about Mistral Belloruus like suitors. All of them were men of dubious origins and even more dubious purpose. Everything they did seemed to revolve around her grandmother. Phryne seldom saw any of them except when they were delivering her grandmother's messages. Such messages were frequent and always couched as admonitions to which she was advised to pay heed. They arrived at odd times and never included even a suggestion that a visit might be nice. But the oldsters were the same, some four or five of them in all—she could never remember which—and the messages were always handwritten on stationery inscribed with her grandmother's name.

This one was no different:

To Phryne Amarantyne:
Please attend on me this midday at my home.
Come alone. Give notice to no one of this meeting.
Be discreet. Be prompt.
Mistral Belloruus

She did not use exclamation points, but she might as well have. Phryne could practically hear the emphasis her voice would have put on her words had she been present to speak them. The oldster conveying the message stayed long enough to be sure that Phryne had read it through and then, without waiting for a reply, he departed. Apparently it was assumed that once she knew what was required, she would act appropriately.

Phryne dawdled a bit that morning, trying out various scenarios for what she imagined might take place at this unexpected meeting. The one that made the most sense revolved around her grandmother's curiosity over why she was working with Isoeld. Mistral Belloruus knew well enough that Phryne did not care for her stepmother, and that there was no good reason evident that she would suddenly agree to work with her. Given this sudden change of heart, her grandmother might have deduced that something important had happened.

Or maybe she had simply decided it was time for her granddaughter to visit her.

Or maybe anything.

Phryne decided to dress for the occasion, choosing feminine, loose-fitting clothes of which she knew her grandmother would approve. She picked flowers from the garden, arranged them in a basket, added fresh apples, and with only minutes to spare set out.

It was a short walk down a main road diverging off into smaller byways, then into worn paths, and finally into trails that wound through the forest trees until they disappeared and you couldn't find your way unless you knew exactly where you were going. Her grandmother did not encourage visitors of any sort, limiting such to those with whom she was familiar. In most cases, even those weren't welcome without having either received a prior invitation or provided acceptable notice of an intended visit.

Her grandmother lived in a large cottage east and south of the main city in woods dedicated to her personal usage and jealously guarded against encroachment. Phryne wasn't sure who did the guarding, since all she had ever seen back there were the oldsters, but she had a feeling that it wouldn't be wise to try to find out. It was rumored that Mistral Belloruus had use of magic. Since Phryne hadn't visited for months, she couldn't really know if anyone was doing the guarding these days. It had been enough to know that her feisty grandmother was alive and well and still dispensing unsolicited advice to her granddaughter.

Still, she felt a certain pleasure in making this visit, knowing that by the time she left she not only would have made some sort of amends for her failure to visit earlier but also would be able to reassure herself that all was well with her grandmother.

She had not told her father where she was going. She had not told anyone, adhering to the admonition contained in her grandmother's message. But afterward, she would tell her father, because even if he wouldn't admit it, speaking only now and again of Mistral Belloruus, he cared about her and worried that they had become so alienated.

Phryne walked up to the porch of the cottage, finding one of the oldsters sitting in a rocker by the door, aged eyes fixed on her as she approached. She couldn't remember his name, although she had known it once. He was small and hunched over and wizened to the point of being dried out completely. His head inclined as she climbed the steps, and he whispered the word "Princess" by way of greeting. She inclined her head in response and walked past him through the open cottage door.

Inside, the rooms were gray and shadowy, curtains closed over windows, shutters canted against the sun, the whole of the interior as still and airless as a crypt. If felt to Phryne as if her grandmother might be trying to acclimate herself to being dead, but that was an unkind thought and she quickly dismissed it.

"Grandmother?" she called out.

"Bedroom!" her grandmother's voice came back, much too strong and abrupt for anyone thinking about dying.

Phryne walked down the hallway and past several rooms to the very back of the house and the chamber in which her grandmother slept. She remembered everything about the house, even though she had not visited for so long, the details familiar enough that she might have left only a day or so earlier. Ancient tapestries and paintings hung from the walls, much of it her grandmother's work. Furniture gleamed with fresh polish, and colorful throws were draped over chair backs and arms. Crystal glittered from a cabinet here; china plates and saucers with intricate patterns rested upright in small grooves notched in the shelves of a hutch there.

A cat wandered by. Crazy Orange, her grandmother called it, a tiger with white feet and a white blaze on its forehead. It never looked at her, on its way to finding better things to do, Phryne supposed.

She found her grandmother propped up in bed, dressed in her good clothes, hands folded neatly in her lap. Her gray hair was pinned up, the wrinkles in her skin powdered over, and her lips painted. She looked younger than her years. Except for lacking a smile, she would have been almost pretty.

"You look very nice, girl," she declared. "I think the colors suit you. Sit over there." She motioned to a chair next to the bed.

Phryne sat. "Are you well, Grandmother?"

"As opposed to what? I am ninety-five years old, well into middle age and looking at the downside of my life. But yes. I am well enough. And you? How are you? Other than lacking a certain respect for your elderly grandmother, a failing that apparently requires no visible remorse for your failure to visit me, how are you?"

Phryne flushed. "I deserve that. I apologize. I should have come before, but I always seem to become distracted when thinking to do so. It is not an attractive habit."

"No, it certainly isn't. But then you make up for it in other ways, so why don't we let all that go. The past is the past, over and done with. Most of it, anyway. How is your father?"

"Well." She hesitated. "He is preoccupied at present with matters of court."

Mistral Belloruus laughed. "Is that how you would put it? 'Preoccupied with matters of court'? You need to work on your language skills, Phryne. Your father is facing the most dangerous moment of the past five hundred years. The valley's protective walls have collapsed, the passes are open, monsters of a sort we haven't seen since we came here have appeared from the outside world, and a Troll army threatens. I should hope he is—if nothing better—*preoccupied!*"

Phryne stared. "How do you know all this? It hasn't been told to anyone. Not even the Elven Hunters who travel north to Aphalion Pass to build the barricades know as much. Only Father and the High Council know. How is it that you've found out?"

Her grandmother smiled and shook her head in what Phryne took to be an expression of disbelief. "You know so little about me, girl. After all these years, still so little. I have eyes and ears everywhere; that's how I know. An old woman doesn't learn much without them. Mine are among the sharpest and most dependable. Remember that when you think of misbehaving again. Some tea, perhaps, before we speak further? Farsimmon! Bring tea, if you please. Even if you don't please, bring it anyway."

Nothing more was said until the old man from the front porch appeared bearing a silver tray with tea service. Solemnly, he poured cups for each of them, bowed to each, and departed.

"A sweet man," Mistral offered when he was out of hearing. "Enamored of me from the moment he laid eyes on me. He never got over the fact that I chose another over him. But now here he is, all these years later."

Phryne took the flowers from the basket she had carried in and handed them to her grandmother, who beamed with obvious pleasure as she cradled them in her arms. Beautiful, she pronounced them. Phryne found a vase, helped her grandmother arrange the flowers, added water from a pitcher, and set the vase on a bedside table.

She reseated herself. "You should be sitting outside, Grandmother. The air is warm and sweet. It's a nice day to be in the sun."

"I imagine it is. But it's better that we keep this conversation to ourselves." The old woman set down her teacup and looked at Phryne. "I mentioned your misbehavior a moment ago, and you didn't blink an eye. Did you hear me?"

Phryne nodded. "I heard."

"You set out with the Orullian brothers and two outlanders from a village south of Aphalion Pass, ostensibly on a tracking exercise, but actually to discover if what you had been told by Sider Ament about the collapse of the protective wall was true. While there, you encouraged your companions to leave the protection of the pass to go out into the world beyond, then encouraged the boy and the girl who were guests to investigate a campsite, which in turn got them captured by Lizards. Excuse me, Trolls—not Lizards. You got the boy back—or rather, he got himself back—but the girl is still a prisoner. That is why your father is barely speaking to you and you are confined to the city. Does that sum things up?"

Phryne started to offer an explanation, but thought better of it and simply nodded.

Her grandmother shook her head and folded her hands in her lap. "I expect better things of you than this, Phryne. Using your status as an Elven Princess, your father's only child, to gain traction over others, especially guests, is unacceptable. Yours must always be the voice of reason and propriety, not the voice of impetuous and foolish impulse. You are a girl becoming a woman, but you are not there yet. You will get there more quickly and smoothly if you question your choices before acting on them."

"Grandmother . . ."

"Please don't try to contradict me or offer excuses. That would make me very sad. You've made a mistake; learn from it. Your father needs you to do that. He relies on you to be his daughter, not some wild child. Your mother would have taught you better and done so earlier, but we've lost her. You may have noticed that I have taken it upon myself to fill her considerable shoes. Your father does much less than he needs to when it comes to your upbringing. He does little enough about many things, as it happens. So I am telling you now. Pay attention to yourself. It is important. These are dangerous times, and they may well become much more dangerous before things settle down again. You must act accordingly."

Phryne took a deep breath, fighting down her embarrassment and irritation at being lectured. "I understand, Grandmother."

"What you mostly understand is how angry you feel when I talk to you like this. But there is no one else who will do so, and I think that someone must." A tight smile flitted across her thin lips. "Enough of this. Let's leave things where they lie for now. Tell me about your work with the healers. Was this your father's idea?"

Phryne nodded. "He says I must work there until he decides he is through being angry with me. I think maybe he put me there so that Isoeld can keep an eye on me. She seems uneasy enough about my being there."

"You don't like her much, do you?"

"Not much." Phryne hesitated. "But maybe I'm not being fair. She spoke to me the other day—confronted me, is more like it. She said I was being unfair and should think better of her. She said all the rumors were lies and she loves my father." She shook her head doubtfully. "I think maybe I *am* being unfair."

"Do you?" her grandmother asked, cocking an eyebrow. "Poor little Isoeld, the dutiful wife and caregiver, so misunderstood, so slandered. I never liked that woman, and I never will. Would you like to know why, Phryne? You won't like what I have to tell you, but at least you will know the truth of things."

"I don't already know the truth?"

"Not enough of it. I've waited too long as it is to speak to you of this, but I kept thinking you would come to see me on your own. Besides, it didn't matter, so long as you were unaffected. I think that might be about to change. So I called you here to set you straight. Doing so may point out, as well, why you need to be more steady in your behavior."

Phryne nodded. "All right. Tell me, then."

Her grandmother took a moment to measure her, looking for something that would reveal her. Not finding it, she shrugged and said, "You should trust your instincts more and your heart less. You might want to think better of your father's new wife, but you would be making a mistake by doing so. She is everything the rumors suggest and worse. She has taken the first minister as a lover, and there were others before him. She connives against and manipulates your father, and she has done so from the moment she met him and saw that he was smitten with her. She might be a simple baker's daughter from a tiny village, but her ambitions are in no way limited by the circumstances of her birth."

Phryne exhaled sharply, shocked and appalled, but also oddly satisfied to discover that she had been right all along. All those pretty words and protestations of innocence—nothing but lies. "But how do you know this, Grandmother?"

"My spies tell me. Old people can go anywhere and be barely noticed. It is both a curse and an advantage. The gentlemen who wait upon me have given me an all-too-thorough report of your stepmother's activities. They are many and various and most do nothing to honor her marriage vows or support your father. You mentioned that she seemed uncomfortable in your presence at work? That has nothing to do with spying on you for your father. It has everything to do with the inconvenience you cause her. By being so near and so attentive, you prevent her from slipping away to her secret meetings with Teonette. You hinder her efforts to be with him, girl. The sooner you are gone back to your old life, forgiven by your father, the sooner she can resume her cheating. Won't you both be happy then!"

Phryne felt her face darken. "If this is true . . ."

She trailed off as her grandmother raised one aged hand. "When you leave, drop by the first minister's chambers on some pretext or other. See what happens."

"Because I am gone to visit you, she goes to visit him?"

"Just do as I say. Reach your own conclusions afterward." She lowered her hand and closed her eyes. "I have to rest now. So you can do what I suggest without further delay. But listen. We are not finished, Phryne. There is something more. Something rather important. I will need to see you again. Can you come back for another visit? Without telling anyone, even your father. I wouldn't tell him about your visit today, either. If you were thinking of doing so, which I expect you were. What you choose to say to your stepmother is your own choice. But leave your father out of it."

Phryne stood up, walked over to her grandmother, bent down and kissed one cool cheek. "I should have come sooner. I am sorry about that. I didn't like hearing all the things you told me, but I guess I needed to. I promise to think about everything you said. I do."

Mistral Belloruus took Phryne's hands in her own. "You are your mother's daughter and my granddaughter, and you are everything we could have asked for. Maturity will come. Wisdom will be gained. You are a special child, and I love you."

When Phryne passed back through the doorway leading out of the cottage and went down the porch steps, she kept her head lowered so that the old man sitting in the chair, rocking slowly, would not see her tears.

■ ■ ■

PHRYNE WASTED NO TIME after leaving her grandmother, making her way back through the woods and along the paths and roadways toward the Council hall and the chambers of the ministers. She could not stop thinking about what her grandmother had told her of Isoeld. All the anger and disdain she had felt earlier for her stepmother, all that she had thought she might be able to let go of, surfaced anew, white-hot and razor-sharp. She had not wanted to believe any of the rumors; she had wanted to dismiss them as lies. When Isoeld had confronted her, she had felt shame and embarrassment at her suspicious behavior. She had wanted to be wrong.

Now what she wanted was something else entirely.

She detoured to the healing center long enough to confirm what she already suspected was true. Isoeld was not there. She had gone home early, fatigued and not feeling well. She worked so hard and cared so much for the sick and injured, the healer to whom Phryne spoke said in quiet praise. It was just too much for her. You can tell she is fragile.

Phryne kept her thoughts to herself and her mouth shut.

She entered the Council chambers and made her way down the hall past closed doorways to the offices of the first minister. When she arrived, she found those doors closed as well, but she put her ear to the door, listened to the silence, and then knocked anyway. Nothing. She waited a moment and knocked again, louder and more insistent. Again, nothing. She stood there, undecided for a few minutes longer, and then turned away. She felt an odd mix of disappointment and relief. Maybe her grandmother was wrong after all.

She left the Council hall and walked back across the grounds of the palace toward her home, pondering. She was almost there, approaching through the gardens, when she saw the door to the toolshed open and Isoeld appear. Carefully, Phryne took one step back behind the screen of a clematis trellis, where she stood perfectly still. Her stepmother glanced about, not seeing Phryne as she did so, and then closed the shed door and walked toward the house in a relaxed but purposeful fashion, brushing back her long blond hair.

Phryne waited where she was, unmoving.

Several minutes passed. Nothing happened. She waited some more. Then the door to the shed opened a second time, and the first minister stepped through. Phryne experienced a sudden, almost uncontrollable urge to scream out, to rid herself of the sudden rush of feelings. She wanted to fling herself on Teonette and choke the life out of him. She wanted to hurt him so badly he would beg for forgiveness.

But instead, she kept silent and waited until he was walking away, moving back toward the Council hall and the trellis behind which she hid, and when he was almost on top of her, she stepped in front of him.

"Good day, First Minister," she greeted him brightly.

Teonette, tall and handsome in a sharp sort of way, was visibly startled. His dark eyes fixed on her with mingled disbelief and shock. "Princess, ah . . . good day to you, as well." He took a steadying breath. "Have you been working in the garden?"

Trying to find out what she had seen. She gave him a smile. "No, I was just returning from a visit and stopped to admire the clematis. And you, First Minister? Admiring the flowers in our gardens?"

The tall man's smile was rigid and uncomfortable. "No, just picking up something from the house for your father. Some papers."

He did not offer to show them, and she did not ask to see them. What was the point? Instead, she nodded as if this were all perfectly understandable and started to turn away.

"Oh," she said suddenly, turning back. "You have something at the corner of your mouth. A smear of color. Are you bleeding?"

Teonette's hand flew to his mouth, rubbing quickly. But when he looked at his fingers, there was nothing there. Phryne smiled brightly when he looked back her. "I think you got it, First Minister. Good day to you."

And she sauntered away, humming to herself.

23

W HEN THE OLD MAN RETURNS, ONLY A WEEK
has passed, and yet to the boy it looks as if his mentor
has aged a lifetime. He is grayer than before, weary
around the eyes, and sad to the bone. The boy doesn't need to ask if the old
man's visit was successful. He can tell at once that it was not.

"He would not heed me," the old man tells him. "He barely listened
to my advice and did not give even the smallest indication that what I said
mattered. He smiled and changed the subject and without saying so dismissed me as surely as if I were no longer relevant."

The old man shakes his head. "He has gone too far inward in his mind.
He no longer sees the world as it is or even himself as he has become. He
no longer understands what it means to carry the staff. He has forgotten the
oath he took and the cause he embraced. He does not say so; he gives no
hint of this. But it is there in his distancing, in the small span of his attention, and in his look. I cannot reach him."

"What will happen now?" the boy asks.

The old man pauses, looking down at his hands and at the black staff
he carries. "Nothing we can prevent," he answers finally.

He says nothing more after that. The boy thinks to ask him of the details of what happened, but he knows the old man does not wish to speak of it. They go back to things the way they were before the old man left. The old man returns to teaching and mentoring, and the boy returns to his studies. The days pass as they once did, and life settles back to what it was.

Until, on a day so bright and clear it suggests that the boundaries of the valley no longer exist and the layers of mist and clouds and rain have dissipated forever, the bearer of the other black staff, the one who would not listen, comes to find them.

The boy and the old man are sitting on a hillside looking out over the valley, talking anew of the way that the power of the staff can alter the bearer's thinking, a subject that seems to be ever present in the thoughts of the boy's mentor these days. Power corrupts, and if not watched carefully, if not kept under control, it will come to dominate the user. This is the risk of wielding it; it is always a danger to the bearer. Caution is necessary, even in the smallest usages, because the power of the staff's magic is an elixir that will build within the body and break down all resistance. Tolerance is possible, but a ready welcoming of the feeling it generates is anathema. It may not seem that there is any danger, especially in times like these, when use of the power is so seldom required. But an understanding of what it means to invoke the staff's power will help keep the bearer safe and alive.

The old man finishes, looks off into the distance toward a forest down the hillside from where they have climbed, and gets to his feet.

"He is here," he says.

At first, the boy does not know who he means. But seconds later a figure emerges from the trees, a gaunt specter bearing a black staff, and there is no longer any question. The Elf has the look of a man returned from the dead, clothes ragged and dirty, features scratched and bruised, shoulders bent as if he bears the weight of his own tomb. The boy stares in disbelief for a moment, not quite able to grasp yet what this unexpected appearance means. But his mentor already knows, and he is advancing to meet the other man, his own staff held at port arms before him.

"Greetings, brother!" shouts the tattered Elf, his voice as ragged and worn as the rest of him. He seems casual and relaxed, an old friend come to visit. But the boy senses instinctively that this isn't so.

"I am not your brother," his mentor replies. "Don't call me that. Why are you here?"

"Because I've done what I said I would do? Surely you didn't think I was lying!"

The old man shakes his head slowly. "No, I never thought that. I hoped you might instead come to your senses. I even warned the King, as I told you I would. It wasn't enough, apparently. Why don't you stop where you are?"

He makes it a command, and the Elf stops. "Nothing you could have done would have been enough, brother. Warning the King only made it harder than it might have been otherwise. But this was a test I sought. I needed to see if I was strong enough, to discover if my power was great enough. I was, and it was. Dozens of dead Elves would attest to this if they could speak from whatever resting place they've found. They came at me in waves once their King was dead. They came at me with everything they had, but it wasn't enough to stop me. So here I am."

"Do you believe yourself strong enough to kill me, as well?"

"I've come to find out."

The boy goes cold at these words and immediately searches for a weapon. But he carries none. There is no need when he is with his mentor, who is a match for anything. Except, perhaps, this time. The boy rises, prepared to do whatever he can to help.

"Your pup would defend you, brother," the Elf says lightly, happily. He almost laughs. "I think I must kill him, as well. I wouldn't want him to come looking for me later, should he be rash enough to do so after I've finished with you. Revenge is such a tiresome business."

"If revenge is so tiresome, you must be weary, indeed," the old man says, shifting the black staff in his hands. "Why come searching for me, seeking my death, if revenge is all you expect to find?"

The Elf cocks his head and thinks on it a moment. "Revenge is not what I seek by killing you, brother. Peace of mind is what I seek. If you are gone and I alone remain, who is left to challenge me? I can be whatever I wish once you are dead. I can be leader of all the Races and reshape the world in whatever ways I see fit."

"You lie even to yourself." The old man's words are so soft they are almost inaudible. "You care nothing for peace of mind. You are here because I would not join you. You seek to make me suffer for refusing your offer.

I would not partner with you in your cause, and so now you would make me pay the price for my temerity."

The Elf's features tighten and his face undergoes a sudden transformation, changing from calm to tense, mirroring rage and frustration and despair all at once, emotions he has kept bottled up inside but now break free. He shifts the black staff in the same way the old man did only moments earlier.

"Shall we find out who shall be judged right and who wrong?" he asks. "Shall we settle this?"

The old man does not reply. "Stay where you are," he says over his shoulder to the boy, his voice soft enough that his enemy cannot hear his words. "Don't try to help me. Don't interfere."

The boy has been taught to obey the old man and not question his directives. But this time he does not think he can do so. He cannot sit by and let his mentor be killed if he can do anything to stop it. He does not like what he sees and hears in the voice of the Elf. He thinks that the old man is in danger. How can he ignore this?

The old man has turned back to face the Elf, who is advancing on him once more. "Do not do this," he says. "We are the last of our kind, the last who bear the staff. Think what—"

But the runes carved into the dark length of the other's weapon are already flaring to life with the power of the Word's magic, and abruptly white fire lances out at the old man. He blocks the strike with magic of his own, but the force of the attack knocks him back two steps. The Elf's laughter is high and shrill as he comes on, the magic preceding him in a steady stream, as if water jetting from a pump. There seems to be no end to it, its power undiminished by loss of either strength or determination in the bearer. The old man has taught the boy that usage of the magic in any single situation is finite, that the supply is not inexhaustible, that it must be expended judiciously. The strength and longevity of the Elf's attack seem to suggest otherwise.

The Elf screams suddenly, an explosion of sustained madness released in primal form, and the magic of his staff grows brighter and its force stronger. The old man is down on one knee, fighting to keep his balance while he fends off the killing attack. The boy, watching, begins to search the empty ground for anything at all that might help, any weapon that he can use.

His eyes settle on a rock that will just fit within the palm of his hand. He picks it up and starts forward.

"You are finished, brother!" the Elf shouts wildly as he sees the old man falter. "Your life is mine to take!"

The fire breaks through and begins to burn the old man. But the boy's mentor continues to fight back, and suddenly the killing fire falters—just a little, but enough that the boy notices. The old man struggles back to his feet, his staff erupting with white fire of its own, fire discharged in fits and starts that hammers into the Elf over and over. The Elf does not bother with defenses, his own attack commanding the whole of his attention. The fire from the old man's staff engulfs him. He screams in pain, but instead of falling under the withering assault, he rushes forward as the magic of his own staff reignites, slamming into the old man with crushing force.

The two stand within six feet of each other, the killing fires of each threatening to destroy the other.

Frantic with the need to do something, the boy draws back his arm and flings the rock in his hand. His aim is true; the rock strikes the Elf in the head, a blow that knocks him backward and for just a moment throws off his attack and leaves him exposed.

The boy's mentor doesn't hesitate. Seizing his opportunity, he uses his magic to hold the Elf fast, sets him ablaze from head to toe, chars him to the bone, and drops him to the ground a blackened husk from which small tendrils of smoke rise like early-morning vapor in the heat of the dawn's sun.

THE REVERIE LOST FOCUS and the memory faded. Panterra Qu, who was watching surreptitiously from where he had been gazing out the window toward the hills east of the castle, could tell. The thousand-yard stare shifted as Sider Ament looked down at the slow-burning fire in the old stone hearth of the reception chamber, and then glanced quickly at the boy. Pan pretended not to notice. The Gray Man preferred things that way. He did not like revealing too much of himself.

It was evening, the shadows lengthening with the sun's departure, the air cool and the breezes dropped off into stillness. The Gray Man and the boy were returning from their weeklong pilgrimage to the villages and towns south and east of Glensk Wood. The response to Sider's warnings had been much as expected. In some instances it was complete disbelief mixed with denial; in others, shock leading to vague promises of help. Most indicated that they would need to secure their own borders first, sending scouts into the passes south to determine if the walls had failed there, as well.

As if that would make a difference if the valley was already open to the north, Panterra thought darkly.

But Sider had warned him going in that help would not be given readily from any of these worthies. Their best chance for finding what was needed would be found where they were now, in the large, fortified town of Hold-Fast-Crossing where Hadrian Esselline ruled as King. An anomaly among the communities of Men, it was the only one that had embraced the Elven model of government by sovereignty. Esselline's direct bloodline could be traced back two centuries, and before then through any number of divergent bloodlines that embraced offshoots of various sorts. The leaders of Hold-Fast-Crossing had settled on choosing a King within the first ten years after the Hawk had brought the survivors of the Great Wars into the valley. They had already seen what they perceived to be the benefits— leadership that promised stability, strength, and organization. The first hints of threats from neighbors had already surfaced, and they were a smaller community than several others living close by. What they lacked in numbers, they would make up for in training and skill. A King would lead and an army would protect. It was a form of government that had worked for the Elves, so there was no reason it could not work for them.

Hadrian Esselline was the sort of King that justified this line of thinking. A seasoned veteran of skirmishes with his neighbors, a warrior and a statesman, he embodied all the best of what people expected in a ruler. Esselline was the strongest of the southern community leaders and the one to whom the others were most likely to look for direction—which was why Sider Ament was here. If Esselline were to agree to send soldiers to help defend the pass at Declan Reach, the other communities would be more inclined to do the same.

And if he did not agree . . .

But Sider pointedly refused any consideration of that possibility, and so Panterra did, too.

Coming to Esselline last was a calculated risk, Sider admitted, confiding in the boy the nature of his strategy. It could be argued that going to Hold-Fast-Crossing first made more sense since its influence among the southern towns and villages was strongest. But Sider believed they would get only one chance at this, and he wanted to come to Esselline without any other commitment in place, giving the King the opportunity to lead by example. The King had a vain side, a sense of pride in his stature, and Sider wanted to play off that in making his case. Esselline would be given a chance at assuming the pivotal role in this matter; to a measurable degree, Sider believed, this would influence his decision, whether he recognized it or not.

But time was slipping away, and whatever impact Esselline might have on the leaders of the other communities must be brought to bear quickly. Still, some things could not be rushed. Having arrived at Esselline's home and been placed in this room, which they had now occupied for the better part of two hours, the man and the boy could only wait patiently for the King's appearance.

It came in dramatic fashion, with Hadrian Esselline bursting through the doors unannounced, robes billowing out behind him, arms extended in greeting.

"Sider Ament!" he boomed out, his voice filling the room. He went to the other man and embraced him warmly. "Look at you! No grayer than the day we met, in spite of all those ugly rumors of your association with wraiths! Sorry to keep you waiting! Matters of state keep me constantly occupied and much less pleasantly so!"

Hadrian Esselline was a big man, tall and broad through the shoulders, a shock of dusky hair falling down about his shoulders, a beard of the same color, eyes as quick and bright and lethal as arrowheads. He was wearing all black with the blood-red crest of his family's coat of arms emblazoned on his chest. Everything about him was bigger than life and twice as real, and when he entered a room it seemed as if he took up all the available space.

"Thank you for agreeing to grant me an audience," Sider replied, gripping the other in return. "I know you are busy."

"Not as busy as you, from what my runners tell me." He glanced over at Panterra. "Who is this boy you've brought with you? Word is, you always travel alone. Don't tell me you've produced an issue?"

Panterra was mortified. He could feel the flush in his neck and cheeks. Sider was grinning. "No issue of mine, though I could do much worse. This is Panterra Qu; he's a Tracker from Glensk Wood and a good one. He was the first to discover what sort of creatures we might be forced to deal with once the mists had failed. He and a friend were tracking two of them when I caught up to them." He gave the King a look. "This boy was held captive by the Troll army that threatens us. He knows about them firsthand."

Esselline gave Pan an appraising look. "Then he needs to be part of our discussion, I think. Is it true, then? Have the mists receded and the protective wall collapsed? Let's sit while we talk of this. Take that chair by the boy. Tell me of the wall. I hear this is the message you have carried to some of the other communities."

"You heard correctly."

"Yet you didn't come to me first? You went elsewhere, to those of lesser stature?"

"Knowing they would turn me down. I wanted to make clear to you when we met how desperately your help is needed. Others equivocate and dither. But you will not, once you hear what I have to say. If you act, they will come around. We are all in the same boat on a very dangerous ocean, Hadrian. As that old saying goes, if we don't hang together, we shall all hang separately. That is what I need for you to believe."

"Oh, I believe it all right." The King nodded emphatically.

"Well, then? Do I have your promise of help?"

"Not so fast. There are other things to consider. Your plan is to keep the enemy out of the valley by bottling up the passes north and hoping the ones south remain undiscovered. I see problems with this. We might close him off from one entrance, but we cannot reasonably think the others won't be found. We might be better off to let the Trolls come in and fight them on our own ground."

"And lose how many of our people in the bargain?"

"Few. We take them all to the strongholds, like this one, and keep them safe until the battle is finished."

"Assuming the battle ends quickly, which I doubt. You haven't seen this army, Hadrian. I have. It's big and well armed. Too many for any of us separately and maybe all of us together. We need to fight it from behind walls and in places like Declan Reach and Aphalion where it cannot bring its full strength to bear. You are a brave man and a skilled fighter. But most in this valley aren't, not even within your own army. We haven't fought a real battle against a real adversary since our ancestors came here. It won't be easy."

Esselline studied him. "So you would trap them in the passes and do battle there? From behind walls? That sounds like a siege to me, Sider. How much longer would that take than a direct confrontation? Besides, you undervalue not only my army, but those of some of the other southern strongholds and the Elves, as well. They will account themselves well if brought to the moment."

"First, we do not simply fight them from behind walls in the passes. That is just where we begin." Panterra watched as Sider leaned forward, assuming an almost confrontational posture. "They will divide their forces to come after us, choosing to attack more than one of the passes. But I don't think they will take time to find the ones they don't know about before they attack. They are impatient and confident in their strength of numbers. They will attack what they know and scout out other choices while they do so. That gives us a chance to slip out of the valley and get around behind them. It gives us a chance to trap them where they cannot defend themselves as they are used to."

He paused. "I do not denigrate the fighting skills and heart of our people. But fighting is not our way of life as it is for these Trolls. You will have to take my word on this. And Panterra's. These Trolls are not like anything we have seen before."

Panterra straightened up as Esselline looked over at him. "What say you, boy? Does he speak the truth as you see it? Are these Trolls really so big and bad as he says?"

"Much worse," Pan answered without hesitating. "They are armored, and they have creatures called Skaith Hounds to track down anything that tries to elude them. And there are more than you think. Five thousand would be a low estimate."

"Yet you escaped them, did you not? Did you fight your way clear?"

Pan shook his head. "I was let go to come back here and arrange a meeting with the leaders of the peoples in this valley. It was a trick to find a way in, and I helped them make it work."

There was a long silence. "Well, you show courage in admitting this, Panterra. And we have all been tricked in ways that make us look foolish, myself included. Although not lately."

"The boy is still learning, but I think he is good at his studies," Sider Ament offered suddenly. "I would not have brought him along if I did not value his advice and appreciate his insight."

"That's good enough for me," Esselline said. He shifted his gaze back to the Gray Man. "You have settled on what needs doing, it appears. You seem to have thought it through carefully."

"As carefully as I can," the other replied. "Though I don't claim your ability when it comes to tactics. I need your help, Hadrian. I can't do enough to keep the enemy out by myself. Even with the northern villages and the Elves, we will be overrun. We need your army to aid us. We need everyone to stand together against this threat. Because, in all likelihood, it is only the first of many, now that the walls are down and we are exposed. We had better set a good example right away or we are likely finished."

Esselline nodded slowly. "It will be done, then. I'll dispatch a force to Declan Reach. I'll lead it myself. I will do what I can to bring the others with me, but I can't promise they will respond as you might like. They will want to make certain of the passes south, first. You know that."

"I do. But if you come and no one else does, we are still a hundred times better off than otherwise."

"Undoubtedly." Esselline smiled. "Are you happy now?"

Sider glanced at Panterra and winked. "Happy enough," he answered.

* * *

TWENTY-FOUR HOURS LATER, they were camped in a glen a day's journey south of Glensk Wood. Twilight had settled in and the last of the day's light was fading west as they went about preparing dinner.

Sider arranged deadwood in a pit, thinking back to his meeting with
Hadrian Esselline.

"Do you think any of them will come?" the boy asked suddenly, as
if reading his mind. "Besides Esselline?"

Sider nodded absently, still looking away. "A few will be influenced
by his decision; they might join him." He shrugged. "Hard to say,
though. Glensk Wood had better plan on defending its own boundaries."

He glanced at the boy, who acknowledged his words with a cursory
nod. "Seems they would want to do more. Why do they think we would
go to all the trouble of coming down there to warn them if it were not
as important as we say it is?"

Sider struck flint to stone, sparked the fire, blew gently on the tiny
flame until the wood was burning, then rose and joined the boy where
he was sitting. "It's not that simple," he said.

"Why not? It seems that simple to me."

He's so young, Sider thought, taking in the smooth face and strong
features. *Like I was when the old man came to me that first time. I didn't
know anything of the world, and this boy knows not much more for all that
he is a Tracker and has the skills of a survivalist. He still doesn't know how
life can turn you around and twist you about and do with you what it will.*

He folded his long, lean frame forward, looking down at his boots as
he spoke. "Not much that seems simple ever is—more so here than in
most cases, I might add. There are alliances, both public and secret, that
dominate the thinking of the leaders of Men and Elves alike. There are
antagonisms between families and towns that have not been forgotten
even after centuries, and these play a part, too. What on the surface
seems obvious and clear is mired in chains of details that are interlinked
and sometimes unbreakable."

He looked at the boy. "A danger from without threatens, a clear and
present danger, and the need is apparent to those of us who live apart
and can reason it through. But most don't live like you and I. They are
part of a larger community of family and friends and fellow citizens,
and a wide range of considerations governs their actions. They are much
more concerned about not doing the wrong thing than doing the right.
They take their time because they are afraid of making mistakes that
will undo them. As I said, it is complicated."

The boy nodded, brushing at his lank hair where it fell across his face. "I guess."

The Gray Man considered him. "How would you like to become someone who could make a difference in all of that?"

The boy blinked. "What do you mean? Make a difference how?"

"Place yourself in a position where you could speak to everyone about the things that need doing, that might have life-altering consequences for everyone, and see to it that the right choices are made. Would you be interested?"

"No one can do that. Not even you."

Sider Ament smiled. "Sometimes, I can. And sometimes is enough to keep me trying."

"But I'm not you. I'm just a Tracker."

"Not just a Tracker, Panterra. You are much more than that. You are special at what you do; you are gifted and skilled. I wasn't exaggerating when I told Esselline I had good reason for bringing you along with me. I haven't met another with your talent in all the time I've been walking the valley and warding its passes."

The boy looked uncertain. "Prue is more talented than I am."

"It might seem so, but she's not. And she is too young. She relies on you. You rely only on yourself. Yours are the greater skills. Even if you don't think so, it is true."

"Well, I don't see—" The boy stopped midsentence and stared at Sider. "What's the point of this conversation? What are you trying to say to me?"

"I am trying to tell you that I think you should be the next to bear this talisman." He lifted the black staff a few inches, drawing the boy's eyes to its rune-carved length. "I think you should become my apprentice and train with me to take my place when I am gone."

Panterra Qu smiled and almost laughed. Sider watched the laugh surface and then disappear as the boy suppressed it. "I don't want to carry the staff," the boy said quickly. "I just want to be a Tracker."

"You would be a Tracker still. You would keep your skills and use them often. But you would do much more, too. You would serve a higher cause than Trow Ravenlock and the people of Glensk Wood."

"No, that's enough for me. Besides, there's Prue. I have to look out for her."

Sider took a deep breath. There it was—the crux of the matter. He gave the boy a smile. "Yes, there's Prue. You consider her your best friend, don't you?"

"I do. You know that."

"Do you love her?"

He hesitated, caught off guard by the question. Perhaps no one had ever asked it. Perhaps he hadn't even considered it. He didn't seem to know what to say. "As I would a sister, yes," he replied finally.

"Nothing more?"

"Not as I think you mean."

"Does she love you?"

Again, the hesitation. "In the same way. As a brother."

"Then there is no difficulty in doing what I suggest. You do not have to stop loving each other as friends and siblings, and you can still be together as much as you choose. Nothing about bearing the black staff prevents this. But . . ."

He held up one hand, palm open toward the boy, as if to stop something he might be about to say. "But something else might prevent it. Not just if you become my successor and the next bearer of the staff, but even if you choose to remain a simple Tracker from Glensk Wood. What you had once envisioned for both of you is finished. That future is gone. It left with the collapse of the magic that warded the valley. It left when the doors opened to the outside world and our survival became a much more perilous undertaking."

The boy gave him a look, and he smiled in spite of himself. "I know how that sounds. But I don't say these things only because the protective wall is down and the passes are open. I say them because I met a man while I was outside the valley, and he told me what the world was like. He described it in detail, and it is not a place that will tolerate weakness or indecision. It is populated by dangerous creatures and infused with the residue of the poisons and the resultant mutations of the Great Wars. Those of the human Race that survived did so by being tougher and stronger than those who did not. The Trolls who besiege the valley are indicative of what's out there. But they are only one example."

He paused, letting the boy think it through. "It isn't hard to see what I am trying to say, is it? A battle for survival is at hand, and it will require more than any of us have considered giving in the past. Life will not be as simple or safe. It will be hard and dangerous, and it will demand a great deal of everyone. You already have a better chance of doing something about that than most. But that chance will increase a hundredfold if you accept my offer. Not only for you, but for those whom you choose to protect."

The boy was silent for a while longer, and then he shook his head doubtfully. "I don't know. I don't know if I can do that. I don't know if I want to."

Sider nodded. "I don't know, either. Neither of us will know until the moment I pass the staff to you. All we can do until then is to try to prepare you for what having the staff means. We can talk about it. We can examine it. You can ask what questions you would, and I can answer them as best I know. This will give you a chance to see if it might be something that interests you—not in the abstract, but in the practice of it. I will try to convince you that you are the right man to bear it. But I will not force you to take it, and I will not expect you to force yourself. It has to be voluntary. You have to feel the need."

The boy shook his head again. "I don't like the idea of it. I don't want to be responsible for so many people."

"How is that different from what you do now? You act as surrogate to an entire village and by proxy for the entire valley in most cases. They depend on your Tracker's skills to ward them, to keep them safe, to see them right. If you fail, many times your own number will suffer as a consequence. Many more lives are in your hands now than ever before because of the danger of an invasion. You cannot pretend that taking up the staff will in any measurable way increase the nature of your responsibility. What it will do is give you a better chance of doing your job as it needs doing."

"Your argument suggests that as a Tracker I alone am responsible for everyone." The boy was standing his ground, thinking it through. "There are other Trackers, equally qualified, equally responsible, and they share my burden. If I become the next bearer of the black staff, I will stand alone."

"You will," Sider agreed. "But how disagreeable do you find that?

Do you not see yourself as standing alone even now? Isn't that how you approach what you do—by telling yourself the responsibility is yours and it doesn't matter if there are others who could do it equally well or who might be called upon to share your burden? You don't think of it that way, do you? You think of it as yours and yours alone."

He could see that he was right. He could see it in the boy's eyes and feel it in his hesitation. "But it still isn't the same," the boy persisted.

Sider let the answer hang a moment, and then he put a hand on the boy's shoulder and squeezed softly. "Why don't we leave it here for now? We can talk about it again later. You can think about what I've said. We should eat something and then sleep."

The boy nodded but said nothing. Sider could tell he was already thinking it through.

THEY PREPARED THEIR DINNER, a rabbit cooked over a fire, some day-old bread they had been given before leaving Hold-Fast-Crossing, some root vegetables foraged and sliced to cook with the meat, and cups of cold springwater. They ate in silence as the last of the light faded from the sky and the stars began to come out.

"Tomorrow, we will reach Glensk Wood," Sider said once the meal was done and they were sitting by the dying fire, listening to the sounds of the night as it closed about them. "I will leave you there and go on alone. I won't be back for several days."

The boy was silent for several moments. "Is this because I won't agree to be your apprentice?"

Sider almost smiled, but managed with some effort to keep a straight face. "It has nothing to do with that. I am going out of the valley to find Prue and bring her back."

The boy looked over quickly. "Then you have to take me with you. I can help."

"Not this time. I know you want to come with me, but I will have a better chance of saving her if I go alone."

The boy shook his head. "It doesn't seem right letting you do this when I was the one who left her. I should be the one to go back."

Sider leaned forward, wrapped his arms around his knees, and looked off into the trees. "You have to trust me on this. You have to defer to my judgment."

He said it kindly, keeping his voice deliberately soft, but he could see the boy wince anyway. He was sorry he had to tell him like this, but time was running out for all of them, especially the girl. Taureq Siq would find out soon enough that no meeting between himself and the leaders of the valley was going to take place. When that happened, he would have no further use for Prue Liss and likely dispose of her quickly.

"What do you want me to do while you're gone?" the boy asked finally.

This was the right question to ask, Sider thought. "I want you to go to Aislinne and tell her what's happened so that she can pass the information along to Pogue. She must let him know that help is on the way. In the meantime, be certain that the pass at Declan Reach is being fortified against an attack. I expect it to come at Aphalion, but we can't take that chance."

The boy nodded. "Will you come back through Declan Reach when you find her?"

"I will."

"Then I'll be waiting for you there. I'll work on the defenses with the others while I do."

There was a momentary pause as the two stared at each other, neither knowing what more to say. "Don't worry," the Gray Man said finally. "I'll bring her back safe and sound."

The boy did not respond, but in the following silence Sider Ament could all but hear the words he was thinking.

You'd better.

24

JUST TWO DAYS AFTER VISITING HER GRANDMOTHER, Phryne was summoned before her father and told that the restrictions placed upon her were being lifted. Her father did not seem either happy or unhappy about this decision, simply resigned. His explanation, however, said everything that needed saying.

"Your grandmother seems to feel that you've been punished enough," he began after sitting her down across from him. "She has sent me repeated notes to that effect. She wants me to put you back to work in a more useful way; she wants me to give you a fresh chance to demonstrate your sense of responsibility."

He paused. "I agree with her thinking, which is saying something. Mistral Belloruus hasn't exactly endeared herself to me over these past few years. She would have me be a widower in mourning for your mother until I die, and even your mother, could she communicate as much, would disagree with her. Life is for the living, and the living have an obligation to carry on."

He paused again, suddenly uncomfortable with what he had said.

"Not that I didn't love your mother more than I will ever love any other woman, Phryne. No one will ever replace her in my heart. You might think otherwise, but that's how it is."

She did think otherwise, but she was willing to give him the benefit of the doubt. She loved him enough for that.

"So I am giving you back your old life, free of any restrictions," he continued. "With the understanding that you will not violate my trust and will exercise good judgment when temptation suggests you do otherwise. No running off on some wild impulse, no throwing caution to the winds to satisfy curiosity, and no going outside the valley for any reason whatsoever. Are we agreed?"

She nodded. "We are."

"This is important, given what I am about to ask of you. Are you certain you can live by these rules?"

"I can live by them."

"Good. Then we will put the last two weeks behind us, and hope that Sider Ament finds a way to rescue that unfortunate Glensk Wood girl from the Trolls."

She cringed inwardly as he said it, but kept her face expressionless.

"As I said, I have something I want you to do. No more work at the healing center for now. Let's leave that to Isoeld."

She cringed anew. That and a few other things she couldn't bring herself to mention.

"I want you to go back up to Aphalion Pass," he finished.

She started, surprised. "But I thought you just got through saying you didn't want me to—"

"Go out of the valley," he finished. "That is exactly right. I don't. What I want you to do is go up to the pass and find out how things are going. Talk to the Orullians and ask them what they think. They're both up there, helping with the barricades. Take a good look around. I need an independent judgment of matters, and you are the most independent-minded person I know. Which is to say, among other things, that you are good at seeing what others miss because you keep an open mind."

He saw the look of uncertainty that crossed her face. "I mean all this as a compliment, Phryne. You won't tell me something just to try to please me. And the truth is what I need. How is the work coming? How strong do the defenses look? What is the attitude of the Elves working on the barriers, now that they know the protective wall is down? That's what I want here. The truth of things. Will you go?"

She rose, walked over to him, bent down and kissed his cheek. "Of course I'll go. Thank you for trusting me to do this."

"Who do I trust, if not you and Isoeld?" he said.

She bit off the reply that was on the tip of her tongue and listened to the rest of his explanation. One of the conditions of her going was that Elven Hunters acting as escorts and bodyguards would accompany her. She agreed without argument; she understood why her father would think it was too dangerous for her to make the journey alone. She was somewhat mollified when he added that she would be allowed to choose their route both coming and going so long as her escort did not think it presented any danger. She would make her own conclusions and deliver her own report when she returned. She was to take no more than three days to do this.

"This is all the time I can give you," he finished. "The deadline for this meeting with the Trolls expires in eight. I will need the balance of that time to muster and dispatch a force adequate to hold the passes. I will have to tell our people something soon. I can't put it off any longer, much as I might like. Time slips away from us, Phryne."

She wouldn't disagree, and since it didn't do any good just talking about it, she left things where they were and went off to pack. Shoving clothes and personals into her backpack, she had a momentary twinge of regret that her companions of the last trip would not be going with her, especially Panterra Qu, about whom she had not stopped thinking since he had departed Arborlon more than a week ago with the Gray Man. Certainly thinking about Pan was preferable to thinking about her stepmother, but her thoughts were generated less as a matter of choice than of fascination. Even now, she remained intrigued with this boy, and although she had tried repeatedly she could not explain it.

She sighed, pondering on it anew as she stood there in her bedchamber, staring at her backpack. Some of her odd attraction to Panterra had to do with his unavailability, she knew. He was human, she was

Elven, and the two did not mix when you were a member of the royal family. He was unavailable to her, and that made him desirable. Some of it had to do with the singular nature of his profession, how remote he kept himself from the rest of the world, how isolated he was. How he could do what he did and be happy, living on his own with no one to talk to but Prue Liss, separated from the rest of his people, immersed in reading sign and interpreting the behavior of nature's creatures.

She knew plenty of Elven Trackers, understood their lives and their need to live free. She had talked with some and listened to their explanations. But Panterra Qu was different, and she could not explain how. Something in the way he viewed the world. Something in the way he spoke and moved. Something in the Tracker part of him that made her feel he could manage in any given situation—which was part of why she had been so quick to cajole him into investigating the campfire that had led to Prue Liss's captivity.

Something in the way he looked at her.

She stopped suddenly, just at the end of closing up her backpack and preparing to set out, struck by a shocking possibility.

Was she in love with this boy? Was that what this was?

She rolled her eyes at the very idea of it and went out the door and down the walkway to the quarters that housed the Elven Hunters. Once there, she inquired after her escort and found that they had assigned Rendelen and Dash to go with her, two who had accompanied her on previous outings in the valley. The former was a veteran, small and tough and smart. The latter was younger, bigger and full of good cheer. They greeted her with friendly waves, their packs already in place, ready to leave.

The morning had not yet reached midday when they set out for Aphalion Pass.

As they walked to the edge of the bluff and started down the Elfitch, she was surprised to find Arik Sarn coming up. The Troll was carrying writing instruments and paper, his head lowered, his mind elsewhere. He did not see her until he was almost on top of her, and when he did he was visibly startled.

"Princess," he greeted in his guttural voice, bowing deeply.

Too deeply to suit her. She still didn't like him. But it didn't much matter because she hadn't seen him once in the time he had been there. Until now, of course.

"Good morning to you," she said in reply. "Taking a walk?"

"Just to the ramp's end and back. I've come from your gardens. We have no such flowers where I live."

"They are beautiful," she agreed. "The gardeners work very hard to keep them so." She glanced at the notebook. "Writing something down about those flowers?"

"Drawing them," he said. He showed her several pages of very good sketchings of early-spring flowers. He smiled. "Helps me pass the time. We don't have these plants outside."

She found it surprising that he liked to draw flowers, but who could tell about Trolls? She left him there with a smile of encouragement and a wave of her hand. She could feel him studying her back.

With Dash and Rendelen as companions, she walked through the remainder of the day at a steady pace, passing out of Arborlon and down through the Eldemeres, making her way across the lowlands to the forest that lay just at the base of the mountains leading up to the pass. The day was cloudy and gray, but the air was warm and the ground soft and dry. As nightfall approached, the trio made camp and ate dinner, and then afterward sat around a small fire drinking ale and telling stories. Phryne might have been born to a privileged and high-ranking family with expectations for her future, but she had not been raised that way. In fact, she had pretty much spurned all of it since she was very young, insisting that she be allowed to spend her time with whomever she wished—which in her case meant with the rough-and-tumble boys and girls being raised as Elven Hunters and Trackers. Her mother and father, seeing how set she was on choosing her own playmates and lifestyle, gave up on trying to manage that aspect of her life early on, settling instead for teaching her what they thought important about deportment and manners and court life in the privacy of her own home. She endured their lessons stoically and structured her life pretty much as she chose.

That became more the case than ever after the death of her mother, when her father, alone now and preoccupied, let her go her own way. Had he known half of the things she did during that time period, even a quarter of the escapades in which she had engaged or the dangerous situations into which she'd put herself, he would have locked her away until she was old enough to know better. Phryne, as her grandmother correctly surmised, had never been very good about knowing better, only knowing what she wanted.

So joshing and teasing with Rendelen and Dash came naturally, just three Elves of similar background and shared worldview, sitting around a fire and passing the time.

Only one area was taboo. No mention was made of the King's personal life or his young Queen. Even Elven Hunters were astute enough to know that this was forbidden territory when it came to Phryne Amarantyne.

They slept soundly until the sunrise woke them, then set out to finish their journey. They climbed into the mountains, bright sunlight washing the landscape as yesterday's weather moved on, the clouds and mists of early morning dissipating, the skies turning clear and blue. By midday, they had reached the slopes leading up to the pass and were met by sentries keeping watch. Within another hour, they had ascended the final section of their climb, moved into the near end of the pass, and could hear the sounds of construction ahead.

The first thing Phryne noticed as they entered the split and saw the first of the staging areas was how close the fortifications were to the near end of the pass. Within minutes, she could see the defenses themselves, braced across a narrows where the cliff walls offered sheer drops of more than two hundred feet. She had envisioned the defenses being set farther in toward the far end of the pass, thinking the Elves would want to fight for every inch of the twisty passageway if the first set of defenses was breached. Clearly, someone had decided otherwise.

She had her chance to discover whom as Tasha caught sight of her from where he was working on fashioning logs into buttresses for the walls and hailed her over.

"Welcome, cousin!" he boomed, wrapping his big arms around her.

A few mouths gaped as he embraced her, for she was a Princess and no one hugged a Princess like that without permission. But Tasha was Tasha, and she expected no less.

"Good to see you, Tasha," she greeted him, hugging back. "I've missed you."

"And me, as well, I hope," said Tenerife, appearing at his brother's side to claim his own hug. "Your father set you free again, I gather?"

"He said he thought I had learned my lesson."

"Which lesson would that be, I wonder?" Tenerife gave her a wink. "How are things in Arborlon? How is Panterra doing without Prue?"

She grimaced. "Must you keep reminding me about that?" She sighed. "Well enough, when he left. Sider Ament took him off to the south to visit the villages there and try to rally support for protecting the other passes. I haven't seen him since. What about here?"

"You can see for yourself, if you want," Tasha offered. "We've gotten the better part of the defensive wall finished. Should be all the way done in three days. Is that why you're here? To give your father a report?"

"Of course not!" She tried to look offended. "I'm only here to see that both of you are safe and sound. But you seem well enough, so I might as well have a look around."

The brothers laughed, and Tasha took her arm and steered her toward the wall. "Come with us, cousin Princess, and see how the working Elves do their job."

With Tenerife in tow, he took her through piles of building supplies and equipment—logs and huge stones hauled up from the valley; chains, clamps, and latching forged by their smiths; and heavy ropes, block and tackle, and pulleys and hoists manufactured by their craftsmen. She looked at everything, still confused by the positioning of the wall. "Why did you build it so close to the near end of the pass?" she asked finally.

Tasha laughed. "Seems like a mistake, doesn't it? But only if you judge the choice without thinking it through. Let me explain." He gestured at the cliffs to either side. "This is the narrowest point in the pass where the cliff walls cannot be climbed by attackers to bypass the fortifications. We've already eliminated some of the climbing paths and footholds farther in, sheering back the wall even farther. On this side, we've hewed out footholds that allow us to place defenders all along the upper stretches of the cliffs, back out of sight of those approaching. Archers will take those positions if we are attacked. Because of time constraints, we decided early on to build a single wall rather than a series. One good wall will have to be enough. We also chose this site based on something a little less obvious. Come over here."

He guided her to the wall, and together the three cousins climbed ladders to parapets and descended on the far side. Tasha led the way forward for perhaps two dozen yards and stopped, pointing up. "Now look up. There, in those clefts to either side."

She looked but didn't see anything. "What am I looking for?"

"What you're not seeing, which is good. We don't want the Trolls to see it, either. We've rigged pins linked to ropes on either side that hold back several tons of rock. If they are pulled, we create an avalanche that will bury anyone caught in the pass on the wrong side of the wall. A last resort, if the walls should be taken. The Trolls will be crowding forward, hundreds deep. There won't be time or space to run. Most will die where they stand."

She nodded. "So you don't think they will see the trap you've set?"

Tenerife shrugged. "You didn't. Are their eyes any sharper than yours?"

"They might have more experience with these things than I do."

"They might be too busy trying to stay alive if they get this far to make a careful study of outcroppings several hundred feet up."

She nodded. It made sense. "Who designed all this?"

Tasha cocked an eyebrow at her. "Ronan Caer. Remember him?"

She shook her head. "But the name sounds familiar."

"It should. He broke your arm when you were five. You were playing with staves, pretending to fight each other. He pretended too hard or you pretended too little, and the result was your left arm in a splint for nine weeks. Do you remember now?"

She did, although she hadn't thought of the incident in years, and she didn't think she had seen Ronan Caer in almost that long. He had moved away from Arborlon when she was still little. "He designed all this?"

"It seems he wasn't wasting his time while he was away. He was studying architecture, particularly as it relates to creating defensive positions. He was exploring, as well. Knew the pass as well as we did.

He set the positions right away. Haren knew his talent from before and called him up as soon as we arrived. Made things much easier."

Haren Crayel, captain of the Home Guard. A good man, one her father trusted implicitly. She hadn't known he was up here, but it made sense that he would be placed in command.

"Enough of ancient history," Tasha declared, taking her arm. "We've got something else to show you besides the fortifications, something that isn't quite so reassuring."

They left the staging areas and the defensive wall behind and proceeded through the pass. Soon even the noise of the construction had disappeared in a baffle of twists and turns that first distorted and then deadened the sound of the noise altogether. They wound deeper into the cut, approaching the wide opening where they had stumbled upon the dragon the last time she was up here.

"Any sign of that . . . ?"

"Dragon?" Tenerife finished for her. "Haven't seen it. Maybe it moved on to less crowded quarters. Maybe there wasn't enough for it to eat in these mountains and it went in search of better feeding grounds."

"Maybe it's waiting for you to get careless," she suggested.

"Maybe," he agreed. "I've been known to do that, but not where dragons are concerned."

They crossed the broad opening, Phryne glancing skyward more than once, caught between wanting on the one hand to be safe and on the other to encounter the beast again. She could not forget the mix of exhilaration and fear she had felt on seeing it for the first time. But the dragon did not appear, and soon enough they were past the widening and back inside the narrows, moving ahead once more toward the far opening of the pass. It took them only a short time after that, and as they neared their destination she caught sight of a handful of Elven Hunters gathered just inside the cut. Sentries warding the mouth of the pass, she realized.

"Any change?" Tasha asked as they came up to the group, glancing from face to face.

"Nothing," one replied. "Take a look for yourselves."

Wordlessly, the Orullians led Phryne forward the last few steps to where the pass opened out onto the foothills and plains beyond. As they neared the opening, Tasha looked over at her. "Look down on the plains, but don't show yourself. Stay in the shadow of the cliff sides."

He motioned for her to go ahead of him, and she did so. When she reached the edge of the light, she stopped and stared out at the broad sweep of the landscape beyond. There were mountains all around, but in the distance, below a ragged clutch of scrub-littered foothills, were plains turned as barren and brown as the rock of their passageway, rolling off to the northwest until they disappeared in the haze of the distant horizon. She scanned from mountains to plains and back again. Nothing.

"I don't see anything," she said, glancing over her shoulder at the Orullians. "Where should I look?"

"There," Tasha advised, coming up beside her and pointing.

She peered out across the foothills and into the hazy air of the plains to the place he indicated. At first she saw nothing but a mix of dark and light terrain. Then she saw what looked like thin, barely noticeable columns of smoke rising out of the largest of the darker patches. She realized that there was movement within the patch, a rippling of life.

"Taureq Siq's army," she said quietly.

"Just so." Tasha's voice was equally soft. "Spread out for several miles on the flats. Been like that for three days now."

Both Orullians were standing next to her, one at either shoulder. Phryne glanced from one to the other. "What's it doing here?"

Tenerife shrugged. "Waiting."

"Waiting for what?"

"That's the question, isn't it?"

"What's troublesome is that it hasn't sent out scouts, not even into the foothills let alone these mountains," Tasha interjected. "The Trolls don't seem particularly interested in investigating. I thought when the army first appeared that it had come to claim the passes. But it hasn't moved since setting up camp."

"Waiting," Phryne repeated.

They stood where they were for a long time as she peered out at the camp, trying to reason it out. The Trolls had struck their old camp and come here, presumably in preparation for their meeting with the leaders Panterra had promised them would come. But would they just sit there trusting to his word without trying to do more? They might, if they thought that his fear for Prue Liss was strong enough that he would do what they had demanded. But how could they be sure he would be able to persuade anyone to come out to meet with them?

How could they be sure of anything?

Something about all of this was deeply troubling, but she couldn't put her finger on it. Apparently her cousins hadn't had any better success.

"Have you gone down to have a look?" she asked.

"And risk incurring the wrath your father visited on you?" Tenerife asked in mock horror. "Of course we have."

"There isn't much to see, even up close," his brother rumbled, easing back a step, as if his bulk made him more visible than the other two. "We saw it all from the rise the last time you were up here while we waited for our chance to rescue Panterra and Prue. Nothing's changed but the location. The Trolls and the tents and all the rest look just the same."

Phryne shook her head. "I don't understand it. Why aren't they searching for a way in? Why aren't they looking for the passes? They know we're in these mountains somewhere."

Tasha snorted softly. "We'll know soon enough. The full moon comes in ten days. If no one appears to negotiate, I'm pretty certain they'll stop sitting around."

"Of course, they could be searching without our realizing it," Tenerife mused. "They were pretty good at creeping up on our Tracker friends without them knowing, and not many are able to do that."

"No," Tasha said, frowning. "We would have seen something. We've had eyes trained on the approach from the day we arrived to begin work on the defenses, and no one has come into the mountains."

"Could they have found another of the passes?" Phryne asked. "Farther south?"

The brothers thought it over for a moment. "If they knew where we were and how to get to us, why bother with requesting a meeting? No, I don't think they know a way in just yet. I think that's what they're waiting for. I just don't know where they think the information is coming from if they don't search it out."

They talked it over awhile longer, but when Phryne was satisfied that she had seen all there was to see, they retreated into the pass. A short time later they had regained the barricades and were observing the progress of the construction once more.

"Will you stay the night?" Tenerife asked as they climbed down from the ladders on the far side.

She nodded. "I want to look around a bit more." She paused. "Did you send anyone to tell my father about the Trolls?"

Tasha shook his head. "Haren decided not to bother. Nothing to tell, he said. It's not as if it's a surprise that they're here. We knew they were coming. If they do something worth reporting, we'll send word then. You can tell your father yourself when you return to the city."

She didn't like it that it had been left to her to do something the captain of the Home Guard should have done, but she guessed it was his decision, not hers.

She spent the rest of the day studying the barricades and listening to the builders explain why they believed them strong enough to repel any attack. She was briefed on the defensive positions and the strategy that Haren Crayel intended to employ if the attack came. Afterward, she had dinner with her cousins and the Elves they were closest to, back to telling stories and sharing ale.

It was late when she rolled into her blankets near a fire they had built for her, the mountain air cold and the wind gusting through the pass. She was tired enough to begin drifting off right away, even though she was still thinking about the reason that the Trolls were making no effort to search for a way through the mountains. Odd, she kept repeating to herself, that they should come so near Aphalion Pass and then do nothing to find it.

If Arik Sarn were there, perhaps he could explain it. She thought of him sitting in the gardens and drawing flowers, and it made her smile. He was pretty odd himself. He would understand the behavior of the Drouj and Taureq Siq better than any of them.

She had almost fallen asleep when the first hint of the answer she had been searching for came to her as a sharp-edged possibility that until that moment she had never considered. Doing so now, she went cold all the way down to her bones.

Within seconds she was shaking Tasha and Tenerife awake.

25

TRUE TO HIS WORD, ON REACHING GLENSK WOOD at midday two days earlier, Sider Ament left Panterra behind and continued on alone for Declan Reach. He took time to reassure the boy that he would do whatever was necessary to recover Prue safely from the Troll camp and would bring her back as quickly as possible. He could read the dissatisfaction and frustration in the boy's face. The boy wanted to go with him and be a part of whatever rescue effort he intended. But Sider had already determined that it would be more dangerous for all three of them if the boy came along and would add nothing to have him there.

"Just do as I asked you," he repeated. "Tell Aislinne what has happened and make sure your report reaches Pogue and the other members of the village council. Confirm that the effort to fortify the pass is under way and if for some reason it isn't, do what you can to change that. Wait for me there if you wish; I'll come through on my return."

Then he was gone, moving quickly away, fading into the trees and not looking back.

He walked the remainder of the day, ascending the steeper mountain slopes toward Declan Reach. By nightfall, he had reached a place at the upper edges of the thinning woods where he could see the entrance. He considered entering the pass itself. In the black silence of the night, he could hear the murmur of voices and see the dim flicker of fires burning within the cut. Someone was camped there, presumably those who had been sent to begin work on the fortifications, and he could have joined them. But he was by nature solitary, and he preferred to keep his own company.

So he stayed where he was, finding a spot where he could make his camp and keep watch. He ate his meal cold, did not start a fire, and long before midnight had wrapped himself in his cloak and blanket to ward against the night's chill and was asleep.

His sleep was deep and dreamless, the first time in a long time, and he woke refreshed and reassured that he was doing the right thing. He hadn't told the boy, but he had a plan. It wasn't fully formed and it depended on the efforts of someone other than himself, but he believed it had a chance to work. Without it, in any case, there was probably little hope for the girl. He had not shared any of this, not wanting to give the boy anything further to think about, hoping his efforts with the fortifications would help take his mind off the matter.

Probably that wouldn't happen, he acknowledged. Probably there was no diminishing the pain of what he was going through.

He departed at sunrise for the pass, gratified to discover that a sizable workforce was in the process of constructing the needed fortifications, a mix of Trackers and builders under the command of Trow Ravenlock. He stopped long enough to make a quick report to the Tracker leader and to reassure himself that Skeal Eile was not doing anything to interfere with his efforts at summoning help from the other communities, and then he moved on. Ravenlock wanted to know where he was going, but he said only that he was going out to scout the movements of the Troll army and left things at that.

He traversed the length of the pass and emerged into the outside world without incident. The landscape he remembered was unchanged, still a mix of barren rock and empty flats spreading away toward distant mountains west and patches of forest that mingled trees both fresh with new growth and withered with death's approach, all beneath skies that were clear and bright and sun-filled. He stood at the opening for a time, just studying the sweep of the terrain, watchful for anything that looked odd or threatening. He saw neither, and even though he knew there would be hidden dangers he felt he was better prepared for them this time.

But he would still need help with the girl.

He reached into the pocket sewn on the inside of his belt and withdrew the tracking device given him by Deladion Inch. *Just press the button until the red light comes on and I will know to come find you,* Inch had told him. Sider had not thought he would ever have need of summoning the big man, but he had kept the device safe anyway.

He pressed the button now, waited for the red light to come on, tucked the device back in his belt pocket when it did, and set out.

What he had remembered even before he recalled the tracking device was Inch's claim to familiarity with the Troll tribes and their movements. If nothing else, he would be able to tell Sider the best way to go about getting into the camp and finding the girl. He would likely know how they set watch and where a prisoner might be kept. Perhaps there were insignia on the tents that identified their usage. If Sider was very lucky indeed, the big man might even agree to help him get inside the camp by going with him. But he wouldn't ask; that would be presuming on a friendship he wasn't sure even existed.

Admittedly, it wasn't much of a plan. But it would give him a better chance than anyone else, including the boy, of managing a rescue. Still, he had to act quickly. Only six days remained before the appointed meeting with Taureq Siq. Sider didn't think the Troll Maturen would show much patience with his prisoner after that deadline expired.

He shook his head at himself. There were so many things that needed doing: rallying the defenders at Aphalion and Declan Reach, speaking with the different Races—he hadn't gone to the Lizards or Spiders at all, leaving that to the Elves . . . *But here I am, doing this instead. All because I promised Panterra Qu I would not abandon the girl, and if I am to have any chance of winning his friendship and trust, any chance of persuading him that he should become the next bearer of the staff, I must first prove that I can keep my word when I make a promise.*

He walked on through the midday light, staying out in the open where he could see anything that approached and hopefully avoid the sort of ambush he had encountered the last time out, all the while moving in the general direction of Deladion Inch's fortress keep. The terrain about him remained pretty much the same—bleak and ruined, stripped of grasses and trees, the earth still toxic from the Great Wars, stark and unwelcoming. Once, far off in the distance, he caught sight of a flat blue glimmer of water, a slender thread wending its way through the countryside, angling off into the haze west. But he couldn't tell the condition of the water or its source. Here and there, clumps of trees grew as fresh and clean as they all must have grown at one time. But they were small islands amid an ocean of devastation, and the bulk of what the Gray Man saw showed little promise.

Once, not so far distant, he saw something much larger than himself shambling through a series of deep ravines, appearing and then disappearing like a mirage. But it was moving away from him, and after a while it was gone entirely.

He found himself wondering how the people of the valley would ever be able to acclimate and survive in this hostile environment. How could they adapt to what they would encounter when they had spent five hundred years closed away in a country where everything was naturally available and almost nothing threatened? He tried to envision how it would happen and failed. It would take new skills and hard-won experience to allow them to make the change. It would take a degree of cooperation and respect that was presently lacking. All the petty jealousies and rifts and differences would have to be bridged and healed.

He didn't know if that was possible. Yet a way would have to be found if those brought out of the carnage of the Great Wars by the boy Hawk were to survive.

The hours slipped away, the afternoon crawling toward twilight, the bright orb of the sun advancing west in a sky that grew increasingly cloudy. Another storm was approaching, coming down out of the north. Sider checked the tracking device, worried that it might have failed. But the red light glowed steadily, so he kept moving ahead. He recognized almost nothing of the land he was traversing, but he carried a compass and his general sense of direction added to its readings told him he was still maintaining his intended course. He just hoped he would get to shelter before sunset or rainfall.

He needn't have worried. He was climbing out of a series of deep ravines toward a line of dead trees and scrub when Deladion Inch appeared above him, clad in the familiar black leathers and metal trappings, the equally familiar Tyson Flechette strapped across one shoulder.

"Sider Ament!" the big man called out in greeting. "Come on up!"

He stood where he was, hands resting on his hips and a bemused expression on his bluff face, watching as Sider finished his climb up the rise and joined him.

"Hello, again," Sider greeted him in turn.

The big man looked him up and down. "Didn't expect to see you again quite so soon. Not that I'm complaining, you understand. I can always use the company of a fellow mercenary. Oh, wait—you don't like it when I call you that. A fellow practitioner of the art of war? Is that better? Well, whatever, I'm glad you came. My tracking device works pretty well, doesn't it? Got your signal on my receiver, and it brought me right to you."

He was rambling a bit, but Sider didn't mind. He was just happy the other man had actually chosen to come find him. "Couldn't have been easier," he agreed.

"Well, then, we're not far from the old homestead, so it won't be any harder from here." Inch glanced at the skies. "I would have reached you quicker than this, but I was out foraging, gone the other direction, and I had to retrace my steps. Sorry about that. Are you hungry?"

Sider nodded. "Thirsty, too."

"Got the cure for both. Come along now, no further delays. Tell me what brings you back out again after I warned you that staying where you were was the better choice. Not that I thought for a minute you'd listen. But I feel an obligation toward those possessed of less common sense than myself. Come, come."

He led the way down the backside of the rise and onto flats that stretched away through miles of ravines and scrub and ruined woods, chatting as they went about what he had been doing since Sider had last seen him. Mostly, he said, he had been working on repairs to the tunnel system in the ruins that served as his shelter while waiting for a message from the tiny village south that had sought his services but was deliberating his price. He was animated and voluble, and he waved his hands with their missing fingers as he talked. Sider gave a mental shake of his head and wondered where all the energy came from.

It was nearing nightfall and the rain was just beginning to fall when they reached the ruins and climbed the stone steps to the rooms that Deladion Inch maintained for himself. They moved inside the buildings, navigating their corridors until they reached a room where there were chairs and a table set in front of a hearth. Within minutes, Inch had a fire going, the dry wood crackling and snapping cheerfully.

"Don't you worry about smoke giving you away?" Sider asked.

The big man gave him a look. "Can't worry about everything. In weather like this, it won't be easy to sort out smoke from mist and rain in any case. Besides, no one could catch me in the maze of tunnels that honeycomb this place even if they wanted to. We're safe enough, smoke or not. Glass of ale?"

They sat before the fire and drank down several glasses, not saying much, just enjoying the warmth and the company. Sider thought that he could live like this, cocooned away, protected from predators, able to come and go as he pleased. He might get the chance to find out since his days of warding the passes leading in and out of the valley were coming to a close.

"I need your help with something," he said finally, setting aside his glass and leaning back.

The big man nodded. "Thought so."

"Understand, I'm not asking you to get involved, only to give me enough insight into what's needed so I might be able to avoid getting myself killed."

Deladion Inch grinned. "In your case, Sider, that might take more than just a *few* insights. But go on, tell me."

Sider nodded. "There's a girl from the valley who's being held captive in a Troll camp. She's a hostage for something that isn't going to happen, and I have to find a way to rescue her before the Trolls figure this out."

"Sounds as if your valley sanctuary might not be so safe anymore. Too bad about that, but I warned you."

"Too bad about a lot of things."

Deladion Inch took a long pull on his ale. "What can you tell me about these Trolls? Do you know which tribe it is?"

"Drouj. Their leader is called Taureq Siq. They've got a camp north of here. They're migrating, they claim, but once they found out about the valley they decided that maybe it might be the home they were looking for. They caught the girl and a boy who managed to get a little too close. A Troll visiting from another tribe made friends with the pair and got the boy out, but not the girl. So now I need to get the girl back. It's more complicated than I'm telling it, but the rest doesn't matter."

"Not to me, anyway," the big man agreed. "Taureq Siq, is it? Now, there's a finely wrought piece of nastiness. Here's what I can tell you. Taureq is not someone you can trust. The Drouj are the dominant Troll tribe in this part of the world. They've subjugated all the other tribes and made them accept Taureq as their Maturen. He's got a serious problem with power, that one. Wants to dominate everything and everyone. If he gets into your valley, you better plan on finding a new home. You say he's camped off to the north?"

"Was a week or two ago. He might have moved closer to the mountains by now. He's expecting a meeting with us in about six days. The girl's being held as insurance. Of course, holding her isn't going to get him what he wants, but I can't just leave her."

"Sounds like you have a reason for rescuing this girl that goes beyond what you're telling me."

"I do. It has to do with the boy. I can explain it, if you want."

Deladion Inch shook his head. "Don't bother. I can get you past the watch and inside the Troll camp, but I don't know about finding your girl. The Drouj are a big tribe—thousands strong. Finding where they've got her won't be easy. You don't happen to speak the language, do you?"

"Not theirs. Our Trolls speak something else."

"Guess you can't ask them where she is, then. Too bad." He stood up. "Let's have something to eat while I think about it."

They set about preparing a dinner, Inch fixing the food while Sider set the table with plates and utensils. He was surprised to see that his host had a large collection of mixed pieces of china and glassware, salvaged somehow from the contents of these ruins or others, all of it neatly stacked and shelved. He wouldn't have thought it of Inch, but then he'd always suspected that the big man was more than he seemed.

They ate, washing down the food with more glasses of ale. Sider was growing sleepy and changed out his ale for water. Deladion Inch laughed on seeing him do so, remarking that his guest had a low tolerance of spirits and common sense both.

"I'm curious about this Troll that got the boy free," the big man said after they had set aside their plates. "How did he manage that?"

Sider shrugged. "According to the boy, he was part of an exchange of eldest sons. His father sent him to the Drouj in exchange for Taureq's eldest. It was some sort of pact to solidify an alliance."

Deladion Inch laughed. "That's a new twist on things. Taureq normally doesn't form alliances; he simply crushes his enemies. What tribe of Trolls did he make this alliance with?"

"Karriak."

"Karriak?" Inch repeated carefully. "You must have heard wrong."

"Maybe. I only heard the story once."

"Reason I say that, the Drouj wiped out the Karriak several years ago. Every last one of them. Taureq and his sons saw to that. I remember hearing about it. Pretty ugly stuff."

Sider stared at him, the first faint twinges of concern surfacing. "Maybe I misheard. Might be another tribe, then? I think Taureq and the Maturen of the other tribe were related. Or the one split off from the other some time in the past."

Deladion Inch studied him wordlessly for a moment, his brow furrowing. "What's the name of this Troll, Sider?"

The Gray Man saw it coming at him through a flash of understanding, but couldn't do anything about it. "Arik Sarn."

The big man nodded slowly. "Interesting. Something you should know. Taureq Siq has two sons. The younger is a bloodthirsty little weasel named Grosha. The older, the more intelligent and dangerous of the two, is called Arik."

The two men stared at each in silence for a long moment, considering the implications. "Arik Siq," Sider said quietly. "And we brought him back into the valley with us, to the Elven home city."

Deladion Inch nodded. "A fox in the henhouse. Sounds like Arik's way. I know them all, the whole miserable family. Grosha has Skaith Hounds for pets. Wanted to feed me to them once upon a time. Would have done it, too, but I had the flechette with me and warned him that his pets would be chopped meat if he set them on me. He hasn't had a kind word for me since."

"Describe the older son to me," Sider said.

The big man did so. The description fit Arik Sarn perfectly. Sider thought it through. The Troll had tricked his captives into thinking he was a friend, using them to gain entrance into the valley, his intention all along. Holding Prue Liss hostage was just a subterfuge. What Taureq Siq needed was a pair of eyes and ears inside the valley to tell him what was going on. His elder son would gather what knowledge he could, and then he would use it against the defenders. He wasn't waiting for a response to his demand. He was preparing for an attack.

Sider told Deladion Inch what he thought was happening, wanting to be certain he was right about this, needing another opinion that he could trust. It was quick in coming. "Always very smart about how best to do things, that one. His father relies on him for that. What are you going to do?"

Sider took a deep breath. "Go back on my word."

"Which word would that be?" Inch looked vaguely amused.

"Promising not to ask you to get involved. Can't keep that promise now. I need you to go into the Troll camp and bring the girl out."

Deladion Inch shook his head, glanced down at his hands and then off into the far corners of the room. Sider waited patiently.

Finally, the big man looked over at him again. "You've got sand, Sider Ament, I'll give you that. All right, I'll go. I haven't anything better to do. I'll bring her out. Where do you want her?"

"I'll draw you a map. Can you leave right away? Tomorrow morning?"

"I can leave now, if you want. What is it you plan to do? Go back inside the valley and find your lying friend?"

Sider nodded. "I don't like the idea of him there another second longer than he has to be. I'm worried that he has something else planned. Maybe I can reach him before he manages to slip away."

"Then we'll both go." Deladion Inch seemed almost eager. "You to your valley and me to Taureq Siq. But first we'll share one last glass of ale, provide us with some additional fortification for what lies ahead. It'll be cold and wet out there, Sider. And it'll be dangerous."

They drank their ale slowly, sitting together in silence, watching the fire die out as it turned slowly to ashes. Sider thought about how blind he had been to the possibility that Arik Sarn might have been using Panterra for his own purposes. He hadn't considered things carefully enough, too wrapped up in the rush to get back into the valley and sound the alarm, too quick to act and not careful enough to think it through. Now he would pay the price. Or someone would. He didn't like thinking about who that someone might be.

Deladion Inch drained the last of his ale and stood. "If you're ready, let's be off. We can take my crawler as far as you want. Then you can walk from there. Solar-powered, fully charged. A beast, left over from the old days. Still works. You should have one for your line of work, too. But mine's the last, so I guess you're out of luck. Ready?"

They walked from the room and down corridors and stairs toward the ground level. Inch was carrying his flechette and another short-barreled, black metal weapon that looked somewhat similar. He wore knives and bore packs whose contents were hidden from view and made no sound as they shifted about inside the canvas. Deladion Inch was a walking arsenal.

"One last thing," the big man said as they stopped at the doorway leading out. "You watch yourself with Arik Siq. He might look harmless, might even seem so, but he's very dangerous. Not impulsive and brash like his little brother. Be careful."

Sider nodded. "I'll do that. You better worry about yourself. You're the one going into a camp filled with unfriendly Trolls. They might decide you're not there for any good reason."

"By the time they figure that out, I'll be gone again. And the girl with me. What's her name again?"

"Prue. Prue Liss."

Inch stuck out his hand and gripped Sider's firmly. "Good seeing you, Sider. It's always interesting. Be looking for you down the road. We'll tell our stories then over fresh glasses of ale."

"We'll do that," Sider agreed.

The two men smiled at each other, broke their handshake, and went out the door into the night.

* * *

ONE THING EVERY ELF WHO KNEW XAC WEN had to admit about him, besides the fact that he was annoyingly omnipresent and intrusive: he didn't miss much. If you wanted to know what was going on in a particular part of the city of Arborlon or even beyond, or if you were curious to know where someone had gone or why, he was the one to ask. His parents had given up trying to keep him under control years ago—forget about during the day when he was all over the place, but even at night when he should have been asleep. Xac Wen told everyone who asked that he didn't need to sleep. A couple of hours were sufficient, and the rest of the time he wanted to be out looking around.

Which was what he was doing when he caught sight of Arik Sarn walking alone down a back road of the sleeping city shortly after midnight. He might have been out for a stroll, but Xac knew you didn't carry a backpack and weapons when you were just taking the air. He might have been on his way to visit someone, but you didn't often go visiting after midnight and you didn't do it in a furtive way. Well, usually you didn't. He was also alone, which meant that for some reason his Elven guards had failed in their duty to keep an eye on him at all times.

This was troubling to the boy, and he watched from the shadows as the Troll moved past, never once indicating that he knew the boy was there. But Xac knew that grown-ups were very good at pretending not to have noticed you when in fact they had. So he waited until the Troll was out of sight, ducked back behind the buildings, and moved through the trees along a little-used path that would bring him out where the road the Troll was following would converge with a larger one.

But Arik Sarn failed to appear. Xac waited until he was sure the Troll wasn't coming, thought about it a moment, and then hurried off to the

Carolan to have a look around. He went swiftly, angling away from where he was certain the Troll must have gone, small and silent as he sped through shadowed trees and down narrow lanes, avoiding houses and people, staying out of the light. When he reached the gardens and the bluff edge, he was winded and breathing heavily. Without showing himself, he dropped down while still out of sight, crawled into the flowering bushes, and lay flat against the ground, listening. He wanted to lift his head for a look, but his instincts warned him against it.

He waited a long time.

Then he heard the soft pad of footfalls from not very far away. They would start up and stop and then start up again. Someone was searching through the gardens and taking their time doing so, looking down every row carefully.

Searching for what?

For him?

He felt chills ripple down his spine at the possibility and inched closer to the bushes next to him, slowly wedging himself under them until they covered him completely. He tucked in his arms and legs. He tried to will himself to disappear.

He waited some more.

Suddenly the Troll appeared at the head of the row of bushes in which he hid, a long knife in one hand as he peered left and right, studying everything. Xac Wen quit breathing. He fought down the urge to jump up and run. He had been right not to risk showing himself, but maybe wrong in coming here at all.

After a long time, the Troll moved away.

Xac waited, still barely breathing, still pressing himself against the earth. He could almost feel the Troll's eyes watching him, could imagine the big hands fastening on his shoulders and yanking him to his feet. He could imagine that and a whole lot more he didn't want to dwell on.

When enough minutes had passed that he felt safe again, he cautiously inched out from under the bushes and began crawling toward the bluff edge. It took him a long time, and by the time he had completed his journey his clothes were torn and filthy.

From his hiding place at the Carolan's rim, he could look down the switchback length of the Elfitch. Nothing looked out of place. The watch was on duty, the torches that lit the ramp were burning, and the ramp itself was otherwise deserted. He glanced from right to left along the edge of the bluff. Nothing in either direction.

He took a deep breath and wondered what he should do.

Then he caught sight of something moving. Below the Elfitch, not far from where the northern boundary of the tree line began, a solitary figure slid through the shadows.

It was the Troll.

Xac Wen watched him until he was out of sight, and then he got to his feet and stood looking down at the darkness, wondering whom he should tell.

26

PHRYNE AMARANTYNE HAD BEEN BACK IN ARBORLON for less than four hours when she got the summons from her grandmother. By then, if Xac Wen was to be believed, Arik Sarn had been gone from the city for twice that long, leaving behind two dead Home Guards and a lot of angry Elves. She had rushed back with the Orullians in tow to prevent just this sort of tragedy, convinced that her revelation about the Troll was no fantasy. She turned out to be right, but she arrived too late to make any difference.

What she had realized belatedly was this: If the Trolls were not bothering with finding a way into the valley, didn't that suggest they already knew a way? But that seemed impossible, given that none of them had ever entered. Except, she corrected herself quickly, for Arik Sarn. He was inside because she and her friends had brought him inside. Put that together with the fact that he was drawing what appeared to be pictures of flowers but could just as easily have been maps, and you had the distinct possibility of a betrayal. After all, what they knew of the Troll was based on what Pan had told them and what little they had observed, which wasn't really very much. Recognizing the possibility had opened the door to the chilling prospect that they had all missed seeing the truth of things—Arik Sarn was another of the enemy that would see them destroyed.

It was no comfort to anyone that Sider Ament had returned, as well, having discovered the truth through a set of circumstances he refused to talk about. Phryne could identify with him; they were bearers of the same message, both of them shocked by the revelation of the Troll's true identity and purpose, both of them furious with themselves for not having recognized it sooner. Not that there was any real way they could have done so, but that didn't make either of them feel any better.

The Gray Man had left again almost at once, tracking the deceiver north in an effort to catch him before he escaped the valley. He told Phryne he fully expected to fail, that his quarry would escape through one of the passes before anyone could catch up with him. Phryne was angry she had not thought before leaving Aphalion Pass to warn the Elven Hunters working on the defenses that the Troll might show up there, but she had been so anxious to reach her father and warn him that she hadn't even considered the possibility. The Orullians told her not to dwell on it; they had all been fooled, all of them equally deceived, and there was nothing to be done about it now but to continue with their plans to defend the valley.

Even so, she thought about it constantly. She wondered how Panterra Qu was going to feel once he learned the truth. He was the one who had been most deceived, having supported Arik Siq as a friend, persuading the others he would be their friend, too. She did not like to think about what it might do to him if Prue Liss was harmed as a result of this treachery.

So receiving the summons was a welcome excuse to think of something besides the turmoil surrounding the Troll. One of the old men brought the invitation: not the same one as before, a different one, another whose name she should have known and could not remember. She took the letter he offered and waited for him to leave. But he shook his head and gestured for her to break the seal and read the contents in front of him. With a dismissive shrug, she did so.

The summons read as follows:

Please come at once to my cottage to speak with me
on a matter of great importance.
The bearer of this letter will accompany you.
Tell no one. Come alone.

There was no salutation and no signature. There was no room for
argument. Her grandmother's imperious attitude was present in every
word of her overbearing command. Phryne sighed in resignation,
folded the letter up again, and tucked it into her tunic.

"Lead the way," she advised the messenger.

They set off through the city, following the familiar roads and
pathways that led to the outskirts and her grandmother's isolated cottage. The day was overcast and gray, a hint of rain in the air, a whisper
of cooling weather. She glanced toward the mountains once or twice
where the trees cleared enough to allow her to do so, wondering if
Sider Ament might have caught up to Arik Siq. She wanted to be back
up at Aphalion Pass, standing with the Orullians at the barricades,
watching for what was now an inevitable attack on the valley. But her
father had forbidden it, intent on keeping her close to him until he
knew more about what was going to happen.

As if being close would make a difference in the outcome of things,
she thought darkly. As if much of anything they did down here in the
city made a difference.

She wondered about Prue Liss, as well, but she could not bear
thinking on the girl's dangerous situation.

The walk to her grandmother's cottage took only twenty minutes,
and when they arrived she was surprised to find her grandmother fully
dressed and sitting in a rocker on the front porch. Her gray hair had
been combed and pinned up, her makeup had been carefully applied,
and her favorite shawl was wrapped around her thin shoulders. She
even managed a small smile.

"Thank you, Gardwen, you may go," she greeted the oldster, giving
him a small wave of one bony hand. "Well done, my dear." As soon as
he turned his back, she shifted her attention to Phryne. "You are very
prompt. I take that as a good sign." She gestured toward the empty
rocker pulled up beside her own. "Sit next to me, please."

Phryne did as she was asked, curious to learn why she had been
summoned.

"Your father faces the worst crisis in the history of the Elven nation since the time our people were brought into this valley by Kirisin Belloruus," her grandmother said quietly, leaning back in her rocker and looking at her granddaughter with a hint of sadness in her eyes. "It is a terrible responsibility."

"Father will know what to do," Phryne said.

"No one knows what to do. It hasn't become clear to anyone yet what is needed." Mistral Belloruus was in no mood for platitudes. "Except perhaps to me, which is why I have summoned you. I am an old lady, Phryne. No, don't say something foolish about how youthful I am or how I might live for many more years. Just listen to what I have to say. I am old. This is not a bad thing, but it does limit what I can do. I still think of myself as young in many ways—still remember being young, for that matter—but I am old. It is important to accept truths, even when they are inconvenient."

She rocked back slightly and looked up at the sky. "So here we are, come to the end of an era and threatened by a grave danger. What are we to do? Most would say they don't know. But I do, Phryne. I always have. Because of who I am. Because of my ancestry."

Phryne had no idea what her grandmother was talking about, and she refused to sit by silently and wonder if an explanation was forthcoming. "What do you think we must do, Grandmother? If you know, then tell me. I am frightened for all of us. I've seen what's out there. The Troll army is massive, and I don't know that we have the strength to stop it if it wants to force its way into the valley. Not even if all the Races agree to stand together, which I don't think they will."

"Very perceptive of you," her grandmother replied. "They won't unite because they don't know how. They will learn eventually, but it will take time. Meanwhile, something has to be done to give them that time. In the old days, it would have been the Knights of the Word that stood foremost. But now they forget their duty. Or at least the descendant of the Belloruus staff did, and paid the price for his foolishness. So there is only Sider Ament, and he is not strong enough alone."

She shifted her eyes back to Phryne and leaned forward. "Help me to my feet, girl. I want to walk."

Phryne rose and took her grandmother's arm, helping her to stand. The old woman felt as light and fragile as fine crystal. But Phryne knew that perception was deceptive; Mistral Belloruus had steel running through the bones of her body.

"This way, down the steps," her grandmother ordered, directing her with small gestures of her thin arms.

They descended, Phryne holding tightly to her grandmother, afraid with every step that she might fall. But the old woman's movements were steady and direct, and she did not falter. They reached the moss-grown walkway and began easing down its spongy length into the gardens planted out back.

"This isn't something I had planned to talk about so soon," her grandmother said as they entered the gardens. "I wanted to wait awhile longer to give you a chance to demonstrate that you were ready, that you had listened to what I told you about growing up and making mature decisions. I wanted you to season a little more. But we don't always get what we want in this life. In fact, we don't get what we want most of the time. We get compromises and settlements, half measures and tamped-down dreams. We get half a loaf baked, half a glass filled. That's what we have here."

Phryne nodded, having no idea what she was talking about. "That might be so, but we don't have to like it."

"We shouldn't have to accept it, either. Mostly, we don't. We understand the odds are against us, but we still strive for something more. We make our best effort each time out because now and then we get exactly what we want."

"Which is what we are going to do here?" Phryne guessed.

Her grandmother glanced at her. "In fact, it is. Both of us are going to make our best effort and hope it works out. Both of us, Phryne." She paused. "You must be wondering what I am talking about."

Phryne grinned in spite of herself. "I'm afraid I am."

"Then I better get to the point and tell you. Lovely flowers, aren't they? On a day like this, with so much to think about, I find it comforting to come out into the garden to do my thinking. Sitting among all this beauty and those sweet smells and bright colors gives me peace. Over here, Phryne."

She directed her granddaughter to a wooden bench settled among a stand of daffodils in full bloom. Phryne helped her find her seat on the bench and then sat next to her.

"Now then," Mistral Belloruus began, and her brow furrowed. "You must be extremely frustrated and disappointed with the way things have been going since it was discovered the protective walls were down. You angered your father by going up to Aphalion on a pretense and then leaving the valley in direct disobedience of his orders. You failed your friends from Glensk Wood. One of them may pay the price for that failure. You helped bring an enemy into our city and then watched him slip away. You discovered that your stepmother is every bit as bad as you had suspected even though too many others see her as an angel. Important events take place elsewhere, but your father keeps you close to home because he fears for your life. Most distressing of all, your role as Princess of the Elven people has made it impossible for you to do much of anything about this."

She paused. "Have I missed anything?"

Phryne was beet red. "I think you've covered it all, Grandmother."

"I don't do this to embarrass you or to add further pain to your life, although I imagine I've done both. I do it to make certain you have a context in which to appreciate the rest of what I have to say. Because, child, how upset you are with all that has happened and how much you want to do something about it is important." She paused. "You would like to do something about all this unpleasantness, wouldn't you? I'm not wrong in thinking that you would, am I?"

Phryne didn't hesitate. "If you can show me a way to right any of those wrongs, to change for the better any of those mistakes and failings, I won't hesitate to do what's needed."

Her grandmother considered her carefully. "Very well, Phryne. I take you at your word. There was a young man who felt exactly as you do once upon a time, and he said much the same thing as you are saying. He even made a vow to help the Elven people when all was said and done. I would hope I could count on you for that, too."

"Grandmother, you have my word that . . ."

Mistral Belloruus brushed away the rest of what Phryne was going to say with a quick gesture. "I know that," she said quickly. "You needn't speak the words to me. You need only speak the words to yourself, in the privacy of your thoughts."

Phryne shook her head in dismay, her frustration growing. "What is all this about? Can't you just tell me?"

Her grandmother's thin face tightened. "The young are so impatient! Oh, very well. When Kirisin Belloruus and his sister Simralin came into this valley, they carried with them, inside the Elfstone known as the Loden, virtually the whole of the Elven nation, together with the city of Arborlon. The Loden had been used before to transport the Elven people when extreme danger threatened, but not for centuries. It was used by Kirisin because otherwise the entire population would have been wiped out by a demon-led army that had surrounded and trapped it. You've heard the story."

"I have," Phryne acknowledged. "The Loden is sealed away in the archives of the palace. Only my father knows where."

Her grandmother gave her a brief smile. "There were three other Elfstones besides the Loden—another form of magic from the old world of Faerie, recovered from the crypts of Ashenell. Three blue Elfstones, which were called the seeking-Stones, one each for the heart, mind, and body of the user. They could defend the user and those he or she warded, and they could find that which was hidden or even lost. Kirisin Belloruus and his sister carried those Elfstones into the valley, too."

She paused. "They were passed down through the Belloruus family from generation to generation, always with two provisos attached. First, the recipient had to agree to keep the Stones safely hidden until they were needed again. Second, the recipient had to swear to uphold a promise made by Kirisin Belloruus to the spirits of the dead that bestowed on him the gift of the Stones. That promise was to keep alive and foster the use of Elven magic as a part of the Elven culture. This manifested itself mainly in the ways the Elves sought to heal and nurture the land and in not forsaking the use of magic as they had during the time of the rise of Mankind. Kirisin and his sister did their best to comply, and some others of future generations did the same. Not all, unfortunately. Nor have the Belloruus family members continued to serve as Kings and Queens, which would have made Kirisin's promise easier to keep. But that is as it is."

Phryne waited for more, and when her grandmother stayed silent,

she threw up her hands in exasperation. "I thought you were going to
tell me what this meeting was all about! I don't know anything more
than when I came here!"

She was aware suddenly of the dark look her grandmother was giving her. "What is it, Grandmother? What am I missing?"

"Enough so that this conversation becomes necessary," her grandmother replied coldly, wrapping her shawl tighter about her. "But here
is a quick summary for you. The blue Elfstones are not missing. I have
them tucked away in my cottage. They were given to the Belloruus
family; they belong to us and so I've kept them. Your father doesn't
know. No one knows except you and me. It was my intention to give
them to your mother as Queen, but then she died. So I left them
where they were and waited for the next member of the family to
come of age."

Her thin hands closed over her granddaughter's. "That would
be you, Phryne. But events have conspired against me, and waiting for
you to come of age is no longer possible. So I intend to give you the
Elfstones now."

◦ ◦ ◦

IT WAS ALREADY DARK when Skeal Eile saw her approaching, coming down the pathway that led to the outbuildings of the healing center where he had been waiting patiently for several hours. She was in
the company of an old woman, a tottering ancient wrapped in shawls
and scarves, bent from the weight of her years. It was the same old lady
that had appeared to Xac Wen on another visit, the same old lady that
was Bonnasaint in disguise. But only the assassin and the Seraphic
knew that.

Arborlon was quiet, its citizens retired mostly, gone to their homes,
their day's work done. Skeal Eile had entered the city with Bonnasaint
shortly after sunset. No one had noticed them; some time back the
Seraphic had acquired the skill to render himself and those with him
invisible. It wasn't so much that no one saw them; it was more that no
one noticed. They would look away or look down. They would sud-

denly find themselves thinking of something else. They would discover a task that needed doing, and it would require their complete attention. But they would not look at him or anyone with him, and if they happened to catch a glimpse of something they would not remember it later.

So entry into the heavily guarded city was no challenge, and finding the healing center even less so. Skeal Eile had been here before on many occasions. His efforts on behalf of the Children of the Hawk had not stopped at the boundaries of the territories occupied by Men but had extended well beyond, although few knew it. He had his followers among the Elven people, too, those who believed in the teachings and found comfort in the power of the Seraphics.

She was one of these.

She was heavily wrapped in a hooded cloak, her head and face covered against what small lamplight burned through the darkness. The moon was down and clouds masked the stars, so the skies were black. But she was taking no chances. She could not afford to be revealed or to have to offer explanations for what she was doing out alone at night. Most especially, she did not want to be caught in his company.

He stepped out of the shadows as she came up to his hiding place, bowing gracefully. "My Queen," he greeted. "How kind of you to meet with me on such short notice."

Isoeld Severine did not look pleased. She lifted her beautiful face to the light and scowled. "I trust this is important. I risk much in coming to you like this."

"You won't be disappointed, I promise."

She took his arm and pushed him back into the shadows. "Must the hag stay with us?" she whispered, bending close.

Skeal Eile leaned past her and gestured Bonnasaint away. The assassin melted into the night. The Seraphic waited a moment more and then turned back to her. "So now we are alone." He gave her his most endearing smile. "You are well, I hope?"

"Well enough. Come to the point."

"As you wish. I've come to make you an offer, one that I think will benefit us both, one that I've been contemplating for some time. It involves your husband."

She rolled her eyes. "Haven't we had this discussion already? There is nothing left to say."

"Only in the abstract, when discussing a future in which he would not be present. We have never conceived of a means by which that future might come about."

"Yes, and for good reason. My husband is a member of a long-lived family, and he shows no signs of slowing down. I will be old and gray and you will be dust in the earth before he dies."

"But you would like him dead, wouldn't you?"

"You already know the answer to that question."

"Let me be direct. When we spoke before, there was always the problem of how to make his death look accidental, how to avoid suspicion falling on you. As well, there was the problem of his daughter, who is next in line for the throne."

"Sweet little Phryne," Isoeld sneered. Her features were no longer quite so beautiful. "I despise the very air she breathes. But I am finally on the verge of winning her over. She speaks civilly to me now and seems persuaded by my words. I may yet find a way to make use of her."

Skeal Eile nodded. "Perhaps you won't need to. What if we could solve both problems at once? What if we could eliminate father and daughter in one stroke and make you Queen of the Elven people under circumstances where no one would question your right to rule?"

She stared at him wordlessly for a moment.

"What would you say to that?" he pressed.

"You could do this?" she asked quietly.

"I think so. Would you like to hear how?"

She considered. "What would you want in return? You worship the ground I walk on, I know. But I suspect that alone is not enough to satisfy you should I become Queen."

A birdcall sounded in the dark, and Skeal Eile pressed himself against the Queen, flattening her close to the wall of the outbuilding, deep in the shadows. On the roadway at the head of the path, a solitary figure walked past without slowing or looking and then was gone.

Isoeld pushed him away. "*That* had better not be what it will take to satisfy you, Seraphic. Though it might prove amusing."

"What I want, my Queen, is your support. My order requires respect from more than the handful of communities in which it is already given. I am expanding its reach into those villages that still do not believe, but it goes too slowly. If the ruler of the Elves were to become an openly admitted member of the sect and urge her people to join with her, that would give me purchase that I could exploit. If their ruler were to acknowledge the value of my order and embrace my teachings, that would give me a way to expand my influence. If I were invited to visit regularly and to speak at a forum provided and endorsed by their Queen, I would gain immeasurable stature."

She gave him a look. "It is one thing to be seen embracing your teachings and your sect. It is another to give you free and open access to my lands. If I open that door, I am inviting the wolf to come in among the sheep. You will devour them all eventually, and where will I be then?"

He smiled. "Better off than you are now."

There was a long silence as they faced each other down.

"Let me clarify," the Seraphic said finally. "What I want has nothing to do with encroaching on your territory. What I want is sufficient prestige to allow me to overshadow those others who claim the title of Seraphic. If I were to become the voice of the Elven people, acknowledged as such by their Queen, I would gain immense influence throughout the villages of Men. That would be enough for me to assume the mantle of supreme leader. Besides, gaining credence for my sect with a majority of the Elves seems unlikely in any case, don't you think?"

He could tell from her face that she wasn't sure. "Are you really so frightened of my influence?" he challenged. "Cannot a Queen find ways to keep her people in line? Cannot a Queen manage to consolidate her power and cement her rule? Can she not put an end to any influence a Seraphic of the Children of the Hawk might wield if bounds once set are overstepped? I would think so, my lady."

"What of this Troll army that threatens us? What difference if I am Queen and you are acknowledged leader of the Children of the Hawk if this horde overruns us?"

Skeal Eile shook his head. "The inevitable is upon us, my Queen. The world is changing even as we speak, the old one fading and a new one arising. Whether we defeat this army and live to fight another day or are driven from our valley into the larger world, our peoples must still have leaders of vision and ability. Would you not rather be one of those than just another follower? Who better to lead your people? Not the King, surely. Not his child daughter. No, my Queen, whatever fate awaits us all, it would be better met if you and I were in power."

"I cannot argue that," she said. She thought about it again, and he remained silent now as she did so. "You would keep your distance from my people save when you were invited to visit? You ask only my verbal support of your position? Do I understand you correctly?"

"You do," he acknowledged, thinking that she was a bigger fool than he had imagined.

She nodded slowly. "I do want to be Queen," she said. "You can make this happen?"

He smiled. "Let me tell you how."

27

DELADION INCH REACHED THE DROUJ CAMP shortly before sunset of the following day, driving his armored ATV down out of the high country where he had dropped off Sider Ament and continuing on toward the flats west. Ament had told him enough so that he would know the girl he was looking for when he found her—as if there could possibly be more than one held prisoner in the Troll camp—and provided a roughly sketched map of the way back up to the pass through which he would bring her to safety. He had accepted both without comment, knowing that either might fail to help in the end, that things might change as they frequently did in a dangerous undertaking like this one.

In truth, although he might have said something to the contrary, he did not really expect they would see each other again. Odds were against it, and he paid close attention to the odds.

But he liked Sider Ament—genuinely liked him—enough that he hoped he was wrong and they would find each other in better times. If he hadn't liked the other, he would never have agreed to this fool's errand. Walking boldly into a camp of five thousand armed Trolls with the express purpose of taking something away from them that they had no intention of giving up—now, that was just plain idiotic. Didn't matter how carefully disguised his intentions or clever his efforts, he was putting his head in the jaws of a steel trap and handing the trigger release to his enemy. You didn't do things like that for anyone but a friend.

Except, of course, sometimes you did things like that for yourself, which was at least partially true here. His friendship with Sider Ament aside, spiriting the girl away would be akin to rubbing the noses of Taureq Siq and his boys in the dirt, and he found the idea immensely attractive.

He watched the Drouj camp grow closer as he eased the big crawler ahead at dead slow, rolling and heaving through the rough terrain like a great beast. Ahead, the first of the sentries appeared from their hiding places. They would recognize the vehicle and allow him to approach without attacking. Word would already be on its way to Taureq Siq, and the Maturen would be ready to receive him when he was escorted in. A part of him relished the meeting; a part of him whispered that it would be a good idea to turn around right now. Taureq Siq was unpredictable, and he had no special love for Inch. He tolerated him and sometimes even used his mercenary skills because the big man had training and weapons that the Trolls did not. As long as he found Inch useful, he would refrain from doing anything bad to him. But all that could turn around pretty fast. It was always a gamble when you got within strangling distance of the Drouj leader.

Well, he thought, permitting himself a wry smile, he hadn't anything better to do with his day.

In some of his darker, wilder moments, those times when he could afford to think about doing things that were so reckless they bordered on idiotic, he imagined riding the ATV into the Drouj camp at full speed with all weapons firing, creating a killing swath of terrible proportions, leveling the hordes that would come against him, tearing apart tents and supplies and finally, ultimately, catching the Siq family in a murderous firestorm that would put an end to them once and for all. He thought about it again now, a momentary indulgence, fueled by a rush of adrenaline at the prospect of what lay ahead. Didn't matter that he would end up dead, too. Didn't matter that he would go the way of the Trolls and be another of yesterday's memories. Sometimes that was enough.

When you were a mercenary of the sort he was, you thought about dying all the time. If it bothered you, it was time to get out of the business.

He rolled the ATV to a stop in front of the pair of Troll sentries who blocked his way, their impassive faces hiding the fear he knew they were feeling, and switched off the engine. Opening the gull-wing door, he climbed out and stretched, taking his time about it. He wore his black leathers and his body armor and carried both the flechette and the spray, one strapped over each broad shoulder. He'd belted knives at his waist and ankles and hooked several flash-bangs to his vest. He looked and felt dangerous.

Giving the sentries a smile, he closed the ATV door and punched the locking numbers on the keypad, alarming and arming it both. Get too close and it would howl like a banshee. Touch it and you risked finding yourself missing a few body parts. Try breaking in and you turned everything for fifty yards in all directions into charred lumps. The Drouj knew this; he had warned them often enough. Once, early on, he had given them a demonstration of his experience with explosives, one that didn't involve any killing or maiming, but made his point about what might happen. It was sufficiently impressive that no one had chosen to test him on his warnings since. No one would today, either.

"*Cudjion!*" he greeted the sentries in their own language, using a general appellation meant as a designation for warriors. He gave them a friendly wave and walked over to greet them as if they were all comrades-in-arms. "*Ejow mik su keshonen Maturen Taureq Siq.*"

The sentries nodded. They already knew why he was there.

Or thought they did.

He followed them into the Troll camp, taller and broader than most, a big man looking easy and confident in his walk. He took his time, forcing the sentries leading him to follow his pace rather than trying to set their own. Once, early on, they had tried to take away his weapons on orders from Taureq Siq. He had advised them in no uncertain terms that they were not to do this. If the Maturen wanted his services, he had to accept Inch on the latter's terms, not his own. Expecting him to give up his weapons while alone and surrounded by Trolls was just nonsense. Besides, what was he going to do? Was he going to suddenly start killing everyone around him when he was one man against so many? Taureq Siq had apparently decided not because he never asked him to disarm again.

If he had known Inch better, he would have insisted on it. He would have realized that the big man always thought about killing everyone around him, just because that was how he kept his edge.

Once, Grosha had tried to take the spray away from him. The boy was a fool, but he was dangerous, too. Inch had knocked him back a dozen feet and leveled the spray at him. He might have killed him, too, if he hadn't thought Grosha so funny at the time. He didn't think him funny now, and sometimes he thought everyone would have been better off if he had just done what his instincts told him when he had the chance.

Maybe today, he told himself. It was a good day for it.

After he found the girl.

The sentries brought him up to Taureq Siq's command tent, where the Maturen was waiting for him, standing in front of the tent flaps with his sycophants and retainers and his miserable younger son. No sign of the elder, which might mean he was still inside the valley. It would be too bad for him if he was. Sider Ament would find him and put an end to him; Inch was certain of it. He'd seen the look in the other's eyes when he'd learned the truth. Revelation, rage, and murderous determination—they were all visible. Scary, even to a seasoned veteran like himself. Sider wasn't the kind you wanted to antagonize, and the Maturen's elder son had gone way beyond that.

Inch came up to Taureq Siq, giving him a friendly greeting in the form of hands outstretched and palms turned up. It signified that he came openly and without bad intentions. A dreadful lie, but what could you do? The Maturen gave him a small nod and nothing more. Trusted nobody, that one. Inch knew why. Taureq was always expecting the worst of everyone and was seldom disappointed. One day Inch, too, would live up to his expectations.

He barely spared a glance at Grosha as he addressed the boy's father in his own tongue. "*Cudjion*, Taureq. Word is you've made plans to make a new home in a valley beyond those mountains." He pointed off to the east, toward where he had left Sider Ament to make his way back. "I thought you might need someone with my skills to help you get settled."

The Maturen gave him a hard look. "How do you know of this? The Trolls don't speak of it."

Inch shrugged. "I met a man, one from the valley. He spoke to me about you. Said you had one of his people. He wanted to know what I could tell him about you, what I knew that might help him decide how to stop you. I told him he had better find a new home far, far away."

Grosha started forward a step, snarling. "You spoke to someone about us?" he demanded. "You gave him information?"

"What I told him, he already knew." Deladion Inch spoke to the father, ignoring the son. "What matters is that I know where to find the entrance to the valley, so maybe that's information you can use. Maybe I can be of service, if there's something in it for me."

Taureq Siq's face relaxed. "We already know how to get into the valley this man comes from. We know everything. Those who live there are not warriors, not trained, not skilled in fighting. They have no army, no unity of their peoples, nothing that would prevent us from taking the valley for ourselves. We don't need you."

Deladion Inch nodded and shrugged. "Maybe you don't. Maybe you know all about their weapons and how to get past them. Maybe you aren't afraid of something that can wipe out half your soldiers before you even get within bow range."

It sounded good, even to him. The secret of the valley's passes was compromised, along with the lack of any standing army trained to defend against invaders. But maybe the discussion hadn't gotten to the matter of weapons.

The Maturen hesitated. "They have the same weapons we do. Except that they have one of the black staffs aiding them, as well. But one man is not enough to stop us."

"One man, no. Fifty fire throwers and a dozen cannons that can reach a target a mile away, yes. Or am I missing something?"

Grosha spit at him. "You lie, mercenary."

"Do I? You know this?"

"I know Elves don't have weapons like that!"

He gave the boy a sympathetic smile. "Elves don't *want* weapons like that. But Men do. What do your spies have to tell you of that?"

It was a calculated gamble, but it appeared to be working. There was a low muttering among those assembled, silenced quickly as Taureq Siq looked around angrily. "Do you know of these weapons?" he asked Inch. "Have you seen them?"

The big man shook his head. "Only heard of them. But I recognize how they work and what they can do from what I know of my own weapons. You don't want to risk facing them without a plan."

"Don't believe him, Father!" Grosha snapped, fury twisting his blunt features. "He would say anything to share in what we have!"

Inch gave him another smile and looked at his father as if to say, *These impulsive boys, what can you do?* "You doubt what I'm saying, little pup? Let's ask the girl, your captive from the valley. Let's see what she says. Go ahead. Ask her."

"We cannot ask her!" Grosha shouted, enraged. "We don't speak the language well enough. Only Arik does. You know that!"

"I don't know anything about it." Inch kept his eyes on the father. "Why don't you let me speak with her? I'll tell you what she says. After all, I've got nothing to gain by lying to you about it. If I do, you'll find out quick enough when you enter the valley and you'll hang me from your tent pole."

Taureq Siq was silent a moment, gesturing for his angry son to be silent, as well. He was clearly conflicted about it, but he was smart enough not to want to risk missing something important.

"All right," he agreed finally. "But if you deceive me, you will die." He gestured toward one of the guards. "Bring the girl."

Grosha turned away in disgust, muttering to himself.

Deladion Inch took a deep breath as the guard departed. He was going to get his chance now, the chance he needed, but he still didn't know how he was going to make this work. Somehow, he had to get the girl through the camp and back to the ATV if they were to have any chance of escaping. But Taureq would have his eye on him the entire time he was speaking to her, so he was going to have to be clever.

A sudden thrumming on the tent roof drew his attention. It was raining, a downpour. Funny, but he hadn't even noticed rain clouds on his way in. He breathed in the fresh smells, the dampness and the cool. He glanced through the gap in the tent flaps; the daylight had faded, clouds covering the sun and masking the sky. It would be dark much sooner. The ground would be wet, and tracks would be hard to follow.

It took only moments before the guard returned with his prisoner. The girl was just a little thing, probably not much more than a hundred pounds, small and slender, with bright red hair and green eyes that looked right through you. She didn't flinch from him when she saw him, clad in black leather and armor, weapons hanging off him everywhere. She simply studied him as she would an interesting specimen, trying to make something out of it.

Inch glanced at Taureq for permission to speak to her, and the Maturen nodded. The big man came forward and knelt in front of her. "You're Prue Liss?" he asked her. "Sider Ament sends greetings."

She stared at him, surprise reflected in her green eyes. "He sent you?"

"He did. He couldn't come himself. Are you all right? Have you been hurt?"

She shook her head no. "What are you going to do?"

"Talk to you a minute. Ask you about weapons that your people in the valley don't have. Pretend you're telling me something about them. Just a quick few words. They don't understand what we're saying, so it's all right. When I'm done, give me a hug. Look frightened. Can you do that? You'll be taken back to where they're holding you, but I'll come for you. Understand?"

She nodded. "I understand."

"Remember the hug," he said.

She nodded wordlessly, eyes fixed on his face.

They talked about nothing, as he had said they would, pretending at questions and answers. It was hot inside the tent, and Deladion Inch could felt the sweat running down his back inside his heavy leathers. Outside, the rain continued to beat against the tent surface, a staccato rhythm. He tried to keep the girl's eyes locked on his, willing her to play along, to make believe with such skill that the Trolls, who were pressing close about them, would not discover their deception. The girl kept looking at him, staring into his eyes, understanding what was needed. She never flinched.

Inch finished, gave her a quick nod, and started to stand up. As he did, she rushed to him immediately and threw her arms around his shoulders and hugged him close. He patted her comfortingly and backed her away.

Then he turned to Taureq Siq. "She confirms what I already told you. But there is some good news. Not everyone has these weapons, only the Men of the larger villages. They have some small fighting forces, too, but they aren't well trained. You can overcome them once you know how to jam their weapons."

Taureq Siq was watching him closely. "You will explain all this to me. But not until Arik returns. He will be here by morning. You will be our guest until he arrives."

Your prisoner, you mean. Inch had expected as much, but he was dismayed that the older son would be back so soon. He would have to act quickly if he wanted to get out of here alive. "I would be honored, Taureq."

They were taking the girl back to where they had been holding her, the guard easing her toward the tent flaps and back outside. Inch glanced her way once, but paid no further attention. "I would appreciate some food and a place to sleep," he told Siq. "I've been traveling all day."

The Maturen nodded to the guards who had brought him in. "Give him what he wants, but stay with him."

Taureq Siq turned away, his attention on something else, the interview over. Deladion Inch moved for the tent flaps, not waiting on his escort. He pushed through quickly, out into the rain, which had diminished from a downpour to a steady drizzle. Twilight had settled in, and torches burned through the gray haze, fighting back against the damp. Without seeming to do so, he scanned his surroundings, just managing to catch sight of the girl's slight figure as she disappeared from view into a maze of tents and bodies. But he marked the direction in which she had gone, knowing it would help him find her later.

His guards caught up and motioned him in the opposite direction, staying well clear as they did so. Inch smiled and nodded, following their lead, taking mental notes of everything as they made their way to a small, shabby tent that was perhaps fifty yards away. The tent served otherwise as a supply dump or an animal shelter, a deliberate comment on his status. On any other occasion, Deladion Inch would have been furious. But it didn't matter here. After tonight, he would never be back.

He ducked inside the tent and settled himself on a sleeping pad amid tent coverings and piles of ties and stays, happy to discover that at least his quarters were dry. His guards brought him food, and he sat down with his dinner. Some sort of stew and warm ale. It was sufficient.

He ate and drank and then settled back to wait.

IT WAS TWO HOURS LATER, the bustle of activity and the drone of voices died down, the rain diminished but the darkness complete, when he peeked through a tiny gap in the tent flaps. His guards stood just outside, looking bored and uncomfortable in their heavy-weather cloaks. There was little movement in the darkness beyond; most of the torches were extinguished, the Trolls were settling in for the night. He couldn't wait any longer. He couldn't afford to be there when Arik Siq returned, and that could happen at any time. He would have preferred it if everyone but the watch was asleep, but you couldn't always have what you wanted in the rescue business.

He called one of the guards into the tent and asked him for a cloak to cover himself and another to lie down on. The guard, under orders to give Inch what he wanted, did not argue. He left and returned again with two all-weather cloaks. As soon as he had gone back outside to his watch, Inch built a dummy of himself out of sacks and covered it with one of the cloaks. Then he moved to the rear of the tent, cut a slit in it with his long knife, slipped on the second cloak with the hood pulled up, peered out to be sure the way was clear, and stepped through.

In the palm of his hand, he held the receiver to the tracking device he had attached to the girl's clothing when she hugged him. A small red light blinked a slow, steady signal. As he got closer to her, it would blink more rapidly and brightly. It would lead him right to her.

Or so he hoped.

He was a big man, but he was among big people, so he wasn't as noticeable as he would have been elsewhere. His cloak and hood hid his features, and the weather and darkness reduced visibility to almost nothing. No one paid any attention to him as he walked through the camp, absorbed in their own business and looking to get in out of the rain.

He glanced down at the signal to make certain it was growing stronger, that he was headed in the right direction. The signal told him he was. He could feel the old, familiar excitement flooding through him. He could feel himself giving in to its intoxicating rush, welcoming it like an old friend.

He checked the signal. It was blinking rapidly. The girl was just ahead.

He saw the guard at the entrance to the tent through the screen of rain, and he knew she was there. No torches lit the entry. No light came from inside. Nothing to draw attention, nothing to suggest its importance. He glanced down at the signal. The blinking orb had grown brighter. There was no question about it; he had found her.

He started toward the tent and the guard.

And suddenly a small billowing of the tent fabric caught his eye, and he changed direction instantly. It might have been the wind and nothing more. But it might also have been something inside the tent pressing up against the fabric. Whichever it was, he didn't like it. It was an instinctual thing, raw and sharp, the sort of internal warning he had learned to trust over the years, the sort of warning that had kept him alive.

He left the tent behind and then circled back from the rear. When he was still several dozen yards away, he stopped beside a rack of spears and studied the tent in the gloom and rain and thought about what he should do. Saving the girl using the direct approach no longer seemed like such a good idea. He needed a different plan, something that would expose the truth about what else was inside the tent. And he was convinced by now that something else was. He felt it in his bones.

The posting of a single guard was a lure meant to deceive him. Kill the guard, slip inside, and get to the girl—that had been his plan and maybe, just maybe, someone had figured that out.

He couldn't have said why, but he thought suddenly that it was more than possible; it was so.

He stood in the rain a moment longer, considering his options.

He could cut through the canvas, slip in from the back of the tent, and take his chances—or he could just walk up to the guard and ask to speak to the girl, say that he needed to check again on something she had said, say that Taureq Siq had sent him.

Neither option appealed to him.

He moved off to the left toward a storage tent he had noticed earlier, a large bulky structure containing food and clothing, perhaps medical supplies, as well, if he remembered correctly how the Drouj kept their camp. What he was about to do was going to place him in considerable danger, but then almost anything he did would do that anyway.

Besides, wasn't that why he was here? Didn't he want to see if he could cheat death one more time?

The idea of it made him smile.

Without further thought, he snatched a torch from its stanchion, walked to the supply tent, loosened the ties on the flaps, and tossed the burning brand inside. The flames found fuel almost immediately, exploding in a bright orange blossom, leaping quickly from the tent's contents to the fabric of its walls. He was already moving away by then, circling back around to the tent where the girl was held captive to see what would happen.

Within seconds shouts and cries of alarm arose, and Trolls began pouring out of their shelters into the gloom and rain, converging on the burning tent. Inch stayed where he was, watching the tent with the girl. After a moment, the flaps opened and Grosha emerged, eyes flicking this way and that, searching the night. Then, abandoning his post, he said something to the guard and rushed off toward the source of the uproar.

Inch didn't hesitate. He went instantly to the rear of the tent and, using his long knife, began to saw an opening in the fabric. The noise around him would hide the sound of his cutting so he didn't bother with taking his time. Speed was important now.

It took him only moments and he was through. Still gripping the long knife, he slipped through the opening and into the tent.

He was attacked almost immediately. A huge dark shape catapulted out of the shadows, slamming into him with enough force to knock him to the ground. Rows of sharp teeth tore at him. A Skaith Hound. If he hadn't been holding the long knife, he would have been dead, but he reacted instinctively, thrusting the knife into the beast's throat and tearing across. Blood gushed out as the beast lurched and writhed, its growl cut short, and then it collapsed on top of him.

Inch threw it off, scrambling back to his feet to confront the guard rushing through the tent flap from outside, a short sword in hand. He blocked the sword's thrust, sidestepped the blade, seized the guard's arm, and wrenched it at the elbow. The bones snapped, the sword fell away from nerveless fingers, and the long knife put an end to him.

Bloodied and angry, his left arm torn open by the Skaith Hound, Inch shoved the dead guard away and searched the tent for the girl. He didn't see her. Panic raced through him, but he forced it down. Either he would find her or he wouldn't, but he had only seconds left to make the effort and then he would have to flee.

The thought was barely completed before he caught sight of movement under a set of blankets stacked in the far corner. Throwing back the coverings, he found her bound and gagged beneath. He cut her loose and brought her to her feet. Her eyes were bright with fear.

"Can you run? Look at me! Can you run?" He saw the fear disappear, and she nodded. "Good. We have to hurry. Stay close to me."

He wrapped her in the dead guard's cloak and took her out through the back of the tent, stepping over the bodies of the hound and the Troll. The fire he had set was still blazing, a bright wash against the darkness. He took her another way, trying to avoid an encounter with the milling Trolls. He walked her steadily forward, resisting the urge to run, keeping their pace slow and steady. Behind them, the shouts and cries continued to rise, but he didn't think the Trolls had discovered that the girl was missing yet.

That changed in the next ten seconds. A fresh cry went up, and now an alarm horn sounded, its deep wail booming out across the flats. His hand dropped to the handle of the flechette, unhooking it from his shoulder, letting it rest against his leg. He didn't want to fire it, knowing that if he did, they would be after him instantly. But he might not have a choice.

The outcries were growing stronger, and the number of Trolls milling about increased exponentially. He knew they had to reach the ATV if they were to have any chance at all. But the vehicle was still a long way off. He pressed on, increasing his pace. Beside him, the girl was a silent black shadow within the cloak, working hard to keep pace. She was tough, that one; she had real iron inside her small body.

Abruptly, a handful of Trolls blocked his path, their hands raised to stop him. He gestured them aside, shouted at them in their own language, and to his amazement they gave way. He hurried on, not bothering to look back, trying to suggest with his body language that his business was important and he should not be interfered with. It worked until he reached the perimeter of the camp. He could just make out the ATV through the gloom when a clutch of sentries converged on him from both sides. He shouted and gestured anew, but this time the Drouj were not giving way.

Pushing the girl behind him, he brought up the barrel of the Tyson Flechette and blew away the two on his left, then swung the barrel right and killed three more. The explosions were loud and the air was filled with the smell of residue from the firing.

"Run!" he shouted at the girl, pushing her ahead of him toward the crawler.

There was no point in pretending now. The game was up. Trolls were converging from everywhere. Ahead, the crawler stood waiting, no sentries in sight. Arrows whizzed by his ears, and he could hear the sound of pursuit. He didn't look back. He ran behind the girl, using his body as a shield.

Several arrows thudded into his back, striking him heavy blows. The body armor and the leathers kept them from penetrating. But if one of them managed to find his exposed head . . .

As they reached the ATV, he wheeled back and fired half a dozen shells into the Trolls coming on, knocking down some, scattering the rest. He punched in the code on the keypad to open the doors and disarm the security devices and shoved the girl inside, diving after her. The doors closed behind them, and he switched on the engine.

There were Trolls all around them in seconds, hammering on the vehicle's metal shell, trying to break through the windows with their heavy spears. He laughed at them as his fingers worked the controls, powering up the engine and engaging the thrusters. The ATV leapt forward, knocking the Trolls aside as if they were made of straw. Rolling and bouncing across the rough terrain, he wheeled the crawler away from the camp, heading south for the flats where he could swing the vehicle east toward the mountains and the pass leading through to the valley beyond.

Inch powered the vehicle out into the night, leaving the Drouj camp and its inhabitants behind. He could see them for a while, blocky forms giving chase, a hopeless effort driven solely by rage, and then they were gone, even their shouts faded away. But he didn't slow, keeping his speed steady, watching the terrain ahead for deep ruts or holes that might crack an axle, determined to put as much distance as he could between themselves and their pursuers before easing off.

He glanced over at the girl. Her eyes were wide, her hands gripping the seat as she pressed herself against its padded back. He had forgotten; she would not have seen anything like this before. It would be a new form of magic for her.

He laughed in spite of himself. "Don't worry! We're safe now!"

Seconds later, the entire vehicle shuddered and broke apart beneath them.

28

IN THE CITY OF ARBORLON, THINGS WERE COMING apart in an equally unexpected way.

Three days had passed since Mistral Belloruus revealed that she had possession of the missing Elfstones and intended to give them to her granddaughter, and Phryne Amarantyne was still struggling with what to do about it. Her initial reaction had been one of shock and anger, and she had told her grandmother that it was her father who should have the Elven talismans, not her. He was King, and they belonged to him. What would she do with them, anyway? She was barely grown and in no way experienced in the uses of magic. It was ridiculous for her grandmother even to consider passing the Elfstones to her.

Her grandmother had let her vent, sitting quietly, saying nothing. But when she was finished, she very calmly and deliberately told her to grow up and be the woman her mother had been. What constituted loyalty to the throne and to the Elven people was a matter of opinion. The Elfstones were never intended exclusively for those who sat upon the Elven throne. Possession of magic that powerful was not a given right, but an earned one. The Elfstones had been passed to Kirisin Belloruus because he had made a commitment to do what was needed to save his people from a demon army and to make certain that the legacy of magic that had once been inherent in the Elven way of life was revived. He had fulfilled that commitment, but those who had gained possession of the Elfstones after him had lost their way. They had accepted blindly that the valley would keep them forever safe and that magic of the sort contained in the Elfstones was unnecessarily dangerous. They had embraced instead the old belief that magic belonged to the age of Faerie and had no place in their world, and so the magic had languished anew.

Her mother had thought differently, but her father had not supported her and so nothing had been done during his reign as King to experiment with the magic. Yes, the Elves still used small amounts to sustain and heal the land, but that was nothing new. It was not the intent of those who had passed the Elfstones to Kirisin Belloruus that usage of the magic should stop there. Had Phryne's mother lived, they would not be having this conversation; the Elfstones would have passed to her. Now they would pass to Phryne—not because she was her mother's daughter, but because she had the strength of character her father did not and that was what was needed if the Elves were to survive.

The session had ended in a shouting match, and Phryne had stormed out, furious with her grandmother and determined to have no part in her misguided scheming.

Yet here she was, just three days later, responding to a summons to return to her grandmother's cottage, another written message delivered by another oldster. In spite of herself, she was going back. She did so for several reasons. For one thing, she loved her grandmother, and no argument between them would ever change that. For another, the recovery of the Elfstones was too important to allow personal feelings to govern her actions. No matter her dismay with her grandmother, she knew she must continue trying to persuade her that the Elfstones should be given to her father. Reason must prevail, and clearly it would have to come from her.

Her grandmother had other plans, of course. She had not tried to give Phryne the Elfstones on the day they first spoke of them—had not even shown them to her, in fact. But this time she produced them shortly after her granddaughter walked through the door. There was no time for arguing, Mistral Belloruus declared as Phryne attempted to pick up where she had left off. What was needed was an object lesson. If Phryne was to persist in her insistence that the Elfstones belonged in her father's hands, she needed to know exactly what that meant.

She marched Phryne outside and through the gardens, going deep into the woods to where they could no longer even see her cottage. They went alone, the old woman making her way with slow, painful steps, the girl holding her arm in case she should trip. It was a measure of her grandmother's determination to win her over that she let Phryne help her, and the girl did not miss what this meant.

When they had reached a place where her grandmother felt comfortable with doing so, she reached into the pocket of her dress and produced a cloth pouch, loosened the drawstrings, and dumped the contents into her hand. Three brilliant blue stones, perfectly faceted and unblemished, their color so extraordinary that Phryne gasped in spite of herself, lay cradled in her palm, the sunlight dancing off their smooth surfaces.

"These are the blue Elfstones, Phryne, the seeking-Stones," her grandmother advised, her eyes fixed not on the Stones, but on the girl. "One each for the heart, mind, and body. They work in unison, drawing on the strengths found within the user. The greater those strengths, the greater the power of the Stones. In effect, the user determines the power of the magic. I see great strength in you, girl. Why don't we find out if I am right?"

Phryne, seeing what was intended, shook her head at once. "I won't do that. The magic does not belong to me, and I don't want any part of it. If you feel so strongly about this, you use them. You are at least as strong as I will ever be. You give the demonstration."

Her grandmother gave her a look. "It doesn't work like that. You don't learn anything by watching me. You learn by doing it yourself. Wielding the magic, experiencing the power, is how you discover what it means to have command of it. Take the Elfstones. Just hold them for a moment."

Reluctantly, still promising herself that she would not use them, Phryne took the Stones. "Why didn't you give them to my mother, if you thought she was the one who should have them? Why did you hold on to them while she was alive?"

"Feel the weight of them?" her grandmother asked, ignoring her. "Much heavier than you would expect. Close your fingers over them and let's see what happens."

"Maybe I don't want to know."

"Don't be afraid. Just do as I ask."

Reluctantly, Phryne did. They were indeed heavier than she expected, and as she held them she could feel unexpected warmth seeping into her skin. Her eyes found her grandmother's. "They feel alive," she whispered.

"They *are* alive. The magic is a living thing. It lies inanimate until a user summons it, until it finds a kindred spirit. It doesn't work for anyone who isn't Elven, and it doesn't respond to anyone to whom it is not given freely—as I have given it to you."

Phryne frowned. "But I didn't accept it."

"You aren't the one who matters. See how quickly it warms for you? That means it knows you are right for it."

"But I don't want this!" Phryne was incensed. She shoved the Elfstones toward her grandmother. "Take them back!"

"Wait, wait." Her grandmother's voice was persuasive, her tone soft and placating. "Let's finish what we started. It won't bind you in any way, I promise. It will only demonstrate what I have been telling you. Now, listen to me. Here is what you must do. For the Elfstones to work, you must picture in your mind what it is you seek. You must see it clearly and you must ask the Stones to find it for you. You must will it to happen. Can you do that? Will you try?"

Phryne did not want to try. She wanted to go back three days in time and start over. But she understood, as well, that if she refused now she would have given up any chance of pursuing her argument that the Elfstones belonged in the possession of her father.

So she said, even more reluctant now than before, "I'll try."

"Remember what I said, child. Your combined strengths of heart, mind, and body will determine the extent of your control over the magic. It will determine how suited you are to its use. This is your chance to discover the truth of things. Use it well."

"I understand," she said, wondering if she did.

"Stretch your hand out in front of you, away from your body. Think of what it is that you wish to find. A person, a place, a creature, anything. Start with something easy. Something you know well enough to see clearly in your mind. You can do much more with these Elfstones than find something with which you are already familiar; you can even find things that you have never seen. But don't start with something that difficult."

She reached for Phryne's hand, folding her own over it. "What will you choose to seek? Tell me."

Phryne didn't know. She wanted it to be something that would test what the old woman said, something that was not too close to where they stood, something that could not be found in Arborlon, for instance.

"What about the young man from Glensk Wood that you seem so fond of?" her grandmother suggested suddenly.

Phryne hesitated. "I don't know. That feels like spying."

"It might help alleviate your concerns for him. Of course, you could seek out the girl instead."

"No!" Phryne said quickly. She did not care to know about Prue Liss just yet. "I'll look for Panterra."

She stretched out her hand, fingers closing about the Elfstones, arm directed southward, in the direction Pan had gone. She closed her eyes to help with focusing her thoughts, picturing the boy in her mind, seeing his face clearly. She willed the Elfstones to show him to her, to reveal his location. She did not press herself, deciding that if the magic was meant to work, it should come easily. She still did not trust what the magic would do. She still was uncertain about its effects. Her grandmother had said nothing that suggested she was in any danger, but Mistral Belloruus had a habit of keeping things to herself.

"Relax, Phryne," her grandmother whispered to her.

She did so, loosening her muscles and going inward to where Panterra's face wafted in the darkness of her thoughts. She floated close to the image, searching for the real thing.

Abruptly, she felt the Elfstones warm within her hand, causing her to open her eyes in surprise and look down. Brilliant blue light seeped from between her fingers, flashing outward in slender streamers that were as blinding as new sunlight. She kept her thoughts on Panterra, watching the light coalesce and then lance outward through the trees and into the distance. She saw it pierce time and space and substance in a tunnel of light that reached for miles beyond where she stood to find the boy from Glensk Wood.

All of a sudden there he was. Panterra Qu. He stood within the high rock walls of a pass in the midst of other workers, all of them engaged in the building of defensive bulwarks meant to span the opening and provide protection against invaders. He was at Declan Reach, she realized, high up in the pass, gone to help with the fortifications.

He was there just long enough for her to be certain of where he was and what he was doing, and then the light from the Elfstones vanished, the image disappeared, and she was back beside her grandmother, standing in the trees beyond her gardens.

She opened her fingers and peered down into her palm where the Elfstones lay twinkling. There was no damage to her skin. There was no pain. She checked herself carefully, wanting to be certain. She had not been harmed.

But something had been done. A rush of exhilaration was flooding through her body, sweeping from head to foot and back again, a sense of warmth and excitement mingling with something she could not define. A satisfaction, perhaps. A glory. It roiled within her like an adrenaline infusion, yet it was unlike anything she had experienced before. She closed her fingers over the Elfstones once more and looked down at her hands as she tucked them close against her body, not wanting her grandmother to see what was happening. But it was useless, she knew. Mistral Belloruus would have tested the Elfstones herself. She would already have tasted what her granddaughter was experiencing.

She looked up again quickly and saw the knowledge reflected in her grandmother's eyes. "Now you know," the old lady whispered.

Phryne handed the Elfstones back, quickly pressing them into her grandmother's hands. "I know. But it doesn't change my mind. The magic belongs to my father. He is capable of handling it much better than I am."

"You are wrong about that, child," the old woman answered.

"You can't know that if you haven't given him a chance to discover it for himself. You owe him that. You did this for me; now you have to do it for him. Then you can make a decision."

"Would you accept such a decision, once made?" Her grandmother waited for her to answer, and when she didn't, said, "I thought not. So what is the point of doing what you ask?"

"You know what I mean."

"I know what you think you mean." Her grandmother smiled and shook her head. "But we needn't talk on it further just now. I only wanted you to understand what having use of the Elfstones meant. There is much more to it than the little you've experienced. You will discover that if you test yourself again, as I think you must. These particular Elfstones are seeking-Stones, but they can also protect the user against other magic and dangers that threaten. They are a powerful weapon as well as a versatile tool. Bearing them carries responsibility; possessing them demands accountability. Few are able to handle demands of that sort."

"I suspect I am not one of those few," Phryne said.

Mistral Belloruus tucked the Elfstones into the pouch and the pouch into her pocket. Then she reached over and took hold of her granddaughter's arm.

"We'll talk about it later, you and I," she said. "We've done enough for now. You need time to reflect on what's happened." She squeezed Phryne's arm gently. "Would you walk me back to my cottage, please? And stay, perhaps, for a cup of tea? I think that would be a very nice end to your visit."

Arm in arm, they made their way back through the trees to the gardens and the old lady's home.

PHRYNE RETURNED TO THE PALACE AFTER THAT and spent several hours brooding. She was not happy about what had happened, but regrets were useless. She should never have agreed to use the Elfstones as her grandmother had insisted, even if it meant an end to their conversation about who should possess the magic. Using them had only confused the issue further. Worse, it had raised questions in her mind that had not been there before. For the first time, she was wondering if perhaps her grandmother was right about giving the Elfstones to her instead of her father. She hated it that she was considering such a thing, aware that by doing so she was betraying him. But was she? Or was she simply doing what was expected of her?

The problem lay with the inescapable truth about her father. In the time of his reign as King, he had done nothing to foster the study or use of Elven magic. He had simply ignored that particular mandate, satisfied that healing and nurturing of the Elven territories was a sufficient use. But the Elves had not survived all these years through healing and nurturing alone. They had not survived the Great Wars and escaped into this valley by taking a passive stance toward the evil that confronted them. Yet here they were, five hundred years later, a new evil at their doorstep threatening to take away their homes and perhaps their freedom, and what fresh magic had they mastered?

None.

The Elfstones were all they had, and if her grandmother was to be believed—which Phryne thought she was—the Elves had ignored that magic completely.

She was also still troubled by her father's decision to marry someone like Isoeld. It wasn't that his remarriage was a betrayal of his vows to her mother; she didn't think that way. It was the clear stupidity of his choice. A treacherous, duplicitous girl too young by half, a girl with no intention of respecting her marriage vows, a schemer with ambitions that far exceeded her concerns for her husband, Isoeld was a poor choice at best and a foolish, dangerous one at worst. That her father seemed so unaware of this, so blind to it, suggested that he had somehow lost his way. If that were so, how effective could he be at wielding the magic of the Elfstones, a power that worked best where the heart, mind, and body must all be strong?

She didn't know. Clearly, her grandmother had made up her mind on the matter. But Mistral Belloruus had never liked her father, even when he was married to her mother. She had tolerated him, but she had never approved of him. It was why, after Phryne's mother was gone, she had cut herself off from him completely.

It was also why she felt her granddaughter was the right choice to bear the Elfstones.

But even if Phryne accepted that her grandmother was right and her father lacked the strength of character needed to use the Elfstone magic, why would she be a better choice? Even if she accepted the gift of the Elfstones, what was she expected to do with them? She hadn't been trained in battle arts. She knew next to nothing about fighting, and she wasn't even particularly strong. Yet if she took the Elfstones, wouldn't she have to stand at the forefront of the Elven army against the Troll invaders? Ultimately, wasn't that what would be expected of anyone who wielded the Stones?

The Orullian brothers would roll over laughing at the very idea. The brothers, her cousins, would never let her live it down if they heard that she was even considering such a thing.

She was so uncomfortable with the idea that she made up her mind on the spot that she was going to reject her grandmother's offer of the Elfstones. Even if Mistral Belloruus was right and her father was the wrong choice to bear the magic, that did not make Phryne the right one. Someone else would better serve the Elven people. Someone with experience and a lifetime of dedication working for the good of the people. It didn't matter that she couldn't think of anyone like that offhand. Given time, she would be able to come up with a name. Or two.

She could.

She was mulling over how to tell her grandmother all this when her father walked into her room and sat down across from her. She looked up expectantly, not sure why he was there.

"I've been summoned to a meeting with Isoeld," he said after a minute, looking unsure of how to proceed with what he had to say. "She says it has something to do with our relationship and my service as Elven King. She wants you there, too. Do you have any idea what this is about?"

This was Phryne's chance to say something about Isoeld's affairs with other men, about her cheating on her husband. After all, it was possible that she had become ashamed enough of her behavior that she was going to do the right thing and step aside as Queen. That was what Phryne would have liked to believe, but she couldn't quite make herself do so. Nothing about Isoeld suggested that the word *shame* was even familiar to her.

So she just shook her head. "I don't."

Her father nodded, looking distracted. "Perhaps I've done something to anger her and I need to apologize . . ."

"Perhaps you've done nothing wrong at all!" Phryne snapped, unable to listen to such nonsense. "Perhaps she's the one who's done something wrong and needs to apologize to you!"

Her father looked startled. "What do you mean? What do you think she might have done?"

Phryne shook her head. "Nothing. I just don't think you should assume you've done anything."

"That isn't how you made it sound." Her father shook his head. "I thought you two were getting along better."

"We are," she lied. She made a vague gesture toward the doorway. "Is she coming here for this meeting? Or are we supposed to go to her? When is it, anyway?"

"Right now, in the family library. Are you ready?"

She would never be ready for anything having to do with Isoeld unless it involved watching her father give the little scut a kick in the backside out the door, but she supposed there was no putting it off. Between the meetings with her grandmother and now this one, she would be grateful if she weren't summoned to anything more than dinner for a month.

They left the room and made their way down the palace hallways toward the library, Oparion Amarantyne leading, his daughter trudging reluctantly behind. Phryne listened to the sound of their footfalls in the silence, thinking it unusually quiet even for late afternoon, when visitors were no longer admitted and the day was winding down toward dinnertime. She mulled over anew her inevitable confrontation with her grandmother, trying to think how to speak the required words. She found it impossible.

The library door was ajar when they reached the chamber, and her father pushed through first, Phryne following. Isoeld stood at the center of the room, right in front of her husband's desk, hands clasped before her, smiling warmly.

Teonette stood beside her, grim-faced.

"Thank you both for coming," she greeted. "This won't take long."

"Why is he here?" Phryne snapped, stepping forward to confront them both. She spoke out of turn, but she was too angry to care. She was incensed at the boldness of this woman, bringing her lover to a meeting with her husband.

"What is this about?" Oparion Amarantyne demanded.

Isoeld took a step forward. "It is about you. It is about taking the measure of a life. Your own, to be precise. Good-bye, Oparion."

In the next instant, a masked figure slipped from the shadows behind the open door and drove a dagger deep into the King's chest. The King cried out and lurched forward, but the assassin locked his free arm about his victim's neck and, holding him tight, drove the dagger in a second and third time. Phryne screamed in shock and rage, but Isoeld was on top of her by now and struck her hard across the face—once, twice, three times—dropping her to her knees, stunned.

The assassin yanked the dagger free from the dying King and allowed him to fall. Without a word, he turned, placed the dagger next to Phryne, and disappeared through the open door.

Isoeld bent close. "Your father is dead, Phryne, and you killed him. A terrible quarrel of some sort, it appears. We may never know the truth of it. But you attacked him with your knife—it is your dagger, you know—and although Teonette and I came running at the sounds of a struggle, we arrived too late to stop you."

Phryne tried to scramble up, but Teonette was behind her, holding her fast. She started to scream, and Isoeld said, "Good, scream all you want! But your anguish at what you've done comes too late for your father. Such a terrible thing, patricide. I imagine we won't be seeing much of you again for many years. That's if they don't decide to put you to death. I'll do what I can to see that they don't. I like the idea of you alive and well and locked away for the rest of your life."

Phryne gasped for breath. "They'll never believe—"

Isoeld struck her across the face several times more. The girl's vision blurred as tears filled her eyes, and she felt everything begin to spin.

"Your father fought back, which is why you have all these marks on your face. He fought hard for his life, even as he was dying. But it wasn't enough. His wounds were too grievous. Drop her."

Teonette let go, and Phryne collapsed to the floor. Isoeld kicked her down all the way and put her foot on her neck. "The King is dead, Phryne," she hissed. "Long live the Queen!"

29

RAIN SPLASHED DOWN ON HIS FACE, CHILL AND stinging, the wind whipping the droplets of water into tiny missiles, and he was conscious again. He lay staring up at a sky that looked like the bottom of a churning cauldron, dark and wild. He turned his head, blinked away the rain, and tried to focus.

What had happened?

Then Deladion Inch remembered, and he was awake instantly. The crawler had inexplicably come apart beneath him. For no discernible reason, a two-ton monster made of iron had disintegrated. That wasn't possible. It wasn't even conceivable.

He felt the pain then, ratcheting through him. He took inventory of his body, a careful investigation that didn't require him to move. His ribs, several broken. His arm, aching badly enough that it might be broken, as well. His head, of course, but when he felt along the skin there didn't appear to be any deep wounds.

Then he remembered the girl.

He looked around, realizing for the first time that he wasn't in the vehicle anymore. He was lying on the ground a short distance away. He had been thrown clear, sustained injuries in the process, and lost consciousness.

But where was the girl?

He sat upright, using his good arm to lever himself off the ground. He found his weapons still attached to him, all but the spray and that was lying not three feet away. The night and the rain formed a screen that turned everything around him hazy and indistinct, including the remains of the ATV, which were all over the place. But he could see the vehicle's cabin off to one side, the doors gone and the windows smashed.

He rolled onto his knees, finding new sources of pain in his legs as he climbed gingerly to his feet. The terrain was much rougher than he remembered, which accounted for the damage he had sustained in the crash. But he couldn't remember any explosion, any flash, nothing that would indicate the vehicle had been struck by a rocket or flash-bang. Besides, no one had those weapons other than himself. Spears and swords and even catapults wouldn't do this kind of damage.

He blinked away the rain, wiped at his face, and took a deep breath. With slow, careful steps he made his way over to the cabin and peered inside. The girl was still strapped to the passenger's seat, her eyes closed, head drooping. He couldn't see any visible damage, but she appeared to be unconscious. He started to speak her name and then realized he couldn't remember it.

"Girl," he called to her instead. "Girl, are you all right?"

Her eyes opened. She nodded wordlessly.

"Unstrap yourself and climb out. You're sure you're not hurt?"

Without responding, she unbuckled the belt that held her in place and slipped down from the seat onto the ground. She brushed herself off, seemed to test her strength, and then looked at him and nodded. "I'm all right. What happened?"

He shook his head. "I don't know."

He stooped down where he could study the undercarriage more closely, tracing the line of the break. Sharp, jagged edges ran all along the frame, as if someone had used a giant saw to sever the body and chassis. He found it again on the axles and gun mounts and even the door hinges.

As if something had cut the vehicle into pieces.

"Acid," he whispered to himself, still not quite believing what his eyes were telling him. Where had the Trolls learned to make acid this strong? When had they discovered the technology?

But they were weapons makers, and they knew a great deal about chemical compounds and the forging of the materials created as a result. Either by experiment or by chance, they had found an acid that could eat right through the strongest metals. That they had used it on his crawler was a clear indication of how far out of favor he had fallen. It wouldn't have mattered if he had come to help them or not; they had intended to be rid of him once and for all.

"Taureq Siq." He was still whispering to himself, still not quite believing what had happened. It occurred to him that he should have given in to his impulses and killed the Maturen and his weasel son when he'd had the chance.

"We have to go," he said to the girl. "They'll be after us and we don't have the advantage of speed or protection anymore. We'll have to rely on being smarter."

She looked at him and nodded. "We are smarter. But I'm still afraid."

"You should be," he said. "Fear will keep you focused on what's needed. What's your name again?"

"Prue."

"Here's the thing, Prue. We still have these." He patted the butt ends of the spray and the flechette. "And these." He touched the flash-bangs and the knives and all the rest. "They don't have anything to counteract my weapons except numbers. We can still get away. Come on."

They set out across the murky, sodden landscape, unable to see more than twenty feet in any direction, the rain and the night shrouding everything. He had thought the rain might let up eventually, but so far it was showing no signs of doing so. At least it would help wash away their trail and conceal their route of passage.

He had started out toward the mountains, intent on following the directions on the map that Sider Ament had drawn leading to the pass, but after only a few minutes he abruptly changed direction and turned south. The Drouj would be using Skaith Hounds to track them. Grosha would be in charge, no doubt, urging his murderous little pets on. The

hounds would have difficulty finding their scent while the rains continued, but when they stopped it would be another matter. In the
meantime, Grosha would expect him to make for the mountains and
the valley within. After all, he had rescued the girl; the assumption
would be that he had done so in the hope of returning her to her people, perhaps for a substantial reward. So Grosha would travel east, hoping to catch up to them or at least to pick up their trail along the way.

But he would be looking in the wrong place, and with any luck at
all he wouldn't figure that out before Inch and the girl were safely
tucked away in Inch's fortress lair. Once there, they could take time to
rest up and heal and could return the girl home later.

It wasn't a great plan, but it was the only one that made any sense.

The problem was, it relied on misdirection and luck, neither of
which Deladion Inch had ever had much faith in. In this case, he
would make an exception. After all, he didn't have much choice. His
ribs and his arm had reduced his ability to defend himself, let alone the
girl, and they would only get one chance at escaping. The Trolls were
not overly bright, but they were strong and durable, and after the disruption he had caused they would be beyond angry.

They had walked only a short distance when the girl saw him
wince. "Are you hurt?" she asked.

"Broken ribs. My arm, too, I think." He didn't want to talk about it.
He just wanted to keep moving. "I'll be fine."

"No you won't," she said, taking his good arm and pulling him
about. "Let me look at you. I know something about healing."

She left the ribs alone, presumably because she did not want to
take the time and trouble to strip off his armor and because she knew
his body was already as well protected as it could be. But she took a
few minutes with the arm, pressing it, watching him for a reaction, asking where it hurt. When she had finished, she told him the forearm
bones were cracked if not broken, and she would splint it. She found a
pair of straight sticks, tore strips of cloth from the hem of her cloak,
and bound up his arm so that the bones were braced. Then she pulled
some leaves from within her tunic and told him to chew them. Surprisingly enough, he felt the pain begin to lessen almost immediately.

They walked on. She offered to carry something for him, but he told her he could manage better alone. He glanced over his shoulder repeatedly, searching the darkness for pursuit, but saw nothing. He took them down streambeds and across wet patches wherever he found them, doing what he could to mask all traces of their passage. He set a steady pace, even though he thought she might have trouble keeping up. She didn't.

Finally, he asked her about it.

"I'm a Tracker, just like Panterra. We were trained to read sign, follow trails, and live out on our own for weeks at a time. We can survive anywhere. I'm very good at it; Panterra is better. The best, in fact, that I've ever seen."

She seemed about to tell him something more, but then thought better of it. "I can keep up with you," she finished.

He marveled to find that she could. A slip of a thing, no bigger than a minute, intense and determined, she was much tougher than she looked. Her red hair was soaked to a burnt umber, and her green eyes gleamed bright even in the darkness and damp. She glanced at him often, perhaps trying to read him. He smiled inwardly. Others had done so before her; none had succeeded.

By daybreak, they were miles away from the Drouj camp, off the flats and into hill country thick with deadwood and scrub and riven with gullies and deep washes. The rains had ceased, but the dampness lingered in the form of mist that snaked down off the distant heights and through the defiles. The temperature had dropped, and both Inch and Prue were chilled in their sodden clothing. It would have been nice to build a fire, but foolish beyond measure.

Even so, Deladion Inch called a halt and had them sit down on a fallen log so they could have something to eat. He could see bits and pieces of the land in the distance, but most of it remained obscured. All night, he had listened for the Trolls and their hounds, but he had heard nothing. He heard nothing now.

"Who are you?" she asked as they chewed on bits of cheese and fruit and some bread that wasn't quite dry.

He told her his name. "I met Sider Ament weeks ago when he came through the mountains tracking an agenahl. Saved his life, matter of fact."

"Why did you come for me?"

He shrugged. "Seemed like a good idea at the time. Sider asked me if I would. I didn't have anything better to do." He flashed her a quick smile. "Sider planned to come for you himself, but his plans changed and he needed to get back inside the valley right away. That Troll that was helping you? Arik whatever he called himself? He's Taureq Siq's older son. He tricked you so that he could get into the valley and find out how things were. Since Sider needed to try to catch up to him before he escaped, I said I would come get you in his place. Things would have gone as planned, too, if the Trolls hadn't discovered an acid that can eat through the steel of a crawler."

"They found that button with the red light that you attached to me," she said. "They didn't seem to know what it was. They argued about it after they found it, so they might not have been certain you put it there. But I think they suspected it was you. Grosha tied me up, shoved me under those rugs, and waited to see if you would come."

He nodded. "I thought it might be something like that. I wanted to give it more time, but I couldn't wait; I had to get you out right away. Arik was supposed to return during the night."

"How would they know that? Can they communicate with each other from that far away?"

He shook his head. "I wouldn't think so. They don't have any real technology beyond ironworking."

She looked down at her hands. "I trusted Arik," she said.

"Don't feel too badly about that. He's good at making people trust him. That's why he's so dangerous."

"So all that business about being one of us, a descendant of a member of the Ghosts, that was just a lie?"

Inch shook his head. "I couldn't say. I don't know anything of the story. The part I know is that he claimed to be the son of a Karriak Maturen given in exchange for Taureq's eldest. I knew that was wrong because the Drouj wiped out the Karriak some years back. Tricked them into thinking they wanted an alliance, persuaded them to let down their guard, and then massacred them all."

She was quiet then for a long time. "I hope Sider catches up to him," she said finally.

He gave her a smile. "I wouldn't bet against it."

THEY SET OUT AGAIN SHORTLY AFTERWARD, still moving south through the mix of haze and gray. The rains returned in a slow, steady drizzle, and the temperature dropped further. The low ground, already swampy and slick, turned to mud covered by large stretches of surface water forming small lakes and connecting waterways. Walking was all up and down, a tiring slog that quickly sapped their energy. The footing was uncertain, resulting in constant slips and slides that cost them valuable time. Everything about them was turning into a morass.

Deladion Inch tried to take comfort in the fact that it would be just as hard on anyone tracking them, but soon grew so tired from picking himself up that he no longer found comfort in anything. His arm had begun to throb anew, pain shooting up and down it in sharp rushes, and the girl gave him some more of the leaves to chew. But his body was aching everywhere by now, not just in the places where his ribs were cracked and his arm fractured, and his misery was pretty much complete. He guessed they were still several hours' walk from his safehold, and they might not reach it by nightfall. He regretted endlessly the loss of the crawler, a dependable rolling fortress he could never replace. He thought of countless ways he might punish Taureq Siq for his part in this, but all of them required that he first get through the day.

Not a sure thing, at all, he decided when he heard the distant baying of the Skaith Hounds.

He cursed under his breath, gave the girl a quick reassuring smile, and kept walking as if the howling didn't matter. But they both knew that somehow, against all odds, the beasts had found their trail and were hunting them and that his efforts at misleading the Drouj had gone for naught. He began measuring their chances of reaching safety before the hounds caught up to them and decided they were slim or none. They would have to find a fresh way to throw off their pursuit or stand and fight.

He decided their best chance was to make use of the chain of waterways and lakes formed by the surface water, wading through in directions that would confuse the beasts. Leading the way, he took the girl into deeper water that covered their feet and ankles and then slogged ahead across vast stretches linked by connecting streams, careful never to step out of the water, never to touch ground that might give them away.

"We could double back on them," Prue suggested at one point, but he quickly shook his head.

"Too dangerous. If they get between us and the fortress, we have no chance at all. We keep going ahead."

She didn't argue. She did not complain or ask to rest. She did not slow. She just did what she was told. He admired this girl.

"How long have you known Sider Ament?" he asked after a time, weary of the silence.

She shrugged. "A few weeks. I only knew *of* him before that."

"That's long enough, I guess. I only met him recently myself. First I knew of anyone living in those mountains. Why didn't your people come out of there before now? What kept you in hiding?"

"It's a long story. We couldn't leave. We were warded by magic that locked us in. The valley was all we knew."

"Bet you wish that was still the case, don't you?"

"It would be easier. But the barrier's down and it won't come back up. We have to face life outside the valley, like it or not." She glanced over, her green eyes unsettling. "How did you become a mercenary?"

He shrugged. "I needed a way to make a living. I didn't have any people, no family, no anything. I'd been on my own since I was ten or twelve. I was living in a village south of here and doing what I could to stay alive. I used to scavenge for things in the ruins that I could barter or sell." He pointed at the weapons slung over his right shoulder. "These brought in good money. I tried using them, found I could, decided to take up a new trade. It made me a valuable commodity to those in search of an edge against their enemies. I liked how that made me feel."

"Don't you get lonely?"

"Sometimes. Everyone does. But I like living alone, being on my own, making my own decisions. Safer that way. Did Sider tell you about what it's like out here?"

She shook her head. "I only met him the one time. I haven't seen him since. But I can guess what it's like."

He laughed softly. "No, you can't."

He proceeded to describe it in detail, a straightforward recitation that left nothing out. He embellished a little, but not much. It wasn't necessary. Things were horrible enough as they were without the need to add anything. She only needed to grasp the gist of it. So he described the killings and the enslavement and the destruction, the basic elements of the savagery that had dominated everyone's life in the aftermath of the Great Wars—or at least everyone who hadn't found the sort of shelter from which she came.

She listened carefully and didn't interrupt. When he was finished, she said, "You're right. I couldn't have guessed at most of it. I don't know how you tolerate it."

"I don't think about it," he said. "I don't let it get too close."

She frowned. "But it's all around you."

"It helps to have these," he said, touching his weapons. "They keep everything at a distance."

From behind them, closer now, the baying of the Skaith Hounds rose and died. Inch glanced over his shoulder. It sounded like the beasts were farther west, perhaps following a false trail. "Let's keep moving."

They walked on for another hour, the day winding down. He thought they were getting close to the fortress, but he couldn't be certain in the shroud of darkness and damp. He didn't usually come at it from this direction, in any case. Everything looked different.

A fresh round of baying rose out of the silence, deep and powerful. The girl stopped where she was and looked back. "They've found our trail. They're coming for us."

"Maybe not," he said, not liking how certain she seemed.

"No, they're coming. I can feel it. It's my gift to know. My instincts warn me when I'm threatened. They're warning me now."

He wasn't sure he believed her, but he didn't see any point in taking chances. He quickened their pace, moving out of the water slicks and onto solid ground again. They needed to get out of the open, to put some walls between themselves and their pursuers. But they would have to hurry. If they failed to reach cover before dark, they would have no chance at all.

The baying rose and fell, continuous now. It was getting stronger, closer. The girl was right. The Skaith Hounds had found their trail. He gave momentary consideration to turning around and waiting for them, setting an ambush to kill them all. Without the hounds, the Drouj would have difficulty tracking anyone in this weather. But the risk was too great. If he failed to kill even one of the beasts, they would lose any advantage they might gain by staying ahead of the pursuit.

He slipped the flechette from his shoulder, released the safety, and clutched the big gun to his chest. He would be ready for them.

All of a sudden there were ruins ahead, a maze of half walls and collapsed roofs, of passageways and rubble. For just an instant he thought they had reached his fortress keep. Then he realized these were only the outbuildings. Still, any sort of protection was better than none. The walls at least gave them something to stand behind when the Trolls caught up to them. Even a piece of a wall would . . .

He was in midthought as the Skaith Hound launched itself at him from out of the darkness, a deadly, silent assassin. The huge beast was on him before he could bring the flechette to bear, knocking him backward off his feet and onto the ground. He only just managed to get the flechette between himself and the hound's jaws, jamming the barrel between the rows of teeth as he fought to fling the animal off. He heard the girl scream, and a second hound appeared, racing across the open ground to join the first. The barrel of the flechette was pointed right at it, and he pulled the trigger while it was still a dozen feet away, the charge tearing into it.

Then he used all of his considerable strength to heave the first beast clear and used the weapon a second time.

He looked around quickly, the barrel of the flechette sweeping the darkness. Nothing else appeared, although he could hear more baying in the distance. There was no hiding now. They would have to stand and fight.

"Inside!" he ordered the girl, gesturing toward the ruins.

She leapt to obey and they hastened through the maze of walls, working their way deep into the cluster of buildings. They were still several hundred yards from the safety of the fortress, but they might reach it if nothing else slowed them down. He found himself laboring as he ran, which surprised him. Then he glanced down and saw the blood soaking his left leg. The first hound had managed to savage it, ripping through the leathers and body armor.

He was bleeding freely, and he could feel the muscles tightening up. He knew what that meant.

Don't think about it!

Guttural cries rose from behind them. Trolls. They had discovered the bodies of the Skaith Hounds. Fresh baying rose and died. It was suddenly silent save for the sound of his breathing and their footfalls. The girl was keeping pace, darting this way and that through the debris, negotiating their passage effortlessly. It made him smile for just a moment. She was a keeper. He'd wondered a moment earlier why he had let himself get into this mess, but now he decided he knew.

Arrows flew past his head, and then one buried itself in his back. But the leathers and the armor stopped its penetration. He snatched at the girl, pulling her down behind a wall just ahead, and he turned, swinging up the barrel of the flechette. He fired three times, booming coughs that ruptured the stillness and ended a handful of lives in seconds. Without pausing to consider the number of dead, he was up and running anew, pulling the girl after him.

"There's more!" she screamed, just as several bodies vaulted a low wall to their left, spears thrusting. They missed the girl, but skewered him, shoulder and leg both. He killed his attackers quickly, efficiently. He bent down and broke off the spearheads and pulled free the shafts. It cost him something to do that, but he didn't hesitate or shy away from it.

Bleeding now from several wounds, he backed away with the girl behind him, watching the darkness. "Anything?" he asked her.

"No. They've fallen back. But not far."

Of course, not far. They had him now. Her, too, if he didn't do something about it. Then all this would have been for nothing.

He dropped behind another wall and knelt close to her. "I want you to go on ahead without me. Don't argue. You have to reach the fortress and open the door for me. I won't have time for that once I catch up. The locks are hidden. But I can show you how to find them. Listen carefully."

He told her where to go and what to do. He made sure she understood. He sketched a quick map in the dirt, which showed her the route she must follow. "Go now," he told her.

She shook her head, the first time she had questioned him. "I can stay and help . . ."

"You don't have a weapon, and you don't have fighting skills. You'll only slow me down if I have to worry about protecting you. Here, take this."

He handed her a Flange automatic, a twelve-shot handgun he had recovered from its hiding place about five years back and restored to working order. He showed her how to use it—how to release the safety, how to hold the weapon steady, how to fire it once or multiple times. "Just in case," he told her.

She nodded once, and then she was off, sprinting away into the darkness. *Good girl*, he thought. She knew, but she wasn't making a mistake by saying so, by staying to argue. He respected her for that. She was worth saving. Sider hadn't made a mistake in asking his help.

He turned back to the darkness, listening for sounds of approaching Trolls. An attack was inevitable, but it might not come right away. He backed into the ruins a little farther, searching the walls and doorways for the right spot. He found it finally, a corner slot formed by adjoining walls beneath a deep overhang. They could only get at him from in front.

He braced himself against the walls once he was concealed in the shadows, reloaded the flechette, and propped the spray up next to him. Then he looped a cord around the firing pins of three of the flash-bangs and fastened them to his chest armor where they could be easily reached. He set two more of the explosive devices on a protruding stone on his left, then changed his mind and moved them to another on the right. His left arm wasn't working well enough to do anything more than brace the stock of whatever weapon he was holding. When the attack came, he would have to move quickly.

He leaned back into the darkened corner and waited. *It was a good run*, he thought. *I don't like that it's ending, but you don't always get much of a say in that sort of thing. You just take what's given you.* He would miss seeing Sider again. But the girl would explain. What was her name? Prue, wasn't it? It fit her.

Time stopped. The night went still, the darkness closed about, and his breath turned to frost on the cold air. He could almost make himself believe he was going to get out of this.

The attack came all at once and without warning. But he was ready, and he fired the Tyson into everything that moved until it was empty, jammed in a second clip and fired again. He was struck repeatedly by arrows and darts, but most failed to penetrate and nothing did any real damage until the Drouj came at him in waves. By then the flechette was empty and he was using the spray, riddling the bodies until they were stacked all around him, Trolls and Skaith Hounds alike.

There was a small lull, and he found himself laughing at the absurdity of it all. He was still laughing when they came at him a final time, too many for him to stop, and as they reached him he pulled the cord attached to the pins on the flash-bangs and everything disappeared in sound and fury.

30

MILES AWAY, ON THE OTHER SIDE OF THE MOUN-
tains, the Gray Man was trekking west toward the pass
at Declan Reach. It was night and he was traveling
quickly. He was no longer tracking Arik Siq; his quarry's destination already known, his course fixed. Matters had taken an unexpected turn
here, too, and here, too, time was running out.

When he had left Arborlon in pursuit of the deceiver, he had begun
tracking him under the assumption that he was escaping the city with
the intention of going back through Aphalion Pass. If his purpose in
coming into the valley in the first place was to gather information that
would aid the Drouj in their planned invasion, he would be anxious to
impart to his father what he had learned before his duplicity was discovered. In order to do that in the fastest way possible, he would take
the shortest route out of the valley, and that meant going through
Aphalion.

So Sider had set out in that direction, not bothering with trying to
pick up the Troll's footprints, choosing instead to sacrifice caution for

speed in order to reach the pass quickly. He did so, only to learn from the Elves on watch that no Trolls had passed that way in the past week. The Orullian brothers, in particular, were adamant that no one could have gotten past the watch they had set at both ends of the pass without someone finding out. Since no sightings or incidents had been reported, Arik Siq must have gone another way.

It was a disturbing discovery, and after doing his own reconnaissance of the terrain surrounding the pass, the Gray Man went back down the interior slopes of the mountains toward Arborlon, this time checking carefully for some indication of where the elusive Troll had gone.

He found it when he was almost all the way back to the Elven city and scouring the terrain above the forest where the boy Xac Wen last seen the Troll going down the Carolan. The tracks he found were clearly made by a Troll, so the Gray Man was able to follow them easily enough. To his surprise, they led northwest upslope into the foothills for only several miles before turning directly west.

Shortly after that, in a dense forest formed by a mix of hardwoods and conifers grown so thick it was impossible to see much of anything once you were in their midst, he found something that caused him both confusion and concern. In a clearing ringed by spruce, he discovered tracks made by dozens of Trolls and a handful of four-footed beasts that had come down out of the high country west of Aphalion. Having joined up with Arik Siq, the entire bunch had set out west along the high slopes, carefully keeping to the shelter of the ridges and forests below the snow line.

At first, Sider couldn't figure out what all the Trolls and their beasts were doing. The pattern of the tracks seemed to indicate that they knew Arik Siq was coming and had waited for him. There were no indications of a disturbance, nothing to show that his arrival was unexpected. But if the Trolls were Drouj, how had they managed to get into the valley without being seen? How had they managed to communicate the details of this meeting with Arik Siq without speaking to him directly?

Sider couldn't be sure of the answer to the latter question, but he deduced an answer to the former pretty quickly. The beasts accompanying the Drouj were Skaith Hounds, which explained almost everything. When he had brought Arik Siq into the valley, there were no defenses in the pass, nothing to prevent anyone living outside from entering. The assumption was that no one could find a way in because no one knew where the passes were. But they had all overlooked the obvious. Simply by returning, they had left a trail. Skaith Hounds could track a quarry anywhere, as Deladion Inch had told him earlier, and since Arik Siq was already planning to betray the valley's secrets, he had simply arranged before leaving camp to have the hounds set on their trail as soon as they were safely out of sight.

Which meant that the Trolls who had gathered to meet with Taureq's duplicitous son could have found Aphalion Pass easily and gotten safely inside the valley long before the first Elves arrived to set watch and build their defenses. They could have prearranged a meeting and waited for its time to roll around by hiding out somewhere high up in the rocks where they would be safe from discovery. How they had managed to decide when and where the meeting was to take place remained a mystery, but it seemed clear to the Gray Man that this was what had happened.

But now that they had joined up, where were they going? What was their purpose?

Sider thought he knew, and it sent a cold spike through his heart. There was only one logical answer. Knowing that the Elves had dispatched a heavily armed force to Aphalion Pass, which very likely would be keeping watch in both directions, Arik Siq had chosen to take a less difficult route out of the valley. The men of Glensk Wood would be working at Declan Reach. They were neither as well trained nor as experienced as the Elves. Declan Reach would offer the Trolls the path of least resistance.

If the Drouj had gone that way, time was precious. They already had the better part of a day's lead on him, so Sider knew he had to hurry if he was to arrive in time not only to prevent their escape but also to save the men who otherwise would have the thankless task of trying to stop it by themselves. In truth, he did not think they were up to it. Even if they were not caught by surprise—which was something of a stretch, given the cunning of Arik Siq—they were not trained fighters.

He also knew there was a good chance that Panterra Qu would be among those working in the pass. He would be at risk along with all the others, but unlike all the others his life had special value.

It was a harsh way to look at things, but Sider Ament could not afford to think of it in any other terms. The boy was the one he had been searching for, the one who would best serve to carry the black staff after him. Panterra Qu might not realize it now, might not accept that it was so, but that didn't change the fact of it. Given time, Sider would be able to persuade him that committing to serve after him and learning how the staff and its magic could help the people of the valley survive was his destiny. He might resist it at first, but in the end he would come to understand that it was the right thing to do.

But any possibility of that happening would be lost if the boy was killed in an attack on the workers at Declan Reach. There was no way to get word to them in time, no possibility of warning them if he didn't do it himself.

A long shot, at best, he admitted. He might already be too late. He might have squandered his chances by assuming that his quarry had gone through Aphalion.

But he couldn't afford to think that way, and so he didn't.

He simply pressed ahead all the harder, his determination sheathed in iron.

PANTERRA QU WAS SLEEPING, rolled up in his blanket, assailed by troubling dreams that ate away at his rest like termites did wood. The dreams were all of Prue, alone among the Trolls, helpless and afraid, fighting to stay calm in the face of catastrophe. She was a prisoner, then an escapee, then a prisoner once more, and so it went, on and on. Her struggles were all the same—desperate, hopeless attempts at finding freedom when she knew no one was coming to save her. He tried to tell her it wasn't so; Sider Ament was coming, and failing that Pan himself would come. He tried to tell her, but he could not speak the words, his voice frozen. He gestured wildly, frantically, attempting to draw her attention, to make her understand he was there for her, but she did not see him. She looked everywhere but where he was, unaware of his presence. He was mad with the need to let her know she was not forgotten or abandoned. But he could read in her face the fear and despair that was slowly, steadily overwhelming her.

As he watched, she began to disappear. It felt as if she were right next to him when it happened. He wanted to scream in warning or snatch her away to safety, but he couldn't move or speak.

Suddenly he couldn't even breathe.

He jerked awake, knowing instantly that something was wrong, his dreams banished in an instant. He stood, stared into the darkness around him, and listened. Nothing. He glanced down. Andelin and Russa were asleep nearby. Parke and Teer were on guard farther up the pass, close to where it opened out onto the rugged slopes of the outside world. The others were sleeping on the valley side of the defensive barriers on which they had all been working for the better part of a week. Overhead, the sky was filled with stars, but he could discern a faint wash of silver light to the east. Dawn was breaking.

Everything seemed all right.

But something felt wrong anyway.

He walked the length of the pass to its far end and spoke with Parke and Teer. There was nothing out of sorts happening there. The world beyond the pass was dark and silent. He shook his head in confusion and moved back down the split to where Andelin and Russa were still sleeping, stopping at the last minute to pick up his bow and arrows, and from there walked on to the defensive barriers. Ladders were propped against the stone and timber walls at a narrows where the pass sloped downward in his direction and leveled out behind where the other men slept. The choice of terrain gave the defenders an advantage in the event of an assault, putting them above their attackers who must come at them over uneven ground. Most of the work was already done. By the end of tomorrow, the wall would be finished and manned by a permanent company of Trackers and others. Trow Ravenlock had already designated those he wished to serve in that capacity. He had done the best he could in making his choices, but the men of Glensk Wood were poorly trained for service as soldiers and fighters.

Shouldering his bow and arrows, Panterra climbed one of the ladders to the top of the wall and stepped over onto the narrow walkway that ran its length. He looked down on the sleeping men. Nothing out of place here, either. He stood where he was, searching for even a brief twinge of the feeling that had brought him awake, trying to make sense of it. If Prue were there, she would know. He did not. His instincts weren't as sure as hers.

But that didn't mean he should ignore them.

He looked for the guard who should have been on post below him and found him standing off to one side in the rocks near the tree line, nearly invisible in the dark, a silent shadowy presence perhaps fifty yards downslope from the sleeping men.

A second later the guard disappeared.

Panterra blinked. It happened so fast that he thought he must be mistaken and kept trying to find him. Then he caught a glimpse of the man's legs kicking wildly as he was dragged back into the deeper shadows.

An instant later shadowy forms emerged from the rocks all across the slopes leading up to the entrance to the pass and crept toward the sleeping men. Some walked upright on two legs and some slouched forward on four.

Trolls and Skaith Hounds.

The Drouj.

He had no idea how they had gotten behind them, but he knew at once who they were. "We're attacked!" he shouted in warning, banging a metal bar on a wooden barrel. "Wake up!"

The response was instantaneous from both sides. The Glensk Wood men rolled out of their blankets, some still sleep-fogged and confused, some quick to snatch up their weapons and defend themselves. But the Trolls and Skaith Hounds were quicker and more focused, attacking up the slope as soon as the warning was given, closing the distance between themselves and their victims in mere seconds. Half the defenders died in the first two minutes, torn apart by the hounds or run through by the Drouj. Panterra tried to slow the attackers, firing arrow after arrow into their midst, killing a couple and wounding as many more. But it wasn't nearly enough. There were too many, and it was still too dark to be accurate with a bow.

Slowly, the survivors fell back toward the defensive bulwarks, searching for a way to escape.

"Up here!" Pan called down to them, drawing their attention. "Climb the ladders!"

A few made it up, quicker than the rest. Most fell in the attempt and were lost. There were perhaps two dozen Trolls and three Skaith Hounds. Panterra concentrated on the latter, trying to bring at least one of them down. But the beasts were agile and quick, and their thick fur was resistant to his arrows.

Russa and Andelin had joined him by now, and were using their own bows. As many as six of their companions had gained the momentary safety of the walls while a handful more still fought to reach them from below. But the Trolls were relentless in their attack, overpowering all resistance. A pair of them reached one of the ladders, forcing the defenders to kick it away. The Skaith Hounds leapt for the ramparts in furious bounds, trying to gain purchase. The men on the walls fell back quickly in an effort to avoid those jaws.

Two more defenders made it up the last of the ladders, and then Russa pushed it away. The Trolls clustered below, shielding themselves from the barrage of arrows raining down on them, searching for another way up. A handful started to build a ramp out of supply boxes and pieces of lumber while the rest hauled out bows of their own and began shooting arrows into the defenders. The men on the walls were exposed and vulnerable. Three of them were killed outright before the rest scrambled over the walls and down the ladders on the other side, abandoning the defenses.

Panterra searched quickly among the survivors for Trow Ravenlock and couldn't find him. Dead, he assumed. Killed in the initial attack.

"Haul those ladders down!" Russa shouted at those with him, not bothering with trying to determine who should be in charge. "We'll fall back to those rocks at the next narrows. If we can, we'll try to stop them from coming over the walls."

No one argued. They raced down the pass perhaps a hundred yards to where an old rockslide formed a second narrows, providing some cover. They numbered seven now, including Teer and Parke, who had finally arrived from their place of watch at the far end of the pass. Fear and confusion showed on the faces of all six of his companions. None of them knew what was happening.

"Listen to me," he said suddenly. They looked at him in surprise, all breathing hard, covered in sweat and blood, their eyes wild. "These Trolls are part of the army that wants to take the valley from us. If they get past us here, they will tell the others how to get in. If that happens, everyone in the valley is at risk. We can't allow that."

"We can't stop them!" one of the men snapped. "Did you see what they did to us?"

"We weren't ready for them before. Now we are. They're dangerous—especially the Skaith Hounds—but they can be killed."

"We'll stop them!" Russa declared. He was a big man with hard features and tree-trunk arms. He looked at the others. "Who's with me?"

Everyone nodded, and the fear and confusion seemed to lessen. "How do we do this?" Andelin asked quickly.

"Block the pass, here at the narrows," Russa declared. "Take positions to either side. Shoot them coming over the wall. Stand until we can't hold. Then fall back to another position. Do it again, if we need to, until they're all dead or we are!"

No one said anything. Nothing needed saying. They would fight to the last man, until they were all killed. Everyone knew the odds against anyone coming to their rescue. No new work parties were due for two days.

"Maybe we can find a way to slip by them," Andelin suggested, looking hopeful. "There are Elves building the defenses at Aphalion Pass. They might send help if someone could reach them."

Russa turned to Pan. "You should go. You've worked with the Elves; they know you. You've been outside the valley, too. None of us has. You'll know better what to watch out for."

Panterra shook his head. "It's too far. I can't get there and back in time to save anyone. Better that I stay with you. If we can't stop them here, maybe I can lead you to Aphalion."

He was thinking suddenly that Sider Ament might come. Perhaps he had rescued Prue by now and was returning with her as he had promised he would, by way of Declan Reach. It was a long shot, but it was the best he could hope for.

Still, he said nothing of this to the others. They had no reason to believe that the Gray Man would help them.

"We'll have a better chance if we stay together," he finished.

Already there were sounds of activity on the walls. Panterra peered around the rocks and saw the Trolls gathering on the ramparts, hauling up the ladders from the far side in preparation for lowering them on the near. A Skaith Hound reared up, its shaggy head swinging right and left, its yellow eyes searching. It lifted its head and howled.

"Here they come!" Russa snapped, his blunt features tightening. "Remember our plan, boys."

Panterra Qu notched an arrow in place and drew back slowly on his bowstring.

* * *

DAWN HAD BROKEN by the time Sider Ament approached the pass at Declan Reach. He had been traveling all night, pushing the pace, trying to make up time and ground on Arik Siq and the Drouj. He was bone-weary and hungry, having eaten nothing since setting out. But his sense of urgency and his determination to reach the pass in time drove him to keep going when common sense would have persuaded another man to rest.

Now that he was here, though, with the pass just ahead, he was aware of the price he had paid for his urgency. If he had to fight now, he might not be as strong as he needed to be.

He trudged up the slope through the scattering of conifers and boulders, wending his way cautiously, listening for sounds that would give away anyone in hiding. He heard nothing. Everything was still. As he drew closer, the dark entrance to the pass visible, he saw the first of the bodies. Trolls and Men both, their bodies twisted in death. He walked up to them, scanning the ground, assessing the visual evidence of what had happened. The Trolls had attacked, caught the Men mostly unawares, and killed many of them while they were still trying to wake up. Some had fought back, but the numbers of dead on each side suggested that the Trolls had gotten the better of things.

He walked past the dead to the bulwarks and stopped. A terrible struggle had taken place here, as well. Arrows sprouted not just from the bodies but from the earth all around them and the timbers of the defensive wall. No one had been left alive on this killing ground.

He saw Trow Ravenlock, lying off to one side, spitted on a Troll lance, his sword still in his hand. Trackers and builders had made a desperate stand against trained Drouj soldiers. Men whose lives revolved around the crafts of reading sign and building homes had failed to find a way to survive.

He took time to look carefully at the faces of the dead, and then scoured the surrounding terrain to make certain he had missed nothing. Panterra Qu was nowhere to be found.

Sider took a deep, steadying breath and exhaled slowly. Perhaps the boy had never been here. Perhaps he was still down in Glensk Wood.

He returned to the wall, propped up a fallen ladder against the ramparts, and climbed to the top. From there he looked over the wall and found more of the Trolls and one of the Skaith Hounds lying dead on the ground below, all of them killed climbing over or within twelve feet of landing. He peered down the shadowy length of the pass for as far as he could see. There were more bodies at a narrows a short distance away.

He descended into the pass using a second ladder, one that had been used by the attackers in going after those defenders they had not killed in the first assault. He moved ahead, more cautious now, taking time to study those sprawled on the ground, not wanting to mistake a live Troll for a dead one. But the three he found at the narrows and the two Men lying next to them—one still clutching a Troll in a death grip—were empty vessels.

There was still no sign of Panterra Qu.

He almost turned back, certain now that the boy either had not come there or had gotten away during the fighting. Instead of wasting his time like this, he should go for help. Someone was needed to man the empty walls of the defenses against a probable attack from the Drouj army. Catching up with Arik Siq no longer seemed likely, and there was nothing to be gained by continuing on.

Yet he did.

Just in case he was wrong, he told himself. Just in case the boy was still at risk.

He proceeded to walk the length of the pass, finding along the way the bodies of two more of the Drouj, another Skaith Hound, and three more of the defenders. All had died fighting, mostly on the run. He checked the faces of the dead, determined that they did not belong to the boy, and then bent down on one knee to read the tracks that continued ahead. Most of them were old, two days or more. But he found the tracks of two men that were new, one following the other, running hard. A handful of Trolls and a Skaith Hound appeared to be following them.

He stood up and continued on.

The pass was still deeply shadowed, but fringes of sunlight were creeping over the peaks and down the narrow draws, seeking out the darker corners. Sider worked his way ahead carefully, still believing that he was too late to help anyone. The fighting must be over, and if any of the defenders were left they had fled to safer places. He regretted that he had failed to catch up to Arik Siq, but consoled himself with a promise that one day he would atone for that.

He was almost to the far end of the pass when he heard something. He stopped where he was and listened. A forlorn voice was crying out weakly. It was distant still, perhaps outside the pass itself, perhaps downslope in the rocks beyond. He started ahead again, listening for more. But the voice had gone silent.

He reached the end of the pass, dropped into a crouch against one wall, and carefully crept forward to where he could see a narrow stretch of rock-strewn slope. He scanned it slowly, searching for whoever was out there.

Nothing.

He hesitated, uncertain what to do. It was dangerous to expose himself without knowing more, but he couldn't stay where he was if he wanted to find out what was happening.

Even so, he hesitated a long time. Then cautiously, he eased his way forward along the rough surface of the rock, inching toward the sunlight. He was just at its edge when he saw a body lying facedown in the rocks, blood everywhere, arms and legs akimbo.

Was it the boy?

He wasn't sure. It was the right size and build; it might be. Then one arm moved just enough to reveal that there remained a small spark of life.

Sider reacted instinctively. He bolted from the pass into the sunlight and raced toward the body. But in his haste, consumed by his fear for the boy, he forgot to summon the protective mantle of the black staff's magic.

He heard someone scream his name and felt a pair of sharp stings on his neck and hand.

An instant later, a Skaith Hound slammed into him from behind, come from out of the rocks in which it had been in waiting, claws and teeth tearing at him. The magic of his staff responded instantly to his summons, keeping the beast from his face and throat. But the magic was weak, a consequence of his own weariness, and the Skaith Hound broke through its protective shield and clamped its jaws on Sider's arm. Sider struggled to break free but could not. Together man and beast tumbled down the rock-strewn slope past the body that wasn't Panterra Qu's—the Gray Man caught just a glimpse of the other's face—and crashed into a pile of boulders. There, on impact, the beast lost its grip. Sider leapt up, deflecting a hail of arrows directed at him from both sides, drove the black staff into the Skaith Hound's chest, sent an explosion of magic down its length, and burned the beast to a blackened husk.

He wheeled back as three of the Drouj careened into him, spears seeking to pin him to the rocks. He blocked their efforts, knocking them aside—first one, then the other two—his body twisting away as he used his magic to shield himself and his staff to crack their bones. But the Trolls were toughened fighters and two of them were back on their feet quickly, in spite of their injuries, swords drawn. Sider used his magic, lashing out at them, turning them aside, and he was on top of them before they could recover. Swiftly he dispatched them.

He faltered then, his muscles gone weak and unresponsive. He was aware of burning sensations where he had felt the stings earlier. He glanced down at his hand and saw what appeared to be a bruise. Then he probed his neck and found a tiny dart protruding from his skin. He had just pulled it free and was examining it when he was struck again, this time in the face.

He dropped into a defensive crouch, pulling out the dart immediately. He saw Arik Siq then, standing in the open now, come out from wherever he had been hiding, a blowgun in his hand.

A single word surfaced in his mind.

Poison.

He fought back, using his magic to slow its spread, armoring himself for what was needed. Then he went up the slope in a rush. Arik Siq put the blowgun to his lips and used it again. But by now the magic was firmly in place and deflected the darts. Twice more the son of the Drouj Maturen used the blowgun before accepting that it was useless. He realized at the same moment that he should have been making his escape. But by now, he was trapped near the mouth of the pass, pinned back against its dark opening, and it was too late to escape the way he had intended. He hesitated only a moment before turning into the pass and fleeing back down its shadowy corridor, back the way he had come, toward the valley.

Sider Ament chased him until his strength gave out and he dropped to the ground, exhausted, his body growing numb as the poison continued to spread. He tried one last time to stop it, to negate its effects, to keep it from his heart.

But it was too late, he realized. The poison was in too deep.

He found himself wishing, as he accepted the inevitable, that he could have told Aislinne good-bye.

31

WHEN ALL OF THE OTHERS WERE DEAD OR dying and he was the last, Pan had broken clear of the pass and made a quick decision. If he ran, they were going to catch and kill him as they had the rest. He needed to get out of their reach another way. So he managed to scale a cliff wall just outside the mouth of the pass that was so sheer and treacherous that neither the heavier Trolls nor the Skaith Hounds could follow. Navigating a series of footholds and outcroppings, he had found a niche that he could squeeze into just far enough that their weapons could not harm him. Once in place, he settled back to wait. There was nothing else he could do. Sooner or later, help might arrive. Or the Drouj might grow tired of waiting for him to come down and leave. There wasn't any reason for them to wait him out, after all. Their sole purpose in attacking the pass was to get back to their tribe and reveal that they had found a way into the valley—of that, Pan was fairly certain. There was nothing to keep them from carrying out this plan now that the defenders were slain. Andelin had been the last; they had dragged him out and left him on the rocks to die. He had still been alive when their attention had been diverted by something happening inside the pass, and they had taken cover.

Then Sider Ament had appeared, alone and clearly unaware of the trap that had been set for him, not realizing that the Drouj had left one of their number on guard inside the pass to alert them to anyone approaching. Pan had shouted his name instantly. But his warning had come too late.

Now he scrambled down out of his rocky perch, rushed to Sider, dropped to one knee, and held him in his arms.

"I tried to warn you," he whispered.

The dark eyes found his. "You did your best."

"Tell me what to do," he begged.

The Gray Man managed a smile. "You're doing it," he said.

Pan braced him with his chest and shoulder and fumbled to bring out his water pouch. He held it to the other's mouth and let him drink. Most of the water trickled down his chin and was lost. Pan could see the color of his skin beginning to change with the onslaught of the poison, taking on a bluish tinge.

"Is there something that will counteract the poison?"

Sider Ament shook his head. "Too much of it . . . is already in me." He swallowed thickly. "Did any of them get out . . . of the valley alive?"

"I don't know. I don't think so. Sider, was that Arik Sarn who attacked you? Why did he do that?"

"Because he's not . . . who we believed. His real name is Arik Siq. He is the Maturen's . . . oldest son. He tricked us . . . into bringing him into the valley. He would take that knowledge . . . back with him. But now . . . he's trapped inside the valley. You . . . can't let him escape."

Pan shook his head. "But why didn't they just leave when they had the chance? Why did they stay?"

"They needed you . . . dead so you . . . couldn't warn the valley . . . about them. Would give them time to regain the pass . . . and bring others to help them." The Gray Man smiled. "You stopped them . . . just by getting away."

Pan shook his head, blinked away his tears. "You were the one that stopped them. I'm to blame for all of this. I'm the one that brought him into the valley in the first place."

The stricken man took a quick gulp of air. "Doesn't matter now. Listen to me. Time doesn't allow for . . . anything more than this. I wish it did. But . . . you have to take the staff from me. No arguments, Panterra. You have . . . to do it now."

Pan stared at him, unable to speak. In the rush of things, he had forgotten about the staff. He hadn't decided if he was going to serve as the Gray Man's apprentice. All that had been pushed aside as the hunt for Prue had begun.

Prue! A chill rippled up his spine. Where was Prue?

"Sider, I can't . . ." He stopped, shook his head. "You have to tell me about Prue. Did you find her? You were going after her. What happened?"

Sider shook his head. "I sent someone . . . in my place . . . when I learned the truth about the Troll. Someone . . . better able than I . . . to save her. Best I could . . . do." He seemed to gather himself. "The staff. Will you take up the staff?"

Pan shook his head in confusion and despair. "How can I agree to this when I don't know if Prue . . . ?"

The Gray Man's hand clamped on his wrist, an iron band that cut off the rest of what he was going to say. "The staff . . . will help you save her. Otherwise . . ." He stopped, choking now, struggling to breathe. "Help you save them all. Men, Elves, all of them. You must . . . give them hope. You have to do what's needed . . . because I can't."

"I don't know if I can!" Pan fought to keep from screaming the words at him. "I'm not you! I don't have your experience! I don't even know how to summon the magic! I've never used it! I don't know anything!"

The hand on his wrist tightened. "You know . . . more than you think. Trust in your instincts. The staff . . . responds to the . . . will of the . . . the user. Just . . . ask for what you need."

He was gasping for air now. Panterra struggled to make it easier for him, holding him upright, trying to find a way to slow the poison. But nothing was helping.

"Take . . . the staff!" the other hissed. Then his gaze shifted. "When you . . . see Aislinne . . . tell her . . ."

The words caught in his throat, his body hunched violently, and then his eyes fixed on nothing. Panterra held him, crying openly now, unable to stop.

"Sider, no," he whispered.

He said it like a prayer, like a plea. It was all he could manage. Then he laid the dead man down, released the hand still clamped on his wrist, and closed the eyes that now seemed to be staring at him.

"Walk softly, Sider Ament," he whispered.

He closed his own eyes, sick at heart and bone-weary, and when he did so the dead man whispered back.

Take the staff.

The words echoed softly in the following stillness.

Take the staff.

THE BOY STANDS WITHOUT MOVING as the remains of the rogue Elf begin to blow away like ashes in a sudden gust of wind. His mentor has dropped to his knees, gripping the staff to hold himself upright. Everything seems frozen—time, place, events, even the boy himself.

But when the old man topples over, the boy breaks free of his invisible chains and runs at once to reach him, the world moving again, time an inexorable, crushing boulder rolling toward them both. He reaches the old man and raises him up, holding him in his strong arms. The old man is so light; he weighs almost nothing. How he could prevail against another bearer of the staff when the other is so much stronger is a mystery.

The old man's breathing is quick and shallow. The boy does a quick study of the broken body. He cannot see any major injuries, anything external. Whatever hurt the old man has suffered is buried somewhere deep inside.

His mentor looks up at him, and nods. "Nothing to see, young one. Just an old man dying."

The boy shakes his head in denial. "No. We can do something. I can find a healer and bring him to you. I can go now."

But the old man holds him fast with his gnarled hands. "I would be dead by the time you returned. Something more important than a futile effort to save my life requires your attention. The staff. It is yours now. It belongs to you. When I am gone, take it."

The boy shakes his head. "I don't think I am ready."

"No one is ever ready for such power. No one is ever ready to command it. But you will do as I have done. You will do your best. Protect the people of the valley, the survivors of the Great Wars. See them to their release or to the passing of the staff to your successor. Great responsibility has fallen to you. You are the last bearer. You have me to thank for that. I am sorry that it must be so."

The boy casts about and then meets the old man's gaze anew. "I have never used the staff. I have no idea what is needed. What if the magic won't come for me?"

His mentor smiles. "I once wondered the same thing. What if I cannot wield the magic? What if I lack the strength and skill? The magic will come when you summon it. You have only to think on it. But your success while using the magic is a different matter. It will be measured by your strength of heart."

The boy is miserable. He wants his mentor to be well again and to teach him what he still needs to know. He wants the rogue Elf never to have appeared. He wants things back the way they were.

"Take the staff from me," the old man says once more.

A moment later he is dead.

The boy stares down at him for a very long time, waiting for him to move, even knowing that he won't. His mind is muddied by his confusion. He will have to travel to the Elves and tell them what has happened. They have already lost their King. Now they have lost their bearer of the black staff. But Men have lost theirs, as well. Unless he does what the old man has asked of him.

Unless he takes up the staff.

It occurs to him then, in a flash of insight that rocks him with its implications, that if he takes up the staff and accepts the terrible responsibility it demands, he will one day be asking another to do the same.

Is this something he can face? Is it something he can bear?

He looks down at the black staff, still gripped in the old man's hand, and for a very long time he does not move.

BEARERS OF THE BLACK STAFF
ends here. The story concludes in
THE MEASURE OF THE MAGIC.